Things You Won't Say

Center Point
Large Print

Also by Sarah Pekkanen and available from Center Point Large Print:

The Best of Us
Catching Air

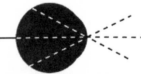

**This Large Print Book carries the
Seal of Approval of N.A.V.H.**

Things You Won't Say

SARAH PEKKANAN

CENTER POINT LARGE PRINT
THORNDIKE, MAINE

This Center Point Large Print edition
is published in the year 2015 by arrangement with
Washington Square Press,
a divison of Simon & Schuster, Inc.

The text of this Large Print edition is unabridged.
In other aspects, this book may vary from the original edition.
Printed in the United States of America
on permanent paper.
Set in 16-point Times New Roman type.

ISBN: 978-1-62899-611-1

Library of Congress Cataloging-in-Publication Data

Pekkanen, Sarah.
 Things you won't say / Sarah Pekkanen. — Center Point Large Print
edition.
 pages cm
 Summary: "An inside look at a family in crisis and a marriage on the
brink after a tragic shooting"—Provided by publisher.
 ISBN 978-1-62899-611-1 (library binding : alk. paper)
 1. Police spouses—Fiction. 2. Large type books. 3. Domestic fiction.
 I. Title.
 PS3616.E358T56 2015b
 813′.6—dc23
                                                          2015012327

For all the book bloggers, librarians, and readers.
Thank you for spreading the joy of reading.

Things You Won't Say

PART ONE

Chapter One

AS SHE APPROACHED THE traffic light, Jamie Anderson prayed it would stay green. She pushed harder on the gas, edging the speedometer's needle as high as she dared—which wasn't very high, because she was a cop's wife and police headquarters was a dozen yards away. Just when she thought she'd make it through the intersection, a slow-moving Toyota cut in front of her, forcing her to hit her brakes. The stoplight blinked yellow, then red.

Jamie held her breath. *Don't look,* she warned herself, even as she felt her gaze being yanked to the right, toward the section of sidewalk that had recently been cordoned off with crime-scene tape. The sidewalk had been scrubbed clean, but she wondered if the dark stains still showed up close.

Her three-year-old daughter's high voice piped up from the backseat: "Pizza?"

"What? No, not today," Jamie said. She gripped the steering wheel tightly. Why was the light taking so long?

"Pizza, please!" Eloise said, her little-girl lisp turning the *l* into a *w.*

"Maybe later," Jamie said.

11

Her husband, Mike, would be returning to this exact spot tomorrow, wearing his dark blue uniform and Magnum boots and heavy patrolman's belt. For the first time, though, his silver badge would be crossed by a black ribbon. A blaring horn jolted Jamie and she pressed the gas pedal again. Being here was wrenching for her. How much worse would it be for Mike to return to the spot where his longtime partner, Ritchie, and a young rookie officer had been shot two weeks ago by a lunatic with a grudge against cops?

But Mike would never quit. Early in their relationship, when they'd been trading stories about growing up, he'd told her that during recess at his elementary school, the boys had split up into two groups: the good guys and the bad guys. The other kids switched between characters, but never Mike. Even back then, he'd wanted to be the one to round up the criminals. It was why he'd turned down a chance at a promotion that would mean more desk work years ago. He loved patrolling the streets, talking to citizens, giving high fives to little kids. Keeping everyone in his little strip of the city safe.

"I hungry! I want pizza!" Eloise's whining had crossed into wailing now.

"Okay, okay." Jamie sighed, knowing she was probably violating a half dozen parenting rules but not particularly caring. She had a little extra time

12

before she needed to pick up her eight-year-old, Sam, and six-year-old, Emily, at their elementary school anyway.

She put on her signal to turn left and stifled a yawn. Mike had endured another nightmare last night, thrashing around before he sat bolt upright and yelled something incoherent, awakening with all the sudden violence of a thunderclap. He'd been sweating and trembling, and she'd gotten up to bring him a glass of water when he said he didn't feel like talking. Neither of them had been able to fall back asleep. Now it was barely two-thirty, and she was exhausted, her feet hot and sore from racing around after Eloise at the playground all morning. She had a trunkful of groceries to unpack before driving Sam to soccer practice, then there would be homework to supervise, lunch boxes to clean out and refill, a dishwasher to unload, the living room to reassemble before the tornado of kids struck again . . . plus her sister, Lou, had left two messages today. Something would have to give, and it might as well be a home-cooked dinner. She'd pick up a couple of pizzas now, give the kids a slice each for an after-school snack, and reheat the rest tonight.

Belatedly realizing she'd achieved victory, Eloise stopped mid-shriek. *A future actress,* Jamie thought. Or an opera singer, given the notes Eloise hit when she was upset.

Jamie found a parking spot near the entrance of

their favorite carryout and unbuckled Eloise from her car seat. She ordered a salad for herself even though she knew she'd end up scarfing a few cheesy pieces from the two large pies she was buying, then she grabbed a Diet Coke from the refrigerated case. She needed caffeine. She needed a housekeeper, a cook, and a part-time driver more, but her budget covered only the soda. She was stretching out her hand to accept her change from the cashier when she heard someone call her name.

She turned around to see a slim woman with chestnut-colored hair who was dressed in black spandex and expensive-looking running shoes. Jamie had on athletic gear, too, but her outfit was chosen only because all her Old Navy T-shirts and shorts—her warm-weather uniform—were entangled in an overflowing laundry basket.

It took Jamie a moment to place the face: another mom from the elementary school. She should know the woman's name; they'd met at a half dozen holiday performances and field trips through the years.

"Hi!" Jamie said, injecting enthusiasm into her tone to make up for her memory lapse.

"It's *so* good to see you," the woman said, moving closer and reaching out to grip Jamie's forearm. "How *are* you?"

The woman was wearing what Jamie had come to think of as a sympathy face: creased forehead, jutting chin, and wide, inquisitive eyes.

"Fine, thanks," Jamie said, pulling her arm away and ignoring the woman's unspoken questions. "Eloise, that's enough napkins. Stop pulling them out, honey."

"It was so terrifying to hear the news," the woman continued. She clutched her chest. "In the middle of the day! I mean, you'd think a police station would be the safest place in the world!"

"Yes, well . . . some people are crazy," Jamie said.

"How is Mike *doing?*" the woman asked.

"He's good," Jamie said, keeping her tone neutral. No way was she going to reveal any personal information. The details would ricochet around the school via an informal gossip tree before her pizza was even out of the oven.

"Oh," the woman said, seeming a little disappointed. "I mean, he was right there, wasn't he? It could've been him!"

Enough. Jamie smiled tightly and reached for Eloise's hand. "Come on, honey, we need to get Sam and Emily."

"My pizza!" Eloise protested, dropping the napkins on the floor.

"We're coming back for it," Jamie said. She left the napkins, grabbed a peppermint from the jar by the cash register to appease her daughter, and rushed them both to the car, feeling the woman's stare on her back.

Yes, Mike had been right there! Was that what

the awful woman wanted, for Jamie to describe the scene she couldn't stop thinking about?

Her cell phone ringing as she was driving to pick up the kids from school—just as she was now. Her hand reaching to hit the speakerphone button and turn down the radio. Mike's voice gasping out terrible words: A man with a hunting rifle lying in wait outside headquarters. Two officers down. A rookie dead on the sidewalk. And Mike's partner and best friend, Ritchie, unconscious and bleeding profusely from a head wound.

Jamie's shaking hand took two tries to fit the key into the ignition.

"Ritchie was right ahead of me," Mike had kept repeating. *"I didn't see the gun! The sun—it hit my eyes . . . Oh, God, I didn't see the gun in time . . ."*

The deranged man had been taken down by another officer who was leaving the same 7:00 A.M. to 3:00 P.M. shift. Later, all the newspapers had reported that in the pocket of the killer's camouflage pants was a rambling note professing his hatred of police.

And now Mike hated himself.

Maybe he should talk to somebody, Jamie thought as she drove toward the school, knowing her husband would never do it. A police counselor had offered therapy sessions, and even suggested Mike start taking antidepressants right after the shooting.

16

"Crazy pills," Mike had scoffed, rolling his dark eyes. Instead he'd tried to lose himself in punishing runs and endless biceps curls and push-ups. He changed the oil in the minivan and added new insulation in the attic. He visited Ritchie in the hospital's ICU nearly every day. He drove Jamie and the kids to bring casseroles and salads to Ritchie's wife, Sandy, and their twins, but while the women talked and the kids played, he mowed the lawn and trimmed the hedges. No matter how hard he tried to exhaust himself, though, the nightmares persisted, and with every passing day, Jamie felt as if her husband was withdrawing a bit more, an invisible casualty of the shooting.

Maybe *she* needed to talk to somebody, Jamie thought.

A housekeeper, a cook, a driver, and a therapist. She sighed. Who could afford any of it?

She pulled into the school pickup line and waited for Sam and Emily to emerge from the red-brick building. Tonight her teenage stepson, Henry, would be staying with them, too. Jamie adored Henry, but she hoped Mike's old girl-friend, Christie, would stay in her car rather than come to the door during the exchange of her son, especially since Jamie's dirty-blond hair was swept up in a messy ponytail and the swipes of mascara she'd put on this morning had long ago sweated off. Henry was the result of a brief fling between Christie and Mike a couple of years before Jamie met Mike. By the time Christie discovered she was pregnant, she and Mike had been on the verge of breaking up. They'd decided to have the baby anyway, and split custody. Against all odds, it had all worked out. Henry was a terrific boy, kindhearted and smart, and even though drama stuck to Christie like a shadow, everyone was on friendly terms. Friendly enough, anyway. At least most of the time.

"Hi, guys," Jamie said as her older two piled into the minivan. "How was school?"

"Boring," Emily answered, flouncing into her seat with a long-suffering sigh. Six years old going on Katy Perry was how Mike always described her.

"I'm starving," Sam said.

"We're picking up pizza in a minute," Jamie said as she pulled back onto the road. She hoped the nosy woman had left the carryout. She couldn't bear another round of questions, especially not in front of the kids, who'd spent so much time with Ritchie and his family. Sometimes Jamie had teased Mike about wanting to socialize with them on weekends. Didn't the two men see each other enough?

Mike and Ritchie were as close as twin brothers, although they looked nothing alike. Ritchie was tall and thin, with horn-rimmed glasses and a prematurely graying Afro; Mike was short and muscular, with wavy dark brown hair. Each knew how the other took his coffee, what his opinion was on mayo versus mustard, and how he reacted in times of stress or boredom or crisis. They even teased each other about reading the sports page on the john. They'd been teasing moments before the shooting, too.

Mike had been about to walk out the building's heavy glass door. But instead, he'd pulled it open and nudged Ritchie in the shoulder.

"Ladies first," he'd joked.

And Ritchie had stepped onto the sidewalk, into the bright sunlight, just ahead of Mike.

It was probably a safe bet that there weren't many people in the world whose dream job included cleaning up elephant dung, Lou reflected as she picked up a shovel and got to work.

But then again, how many people had the chance to walk through the tall metal gates of a zoo in the dawn of a lush summer day, listening to the calls and chatter of the tufted capuchin monkeys, or the bone-shaking roar of a Siberian tiger? Bearing witness as the zoo came alive was a transformative experience, one that became even more meaningful to Lou as she got to know the animals, to recognize their individual sounds and gauge their moods.

"Tabitha ate about a crate of sweet potatoes last night," another keeper called as he hosed down the adjoining pen. The four Asian elephants were out in the yard, rolling around in mud, which was their morning ritual. The early June day promised to be another hot, sticky one, and the mud would protect the mammals' skin—more evidence to Lou that when it came to common sense, elephants trumped humans any day. Take all the women who greased themselves up in search of a perfect tan and then, a few years later, injected chemicals into their faces in an effort to undo the damage. Which was the smarter species?

"I can tell Tabby binged," Lou said, scooping up the last of the impressive mess. "But she lost fifty pounds last week, so she needs to put a little back on." Especially since the great mammal was pregnant. Lou always watched her animals closely, but Tabby required extra attention these days.

"Any big plans for the weekend?" the keeper asked.

"Nope," Lou said. She knew she was supposed to lob back the question, but she let it drop. Lou didn't like chatting while she was working at the zoo—it interfered with her time with the animals, and small talk felt draining to her. Besides, she had to make enough of it at the coffee shop where she worked part-time as a barista to supplement her salary. She spent her mornings and early afternoons wiping down enclosures and weighing out food and making sure the elephants were happy. She spent three evenings a week wiping down counters and measuring out coffee grounds and making sure her customers were happy. She supposed there was a kind of symmetry to the services she provided.

Lou finished cleaning the pen, rinsing her boots last. They'd still stink badly enough that she'd have to leave them on the balcony of her apartment tonight, she knew from experience. She was immune to the smell, but she'd learned from the looks she'd received when she popped into CVS one day directly after work that not everyone was. Now she kept a spare pair of flip-flops in her car.

She'd been a full-time animal keeper for a few years, but it had been a long road to achieve her dream, inconveniently realized shortly after she'd graduated from college with a degree in accounting. She'd gone to night school to get another degree—this time in zoology—and had started volunteering on the side, knowing practical experience could be a deciding factor when her résumé was in the middle of a tall stack. First she'd worked for a local vet, then the ASPCA, and finally, she'd begun helping at the zoo. She'd given up her accounting job because the hours weren't compatible with her volunteer work. Turning in her notice made a twenty-pound boulder she hadn't realized she'd been carrying around drop off her shoulders. Lou wasn't cut out to sit in a sterile office, willing the clock to hit 6:00 so she could feel alive. She had school loans she wouldn't be able to repay for a couple of decades, her muscles constantly ached from the hard labor that accompanied her job, and she'd been bitten by a zebra, peed on by a giraffe, and hit on by a horny llama, among other indignities.

She'd never been happier.

Lou leaned on the handle of her shovel, watching as Bailey filled his trunk with water from the pool. Lou preferred the company of animals to just about anyone else's, except maybe that of her sister, Jamie, and her family. Elephants were gorgeous, complex creatures with rich emotional lives. They cherished their young, communicated in rumbles that could be understood a mile away, and had personality quirks to rival any human's. Take Bailey—he acted like a tough guy, but he was terrified of squirrels and cowered in a corner while they snacked on his food. Sasha was a scamp who liked to squirt the others with water, and Martha would meticulously mix her meals together, like she was making a salad—a bit of hay, a carrot, a few apple slices. Then there was Lou's favorite: big, sweet Tabitha, the most utterly lovable creature on the planet. She hoped the baby had Tabby's temperament. Give that girl a few words of praise and she was in heaven.

In a little while, Lou would let the elephants

out to explore the more than five miles of trails that constituted their habitat. Lou knew other keepers loved their elephants just as much as she did, but she couldn't bear to visit zoos that had inadequate spaces for elephants. The gentle, intelligent creatures needed plenty of room to roam. Here, she could place hay and vegetables in different locations every day, scattering meals throughout the exhibit and hiding the food, so the mammals could forage for it as they did in the wild. There were two pools—one for wading, and a deep one for swimming—and shady areas to rest. But the best spot was the back-scratching tree. The elephants loved to rub themselves against the low-hanging branches, and Lou could practically hear them sighing in relief.

Lou's cell phone buzzed in her pocket and she dug it out, belatedly realizing she'd smeared traces of elephant poop on her cargo pants. Not the first time; most of her clothes sported faint green and brown stains.

"Sorry to call so early," Jamie said. "But I knew you'd be up. Is it really only seven? I meant to phone you back yesterday but things got crazy. Emily ate too much pizza and had a stomachache, so I was up half the night, and I swear it feels like noon. At least I hope her stomachache was from too much pizza. This is the last week of school before summer break and if she has to miss a day I'm going to cry."

"How much coffee have you had?" Lou asked when Jamie paused for breath.

"Don't ask." Jamie sighed. When she spoke again, Jamie's voice was tremulous. "Mike's going back to work today."

"Is he okay with that?" Lou asked.

"You know Mike," Jamie said. "If he isn't, he'll never let on."

That was true: Mike was hardly the type to engage in long, emotional talks. Sometimes Lou felt like she had more in common with her sister's husband than with her sister. Then again, she'd always felt more comfortable around guys. Maybe her father was the source of that. He'd insisted he didn't miss having a son, but he'd nicknamed his daughters Jamie and Lou. Who did he think he was kidding?

"So what's up with you?" Jamie asked.

"Donny has a new girlfriend," Lou said.

"Hmm," Jamie said. "What's she like?"

"Okay, I guess," Lou said. "I haven't talked to her much. But she seems nice."

"Does it feel weird?" Jamie asked. "I mean, you guys haven't been broken up that long."

"Long enough," Lou said. "I think they're getting serious. They've been together almost every night this week."

"Do you think he's going to ask her to move in?" Jamie asked.

Lou considered the possibility. She didn't love

Donny any longer—in retrospect, she wasn't sure if she ever had or if she'd been swept up in his desire for a relationship, like a swimmer in a fast-moving current—but she sure loved renting the extra bedroom in his apartment. It was close enough to the zoo that she could walk here in the mornings. If the new girlfriend moved in, would that mean Lou would need to move out?

"Let me know if you want to find a new place," Jamie was saying. "I could help you look—Oh, honey, let me pour the syrup. No! Okay, fine, you can help. We'll pour it together. Shi—shoot. Can you grab a paper towel? No, not the whole roll, just one."

"Sure," Lou said. "In all your spare time." She didn't think she'd had a conversation with Jamie in the past six years that hadn't been interrupted by a child. She'd wanted to ask for advice on how to act around the new girlfriend—sometimes it was a little hard for Lou to read the social cues that other people instinctively grasped—but it was clear this wasn't the time. "Is Sam around? Can I talk to him?"

"Sure, hang on."

Lou heard heavy breathing a second later. Sam still hadn't mastered the art of salutations.

"Do you know elephants are the only mammals that can't jump?" Lou asked.

"What do you call an elephant that never takes a bath?" he responded.

"You got me," Lou said.

"A smellephant."

Lou laughed. "Have a good day at school," she said. "Actually, forget I said that. That was just a stupid adult thing to say."

"You want me to have a bad day at school?" Sam asked.

Lou adored this kid. "I'll bring you to the zoo in a few weeks to see the cheetah babies," she said. "They're so fuzzy and cute."

"Really?" Sam asked.

"Pinkie swear," Lou said. She wished her conversations with Jamie could be like this— light and easy and fun. But Jamie was always fixing things—meals, messes, boo-boos—and sometimes Lou felt as if Jamie was eyeing her as another project. Little sister Lou, unmarried at thirty-one, with a bad haircut (even Lou had to admit it looked deliberately unflattering, but what could she expect when she'd paid $12.99 for it?) and an extra twenty pounds and a fondness for fart jokes. Maybe she *should've* been born a boy—guys could get away with all that stuff a lot more easily.

Lou supposed it wasn't Jamie's fault, though. Their mother had died of a staph infection when Jamie was fifteen and Lou was twelve, and Jamie had stepped into the role of maternal figure, cooking meals and explaining what it would be like when Lou got her period and teaching Lou how to shave her legs (a practice Lou stopped a few years later. Why bother?).

It was strange, Lou thought as she began rinsing off the shovel she'd used to clean Tabby's enclosure. She had lots of memories of being with Jamie while growing up but virtually none of her mother. Once, when Lou had been leaving work, she'd passed a group of tourists who were viewing the small mammal exhibit. Without realizing it, Lou had stopped and edged closer to one of the women. *That perfume,* she'd thought. The floral scent had tugged at the edges of Lou's consciousness, making her feel as if there was something she vitally needed, something just beyond her reach. Had her mother worn the same fragrance? She'd wanted to ask the woman the name of the brand so she could buy a bottle and uncork it and try to coax out the memories that had to be lingering in the recesses of her brain, but she hadn't known how to explain her request. While she was still fumbling for the right words, the woman had taken her two young daughters by their hands and headed off. Lou had stared after her, an ache forming in the center of her chest.

Now Lou began to make notes on the elephants' charts, then set the paperwork back down. Jamie's question hung in the air. Of course Lou couldn't stay with Donny and his new girlfriend. Come to think of it, he'd mentioned the other day that there was a woman in his office who was looking for a roommate. Now she realized he hadn't been making idle conversation. She wondered why he hadn't simply asked her to move out. Had he and his girlfriend been talking about it, hoping she'd take the hint? It was a little embarrassing.

This was why Lou loved kids and animals best. They told you what they thought, in the most direct terms possible. If kids were mad at you, they yelled. If elephants were mad at you, they charged and stomped you to death. Simple and straightforward.

Maybe she should see if another keeper needed a roommate—after all, they couldn't complain about the smell of her boots.

Lou walked over to the barrier that separated keepers from the elephants and pulled a red apple out of her pocket.

"Come, Tabitha," she called, and the elephant lifted her massive head and ambled over. Lou tossed her the apple and watched it disappear. The elephant caught her eye, and Lou held her gaze for a long moment.

Sometimes she wished that she could just live here, where life was less complicated.

Christie Simmons twirled the straw in her strawberry margarita, knowing without raising her eyes that the balding guy across the bar was staring at her. She fought the urge to check the time on her cell phone. Simon was late. Again.

"Excuse me."

Baldie had made his move and now leaned against the bar beside her. He'd been there for only two seconds, and already he was crowding her.

Christie glanced up, putting a question in her eyes.

"Buy you a drink?" he offered.

She deliberately looked back down at her full glass.

"After that one, I mean," he said.

He wore a nice suit—nothing custom-made, but a good-quality pinstripe—and his fingernails were clean. Those things were important to Christie. He took out his wallet and removed a gold AmEx card and waved it at the bartender. "I'll start a tab," he said.

Seven years ago—maybe five, on a good day— Christie would've drawn the eyes of the rowdy, younger guys playing pool in the corner. They would've put down their cue sticks and wandered over, loud and sloppy, flirting artlessly while she threw back her head and laughed, keeping her back perfectly straight so they could admire her curves.

But now she was thirty-seven, technically old enough to be their mother. So instead of being surrounded by muscles and hair flopping into eyes and offers of a slippery nipple shooter, she was left with this: a poseur trying to impress her with the color of his credit card. Which matched the color of his wedding ring.

"I'm meeting someone," Christie said.

Mr. Married leaned in closer. His breath smelled sour, as if he'd been drinking whiskey all day. Maybe he had.

"Well, it doesn't look like he's meeting you," Mr. Married said. His smile didn't reach his small, flinty eyes. "You've been sitting here for half an hour."

She hoped the stab of hurt she felt didn't reveal itself. She didn't want to give him that triumph. She knew this guy's type: She'd flirted with him, dated him, hell, she'd even *married* him once in a spectacularly bad decision that she'd reversed six months later. He'd never made it to the top tier of his profession, and it rankled him. Maybe he had a decent house, and a 401(k), but every day, he had to answer to someone who held the job he coveted, the lifestyle he'd been denied. His anger and frustration mounted, and he released it in passive-aggressive ways: Pretending he had to work late while his wife waited at home. Loudly joking with the barista who made his four-dollar latte to prove he was a good guy, then deliberately cutting off other drivers in traffic. Oh, yes, Christie knew his type intimately before he'd even spoken a word. In bed he'd be a little rough and a lot selfish.

Christie's cell phone rang, but she made herself

wait a few beats before picking it up. She angled herself so Baldie couldn't see her face. If he shifted another step or two forward, they'd be spooning, she thought as she suppressed a shudder.

"Hey, gorgeous." With those words, she knew Simon wasn't going to show up. She'd gotten her hair highlighted—she'd been a little worried it was getting too blond, but her hairdresser had insisted no one could ever be too rich or too blond—and she'd splurged on a bikini wax. She'd applied her makeup carefully, using tricks she'd added to her arsenal over the past few years: a line of white on the inside of each eyelid, to make her eyes appear bigger and brighter, concealer that promised to hide fine lines as well as dark circles, a lip-plumping gloss that stung with the intensity of hot peppers but did seem to make her lips appear fuller. She'd even remade her bed with fresh linens.

"Hi there," she said. She could hear Mr. Married breathing behind her, so she blocked the pique from her voice.

"Something exploded at work," Simon said. "Rain check?"

She wondered if Mr. Married had given his wife the same excuse. But Christie wasn't even a wife. She was a girlfriend, and not a demanding, jealous one, either.

"Sure," she said.

"Love you," Simon told her. It rankled her that he never added the *I,* but she let it go, like she always did.

She waited until she heard him hang up, then she added, "Oh! I thought you said the bar at the Ritz! Okay, I'll meet you in a few."

She put her phone in her purse and stood up. She didn't meet Mr. Married's eyes; she suspected he'd seen through her charade. She left the bar and entered the bathroom and stood in front of the mirror, blinking hard as she assessed herself: long hair styled in beachy waves, tanned skin, false eyelashes applied individually so they looked really natural, and a body that tilted toward lush in all the right places, effectively highlighted in her short black skirt and black tank top. True, her nose was a sharp triangle and her chin was a little weak, but she was still the prettiest woman in the bar, she thought.

She exited the bathroom and stood in the hallway, wondering what to do next. Maybe she'd get a salad in the dining room, even though a woman eating alone seemed pathetic.

"Excuse me."

She whirled around, expecting to see Mr. Married. But it was a different man, one who looked a little older and rougher around the edges. He wore a white button-down shirt and soft-looking tan blazer, cowboy boots, and one of those leather bolo ties with a big sterling silver and turquoise pendant. The outfit didn't quite work here in D.C., unless he'd tied up his horse in the parking lot.

"I was hoping to talk to you about a business proposition," the guy said.

"Are you kidding me?" She felt her heartbeat quicken in fury. "You think I'm a hooker?"

"No, no, not at all," the guy said quickly. His brown eyes were a little watery-looking behind his glasses, and he had the beginnings of a gut. "I think you're a businesswoman. I wanted to talk to you about a job—a real one."

The guy held up a briefcase. Like him, it had seen better days. There were scuffs around the edges and the metal lock had dulled. "I can explain. I've got all the paperwork here. I'd offer to buy you a drink but I saw how you responded when the last guy did that."

"A job," Christie repeated. "Are you for real?"

The guy nodded vigorously. "It pays well and it isn't illegal or unethical. And you'd be doing a service for womankind."

He seemed sincere. Christie could usually sniff out a creep a mile away, but this guy didn't exude weird vibes.

She couldn't help blurting: "Why me?"

Later, when she found out what he wanted her to do, she'd think about his answer and wonder if it was the nicest compliment she'd ever received or a degrading insult.

"Because you're absolutely perfect for it," he said.

Chapter Two

JAMIE AWOKE SUDDENLY, FEELING as if the house had tilted off-balance.

She sat up, listening with a mother's ears. She hadn't slept deeply through the night since her children were born. She always awoke at the first cry—sometimes she even felt as if she'd been jerked out of sleep right *before* the cry, alerted by a subtle gathering change in the atmosphere signaling a sick or scared child.

She quickly realized what was amiss: Mike's side of the bed held only the rumpled comforter. He'd probably gone downstairs to click on ESPN, as he had so many nights recently, Jamie thought. Strange, though. She couldn't hear the sound of the television through their house's thin walls.

Suddenly, she was wide awake. She almost called out her husband's name, then stopped before the single syllable escaped her lips. Something told her not to speak. She slipped out of bed, still craning to hear whatever it was that had awoken her, an electric tension snapping through her body.

She walked along the hallway and crept down the stairs, moving quietly in the shadowy space. She almost tripped on a toy car one of the kids had left on the second-to-last step, but she caught herself on the banister.

There weren't any lights on in the main level of the house, either. Could Mike have taken his police cruiser and gone somewhere?

She crept toward the kitchen, her heart thudding so powerfully it almost hurt. When Mike stepped out of a corner and grabbed her arm, she nearly screamed, but instead released a tiny squeak.

Mike was naked except for his boxers, and he was holding his police-issue SIG Sauer. He raised a finger to his lips and pointed toward the sliding glass doors that led to their small wooden deck and, one flight below it, the backyard. There was a gap of a foot or so between the two doors. Jamie could feel the gentle breeze against her cold skin.

Mike put his lips close to her ears. "I heard someone," he whispered.

The kids. Jamie's eyes darted toward the stairs, but Mike shook his head. "I think he's in the living room," he whispered. "Stay back."

He started moving slowly, his gleaming black gun leading the way. Jamie began to tremble. Why was Mike going after the intruder? They needed to barricade themselves upstairs! For one wild moment she wondered if the shooter from the police station had tracked Mike down, but that was impossible—the man had been killed instantly. But he could have a father or brother who was seeking revenge.

Mike took another slow step toward the living room. He was too far away for her to reach him now. She was torn between going after her husband, to try to protect him, and getting to the kids.

She chose her children.

She hurried back upstairs, stopping to grab the cordless phone and dial 911. "Intruder," she gasped, giving their address as she checked each of the bedrooms and strained to hear what was unfolding one floor below. Sam was sleeping soundly, his ragged stuffed bunny against his cheek, as were Eloise and Emily, who shared a room. Henry was sprawled on the top bunk bed in the tiny far bedroom, snoring softly. The moment she realized they were all safe, Jamie began shaking so profusely the phone banged against her cheek.

"How many are there?" the emergency operator was asking.

"I don't know," Jamie whispered. She was standing guard in the hallway, which gave her the best vantage point of all the bedrooms. "But my husband is a police officer. He has a gun. He's the one wearing boxers. Oh my God, please tell them not to shoot him."

"Officers are on their way," the operator said.

"Jamie?"

Mike's voice floated up the stairs, sounding normal now. She pressed the button to hang up the phone as she rushed to his side, no longer worried about making noise.

He was standing in the living room, the overhead lights blazing, holding a fuzzy red Elmo doll that gave a bleat as it feebly lifted an arm above its head. "The batteries are dying in this," he said.

"Was that the noise?" she asked.

"I don't think so," he said. He tossed the Elmo doll back into a toy bin. "The door was open when I came down here. I checked the rest of the house. It's clear now."

"Did they take anything?" Jamie asked. She saw her iPad still sitting in plain view on the kitchen counter and the laptop Henry used for homework on the couch. "Mike? Can you put away your gun?"

The sight of it made her feel a little ill.

Mike stared down at it as if he hadn't realized it was in his hand. "Yeah," he said, and he started to go upstairs. Since having children, he always unloaded it and kept it in a small safe in their closet.

"Maybe you should put on some pants. I called nine-one-one," Jamie said, just as the flashing lights of an approaching cruiser spun swaths of blue and red through the house, illuminating Mike's face.

"You did what?" he asked. Something shifted in his expression. Was he angry with her?

"I thought someone broke in! We've got kids in the house, Mike!"

He hurried upstairs without a word, and Jamie went to open the front door for the responding officers. She could see the neighbor across the street come to stand on her front steps, and Jamie waved at her, wishing she'd had time to put on a bathrobe over her long T-shirt.

She didn't recognize the two young officers who stepped out of the patrol car, but when Mike came back downstairs, he seemed to.

"The sliding door was jimmied open," Mike said. "But I cleared the house."

"We'll do another check," said the officer with glasses, the one Mike had called Stu. He looked fresh out of the academy. No wonder he'd drawn the overnight shift.

"Our kids are sleeping upstairs," Jamie said. "Please try not to wake them . . . I think they'd be scared if they saw you."

"Of course, ma'am," Stu said.

"I'll go with them," Mike said. He was barefoot, wearing jeans and a red Washington Nationals T-shirt now, and his thick, dark hair was unruly.

"Just stay behind us, please," Stu said.

Jamie could see Mike tense at that. He probably had ten times the experience of these guys. But he followed the men as they checked every room, closet, and cupboard. Their house had four bedrooms and two baths upstairs and a kitchen, dining room, and living room on the main level, but all of the spaces were small, and the search didn't take long. Remarkably, the kids never stirred. But then, Jamie had once burned cookies she was baking for a PTA fund-raiser (*baking* being a loose term—her effort involved slicing dough off a premade roll) and the smoke detector had blared for the better part of five minutes. That hadn't roused the kids, either.

"Let's take a look at that back door," Stu said.

"I didn't touch it," Mike said. "It's still like I found it."

Jamie followed the men through the living room and watched them kneel down to examine the door.

"No marks," Stu said. "Good solid lock, too. The intruder would've walked through the yard . . . hang on . . ." He bent down and pointed to a small clump of dirt on the mat just inside the door.

"That could be from our dog—" Jamie started to say, before cutting herself off. "Wait—where is she? Wouldn't Sadie have barked?"

Mike always let Sadie out in the backyard at night just before coming to bed. It was one of the rituals they'd fallen into by unspoken agreement: Jamie turned on the dishwasher and set up the coffeepot, Mike let Sadie out and locked up.

"Where does the dog sleep?" Stu asked.

"Upstairs, on the floor in one of the kids' rooms," Jamie said. Technically, Sadie usually climbed onto a bed at some point during the night—dog and kids coconspirators against Jamie's halfhearted rules—but Sadie never would've let the two officers go near the kids without putting up a protest.

Jamie ran back up the stairs and checked every bed, but their little tan-colored mutt was gone. She took a moment to grab her bathrobe before heading back downstairs.

"She isn't there," Jamie said.

"Could she have gotten out when the intruder came in?" Mike asked.

"It still doesn't explain why she wouldn't bark," Jamie pointed out. "You know she always goes nuts when someone new comes into the house. I would've heard her."

Her head snapped up and she looked at Mike. "Are you sure you locked the sliding doors after you let her out?"

Mike's brow furrowed. "Yeah."

"Because if there's a crack, she can nudge them open with her nose."

"I locked them," Mike insisted.

Jamie leaned out through the opening. "Sadie!" she called loudly.

A moment later, the dog came bolting up the deck's stairs and back through the sliding doors into the house. She immediately began barking at the two officers. Stu knelt down and let Sadie sniff his hand. She gave two more yips before allowing herself to be petted.

"Hard to believe an intruder would get by this

killer," Stu said. "For such a little thing, she makes a lot of noise."

Instead of responding, Mike rubbed his eyes. Jamie could see it happening: Mike, bone-weary and stressed, one eye on the television as he let Sadie in for the night, reaching to slide the doors shut but not locking them. Sometimes during the day, they let Sadie out in the backyard and didn't bother locking up, especially if the kids were running in and out to the play set. It was possible—natural, even—that he'd forgotten at a time like this, when their lives had been upended.

But why had Mike immediately grabbed his gun and assumed the worst?

"Anything missing?" Stu asked.

"Not that I can tell," Mike said.

"Our electronics are still here," Jamie added, gesturing to Henry's computer.

Stu cleared his throat and glanced at his partner, then looked down at his feet. "Probably some teenagers playing a prank," he said. "Summer vacation's just about here. They're getting antsy."

"One of them stole a street sign a few miles away this week," the other cop added.

Stu was a terrible liar. He'd come to the same conclusion she had: Mike had forgotten to lock the doors, then overreacted. Jamie was just glad the officers hadn't seen Mike cutting through the house in his boxers, aiming his gun at the squeaky

Elmo doll. He never would've lived it down at the station.

But the way the officers *weren't* looking at Mike was almost worse than teasing. Mike reached out and pulled the sliding doors closed, then locked them, the clicking sound echoing in the sudden stillness.

"Teenagers," Jamie said, nodding. "We've got a fourteen-year-old here tonight, so maybe they were planning a prank like you said."

She'd made it worse, Jamie realized. She'd been the one who'd suggested it was Sadie, and her sudden reversal was too obvious.

"Can I get you guys a cup of coffee?" she offered quickly and was relieved when they shook their heads and said they needed to get going.

"Let you two get some sleep," Stu said. Mike reached out and slapped his palm.

"Thanks for coming," he said. "Sorry my wife called you in. I figured it was nothing."

Jamie could feel her cheeks heat up, but she kept quiet. She knew Mike needed to save face. She closed the front door behind the officers and locked it, then turned to her husband. He looked a little dazed, as if he'd just awoken from a vivid dream and felt disoriented.

"Coming to bed?" she asked. She knew she probably wouldn't be able to get back to sleep tonight, but maybe Mike could. And she'd welcome the chance to lie beside him and feel his warmth, to try to get physically close to him to compensate for the emotional distance that had begun to creep between them, like a fog, since the shooting.

But he shook his head. "I'm going to get some cereal."

"Okay." Jamie waited until he'd turned and walked toward the kitchen, then she headed upstairs. She stopped in each of the children's rooms again, putting her face close to Eloise's head so she could inhale her daughter's sweet smell and picking up the doll on Emily's floor and placing it on top of her bureau. Sadie was curled up in the crook of Sam's knees, and Jamie gave both of their heads a stroke. She stopped in at Henry's room and pulled up the covers he'd kicked off.

Finally she went into her own room and climbed into bed. She lay there for a moment, then she got up to do something she never had before in all the years she'd known Mike.

She pulled on the safe's door to make sure he had locked it after putting away his gun.

Lou's weary body craved a long, hot soak in the tub. She'd worked at the zoo that morning, then hurried to the apartment for a quick shower and change, then she'd caught the Metro to the coffee shop, where she'd stood for a five-hour shift, steaming endless stainless-steel carafes of milk and dousing iced drinks with whipped cream and caramel sauce. After her bath, she'd make a thick sandwich, then collapse in front of the television. Maybe an old black-and-white movie, or the History Channel, she thought as she fit her key into the apartment's lock.

She inhaled the scent of roasted garlic as she opened the door.

"Yummy!" she called. Maybe Donny had gotten carryout. He always bought enough for two and insisted she dig in, pretending he'd overordered. He knew she didn't have much money, and it was one of the many kindnesses he'd shown her during their relationship and in its aftermath.

But the face that appeared around the hall corner belonged to Donny's new girlfriend. Mary Alice was holding a glass of red wine and wearing a pretty red top, as if she'd coordinated the two. Mary Alice was fifteen years older than Lou—as was Donny—which was all Lou knew about her. That and the fact that the two of them had met at a Forties and Fabulous! social group that gathered for things like nature hikes and hot-air balloon rides.

"Hi," Lou said. "What smells so good?"

"Donny's making chicken cacciatore," Mary Alice said.

"Wow," Lou said. "Impressive for a Thursday night."

Lou pulled off her clogs, sighing as she wriggled

her toes, and tucked the shoes into a basket by the front door before walking further into the apartment. The dining room table was set with real china, and there was a bouquet of red roses in a vase. Classical music soared from speakers.

"Hey," Donny said, wiping his hands on the apron tied around his middle. Lou had bought it for him the previous Christmas, along with a new cookbook. "I thought you were doing the late shift."

"I was," Lou said, suddenly remembering how Donny had asked about her schedule earlier in the week. "But someone asked me to switch."

Donny glanced at Mary Alice, then back at Lou. "Are you going out tonight, or, um . . ."

"Tonight?" Lou asked.

She looked at the two plates on the dining room table, the flowers, the glowing candles.

"Oh! Yes, I'm meeting a friend to—to see a movie," she lied. "I just came home to change."

The relief on Donny's and Mary Alice's faces was almost comical.

Lou hurried into her bedroom and pulled off her T-shirt, slipping on a clean one. She freed her honey-colored hair from its ponytail and ran a brush through it, then rubbed on a little lip balm. She never wore makeup, so she didn't need to freshen her face. She sniffed her armpits and decided she'd have to make do with another swipe of deodorant instead of that bath. She gave her small, cozy bed a longing look, then opened the door. She half-expected to see Donny and Mary Alice waiting there, holding out her clogs, desperate to hurry her along.

Lou covered a yawn with her hand, then injected energy into her voice as she called out, "Good-bye!"

"Bye!" Donny called back.

Lou stepped out of the apartment building and felt a fat raindrop splatter onto her head.

"Perfect," she said.

She hurried to the bagel place a block away, but it was closed. The rain came down harder, soaking her hair and streaming into her eyes. At least the night was warm, she thought. She walked a bit farther and found an open bar, its pink neon sign flickering in the dusky light. She stepped inside and saw one vacant stool. She collapsed onto it gratefully and reached for the menu.

There wasn't much here she could eat; she'd become a vegetarian around the same time she'd started working with animals. She scanned through the offerings: buffalo wings, loaded potato skins, hamburgers . . .

"Help you?" the bartender asked. Maybe he was too busy to form a complete sentence; this place was packed.

"Do you have veggie burgers?" she asked, straining to make herself heard over the blaring music.

The bartender shook his head. He had a silver ring piercing the tip of his nose, and Lou idly wondered if it ever got caught on anything. She thought about asking, but he already looked impatient.

"Um, can I get the potato skins without bacon?" she asked.

He shrugged. "Dunno. I'll check. Drink?"

"A Sprite, please," she said.

She grabbed a cocktail napkin and wiped the dampness from her face, then glanced around. Almost everyone was dressed in black, tattoos abounded, and a few folks had facial piercings. It was a young, hip crowd. Lou was wearing shorts and a blue-and-white striped T-shirt that was a little big—tight-fitting clothes chafed her skin— but she wasn't uncomfortable. She'd long become inured to the sensation that she didn't fit in.

Donny and Mary Alice seemed like a good match, she thought as the bartender brought over her soda. They were both soft-spoken, with salt-and-pepper hair and silver-rimmed glasses, and Lou could picture them settling into the same easy routines she and Donny used to enjoy: walks after dinner on mild evenings, Sunday mornings on the couch with the newspapers spread out between them, the radio station in Donny's Acura tuned to NPR while they discussed the day's stories.

The apartment had two bedrooms, and Lou

wouldn't have a problem with them all sharing the space, but she suspected Mary Alice might not like it. Most new girlfriends didn't relish having old ones around. Look at the issues Jamie had with Christie, even though Jamie and Mike had been together for more than a decade.

Lou polished off her Sprite, thirsty from her long day in the heat, and tried to puzzle out the lyrics to the song blasting through the speakers. It seemed to involve betrayal, but ennui could also be the lead singer's main complaint. When her potato skins finally arrived, they were topped with bacon bits. Lou used another napkin to pick them off. The potato skins tasted as stale as if they'd been made the previous week and abandoned under a warming light, but she was too hungry to care.

Was the music getting louder? A pulse in the side of her head throbbed in time to the frantic drumbeat. She ate her meal quickly, then paid her bill (Four dollars for a soda? Really? Maybe hipsters were richer than they looked) and slid off her stool. It was raining harder when she walked back outside and took a look around. A movie theater was a few blocks away, but a quick check on her iPhone revealed she'd missed the beginnings of the two shows playing.

She couldn't go back to the apartment this soon, and there weren't any libraries or bookstores within walking distance. She didn't have a car, so her options were limited. She found herself heading toward the theater, her heavy clogs splashing through puddles. But when she tried to buy a ticket, she ran into trouble.

"One for whatever's showing now," she said.

"The next movie's at nine o'clock," the teenage attendant said.

"I know," Lou said. "But I want one for the movie that's playing now."

"It started forty minutes ago," the attendant protested. He frowned at her from behind the glass window of his booth.

"I don't care," Lou said.

"But you missed half of it," he said. "I can't give you a discounted price."

Lou leaned forward. "Look, I'm getting rained on and I can't go back to my apartment for at least two hours because my roommate has his new girlfriend there and I'm pretty sure they want to have sex. Two hours is enough time, right? I mean if they have dinner first."

The attendant reared back, and Lou realized she'd probably overshared again. Jamie had suggested, more than once, that Lou didn't always need to be brutally honest or say the first thing that popped into her head. "Most people don't mind if you tell them a few white lies," Jamie had said. "They expect it, even." This particular conversation had come in their high school lunchroom, after one of Jamie's best friends had asked if her new jeans made her look fat. "Yes," Lou had said.

"Jeez, Lou," Jamie had snapped after her friend had run off to the bathroom in tears. "Think before you speak sometimes, okay?"

"I figured she'd want to know," Lou had protested. "Maybe she can return them."

"But there's a gentler way of telling people that stuff," Jamie had said. "You can't just blurt it out."

"She asked," Lou had pointed out, but Jamie had just sighed and gone to comfort her friend.

"The computer won't sell you a ticket to this show," the attendant was saying. "It will only sell you one for the nine o'clock show."

"Okay," Lou said. The solution was easy enough once she had a little more information. "I'll take one ticket for the nine o'clock show." By now she was completely drenched.

She walked through the double glass doors and handed her ticket to another attendant, who tore it in half without commenting. She found a seat near the back of the theater and sat down, shivering in the frosty blast of air-conditioning. She glanced around. Everyone seemed to be part of a couple. Even the pretty young star on the big screen was closing her eyes in anticipation of being kissed.

Lou could almost hear Jamie's voice in her head, cajoling her to get out and meet someone new, to join a cooking class or a gym, to claim an empty spot in a book club. But Lou felt like she had enough filling in her life. Along with Jamie's family, there was her family of animals at the zoo. Plus she talked to her father every couple of weeks and visited him and his new wife in New York once a year or so.

Sometimes she wondered if their dad still missed their mother. He didn't talk about her at all anymore, but Jamie had told her they'd been deeply in love. "Don't you remember them dancing in the living room?" Jamie had asked. "We'd tiptoe down and watch them when we were supposed to be in bed." Lou strained as hard as she could, but the images refused to bloom for her. She'd been twelve when her mother died, not a toddler. Why couldn't she remember? "And the parties they had!" Jamie had once said. "Mom would always sneak onto the front porch to smoke with her friends." Maybe that was why Lou had never minded the smell of cigarette smoke, even though the habit held no attraction for her.

Their father had remarried three years after their mother's death, and Lou was glad her dad had found someone. His new wife, Kathy, was nice enough, but Lou had never felt particularly close to her, probably because she'd entered their lives just a few years before Lou had left for college.

She'd missed too much of the movie for it to

make any sense, so Lou huddled lower in her chair and closed her eyes. The next thing she knew, someone was tapping her shoulder.

"You're snoring really loudly," the girl behind her whispered.

"Sorry," Lou said. She could hear giggling and she sat up straighter. Her clothes were damp and she could feel goose bumps rising on her skin. She stole a glance at her watch and realized she couldn't go home for at least an hour. She wrapped her arms around herself and wished more than ever for that hot bath.

She needed to find a new apartment, fast.

She, Christie Simmons, had a job!

A real job, too—not like the hostess and receptionist gigs she usually floated between, or the "modeling" assignments she'd taken in the past that required her to walk around in a bikini at car shows. This was regular, steady, *enviable* work. Elroy had even mentioned an expense account. Bolo-tie-wearing Elroy wasn't a misplaced cowboy after all. He was a private detective who specialized in infidelity cases, and Christie was going to help him gather evidence. She'd be working undercover. The best part, though, the thing that made her lips curve into a secret smile, was that she'd be playing off the assumptions of people like Baldie with the wedding ring from the bar. Just because a woman was single and sexy, some guys assumed she was easy, a throwaway sort of girl. And during the past few years—the same stretch of time in which she'd begun to feel a slight ebb in her energy and notice a slight sagging of the skin around her eyes and jawline—she'd realized it had begun to bother her deeply. Christie wanted a lot of things, including a nice house and car, but something else had edged its way to the top of her wish list, something that couldn't be bought.

Respect.

Only one man in her life had ever treated her with true dignity: Mike, the father of her beautiful, perfect son, Henry. Christie had met Mike at a bar—because let's face it, girls like her didn't hang out at the library or health food store or hiking trail—and he'd offered to buy her a drink. But then the familiar script had strayed from its usual path: he'd kept his eyes on hers instead of focusing them twelve inches lower, and he'd spoken her name when he handed her a glass of Chardonnay. Back then she thought wine tasted sour, but she'd been twenty-three and figured the drink sounded classy.

Mike had been so beautiful—intense brown eyes, a blunt nose, and broad shoulders. A triangle of springy black hair peeked out from the top of his polo shirt. He wasn't very tall, but he seemed to take up a lot of physical space.

"Can I take you out to dinner?" he'd asked,

while her friends gave her the thumbs-up and made obscene gestures behind his back.

"Dinner?" she'd repeated. She'd licked her lips, glossed in a shade called Kitten Pink, and lowered her eyelashes, hoping he appreciated the four coats of mascara she'd painstakingly applied.

"Tomorrow night," Mike had said. "Italian sound good to you?"

"Are you telling me you're Italian?" Christie had asked.

It took Mike a moment, but he'd gotten the joke. "You're a firecracker," he'd said.

"And what are you?" she'd asked.

"A cop," he'd said. She'd seen the way he stood up a little straighter with the release of those words. She'd almost made a joke about his handcuffs, but she'd refrained. For some reason, she didn't feel like bantering with him the way she did with other guys.

"I do like Italian," she'd said instead. "In all its forms."

"So I'll pick you up at seven." That was Mike—confident, direct, steady. He'd shown up five minutes early, held open the car door for her, and asked her what she liked to eat as she studied the menu at the restaurant.

"Nothing too heavy," she'd said. She was a size eight, and wanted to stick to it for as long as possible. Which might be only until she turned forty, given that her mother now resembled a blowfish. But her mother subsisted on a steady diet of junk food and junkier television, and Christie was determined to avoid that path. Well, at least the fast-food part.

"The angel hair's nice," he'd said, in a voice so low and deep it was almost a growl. "Maybe with clams and a little red sauce."

She'd nodded, and when the waiter arrived, Mike had ordered for her. It had made her feel taken care of, but not in a creepy, father-figure way—especially since she'd slept with Mike that night. Mike may have been a gentleman, but he wasn't *that* much of a gentleman.

He was good in bed, if conventional, and eventually that was his downfall: being too traditional in other ways, as if he was rushing toward middle age, arms stretched out in a welcoming embrace. Mike wanted the white picket fence and Sunday afternoons helming the barbecue grill. Christie wanted nights out dancing and spontaneous trips to Vegas. She was far too young to settle down, and if she were being perfectly honest, Mike didn't seem all that eager to settle down with *her,* either. His calls came less frequently after the first few weeks.

They probably would've drifted apart, their memories of each other fading with each passing year. Maybe after a decade or two, one of her friends might've said, "Remember that cop you used to date?" And Christie would've replied, "Oh, yeah, he was cute," and struggled to conjure his name.

But she got pregnant.

It was her fault. She'd told Mike she was on the pill, which was the truth, but what she didn't reveal was that sometimes she forgot to take it, especially after a night of drinking.

She'd broken the news to him because she wanted him to help pay for the abortion, but part of her also wanted to say the words because she didn't have anyone else in whom to confide. Her mother would've erupted—she'd had Christie at eighteen and was vocal about questioning the wisdom of that decision—and her father was nothing but a faded photograph Christie kept hidden in a dresser drawer. At least she thought the picture was of her father. The guy in it had an arm around Christie's mother's shoulders, and she could tell it was taken at about the time she'd become pregnant, because they were in the halls of their high school. Sometimes Christie thought she could see bits of herself in the shape of his eyebrows and the straight lines of his nose, but she'd never met him, so she couldn't be certain. Apparently he'd entered the military after graduation, and hadn't responded to the letters Christie's mother had sent. If Christie's mother had thought the news of a baby would lure him back, all handsome and official in his Navy whites, like a scene out of *An Officer and a Gentleman*, it had been the first of many disappointments in her life.

Christie didn't know what kind of reaction she'd expected from Mike when she told him about the two lines on the E.P.T. test, but he'd merely nodded without changing expression. Maybe that went hand-in-hand with being a cop —you couldn't freak out when someone confessed to something big, like a murder, or you'd blow the whole case.

After a moment, he'd quietly asked, "Do you want to get married?" She'd almost fallen off the couch. What twenty-three-year-old guy would ask that of a girl he'd been dating for less than four months?

By then Mike's steadiness had become boring, and the thought of being yoked to him for the rest of her life made her feel claustrophobic. He laughed too loudly when he watched television —which he was content to do most nights while he drank a Budweiser—and he owned only one suit, a blue number with a disturbing sheen.

"No," she'd said. "And I don't think I want to keep it."

He'd gone pale then, and had put a hand to his own stomach.

"I'm Catholic," he'd said.

That explains a lot, she'd thought.

"Just—wait, okay?" he'd said. He'd dropped his head into his hands for a long moment. They were in his condo, sitting side by side on the black leather couch, untouched cartons of Chinese food in front of them. Christie couldn't eat because morning sickness had struck with a vengeance, except it was all-day sickness. That, along with her missed period, had been what prompted her to pick up a test at CVS.

"What if you kept it?" he'd said. "*We* kept it."

"I told you I'm not getting married," Christie had said. *Not to you, anyway,* she'd refrained from adding.

She didn't know why, but suddenly she'd felt angry with him. "I was going to break up with you," she'd said. "You bore me."

"Don't do anything yet, okay?" he'd said, and it had made her even more upset that he hadn't reacted to her declaration. "It probably has arms and legs by now. Hair, too."

"Of course it doesn't," she'd said, even though she had no idea who was right. She'd stood up, fury shaking through her. "It's a blob. A tiny little blob!"

She'd stormed out and driven home, where she'd poured a big rum and Diet Coke, which she vastly preferred to the stupid, cheap wine Mike always offered her. She wasn't keeping the baby, so what did it matter if she drank? But she couldn't swallow more than a sip. The alcohol felt metallic in her mouth and made her stomach heave. She'd poured it down the drain instead, and cursed Mike.

An hour later he'd knocked on her front door, breathing hard, as if he'd run the whole way there. "The baby's got fingers and toes. I checked. He or she is the size of a kidney bean about now."

And Christie had burst into tears.

She and Mike didn't last, of course. They'd already broken up by the time of her first ultrasound. But the arrangement Mike had suggested was surprisingly successful. He took the baby most of the time when he wasn't at work, and he paid for part-time day care. Christie had Henry only three nights a week and one weekend day. Mike also gave her five hundred dollars a month in child support. Christie had complained about having to drop out of hair-dressing school, since her all-day sickness was so overpowering and the smell of chemicals made it worse, but she'd never regretted their decision. The truth was, Henry was an angel. He slept through the night the very first week, happily ate whatever was offered, and rarely got sick. She loved watching TV with him cuddled on her chest, smelling of soft, chalky talcum powder and feeling as cozy as a hot-water bottle. Henry was good company right from the start.

Later she figured out why she couldn't go to the

abortion clinic. It wasn't because of the haunted look that had come into Mike's eyes, or the thought of those tiny fingers and toes wiggling inside of her. It was because the moment she learned she was pregnant, the hollow, aching feeling Christie had grown accustomed to carrying around had finally disappeared. It was only after it had vanished that she'd been able to identify it as loneliness.

Now Christie pulled her Miata into the cul-de-sac where Mike and Jamie lived. Mike had built the white picket fence around their brick rancher himself. When he'd told Christie, she'd faked a coughing fit to hide her laughter. The front yard, as always, was littered with scooters and a tricycle and squirt guns. Even before Jamie opened the door, Christie knew what the interior would look like: sports equipment piled haphazardly by the front door, a beaten-up sectional sofa around a television that was too big for the space, a bunch of kids wandering around, including a neighbor or two . . . Strange how all the things she'd bristled against fifteen years ago didn't seem quite so terrible now.

She knocked on the door, and Jamie answered, pushing her bangs off her face with one hand while she pulled open the door with the other.

"Hey," Christie said. Mike's wife was only a few years younger than Christie, but Jamie looked about twenty-five, with her unlined, softly rounded face and baby-blue eyes. She probably still got carded.

"Hi, Christie." Jamie smiled without showing her teeth.

Christie may not have made the honor roll in school, but she had an unerring sense about people. Jamie tolerated her only because of Mike and Henry.

"Is that a new shirt?" Christie asked.

"This?" Jamie looked down like she'd forgotten she was wearing clothes. When she looked back up, she also wore a suspicious expression. "No, I've had it forever."

Christie didn't know why she'd said it. Obviously the shirt wasn't new; the neckline was a little frayed. She never knew how to act around Jamie, so she usually ended up saying or doing the wrong thing.

"So is Henry around?" Christie asked.

"Yeah, hang on," Jamie said. "Henry!" she called up the stairs. A minute later came the thudding of heavy footsteps and the sight of her son.

"Hey, Mom," he said, moving easily and fluidly despite the fact that he seemed to be all knobby elbows and gangly limbs. Henry played three sports: baseball, basketball, and soccer. He got mostly As with a few Bs sprinkled in like seasoning. He said "please" and "thank you" without being prompted. He was a golden boy.

"Burgers sound good for dinner?" she asked.

"Actually, we had that last night," Henry said, glancing sideways at Jamie. "But I don't mind twice in a row."

Christie pulled him close for a quick hug, noticing again the fine light-brown hairs that had begun to sprout above his upper lip. She was five foot five, but he'd officially passed her a year ago. She wasn't a sentimental person, but tears had stung her eyes on the day she'd realized she had to look up at her son.

"Bye, Jamie," Henry said. He gave his stepmother a hug, too—he was the human version of Switzerland—and stepped out the door, his huge backpack slung over one shoulder.

"Love you!" Jamie called after him, and Christie felt herself soften. No matter what she thought about Mike's wife, she had to give her this: Jamie had never been anything but good to Henry. Once Christie had asked Henry about the time he spent with Jamie. "Does she ever say anything about me?" she'd asked, keeping her voice casual.

"Yeah," Henry had said, and Christie had braced for it.

"At night, when we say our prayers"—this was something Christie hadn't authorized, but she couldn't control what Mike did with their son—"Jamie tells me to include you."

"Oh," Christie had said. For a moment she

wasn't sure how to take that revelation. Did Jamie think Christie needed saving? But Henry's voice was sweetly innocent, and she'd decided it was a compliment of sorts. Even though Christie didn't believe in God, she liked the idea that someone else was putting in a good word for her.

"I've got some cool news," she said as they climbed into her Miata. "I got a new job."

"Yeah?" Henry said. "Where?"

"It's undercover," Christie said. "A private detective hired me."

"Seriously?" His face brightened.

"I know, right? You've got a cop for a dad and an undercover investigator for a mom."

"So what are you gonna investigate?" Henry asked. "Drug deals?"

"No," Christie said, amending it when she saw Henry's disappointment. "At least not at first. I'm going to catch gross guys who cheat on their wives."

"Like with wiretaps?"

"Probably," Christie said, even though she had no idea. Elroy hadn't given her all the details; they were meeting in a few days to go over them. "I'll probably have a hidden microphone when I talk to the guys. Maybe a secret camera, too." And possibly a sexy trench coat, Christie decided. She might as well start breaking in her expense account.

"That is so awesome," Henry said.

"I know, right?" Christie said, and she experienced the same warm burst of pride Mike must have felt on that long-ago night when he'd told her he was a cop. Her new job paid sixty bucks an hour, which was a heck of a lot better than the fourteen she currently earned as the receptionist at a hair salon.

She felt as if the fates were finally turning in her favor, after all those bad relationships and overdue credit card bills and the sense that somehow, without her being able to pinpoint exactly when or how it had happened, the life she'd meant to live had slipped past her, carrying along a tide of people who were laughing and clinking champagne glasses and waving as she stood on the shore.

Screw her passive-aggressive scale, she thought, and she said, "Should we go get hot fudge sundaes to celebrate?"

Chapter Three

SUMMER WAS OFFICIALLY HERE. Hot, sticky, languid summer. It was 10:00 A.M. on June 22, and a flurry of teacher appreciation events and picnics and field days had ushered in the end of the school year. Now Jamie was wondering why teachers didn't earn million-dollar salaries. All they'd have to do was stage a strike, and after a few days, parents would be pulling money out of their wallets to make up the difference. Jamie could barely handle *three* little people—how did anyone control a pack of twenty-five or thirty without tranquillizer darts?

A shower, she thought longingly as she bent down to wipe up something brownish—best not to examine it closely—off the floor. Before kids, bathing used to be an uneventful part of her morning routine. Now ten minutes alone with sweet-smelling shampoo and hot water coursing over the knots in her shoulders felt as luxurious as a week in the Bahamas. But her plans to get up early and sneak one in had been thwarted when Eloise awoke at 5:45, having soaked through her nighttime diaper. Jamie had started to throw the wet pajamas and sheets into the wash, then she'd realized there was already a load in the machine. It smelled funky—it must have been moldering there for a few days—so Jamie had dumped in a little more detergent and pulled the dial to rewash it, then come upstairs to encounter the stain on the floor. By then Eloise was flopped on the couch, her hair sticking up and her eyes bleary, loudly asking for Barney on TV.

"Shhh, honey," Jamie said. Was she actually panting from the brief exertion of running up the stairs? She really had to figure out a way to exercise regularly. "No TV this morning."

Eloise started wailing. Her flair for drama always took a sharp uptick when she hadn't gotten enough sleep.

"You're going to wake up Sam and Emily!" Jamie chided. As if Eloise cared; Jamie would have to turn to her arsenal of bribes and threats, another violation of parenting rules. The thing about the "experts" on TV, though, was that they were always rested and fresh—not to mention that most of the nannies on those parenting shows weren't actually parents. They were like sportscasters who'd been cut from their high school teams, called in to nitpick the performance of professional athletes.

"Want some chocolate milk?" Jamie offered. Eloise considered it, then nodded. Jamie fixed the milk in a sippy cup, grabbed Eloise's favorite chunky board book and a few toys, and set everything on the couch next to her daughter. That might buy her enough time to rinse off—she was pretty sure she smelled like pee now.

But then Sadie started barking at an invading squirrel in the backyard, and Jamie rushed to shush her, too, and seconds later Emily awoke and immediately began bickering with Eloise . . . seven pancakes and one mostly uneaten bowl of fruit later, the kitchen was a disaster, Jamie was limping from stubbing her toe on a chair's leg, Sadie had managed to overturn her dish of water, and Mike had gone to work, wearing his shiny badge with the black ribbon that made Jamie feel as if someone was grabbing her heart and squeezing it whenever she looked at it. And her shower shimmered like an oasis, forever just beyond her reach.

Jamie stole at look at the clock. Had the hands stopped, or could it really be this early?

"Let's go to the pool," she suggested. Forget the dishes and laundry and all the other chores waiting for her attention. She'd combust if she stayed in the house for another minute. They all needed to be outside, in the fresh air, even if it was so muggy and thick it felt like a wet sheet wrapping around her every time she stepped out the door.

She gathered up sunscreen, towels, bathing suits, goggles, and some water toys and bundled everything into a giant beach bag. Then she filled a cooler with sandwiches and pretzels and drinks. The kids would beg for lunch from the overpriced snack bar, but if she didn't set a precedent now, her bank account would be empty by the end of the summer. She'd allow them one Popsicle each, she decided.

"Are Finn and Daisy coming?" Emily asked.

"I was just going to call them," Jamie said. A carefree day might be exactly what Ritchie's wife and kids needed.

She reached for the phone and dialed the number she knew by heart. Sandy answered on the third ring.

"Hey, hon," Jamie said. "Up for a day at the pool?"

She kept her tone light, not letting on that hearing Sandy's high, crisp voice with the hint of a Boston accent, an inheritance from Sandy's hometown, conjured so many turbulent feelings in her—relief that it hadn't been Mike who'd walked out the door first, guilt for the same reason, dread that Mike could be next. When Jamie had rushed into the hospital after Mike's call, the first thing she'd seen was a wall of blue. Dozens of officers lined the hallways outside the area where surgeons frantically fought to save Ritchie by removing the bullet from his skull and reducing the pressure around his brain. By then everyone knew the rookie nicknamed the Kid was dead. His eyes were open and unblinking as he lay on the sidewalk, Mike had told Jamie after he'd awoken from one of his nightmares, gasping and shuddering. That was before he'd stopped talking to her about the shootings.

Jamie had torn down the hallway, past the officers who were stoic and the ones who were crying, because she'd caught sight of her husband and in that desperate, blurry moment she'd thought Mike had been shot, too. But the blood darkening his shirt had belonged to Ritchie. Moments after Ritchie had fallen, Mike had leapt on top of his partner, covering him, trying to shield his best friend from a second bullet.

It wasn't until the surgeon came out into the hallway to announce that Ritchie was still alive that Sandy had broken down in Mike's arms, her husband's blood leaching off Mike's uniform to stain her face, sobs exploding from her thin frame. Jamie had patted her back, trying to whisper words of comfort through her own tears. Sandy had pulled herself together when the surgeon added, "But he's not out of the woods. And there are going to be some complications if he makes it."

Complications. Such an innocuous word. A complication was a traffic jam, a malfunctioning coffeemaker, two meetings scheduled for the same time. It didn't begin to describe Ritchie learning to fasten the Velcro on his new shoes and feed himself. It didn't encapsulate the brain trauma that revealed itself in his halting speech, or memory lapses.

Ritchie *had* died that day, a part of him anyway.

Jamie had tried to reassure Mike that his brief hesitation wouldn't have made a difference; that the shooter was already in position and the two rifle cracks had sounded within seconds of Ritchie exiting the building. But Mike felt as if he'd betrayed the sacred oath of his profession. He wore his guilt like a shroud, and Jamie was beginning to worry that it would always shadow him. At least Sandy put the blame squarely where it belonged: on the shoulders of the shooter.

Maybe Sandy cried at night, when she was alone in the bed she'd once shared with her husband, but Jamie had never again seen her break down. Sandy was a cop's wife, which meant uncertainty and worry had always been familiar companions. Everyone who married a police officer knew that the moment a certain call came over the radio— say a 10-33, code for an officer in trouble—their lives could irrevocably change. Sandy might have been mentally preparing for this ever since she'd said her wedding vows, or maybe, like Jamie, she'd tried to block out the fear that was an unwelcome adjunct to her husband's job. Jamie didn't know because they'd never discussed it. Doing so would have seemed like tempting fate.

"The pool sounds good," Sandy was saying.

"Just grab your bathing suits and I'll swing by

and pick you up," Jamie said, pulling the jar of peanut butter back out of the cabinet and opening the refrigerator to find the bread. "I've got lunch for everyone, too."

"I made some chocolate chip cookies this morning," Sandy said. "I'll throw those into a Tupperware and bring them along."

"Perfect," Jamie said, marveling at Sandy's competence, especially now.

After hanging up and making more sandwiches and managing to shepherd everyone into the minivan, then immediately circling back home to pick up Eloise's sandals, despite the fact that Jamie argued they were just going to the pool and didn't need shoes (knowing, even as she spoke, that it was impossible for anyone to win arguments with three-year-olds, who were as determined and illogical as drunks), they drove the two miles to Sandy and Ritchie's house.

Jamie could see a few off-duty officers working in the front yard, carrying planks of wood from a pile on the lawn to the side door. They were building a wheelchair ramp, she realized. Ritchie would be in one for a few months when he came home. Jamie had no doubt the officers would be back to tear down the ramp when it was time for Ritchie to graduate to a walker. Doctors were hopeful he would be able to stand on his own within six months or so, but they were less willing to predict how quickly he'd recover mentally—or if there would ever be a complete recovery.

Sandy came out the front door, a beach bag in her hand and Finn and Daisy by her side. One of the officers picked up Finn and flipped him over his shoulder. Finn squealed and laughed, especially when the officer pretended to put him on the hood instead of inside the minivan.

The brotherhood in blue, Jamie thought. Stories about police brutality and corruption always made headlines, but overlooked were these quieter truths: the fierce loyalty and unexpected kindnesses members of the force shared. Sure, they teased each other, often viciously: One pudgy detective was nicknamed Stay Puft in homage to a brand of marshmallows, and another officer, who'd tried to pull open a door marked PUSH during his first day, would forever be known as Einstein. Mike was jokingly called Rambo, because of his dark hair and muscles. Insults flew fast and furious around the building at morning roll call, yet whenever someone was hurt or suffering, the force appeared, steadily as the ocean tide coming in.

"Hey, girl," Jamie called, pressing a button to open the minivan's side door for the kids. That automatic function was the only upgrade she'd wanted when they purchased the vehicle from a used-car lot. Forget heated seats and sunroofs— when you were carrying one kid and holding the hand of another while juggling three grocery bags and dodging cars as you wove your way through a parking lot, that was the feature that won a mother's heart.

Sandy climbed into the passenger's seat and leaned over to give Jamie a hug. "Thanks for this," she said. Sandy's dark brown skin was as fresh and unlined as ever, but her eyes looked tired.

She was drawing on a deep reservoir of courage and strength for Ritchie and the kids, Jamie thought. Would she be able to do the same, if their positions had been reversed? If Mike hadn't nudged Ritchie out the door first? Jamie pushed away the invading thought.

"I'm so glad you were free!" Jamie said. She waited until the kids strapped themselves in, then waved good-bye to the officers and put the van in gear. "How's Ritchie?"

"We're going to have dinner with him tonight," Sandy said. "He's getting pretty good with a spoon."

"That's great!" Jamie said. Tall, strong Ritchie, who did triathlons and baked his own kale chips before it was fashionable—his nickname was Tree Hugger—was learning to master a spoon. She wouldn't cry, Jamie told herself. If Sandy could power through this, everyone else should be able to as well.

"A fork's still a challenge, though," Sandy said.

"He'll get there," Jamie said. "I thought I'd go with Mike when he visits this weekend . . . so if you need a break to get things done around the house or whatever, let me know. I can time it to then so you'll know Ritchie has company. And you can drop off the kids on Sunday if you want to visit him alone."

"Thanks," Sandy said. "They usually like to go with me, but maybe I'll take you up on it sometime."

Jamie hesitated, not knowing if bringing up happier memories of Ritchie would be painful or welcome. Maybe Sandy just needed a day off from thinking . . . But in the end, she decided to risk it.

"Remember when the guys answered the call from the woman who was in the shower and had heard a man's voice in her room? And it turned out to be the woman's father on the answering machine?"

Sandy laughed and seemed to relax a little in her seat. "They were so mad. They thought it was going to be their first big arrest."

"And then the next day someone attached an old answering machine to their lockers with evidence tape," Jamie said.

As they traded memories about their husbands' early days on the force, Jamie thought about how she and Sandy had gravitated toward each other at softball games and annual picnics, knowing their friendship was inevitable because of their husbands' bond. Some officers switched partners a few times before finding a good match, but as different as they were, Mike and Ritchie had hit it off immediately. Maybe that was *why* they'd hit it off. Ritchie was calm and placid, whereas Mike's temper could run hot. Ritchie liked classical music, Mike liked classic rock. Mike once lost a bet and had to eat a kale chip; he'd ended up spitting it out on his dashboard. But through the years, Mike had turned into a fan of NPR's *Morning Edition*, and Ritchie had recently declared the Kiss song "Beth" one of his top ten favorites.

"Is a bad guy going to shoot my daddy, too?"

The little voice cut through the air.

Jamie froze, but Sandy recovered quickly and answered Eloise, her voice warm and reassuring. For that, Jamie would forever be grateful.

"Of course not, honey," Sandy said, twisting around to look at the little girl. "Your daddy is very safe."

Jamie waited for Eloise to continue the conversation, but she didn't. Kids were remarkable that way; they often spoke truths that adults were too scared to address, then they moved on. At least Jamie thought Eloise had moved on. She and Mike had told the kids about Ritchie's injury in vague terms, assuring them the bad guy was in jail (the lie seeming less upsetting than the alternative). They'd promised that the doctors would help Ritchie get better. But Eloise's question seemed to pierce through Jamie like a sharp-ribbed arrow, deflating the sense of optimism she'd tried to conjure for the day.

Jamie pulled into the pool's crowded parking lot, finally finding a space near the back. "We're here!" she announced unnecessarily, wanting to fill the quiet.

Mike had never been shot—but he'd been stabbed once, by a junkie he and Ritchie had taken in after the woman lay down in the middle of the road for a nap. Mike had made the mistake of letting down his guard because she was young and female, but he'd spotted the knife arcing toward his chest in time to deflect it with his forearm. He'd needed twelve stitches, and a white scar still bisected the skin above his elbow. And now he was back at work, a weakened version of himself, patrolling the streets that seemed more unsafe than ever.

"It's so hot!" Jamie said as they paid the attendant at the front desk and pushed through the turnstiles that led to the public pool. "Let's get changed and then I'll lather you all up with sunscreen and you can jump in the water."

It *was* going to be a wonderful day, she told herself almost fiercely. Sandy deserved it. Jamie had tucked an old issue of *People* magazine in her bag at the last moment. She'd put it down on a chair and insist on watching the kids so her friend could have a break.

As they walked up the cement path that led to the pool, Jamie felt something: a gentle tug on her hand.

It was Sam, her anxious kid, the one who sometimes chewed the collar of his shirt. He'd listened to her and Mike talk about Ritchie and his injury and he'd seemed to be okay. He hadn't asked any questions, so they hadn't elaborated. But now she saw Sam hadn't taken the news in stride, not at all. None of them had. Mike with his workouts, she trying to stick to their usual routines, Sandy with her bright reports of Ritchie's progress, the kids with their laughter and arguments . . . normal life wasn't normal any longer. Maybe it would never be again.

Her son's hand was cool on this warm day, and that was what broke her heart.

"But what if it happens again?" Sam said. Jamie didn't have to ask him what he meant.

The question Eloise had unleashed was the same one echoing in Jamie's head.

Lou gave a quick knock on her sister's front door, then pushed it open. She saw Sadie charging toward her, and she raised her right knee so that her leg was at a ninety-degree angle. That blocking maneuver was all that was needed to keep Sadie from leaping up and jabbing her nails into Lou's thighs. Lou had tried to explain to Jamie that it was relatively simple to train a dog, but Jamie had waved away Lou's suggestions. "I can't even train my kids to put their dirty laundry in their hampers," Jamie had said. "Can we start with that and work our way down the priority list?"

Lou gave Sadie a quick scratch behind the ears, then called out, "Who wants candy?" The sudden pounding of feet on the stairs sounded like a mini-avalanche. "Sorry, did I say candy?" she asked as the kids swarmed around her. "I meant Brussels sprouts."

Lou fended off the mock attack from the children, laughing. She'd never felt a maternal longing or heard a biological clock ticking in her midriff or experienced whatever it was women were supposed to feel when they hit thirty. But oh, did she adore being an aunt—the kind who told silly jokes, threw the first snowball, and took the kids to see Pixar movies and let them load up on popcorn and tubs of soda. Lou didn't do all that stuff to make the kids happy—she truly enjoyed it, too. Sitting around a dinner table discussing politics and home renovations with adults was the most boring experience she could imagine. Kids had so much more life in them, at least until life itself sucked it back out.

"After dinner!" Jamie was calling, confiscating the Hershey's Kisses Lou was tossing into the air and letting the kids catch like raindrops. "Come on, guys, I just made you all hot dogs . . . Eloise, I saw you put that in your pocket. Give it back! Lou, can you stop that?"

Buzzkill, Lou thought. Jamie used to go nuts over her Halloween candy as a kid—endlessly sorting it and awarding each piece a number of stars and scheming about how to get maximum enjoyment from the bag of sugary snacks. How had her big sister forgotten about the simple magic contained in a square of crinkly foil?

"So what's the plan for tonight?" Lou asked the kids. "A game of Hullabaloo? Or hide-'n'-seek? Or how about a massive pillow fight? I'll take you all on!"

"Maybe a pillow fight isn't such a great idea," Jamie said, scooping the candy off the floor. "Remember a lamp got broken last time, Lou?"

"Oh, right," Lou said. "Well, we can move the pillow fight outside."

"Dinner first," Jamie said. She led the way into the kitchen, and Lou hid a smile when she saw Eloise pull a Kiss from her other pocket and gobble it down.

"Thanks again, Lou," Jamie said as she picked up a piece of paper off the counter and handed it to her sister. "I wrote everything down, but it should be pretty simple. They just need to brush their teeth before bed, and make sure everyone goes to the bathroom, too."

"What if they don't have to pee?" Lou asked

solemnly. She peered at the paper: "Oh, it says right here that I have to make them do push-ups until they obey!"

Sam began laughing so hard he practically fell out of his chair.

"Get down and give me twenty, child!" Lou ordered, pointing at him. Sam's laughter turned into coughing and he spat something onto his plate.

"He's gross," Emily said, crinkling her nose. "Can I go eat in front of the TV?"

"Take it easy," Jamie said to Sam. "Did a piece of hot dog go down the wrong way? Have a sip of water . . . there, that's good . . . Emily, come back here. You need to eat at the table."

Jamie turned to Lou. "She keeps trying to watch *Pitch Perfect* because it's on HBO now, but it's way too old for her."

"Annabelle saw it," Emily protested.

"Who's Annabelle?" Lou asked.

"She's in Emily's grade," Jamie said, before whispering to Lou, "Annabelle also wears shorts that barely cover her butt."

"Why do they even make clothes like that for kids?" Lou asked, and Jamie shrugged. "You got me. But all it takes is one queen bee wearing them and you've got a trend."

Lou watched as Jamie walked over to the refrigerator, grabbed a bottle of white wine, and poured a few inches into a glass.

Jamie glanced at the kids, then moved a few feet away and lowered her voice again. "I'm nervous," she confided. "I don't know why . . . I saw Ritchie a dozen times in the hospital . . . It's not like rehab is going to be that different."

"Auntie Lou, can I sit on your lap?" Eloise asked.

"Let me talk to your mom first, okay? You guys finish dinner and then we'll play," Lou said. "Go on, eat! But don't choke like Sam. Chew your food, like elephants do."

"I didn't know elephants had teeth," Sam said.

"Twenty-four pearly white chompers," Lou said. "Actually they're kind of yellow. Elephants don't brush enough. Obviously your mom didn't give them a bedtime list."

She winked at the kids, then turned back to her sister and, following Jamie's lead, kept her voice low. "He's still the same guy," Lou said.

"But he isn't, exactly," Jamie said.

Lou didn't know what else to say. She wasn't nearly as good as her sister at providing comfort. So she just tucked a handful of Kisses in Jamie's purse, which was stuffed almost to bursting, even though it was the size of the carry-on bag Lou took on airplanes. Lou found purses bizarre and unnecessary encumbrances. She kept her driver's license and a credit card tucked into her iPhone's case in one pocket, and her keys in another.

"Thanks," Jamie said. She unwrapped a Kiss and slipped it into her mouth, keeping her actions covert so the kids didn't see. That was the Jamie that Lou remembered. "I'm armed with wine and chocolate," Jamie said. "What more could I need?"

"How does Mike feel about it?" Lou asked. "Is he upstairs chugging a beer and smoking a cigar?"

Jamie smiled, which had been Lou's intention. "He's getting out of the shower. He went for a long run again today."

Lou nodded. Jamie didn't look so good, even though she was dressed up—well, dressed up for Jamie, which meant a simple khaki skirt and blue sleeveless top, but for Lou that would've been practically black tie. Jamie's face was strained, with smudges of purple beneath her eyes, and she was twirling a lock of her hair around her index finger. That was a nervous habit dating back to her childhood. Once Jamie's hair had gotten so ensnarled that their mother couldn't remove the knots and had to cut out a chunk. Jamie had cried, and her mother had done something to make her feel better. "What was it?" Lou had asked. "I can't remember," Jamie had said. "Did she make a face? Sing a silly song?" Lou had pressed, but Jamie had just shaken her head and shrugged. The memory seemed a fingertip beyond Lou's reach, and the more she strained, the faster it slipped away, like a dream that began to fade the instant one awoke. A few sharp fragments were all Lou could cling to: the smell of some-thing sweet—fresh flowers in a vase? or that perfume?—and the pink headband Jamie had worn for weeks to disguise her missing chunk of hair.

"Mike hasn't been sleeping," Jamie was saying. She took another big sip of wine. "And at work they tried to pair him with a new guy, who talks all the time and drives Mike crazy."

"Can't he switch?" Lou asked. She reached into a kitchen cupboard for a glass and filled it with water from the Brita pitcher on the counter; she was as familiar with Jamie's kitchen as she was with her own.

"Yeah," Jamie said. "But I'm not sure that will solve the problem. I think partnering with anyone who isn't Ritchie is going to be difficult for Mike. It would be like having your beloved husband leave you, then having a new guy move into your house the next day. Can you imagine how strange that would feel?"

"Probably not the best analogy for me to relate to," Lou joked.

"I'm sorry—" Jamie began, but Lou waved away the apology. Why did people, even her own sister, automatically assume she wanted to get married and have kids? Children didn't sleep nearly as much as animals, and they were a lot louder.

"So how bad is Mike's insomnia?" Lou asked.

"Awful. He watches TV most nights and dozes on the couch," Jamie said. "Or if he starts out in our bed, he comes downstairs for a snack at three A.M. He's just . . . I don't know if it's depression. Maybe the beginnings of it. The other day he was staring out the window and Emily was trying to get his attention and she had to call out, 'Dad!' three times."

"Maybe he needs a little more time off," Lou suggested.

"I don't know," Jamie said. "I'm thinking the opposite. That he needs to stay busy. And having other cops around who know what he's going through might help."

Lou started to say something, but she heard footsteps approaching. When she turned around, there was her brother-in-law, his broad shoulders filling the doorway to the kitchen.

He reached out and gave her a hug, like he always did. He smelled of soap and felt like a brick wall. Lou adored Mike. He was just easy; he put his feet up on tables and drank beer straight from the bottle and didn't feel the need to make constant conversation—all traits Lou shared.

"Steroids, huh?" she joked, squeezing Mike's huge biceps, and was rewarded with a grin.

"Kids, thanks for babysitting Lou for us tonight," Mike said.

"We're going to make you pee before bed-time!" Sam yelled.

"Don't ask," Lou told Mike.

"Not sure I want to know," he joked as he reached into the refrigerator to grab a Red Bull.

"I'm finished," Sam said. "Do I get my candy now?"

"Dishes in the sink first," Jamie said. "Don't forget your silverware . . . you, too, Emily. Lou, you've got my cell number if you need it, right?"

Lou furrowed her brow. "You mean that thing you call me on all the time?"

Jamie rolled her eyes and gave Lou a quick hug. "I love you, you know."

Mike was reaching into his pocket and frowning. He checked his other pocket, then looked at the kitchen counter.

"What're you missing?" Lou asked.

"My keys," Mike said.

"Did you leave them on the hook by the door?" Jamie asked.

Mike shrugged and went to look. Lou followed him with her eyes, feeling a tinge of worry. When she'd first glimpsed Mike in the kitchen doorway, she'd noticed his sheen of good health —he was tan and fit, his hair still damp from the shower, his black thin-knit shirt straining across his chest. But then he'd moved closer, and she'd noticed the dull exhaustion in his eyes, and the lines in his forehead that seemed to be permanently etched. How many of those caffeinated beverages was he drinking a day? she suddenly wondered.

"I'll go help Mike look," Jamie said.

Lou turned her attention back to the kids, and eventually Jamie found a spare set of keys and they headed out. It wasn't until the kids were asleep and Lou was reaching into the refrigerator to find a snack that she solved the mystery.

On the middle shelf, next to the eggs, were Mike's keys.

"Say a wife suspects her husband is cheating," Elroy said as he dipped a French fry into a pool of ketchup and ate it as daintily as a cat. The fries looked incredible—crisp and plump and golden brown. They'd probably been deep-fried in a hot bucket of fat. But Christie's scale had betrayed her again this morning, inching up another pound for no good reason, so she'd just shaken her head when Elroy offered to share.

"She needs proof, right? Because if she confronts him he's gonna say no. Or maybe she already has, and he's got excuses. Too many excuses. His BlackBerry is for work and if she asks him for the password all of a sudden, he'll know she's onto him and he'll delete all the messages. She can't follow him around without being spotted. She's picking something up, something she can't quite prove but she knows is real. That's when she comes to me. It's like when birds sense a storm is coming and they suddenly strip a bush clean of its berries. Who knows how they know? Maybe an invisible change in the air. But they're always right."

Christie nodded as Elroy nibbled on another fry. She'd never seen a guy eat so slowly; most men she knew wolfed down their food. The combination of his soft voice with the hint of a southern accent and his deliberate movements was oddly hypnotic.

"Some of the time they'll have another woman in mind. A co-worker, a neighbor, an old girl-friend—someone who gives off weird vibes. I tell you, bloodhounds got nothing on women when it comes to sniffing this stuff out. So they want us to follow hubby and see if he's up to no good. But maybe he only sees the other woman once every week or two. That's a whole lot of money to be paying for stakeouts; my rate's a hundred an hour plus expenses. Most of them can't afford it for too long, and their husbands would notice if thousands suddenly disappeared from the bank account."

This was fascinating stuff, better than watching soap operas. Not that she did that. Regularly, anyway. Christie leaned in closer, which meant she got a mouthwatering whiff of the fries. She cursed the sadist who'd invented carbs and tried to breathe through her mouth.

"So what do they do next?" she asked. "The wives, I mean."

"That's where you come in," Elroy said. He used his napkin to wipe each of his fingertips in turn, then he took a small sip of water and pushed away his mostly full plate, which meant it was that much nearer to Christie.

"In my experience, a guy who's already cheating isn't going to turn down another opportunity, if you get my drift," he said, giving her a meaningful look.

"You're not that subtle," Christie said.

Elroy smiled. "The thing is, you gotta walk a careful line. A girl like you—if you throw yourself at a guy, he's going to say yes, unless he's the Pope."

A girl like you. Christie soaked in the compliment like a hot bath. Simon hadn't called last night, and when she'd called him at 10:00 P.M.— the three glasses of wine she'd drunk had been coconspirators, urging her to do it—her call had gone straight to voice mail. She'd waited up, but he hadn't phoned back. Then this morning, a bouquet of flowers had arrived with a note typed by the florist: *Sorry I missed you.*

It wasn't even an extravagant bouquet. There was baby's breath filling a lot of spaces. What was it Elroy had said? A change in the air.

"So what do I need to do?" Christie asked, shoving the fries back toward Elroy.

"We trail the guy," Elroy said. "Find a place for you to bump into him. An elevator, a sidewalk. Maybe you drop your purse to give him an excuse to help you pick it up. You send out signals— nothing too flashy, but you'll let him know you might be interested—and see if he responds."

"Isn't that entrapment?" Christie asked. She was proud of herself for remembering the word; she'd heard it on a recent episode of *CSI.*

"Nope," Elroy said. "We're not arresting any-one here."

"Okay," Christie said. "So if he responds, then what? Exactly how far do I take this?"

She fixed her eyes on Elroy and folded her arms over her chest. He'd better not expect her to actually fool around with a mark. She liked her new identity as a businesswoman, someone smart and strong and capable. Someone who didn't get screwed by men physically *or* emotionally.

"You say you're in town for a few days on business. Maybe he wants to meet you at your hotel for a drink. You set a time for him to come by and I get to the hotel first to set up my camera and recording equipment. You meet him in the room, get him to talk about what he wants to do to you—"

At Christie's expression he hurriedly continued, "Just talking, no touching—then I knock on the door and call out 'Room service.' You tell him to sit back and relax, that you ordered champagne. Then you open the door and boom! You're gone."

Christie turned the plan over in her mind. "How do you know when to knock?"

"I listen in on the recording equipment. I've got a good hotel in mind; there's a coffee shop next door. After the job we wait there. Or I wait there, because you're done, so you can take a cab home. When the dude's gone I gather my stuff and write up a report for wifey."

"Who pays for the cab?" Christie wanted to know.

"The client," Elroy said. "All your expenses plus sixty an hour, like we talked about. Most jobs will probably take about four hours, start to finish, including your transport time."

Christie drummed her nails on the linoleum table. "It sounds too easy," she said.

"You'd be the third girl I've hired for this job, and none of the others complained."

"Why did the other two quit?" she asked.

"The first one moved away," he said. "She was with me for three years. The second one married one of the guys we'd set up when his wife divorced him."

"You're kidding."

Elroy shook his head. "Wish I was. She was good at what she did. So, are you with me? We'll probably work four, five jobs a week."

"That many?" Christie asked. Five jobs a week,

at four hours per job, and sixty dollars an hour would be . . . let's see, about . . . Well, it would be a lot of money. Plus expenses!

"You wouldn't believe how many more people are having affairs since Facebook," Elroy said. "The number of folks who hook up with exes . . ."

Christie suddenly wondered if Simon had a Facebook account. "Do you ever trace people?" she asked.

"What do you mean?"

"Like put a tracker on their car."

Elroy shook his head. "Nah. But I did put up an ad on Facebook. My clients have doubled since then."

He regarded her for a moment. "Any questions? Any moral objections we need to get out of the way?"

"Are you kidding?" Christie shook her head. "My mother cheated on my stepfather—or make that stepfathers, plural—the whole time I was growing up. Once she and one of the guys took me to the movies. They told me they were going to sit in the back row but I should sit up front, where I could see the screen really well." She rolled her eyes. "Like that was what they were thinking about. They just didn't want me to see *them* pawing each other. I finally told my stepfather when I was twelve."

"What happened?" Elroy asked.

Christie looked down at her Diet Coke and

swirled her straw around a few times. She cleared her throat before answering. "He left," she said.

"Do you regret telling him?" Elroy asked.

"I regret not doing it earlier," she said. He had been the nicest of the many men who'd shared her mother's bed. He'd bought her a harmonica once after she'd seen a guy on the street playing one and thought it sounded pretty. It was just a cheap toy, but he hadn't given it to her until her birthday, which was weeks after they'd watched the street performer. She didn't know what had surprised her more: that he'd remembered how much she liked the sounds the tiny instrument made, or that he'd noticed her enjoyment in the first place.

Elroy opened his battered briefcase and pulled out a file. He withdrew a photograph and slid it toward Christie. It was of a nice-looking guy, maybe in his early forties, the sort you'd see tossing a baseball to his kid at the park on a Saturday morning. Christie didn't know what she'd expected, but it wasn't this sandy-haired, smiling guy with freckles on his nose.

"Say hello to your first client," Elroy said.

Chapter Four

RITCHIE'S ROOM IN THE rehab facility wasn't as intimidating as Jamie had expected. She'd thought it would be white and sterile, with sharp edges and high-tech machines—similar to the hospital room where she'd visited him—but it seemed almost homey. This was a space for patients who were here for the long haul, she thought. There were curtains on the window, and family pictures atop the nightstand.

Ritchie was propped up by pillows in bed. He was holding one of those squishy stress balls and seemed to be struggling to make a fist around it.

Jamie paused in the doorway, tears rushing into her eyes, memories rushing into her mind: Ritchie racing around his backyard on the Fourth of July, holding a silver sparkler and being chased by all the kids; Ritchie putting his arm around Sandy and kissing the top of her head as she leaned into him one weekend when they'd all gone to the beach together; Ritchie and Mike, side by side, standing straight and proud as they received an official commendation for apprehending an armed robbery suspect.

"How are you, handsome?" Jamie asked. She

walked over to Ritchie and kissed his cheek. Only his brown eyes were the same. His face was still swollen, and a worm-like scar curved around his right ear, cutting into his skin. His hair had been shaved for surgery and hadn't completely grown back in yet. He'd lost weight, too.

"Good," Ritchie said.

"Old buddy," Mike said, coming closer and giving his partner a fist bump. "We gotta bust you out of here!"

"The doctor . . . said . . . another few months," Ritchie said, his cadence much slower than usual, as if he were speaking a foreign language and first needed to translate the words in his head.

Another few months, Jamie thought. But then there would be outpatient physical and speech therapy. And after that? Nothing was clear. Brain injuries were notoriously complicated, and it was hard to predict if Ritchie would ever be able to return to the force. Sandy had talked about it at the pool, and Jamie had been glad she couldn't see her friend's eyes behind her dark sunglasses. She knew they'd look shattered.

"Yeah, but you like a challenge," Mike was saying. "I'll give you two weeks before they're kicking you out."

Ritchie smiled but didn't say anything.

There was a small silence.

"I saw Sandy and the kids the other day," Jamie said, her voice too bright. "We all went to the pool. Daisy is such a terrific swimmer! She's a little fish."

"Yeah," Ritchie said. He frowned. "I was working with her . . . Last month? No, maybe last summer . . . I can't remember . . ."

"Well, we need you to give our kids swimming lessons!" Jamie said quickly. "Eloise is still afraid to put her face in the water."

"You need anything?" Mike asked. "Kale chips, maybe?"

Ritchie smiled and started to shake his head, but he immediately stilled the motion. Jamie wondered if the slight movement hurt.

"Did they give you . . . a new partner yet?" Ritchie asked.

"First of all, he isn't my partner," Mike said. "He's a stand-in until the real thing comes back. And he's a moron. My standards aren't all that high, given what I put up with for the past decade, but even I can't deal with the guy."

"You're used . . . to per-perfection," Ritchie said.

Jamie turned as an orderly came into the room, carrying a food tray. He set it on the edge of Ritchie's bed, checked the level of water in the giant plastic cup on Ritchie's nightstand, and exited quietly.

"Want some . . . pudding?" Ritchie asked Mike. "It's awful. That's why . . . I offered."

"Sounds tempting," Mike said. He reached for

one of the containers, peeled back the foil lid, and used his fingers to scoop up a taste. "Christ. They're trying to kill you, aren't they? They give life, then they take it away."

Ritchie's laugh was weaker than usual, but it was one of the most wonderful things Jamie had ever heard.

"Go ahead and eat," Jamie said. "Get strong!"

"Gotta use this, ah . . ." Ritchie said, holding up a strange-looking fork. The handle was thick and there were two wide prongs instead of four.

"A spork?" Mike asked, quickly filling in the word when Ritchie stumbled over it.

In a moment, it became clear why he needed the special utensil: Ritchie's movements were similar to those of a young child learning to eat on his own. He dropped more penne noodles than he managed to ferry to his mouth on his first bite.

"Crap," he said, looking down at the mess he'd created. Luckily all of the noodles had landed on the extra-large tray; they must've made them big for a reason.

"Hey, don't worry about it," Mike said. "What the hell kind of hospital serves noodles to someone who just got shot and is getting his reflexes back?"

Mike was furious, Jamie saw. Or not exactly furious—his rage was on the surface, covering something fragile and turbulent underneath.

"Forget this," Mike said. He pulled the tray

away from Ritchie in a jerky movement. "I'm going to get you one of those cardboard veggie burgers you love, okay? Extra pickles and tomato. I'll be right back."

Jamie wondered if the pasta wasn't precisely the point—if Ritchie were being given challenging foods so he could practice fine-motor control—but she remained silent. This wasn't about Ritchie's dinner.

"Do you want me to go pick it up?" Jamie asked.

Mike shook his head. "I'll be fast."

Jamie watched Mike exit the room and thought about Lou's suggestion that Mike needed some more time off. Maybe her sister was right. She didn't know anymore; she'd lost the ability to read her husband. She and Mike had had their ups and downs—what couple didn't?—and during some periods, especially in the bone-wearying, endless stretch of time when Eloise was a baby and Sam and Emily were careening through toddlerhood, she'd felt a distance wedging itself between her and Mike. She'd been consumed with constant, draining caretaking, with feeding little mouths and cleaning hands and bottoms and settling squabbles and soothing boo-boos and running endless loads of laundry and dishes. She knew Mike's job was stressful, but she couldn't help feeling resentful when he came home after sharing a pizza and a pitcher of beer with the guys from his shift when she couldn't even manage to drink a cup of coffee while it was hot.

Just last year they'd gone three days without speaking after a ridiculous fight sparked by whether Emily was old enough for a sleepover. They'd bickered over countless small things, and once Jamie had thrown one of her sneakers at Mike, incensed that he hadn't discouraged Christie from flirting with him. Mike had slept on the couch that night before climbing back into their bed the next morning as she showered. He'd still been wearing the Homer Simpson boxer shorts Henry had given him for Christmas, a memory that always made her smile.

So yes, they'd weathered anger and pain. But an invisible, powerful connection had always linked them. This time things felt different. It was as if a wall had sprouted up in front of Mike, too wide and tall for her to reach around and touch him.

In the six weeks since the shooting, she'd learned what it meant to miss her husband, Jamie thought as she sat down next to Ritchie and smiled to cover her sadness. She missed rolling over in the middle of the night and pressing up against Mike's warm body. She missed having him walk through the front door and effortlessly scoop up a kid in one arm and reach the other around her waist as he dropped a kiss on the back of her neck. She missed the way they'd try to stay up together to watch reruns of *Modern Family*, and she'd invariably fall asleep against his shoulder, and he'd tease her about her snoring.

"Sir? Can I help you?" Jamie heard someone ask loudly.

Jamie became aware of a rhythmic, thudding sound coming from the hallway. She felt a cold tingle work its way down her spine as she stood up and walked to the door and looked down the hall, toward the noise. Mike was still standing there, waiting for the elevator. His head was down, and his hands were clenched by his sides. He was ignoring the nurse frowning at him.

As she watched, Mike's foot drew back, then kicked the closed doors of the elevator again.

"So," Lou said, looking at Donny.

"So," he repeated, looking back at her.

They were seated on the couch, a healthy distance separating them, like sitcom actors depicting a strained relationship.

"Did you want anything to eat or drink?" Donny asked, as if she was a guest. It made her think her instincts about the contents of this conversation were right. He was going to ask her to move out.

"No thanks," Lou said. "I'm good."

This was one of the problems in their relationship: they both hated conflict. So they never discussed problems. Lou hadn't even known that Donny was unhappy with their relationship until he suggested a break. She hadn't even known that *she* was unhappy until she felt relief at his suggestion.

Lou wondered if he'd ever really loved her, or if she'd loved him. Donny didn't even like animals! Whenever he came with her to Jamie's, he'd pet Sadie once or twice, then discreetly sniff his hands and hurry away to wash them.

"Mary Alice and I . . ." Donny cleared his throat.

"It's okay," Lou said. She might as well make this easier on both of them; Jamie probably wouldn't mind her being blunt in this case. "Is she moving in? Do you want me to move out?"

"We're getting married," Donny said.

"Oh!" Lou said. Now, that she wasn't expecting. What did you say to your ex-boyfriend and current roommate upon learning that he was engaged? Luckily she settled on the right word: "Congratulations."

"Thanks," Donny said.

Back when they'd first met, after Lou had handed him a latte and he'd asked for her number, she'd been flattered. Guys weren't exactly lining up to sleep with her. She'd been with only two in her entire life. And Donny looked a little bit like the late actor Robin Williams, whom Lou had always liked. Now Lou waited for whatever feelings might come—regret, loss, relief—and realized she didn't feel much of anything.

"There's this woman who works in my office,

Kelsey," Donny was saying. "She's looking for a roommate."

"Have I met her?" Lou asked. Donny was an actuary, someone who specialized in analyzing the financial risks of business decisions. She sometimes wondered if he did the same with emotional decisions.

"I don't think so," Donny said. "She's new."

"Okay," Lou said. "I'll call her."

Donny looked relieved. He stood up and pulled a piece of paper out of his pocket. "You can probably see the room tonight, if you want," he said.

"In a hurry to get rid of me, huh?" Lou joked.

"No, no," Donny protested, a bit too fervently.

Lou swallowed hard. "I'll move out as soon as I can."

"So what are you thinking?" Donny asked. "A couple weeks?"

She blinked. "Um, yeah," she said. "A couple weeks probably."

Donny sighed, and his whole body seemed to deflate. He was a good man, Lou thought. But she already knew she wouldn't miss him. When she spent the weekend with Donny, she missed the elephants.

"You could call her now," Donny said.

"Who?"

"Kelsey. The woman with the apartment."

"Oh, right," Lou said.

Donny was looking at her expectantly, so Lou reached for the phone and dialed the number. It rang twice, then someone answered.

"Hi. I'm trying to reach Kelsey. This is Lou. I'm a . . . a friend of Donny's?"

"Oh, yes. Did you want to see the apartment tonight?"

"Um, sure," Lou said. Had Donny told Kelsey how desperate he was for Lou to move out? She felt a little hurt by the thought.

"You can come now."

"Now?" Lou said. She looked at Donny. "Okay." She scribbled down the address, then hung up.

"So I'm going to check out the apartment," she said, unnecessarily. She looked down at the piece of paper in her hand. She recognized the name of the street and could visualize the route. "It's just a mile or so away."

"Great!" Donny said.

She stood up and put on her clogs, then headed out the door. What she'd like, ideally, would be a sunny little studio close to the zoo. She'd have a teakettle and toaster and microwave, and the apartment would allow pets (Donny's didn't). She'd get two cats, so they'd keep each other company while she was out. But D.C. real estate was exorbitant, and zookeepers didn't make much money. A place of her own would have to remain a distant dream.

She strolled through the streets, passing a

bakery and Thai and Ethiopian restaurants, enjoying the sounds and smells. She bought a veggie burrito and a bottle of water from a food truck and ate while she walked. A few minutes later, she reached Kelsey's building and stood looking up at it. The building was old but seemed well maintained, with wide, gray stone steps curving to the main door. She climbed them and buzzed the number for the apartment.

A voice came over the intercom: "Who is it?"

"It's me. Lou," she said.

There was a pause. "I'm here to see about the room?" Lou added.

A buzzer sounded and she pulled the door open and took the stairs up to the third floor. She knocked and waited for what seemed like an abnormally long time before the apartment's door was opened by a short, wiry woman who looked to be in her mid-thirties. The woman's waist-length black hair was so straight that Lou wondered if she ironed it, like Jamie had once tried to do back in junior high school. The smell of singed hair had stunk up the house for days.

"Hi," Lou said.

"Sorry, I was just straightening up," Kelsey said.

"Well, I hope you didn't do that on my account," Lou said. "A little mess doesn't bother me."

"It doesn't?" Kelsey frowned, then opened the door wider, the expression on her face indicating it might be against her better judgment. "Come in."

Lou stepped into the narrow hallway. It was empty except for a wooden table with skinny legs that looked like an antique.

Kelsey was staring at her oddly. "Can you take off your shoes?" she asked. "I'd rather you didn't track dirt and germs in here."

"Oh, sure," Lou said. She slipped out of them and followed Kelsey into the living area. Immediately she wondered what Kelsey could've been cleaning; the place was spotless. There was a gray couch with angles so sharp it looked as if it might cut the behind of anyone who sat on it, and a glass coffee table, and a little cube that could've been a chair but also could've been a footrest. Exactly two magazines were placed on the coffee table, so crisp and glossy they appeared untouched.

"Living room," Kelsey said unnecessarily. She gave a little wave of her hand. "Kitchen."

Lou peered into the galley kitchen. A lone gerbera daisy stood in a slender glass vase on one of the shining granite counters, and the fruit bowl held one orange and one red apple.

"Your room would be here," Kelsey said, walking down a short hallway and pointing into a doorway. She seemed to be checking Lou out in quick, sidelong glances. Lou wondered if her burrito breath was soiling the sanctity of the apartment. "I'm using it as a guest room now, but I don't have a lot of guests."

Lou followed Kelsey to the small, rectangular space. A four-poster bed dominated the room, and there was a matching bureau opposite. Lou opened a door and found a tiny bathroom, then she looked into the closet. It was probably a good thing she didn't have a lot of clothes.

"It's nice," she said.

"It's seven hundred a month plus utilities," Kelsey said. She handed Lou a piece of paper. "Here are some ground rules."

Lou began to read the typewritten words: *Rent will be paid on the first of the month. Quiet time will commence at 10:30 P.M. and continue until 5:45 A.M. All guests must be approved in advance. No sleepovers will be permitted. Food in the refrigerator should be clearly labeled and renter will only eat and drink his/her groceries. No dishes will be left in the sink; they must be immediately washed and put away in the appropriate space in the cupboard . . .*

Lou looked up. "Sleepovers?"

"Guests of the opposite sex," Kelsey said, then quickly clarified, "or the same sex. I don't have a problem with that. Actually, I do—not the same-sex part. The sleepover part."

She leaned closer and peered at Lou. "You've got a . . ." She made a brushing gesture against her own cheek.

Lou reached up and felt something slimy. "Guacamole," she said, wiping her fingers off on her cargo pants. Kelsey looked ready to gag. She reached over and plucked a tissue from a box atop the dresser and let it flutter into Lou's outstretched hand.

Lou could envision what her life would look like if she lived here. She'd have to tiptoe in after late shifts at the coffee shop, and wash her clothes before Kelsey caught the scent of the zoo. If she took an unauthorized swig of orange juice, she'd probably be Tasered.

But what other choice did she have? The apartment was reasonably priced—at least by D.C. standards—convenient, and available. She thought of heading back home and seeing Donny's eager face as he asked how it went.

"Okay," she said, handing back the list of rules. "When can I move in?"

"The first of next month. I'll need a security deposit, too," Kelsey said. "And I want to give your room a deep cleaning first."

Lou said good-bye and trudged toward home, feeling her shoulders slump. She'd just avoid Kelsey as much as possible, and start looking for a new place after a few months. This would be temporary, she consoled herself.

On impulse, she turned down a side street. It was almost dusk now, but if she hurried, she'd arrive before closing. As she got closer to the zoo, she found herself running, her stress peeling away and being replaced by a sense of exuberance.

"Weren't you here all day?" one of the volunteers asked as he drove by in one of the golf carts used by employees. Lou just gave him a wave and ran faster.

She reached the elephant enclosure area in time to see Tabitha enjoying her dinner. As if the elephant sensed her presence, Tabitha looked up and caught her eye. Lou waved to her but didn't call her over. She didn't want to interrupt Tabby's meal. She was eating for two, after all.

The sinking sun suffused the sky with rose and violet streaks. Martha and Bailey ambled through the yard, their slow, steady gaits echoing Lou's heartbeats. When Lou looked at the creatures, she experienced the same overpowering sense of peace and awe that some people reported feeling when they viewed the ocean for the first time, or the Grand Canyon. Lou wasn't religious, but being around the elephants elevated her to a near-spiritual experience. The presence of their dignity and wisdom felt healing.

Tabitha wasn't finished eating, but she abandoned her dinner and walked closer to Lou. Lou felt tears form in her eyes.

"Good girl," she said softly, but loud enough for the elephant to hear. Tabby understood more than two dozen words, and these were the ones Lou made sure she heard the most.

She supposed she should get home and begin packing. But she didn't want to leave. She'd like nothing more than to curl up on a bale of hay and sleep here, out under the night stars, cocooned by familiar smells and sounds.

The thought of moving in with scary, bossy Kelsey was so daunting. She knew she'd do something wrong—be too loud or track in dung or walk around with more guacamole on her cheek. She imagined her new roommate's face tightening every time she walked into the apartment, just as Donny's did now.

"Hey there," another keeper said as he passed by. "Did you hear about Tabby's tail?"

Lou shook her head. "What?" she asked urgently.

"She broke off a few hairs when they got tangled in something. I think it just happened an hour or so ago."

Lou straightened up, trying to get a better look at Tabby's hind side. It wasn't as innocuous as it sounded; the tuft at the end of an elephant's tail, used to swat away insects, was composed of individual hairs that were as strong and wiry as guitar strings. If one broke off at the quick, it could lead to an abscess or infection.

"Did someone get antiseptic on it?" Lou asked.

"Yeah," the keeper said. "It's in her chart."

Lou was glad the charts were scrupulously kept, but she knew she'd never need a reminder to check on an animal's injury. In fact, she wanted to take a look now, to make sure the tail wasn't too bad. She'd hang out at the zoo for a few hours and keep an eye on Tabby, just to be sure.

Lou didn't know much about Tabby's history—no one did, since she'd come to the zoo via an overcrowded sanctuary—but she sensed the elephant had been treated poorly at one time in her life. Maybe that was why Tabby seemed so grateful for the gentle care Lou provided now.

"Good girl," Lou told her favorite elephant again. In a few months, Tabby would give birth, and Lou knew the experience could be traumatic. She'd be here for every moment of it. She'd protect the elephant and her baby as best she could, for the rest of their lives.

It was the least she could do for the beautiful creature that had given her so much.

Christie assessed herself in the mirror, then dabbed on a little more lipstick and adjusted her new black wig. She slipped into her short trench coat and belted it tightly around her waist. Maybe the coat wasn't a necessary expense, but she was planning to ask Elroy to divide the cost among several clients. After all, she was a bona fide private detective now. She might not have a license, but she was at the center of real investigations, a vital player in uncovering deceit. She needed to look the part.

Elroy had shown her the photo of the man he'd called her first client, but Elroy had been wrong.

Simon was going to be her first client.

He'd texted that he was working late again and would meet her at her apartment around 10:00 P.M. In the early days of their relationship, he'd taken her to dinner or the theater. Now she was nothing but an occasional booty call. She'd typed back something flirty and brief, to avoid making him suspicious. Then she'd put on her disguise.

She slid her camera into her shoulder bag, put on her sunglasses, and headed to her Miata. She figured he wouldn't be leaving the office before 6:00 P.M., since he'd never ducked out early even during the hot, heady days of their relationship. His office was on K Street in downtown D.C., a busy avenue where you couldn't park during rush hour. Her plan was to drive to the Metro, then take the train downtown and linger near the glass-walled lobby of Simon's building. That way she could observe him if he left on foot, but she could also keep an eye on the exit to the garage in case he drove somewhere.

She didn't know what she'd do if he took off in his car. D.C. had plenty of cabs, but it wasn't like New York, where ones sped by with the regularity of seconds ticking past on a clock. At least traffic would work in her favor; most streets were gridlocked during rush hour, which meant if she hurried, she could probably keep an eye on Simon's car until she managed to wave down a cab. It wasn't a foolproof plan, but it was the best she could come up with.

Forty-five minutes later, she was outside Simon's office, sweltering in the heat. Why hadn't she considered the fact that it was summertime before she'd put on the trench coat? She positioned herself so that she was out of the line of view of the security guard manning the desk in the lobby, took out her iPhone, and prepared to wait.

After an hour, though, her calves ached, her scalp was soaked with sweat under her wig, and she could feel blisters forming on her heels. She was certain Simon hadn't left yet. She'd seen dozens of men exit the building, all looking vaguely alike in their dark suits and wingtips, but Simon wasn't among them.

Was it possible he'd been telling the truth?

Simon wasn't anything like the men she'd dated in the past. She usually went for strong, silent types, bad boys who took her to pool halls or pressed up against her at bars. She'd been on the back of more than one motorcycle, and she'd had her name tattooed on two different biceps. Simon was different. She'd met him at a bookstore, of all places. She'd taken Henry there on a Saturday afternoon because he'd gotten a gift certificate for his birthday, and she'd gone to the little coffee shop to get a latte. Simon was sitting there, reading *The Wall Street Journal*, wearing jeans with ironed creases down the front (after their third date, she'd gently suggested he have his cleaning lady stop doing that). The café was busy, and when Christie got her drink, she'd stood there for a moment, wondering where to sit. Simon had looked up, assessed the situation, and gestured for her to take the empty chair at his table.

"Thanks," she'd said. As she put down her latte, a little liquid had sloshed over the rim of her cup, onto the table.

Simon had put down his newspaper and reached for his napkin, which was as crisp and fresh as the rest of him.

"Thank you," she'd said, giving him a closer look as he cleaned up the spill. He wasn't ugly; he was just bland. He was on the thin side and wore his straight, gingery hair combed from a side part. He had on wire-rimmed glasses, a watch that was so plain it had to be expensive, and a striped oxford shirt. His teeth were very white and had obviously been coached into a perfect arc by an orthodontist. She ran her tongue over her own top teeth—one of the front ones tilted in toward the other, but some men told her it was sexy— and decided she could use a little more politeness in her life. The last guy she'd dated had called her a bitch when they'd argued about what movie to see.

When Simon didn't pick his newspaper back

up, she'd known he was going to ask her out, and he had, after they'd chatted for a few minutes. After giving him her phone number, she'd excused herself and gone to look for Henry, before he could come to her. She wasn't planning to hide her son forever, but there wasn't any need to advertise the fact that she had a teenager just yet.

They'd gone to dinner a few nights later. She'd been waiting in the lobby of her apartment building when he pulled up, because she wasn't ready to let him see her place, either. She'd walked outside as he stepped out of the car, and he'd hurried to open the passenger-side door of his Porsche before she reached it. Christie knew about cars; enough of the men she'd dated had been obsessed by them. One had even had a photograph of Simon's exact vehicle pinned up in his garage.

He took her to a restaurant with gleaming wooden booths and dim lighting and hushed voices, and when the waiter handed him a thick wine list bound in leather, Simon didn't need to look at it. "Do you like Argentinian reds?" he asked Christie. "The Casa Lapostolle is good, if we want to go with a Cabernet. It's smoky, with hints of berry. Or we could try a Pinot Grigio if you're in the mood for a lighter meal . . ."

"You choose," she said, feeling unexpectedly shy. Were you supposed to put the napkin on your lap the moment you sat down, or were you supposed to wait until the food arrived?

When the waiter brought the wine, Simon went through the ritual of smelling the cork and tasting a sip before crisply nodding his approval. Something about his authority gave him a shot of sex appeal, Christie thought. The waiter poured her a glass and she raised it to her lips. It felt velvety against her tongue, and tasted so different from anything she'd had in the past. She didn't dislike wine; she'd just never had any worth drinking, she realized.

She took another swallow, a bigger one this time. Simon had chosen the red, and she hoped it wasn't staining her teeth.

Two glasses later, her confidence had come rushing back. She could tell Simon was a little intoxicated, and not because of the alcohol. He couldn't stop staring at her. She was wearing a patterned wrap dress from T. J. Maxx, cut low enough that every time she leaned forward—and she made sure to do that often—her creamy, lush breasts were on display. They were absolutely her best feature, even if they'd begun to droop a bit. But a lacy push-up bra took care of that issue.

She visualized the type of woman Simon had dated in the past: yardstick-thin with hair severely scraped into a bun; wearing pantsuits and frowning as she earnestly discussed her rose garden and blue-chip stocks.

Yawn, she thought, and she launched into a story of her co-worker at the hair salon, the woman who'd accidentally cut a customer's finger with scissors when the customer had put her cell phone to her ear.

"I mean, it wasn't her fault!" Christie said, giggling. Simon was laughing, too. "She whipped out that phone the second it rang. I bet the person on the other end was surprised to hear her scream instead of say hello."

Over tender filet and lemony asparagus, she asked him about his work. "Boring lobbying stuff," he said. "I'm a partner at a law firm."

"Oh, I doubt it's boring," she said. She'd already Googled him, and she knew he was a name partner at one of the biggest firms in town.

"No, trust me, it is. You'll fall asleep in your plate if I tell you more. So about your job . . . What is it you do there?" he asked.

The lie slipped out quickly: "I'm the manager."

What was the harm in one tiny fib? she wondered as the waiter refilled her glass again. She swirled it around, as she'd seen Simon do, and took another sip. He was right; she could distinguish the hint of berries, and the not-unpleasant taste of smoke.

The waiter cleared away their plates, and she protested that she couldn't possibly eat another bite, but Simon ordered a slice of cheesecake and insisted she try it. It was impossibly tart and airy, the best she'd ever eaten, and she closed her eyes while she sucked the last bite off her fork. When she opened them, she saw Simon looking at her with the expression she imagined she'd worn when she glimpsed the decadent cheesecake. The bill came and Simon pulled out his wallet and put in a credit card without even checking it, but not before Christie had seen that the three-digit total started with the number two.

The valet brought around the Porsche and Simon handed him a folded bill, then tucked Christie into the passenger's seat like she was a delicate present. She looked over at his profile as he navigated the dark streets, his hands steady on the wheel, the moonlight glinting off his glasses. His shoulders were sloped and his ears seemed a little too big for his head, but Christie knew she could get past that.

"Would you like to come up?" she suggested when he parked in front of her apartment building. She'd been in Simon's world for the past few hours, where everything was posh and orderly. Now it was time to introduce him to hers, and shake him up a little.

She'd already set the stage earlier in the day, dimming the lights to hide the fact that her apartment was a little shabby, with a stain on the couch and cheap Formica kitchen counters. She'd gathered up all her crap—shoes, clothes, dirty dishes, old magazines—and returned everything to its proper place. She'd even set up a John Mayer CD that would play at the touch of her remote control's button.

Simon looked a little surprised when she led him through the apartment's lobby. She wondered what he'd expected—a butler and glossy marble floors instead of linoleum? She was a single mother who worked for not much above minimum wage. But of course, Simon didn't know that. He didn't know anything about her, and she was beginning to think it would be a good idea to keep it that way for a while.

She unlocked her front door and quickly turned on the music. She didn't want Simon to spend too much time examining her apartment. She stood in the middle of the room and held Simon's eyes with her own as she untied her dress, her hips swaying to the languorous beat of the music, the dress slipping to the floor. His gasp was her reward. She was wearing a black lace thong that matched her bra, and thigh-high stockings. She left on her heels as she beckoned to Simon, seeing his upturned face alight. He was like a little boy getting his first glimpse of the Ferris wheel at the county fair.

He hadn't stayed over that night, but she hadn't wanted him to. The sex was mediocre, and it was over far too quickly. She'd had better nights with her vibrator and a Showtime movie, which she planned to turn to after he left.

But the next day, flowers arrived. The arrangement was so big she couldn't see the deliveryman's face behind it. Simon called a few hours later and invited her to see a play that weekend. A play! She hadn't been to one since her high school's production of *Grease.* It was excruciating—a single actor put on different hats and prattled on for ninety minutes—but afterward there was a late dinner with a cheese course for dessert, another novelty for her.

Simon couldn't get enough of her, at least in the beginning. Once he'd dashed out of work for a quickie when she told him she was standing in front of his office building, wearing absolutely nothing beneath her dress, but now he took a while to return her calls. She knew each brought something fresh to their relationship, something that had been previously missing from the other's life. She offered excitement and passion to Simon, and in return, he gave her luxury and security.

At least, early on that was their relationship's equation. But then one night, after a few drinks, they'd been in bed together and she'd told him about not knowing her father. Simon had stroked her hair and murmured that he was sorry, and she'd found herself crying. He hadn't tried to have sex again with her that night, even though he usually wanted to a second time. He'd just held her until she fell asleep. Something within her had shifted during the course of those hours. She realized his ears were actually a fine size. She left a few things at his town house in Georgetown, hoping he might offer her a drawer or some closet space. She even bought a book about sex, thinking they could work together to improve things.

Why had Simon begun to slip away just as she'd started to truly care for him?

Stakeouts sucked, she decided as she sighed, slipped off her shoes, and rested her sore feet against the hot pavement. She was contemplating going home when she caught a glimpse of movement to her left and realized Simon's Porsche was exiting the garage. She almost couldn't believe it, even though she thought she'd been expecting the betrayal. She glanced around wildly for a cab, but the only one she spotted had a passenger in the backseat.

Luckily traffic was terrible, just as she'd anticipated. She pulled on her shoes again and broke into a jog, avoiding the subway grates that could snag her heels, and headed north. Then a traffic light that was holding Simon's Porsche back turned green and he cut into a faster lane, moving a block ahead. She was in danger of losing him. She felt her wig start to slip, and she anchored it with one hand. It must be close to ninety degrees, and sweat dripped down her face and stung her eyes. The edges of her shoes cut into the tender skin around her heels, but she forced herself to run harder, even when a passing bus exhaled a gray plume of sour-smelling exhaust into her face.

"Someone's in a hurry!" a guy called after her. She gave him the finger and kept scanning the area for cabs, finally spotting one going the wrong way. She flagged it down anyway and leapt inside, breathing hard.

"Make a right and go around the block!" she said. She craned her head out the window, trying to keep Simon's car in view for as long as possible. "I'm trying to follow someone."

She'd expected a reaction from the cabbie, but maybe he was used to this sort of thing, or had seen too many thrillers, because he just nodded and continued arguing with someone over his headset.

For a few minutes she was certain they'd lost Simon. But the cabbie was adept at finding tiny, opportunistic pockets of space, and he managed to move ahead, weaving through the cars clogging the streets.

"There!" Christie shouted.

She could see Simon's car one lane over. He drove as unimaginatively as he made love, so it was easy for the cabbie to maneuver closer to him. What a waste of a Porsche, Christie thought.

Simon took a few more turns, heading toward Georgetown, then pulled up in front of the Four Seasons Hotel. He gave his car to the valet, and as he stepped out, Christie noticed he was carrying pink roses. The bouquet was enormous. Her throat tightened.

She gave the cabdriver a ten and climbed out, keeping a steady twenty yards behind Simon. He wasn't checking in to the hotel after all, she realized as he passed the reception area. He walked through the lobby toward the Bourbon Steak restaurant. He spoke briefly to the hostess—Christie couldn't overhear the exchange—then was led away. Christie waited until he'd disappeared from view, then she entered the restaurant.

"May I help you?" a passing waiter asked, but Christie batted her hand at the man. "I'm meeting someone," she said.

She glanced around and saw Simon leaning down to kiss a dark-haired woman on the cheek before handing her the roses and taking the seat next to her. She couldn't glimpse the woman's face; her back was to the door. Christie stalked toward them, feeling the glances of other diners. She stood next to the table, but Simon was engrossed in conversation and didn't notice her.

"How's work?" she asked sweetly.

Simon's head snapped up. He blinked a few times, then his brow creased. "Christie?" he asked.

She glanced at his date and was struck by the fact that the woman was at least twenty years older than Simon. There was a blue Tiffany box on the woman's plate. What was going on? Could he possibly be proposing to this old crone?

But no, the box was too big. It might've held a bracelet, but not a ring.

And Simon and the woman weren't alone, Christie realized. They were at the end of a table filled with people of various ages. From her vantage point across the room, Christie hadn't noticed they were all together.

Simon stood up, his manners apparently so ingrained that they stuck with him even when he was unexpectedly confronted by a wig-wearing lover. "This is my mother, Eleanor. Mother, this is—this is Christie."

"Your mother?" Christie echoed.

Why hadn't Simon simply told her he was going to dinner with his mother?

"And my younger brother, David, and his girlfriend, Morgan," Simon said, gesturing around the table as everyone looked up, naked interest spreading across their faces. "Our dear friends the Griffins . . . the Simpsons, who are longtime neighbors . . ."

"Chrissy, was it?" Morgan asked. She was one of those too-thin women who seemed like they filled their leisure hours with horseback riding and bridge games, exactly the kind Christie had imagined Simon had previously fallen for.

"Christie," she corrected. Her name hung there

for a moment as everyone looked up at her.

"Are you on your way to a costume party?" Simon finally asked.

Simon's mother appraised her coolly as Christie slowly became aware of how she must look: her makeup smudged, her wig askew, her armpits sweating so profusely they'd stained her trench coat with dark, sticky patches.

"Yes," she said.

"Oh! Well, have fun," Simon said. "We're celebrating my mother's birthday, so . . ."

He obviously expected her to walk away. But this wasn't an intimate dinner; there were ten people at the table. A few weeks earlier she'd introduced Simon to the most important person in her life—Henry. They'd watched *The Matrix* and had shared a giant bowl of popcorn. Yet obviously, Simon wanted to keep her removed from his family.

Everyone else had gotten a description when he'd introduced them, she thought as she felt her cheeks burn. Dear friends. Longtime neighbors. *A girlfriend.* But she was just Christie, someone who could be an acquaintance—a secretary at his office, a waitress at one of his regular restaurants. Maybe he'd hoped everyone at the table would draw that conclusion.

The knowledge slammed into her: Dorky, premature-ejaculating Simon was ashamed of her.

She felt her fury gather as she wondered what transgressions had relegated her to outsider status. Had he seen her checking her iPhone during the play? Maybe she'd used a wrong fork, or had walked on the outside of the sidewalk instead of the inside.

"Let me escort you out," Simon said.

"Escort me out?" Christie's voice rose, and she could see people swiveling to watch. She picked up the nearest beverage and tossed it at Simon. He gave a little girlie screech and reared back. "Screw you, Simon. Because you sure won't be screwing *me* again with your little dick."

A waiter hurried over. "Miss, I'm going to have to ask you to leave," he said. "You're disturbing our guests."

"Don't bother," Christie said. She pointed at Simon: "And don't ever call me again."

She'd meant to deliver her exit line in a chilly tone, the one the rich people on *Downton Abbey* used when they were upset.

But instead, her damned voice broke.

Chapter Five

THE CALL CAME IN at 2:05 P.M. on the hottest afternoon of the year.

Earlier that day, a thunderstorm had unleashed its power and temporarily washed the heat out of the air. But now the sun was blazing, seemingly furious that it had been blotted out by the storm clouds, acting as if it was trying to make up for lost time. Jamie was in the kitchen, reaching into a shopping bag for the milk she'd just picked up at the grocery store, when the phone rang.

Their air conditioner, which they'd used only sparingly until today, had been blasting away—until it suddenly stopped. Jamie had called the HVAC company and wasn't reassured by the receptionist's response: Everyone had started using their air conditioners full force today, meaning that all the electrical issues that had quietly developed over the past few months had exploded. A technician probably couldn't be there for two days, the receptionist had said.

"Two days?" Jamie had said. "We've got kids, and a dog . . . please, is there any way he can come sooner?"

"I'd go to a hotel," the receptionist had advised, unhelpfully. "One with a pool."

Jamie had begged a little longer, and the receptionist had promised to call back if there was an unexpected opening. So at the sound of the ring, she snatched up the receiver, hoping for a miracle.

"Mrs. Anderson?" The voice was male, unfamiliar, and official. "This is Officer McManus. Am I speaking to the wife of Mike Anderson?"

Her knees almost gave way before she remembered: If Mike had been killed in the line of duty, officers would've appeared at her door instead of calling. She'd know instantly when she glimpsed their faces; there would be no need for them to utter a single word.

She gasped for breath. "Yes," she said. "Mike. Is my husband okay?"

"He's safe, ma'am," the officer said.

Her head spun; the officer's voice wasn't reassuring. Was Mike hurt, then? She thought about the blood on his uniform at the hospital, that black band on his badge, his late-night drifting around the house. He shouldn't have gone back to work; he wasn't ready. Why had she let him? His reflexes were too slow. He didn't even hear his own children calling him. Suddenly she was certain he'd missed a threat, one he would've spotted just a few months ago. She thought of Ritchie in the rehab unit, struggling to eat, and she staggered forward and clutched the kitchen counter.

Please, she thought, her lips forming the word.

"What happened?" she asked, and she squeezed her eyes shut, as if that could cushion her from what would come next. Even when Mike had been stabbed by the junkie, there hadn't been an official call. Mike himself had phoned from the hospital just before he'd gotten stitched up.

When the words finally came, they bounced off her without penetrating. It was as if the officer was speaking underwater, or in a foreign language, or through a scrambled radio transmission. She could hear the sounds he was making, but comprehension eluded her.

"Mike shot someone in the line of duty. A teenage boy," the officer said. "He's at the station now."

Jamie gasped. "Did Mike get shot, too?"

"Mike wasn't injured," the officer said. His sentence seemed to dangle there, with the most important part unspoken.

"The boy," Jamie said. A teenager. Was he close to Henry's age? "You said he was at the station."

"No, ma'am," the officer said. "I meant Mike is at the station."

"Should I come there?" Jamie asked.

"No, that wouldn't be a good idea," the officer said. "There are still some . . . formalities to go through."

His tone was telling her something his words weren't. Jamie leaned forward, resting her head against the door of a cabinet, feeling her throat thicken. "Is the boy . . . ?"

She couldn't finish her sentence. But she didn't need to; she knew the answer before the officer spoke in a voice that seemed heavier than it had been a moment before.

"He's dead, ma'am."

Lou was measuring out the elephants' evening meal when her cell buzzed in her pocket.

"Hey, Sis," she said, cradling the phone between her ear and shoulder while she threw another armful of leafy greens onto the industrial-size scale.

"Lou."

Jamie's voice sounded strangled. "Mike . . ." she began, then her voice trailed off into a high-pitched squeak. Lou's heart began to pound.

Nonononono, she thought, the words building like a scream in her mind. Not Mike. Please not Mike.

"He shot someone," Jamie whispered.

Lou's mind swam as she fought for clarity. "Mike. He wasn't hurt?" she finally asked.

"No," Jamie said. "They told me he was safe . . ."

"Good," Lou said. She tried to unknot her thoughts. "That's good, right?"

Jamie's breathing was ragged, as if she was

running hard. "It was a teenage boy—Lou, I don't know what kind of state Mike is going to be in. He's never hurt anyone before."

Lou slumped down on the hard floor. Mike had shot a teenager?

"It's so hot . . . I can't breathe," Jamie said. "The air-conditioning. I thought they were calling about the air-conditioning."

Jamie didn't sound like herself. Could she be in shock?

"Do you want me to come over?" Lou asked. Her shift was ending soon, and she'd already treated Tabby's tail, which seemed to be healing.

"I—I don't know," Jamie said. "Mike might want to be alone . . . I don't know when he's going to get home. And I need to—The milk is spoiling. I was just putting everything away. Oh, God, Lou, he wasn't hurt. He's safe."

Lou listened to her sister sob and tried to think of the right thing to do. "I think I should come over," Lou finally said. "I can be there in twenty minutes."

She stood up and reached for a pad of paper and, with a shaking hand, scribbled a note detailing the rest of the work that needed to be done for the elephants. She found another keeper and gave him the piece of paper. She saw him read it and nod, then she ran for the exit, her phone pressed tightly to her ear.

"The kids," Jamie said. Lou could hear her

blowing her nose. "I put *Finding Nemo* on after the call . . . What am I going to tell them, Lou?"

"I don't know," Lou said, wishing she could give her sister the right answers.

"Maybe I should wait for Mike to talk to them," Jamie said.

"That sounds like a good idea. I'm going to take a taxi," Lou said. "I'm on Connecticut Avenue, so I should be able to hail one pretty fast."

"Do you think Mike will need to stay a long time?" Jamie asked.

"I don't know," Lou said again. She spotted a taxi and waved it down.

Jamie's breathing still sounded jagged and she made a little whimpering sound. "I can't believe this happened. Mike's never going to get over this. And that boy . . . his family . . ."

"I'm coming as fast as I can. I love you," Lou said before she hung up. "Just take some deep breaths, okay?"

She climbed into the cab, leaned back against the vinyl seat, and closed her eyes, then opened them again when she felt a sudden rush of hot wind on her face from an open window. The cabbie was looking back at her and wrinkling his nose.

She closed her eyes again and tried to follow the advice she'd just given Jamie and breathe, but then a breaking announcement came over the radio.

Lou caught the first few words and leaned forward. "Can you turn that up?" she asked.

The radio announcer's voice filled the small, enclosed space: ". . . breaking up a gang fight when the shooting occurred. The deceased's name is currently being withheld pending notification of his relatives, but he is described as a fifteen-year-old Hispanic male. Sources say the Metropolitan police officer who fired his weapon was the partner of Officer Ritchie Crawford, who was seriously injured in a shooting outside police headquarters just a few months ago."

The taxi was still moving, but Lou felt as if it had slammed into a concrete wall.

The cabbie shook his head. "These police, they shoot too much. Out of control."

Lou thought of Mike on the couch, his arm slung around Henry, ruffling the boy's hair as Mike teased his son about liking a pretty girl in his class. She could see Mike charming Eloise out of a temper tantrum by quacking like Daffy Duck, and tossing Sam in the air and pretending to bobble him after he caught him. Then she remembered Mike with the dead eyes, leaving his car keys in the refrigerator.

Lou wrapped her arms around herself and bowed her head.

The report cut to a sound bite from someone—Lou didn't catch the name: "How many times does a young man of color need to be murdered by police before we as a country demand that it stop? Police are there to protect all of our citizens, especially the vulnerable. Especially the young. Tonight a family is grieving for no reason other than the actions of a trigger-happy police officer who decided to be the judge, jury, and executioner when he saw a brown face."

"Turn it off!" Lou shouted.

The cabdriver obeyed without a word. The silence pressed down around her.

Lou reached for her phone again and dialed Jamie's number.

"Lou?" Jamie's voice was thick with fresh tears.

"Did you hear it?" Lou blurted.

"Hear what?" Jamie asked.

"Nothing," Lou said quickly. "Are the kids watching *Nemo* on TV or is it a DVD?"

"What?" Jamie asked. "I think—It's a DVD. Why?"

"Just don't turn on the TV or radio until I get there, okay? I'm in a cab now. I'll be there in ten minutes."

"Okay," Jamie said.

Lou could sense the cabdriver watching her. She looked up to see his dark eyes with heavy brows in the rearview mirror.

Lou had offered to help, but the irony was, Lou needed Jamie to instruct her on what to do. Jamie would be good in this situation—she'd keep everybody calm, and figure out the next step.

She'd fix something to eat and tuck in the kids and sit down and start making a plan. But Jamie was drowning now; Lou could hear it in her voice. For the first time, her big sister needed saving.

Lou would do anything for Jamie, but she wasn't sure if she could do this. She didn't know how.

The cabbie finally reached Jamie and Mike's modest brick home, and Lou swiped her credit card through the electronic payment device.

"You know him?" the cabbie asked as Lou opened the door. "The cop?"

Without even thinking about it, Lou blurted "No" and slammed the door.

Instantly she felt a crush of guilt. She wanted to call back the cab, to yell, "Yes, and he's the best guy I know! He didn't do it—not like they said on the radio!"

But the cab was turning the corner and disappearing, and Jamie was throwing open the door. She must have been standing by it, watching for Lou. Her eyes were red-rimmed, and she looked smaller somehow. Diminished.

Lou finally knew what to do—at least for now. She hurried toward her big sister, stretching out her arms.

Christie was giving herself a manicure when her cell phone rang, startling her and making her smudge her thumbnail. She swore softly, then answered, already irritated at whoever was calling. It had better not be Simon, although she was furious he'd taken her at her word and hadn't called. She'd never go out with him again, but a little groveling would be nice.

"Hi, is this Mrs. Anderson?"

Christie frowned. "No," she said. "It isn't."

"Oh—I'm sorry. This is Sara James. Henry gave me this number for his mom. He's over here hanging out with my son Jake."

Christie poured a little polish remover onto a cotton ball and began to wipe her thumb clean. She'd have to redo it.

"This is Christie Simmons," she said. "Henry and I have different last names."

"Oh, me, too," Sara said. "I never took my husband's name, either."

And I never married Henry's father, Christie thought. Who cares?

"Anyway, I'm calling because Henry was supposed to be picked up an hour ago. It's no big deal, but Jake has swim team tonight, so . . ."

Perfect Jamie had forgotten to pick Henry up? Christie could hardly believe it.

"I'll swing by and get him," Christie said. "Sorry about that. Henry's stepmother must have forgotten."

She relished saying those words. Maybe Sara would repeat them to a few other mothers, let Jamie be the one to look bad for a change. Christie knew she was the subject of gossip among some of the other parents, who assumed Jamie was Henry's biological mother until she corrected them. Christie stood out—she brought cupcakes with nuts to one of Henry's classrooms, not realizing there was a kid with a potentially fatal allergy in the class, cheered too loudly when Henry shot a basket or caught a foul ball, and stood up to take pictures at the holiday pageant until a pinched-faced woman tapped her on the shoulder and asked her to sit down.

You just don't want your husband looking at my ass, Christie had thought. Maybe her black leather skirt was a touch tight, but she liked it that way and guys sure seemed to as well. No way was she going to turn into one of these Stepford mothers in a pastel sweater set and chinos. She'd unleashed a little shimmy as she sat down, just to piss off the wife. But later that night, when the pageant ended, she'd said good-bye to Henry, who was going home with Mike. Jamie was talking to the sour-faced woman, and Christie wondered if she was the topic of conversation. A lot of husbands were going to get the cars and warm them up and bring them back for their families. She overheard people making plans to go out for hot chocolate as she walked past parents posing for pictures with their kids. Her car was at the far end of the parking lot since she'd arrived a few minutes late, and by the time she reached it, her toes felt like cubes of ice in her thin boots. She'd gone to a bar with a friend and had ended up sleeping with a guy. The next day, she'd awoken with a headache and no recollection of his name.

After Christie wrote down the address and promised to come pick up Henry, she took a moment to finish painting her nails (in Essie's Forever Young, and if Freud had anything to say about that, he could screw himself). A few minutes later she headed out, blasting her favorite Dave Matthews CD all the way Sara's house. She found Henry and his friend tossing around a football in the front yard. The front door of the expensive-looking Tudor was open, and Sara stepped out and locked it behind her, then hurried toward Christie.

"Thanks for coming so quickly," she said as Christie got out of her car. Christie felt herself standing up a little straighter. She was the good mother in this scenario, the responsible one.

"I just can't imagine why Jamie forgot," Christie said, shaking her head. She was thoroughly enjoying this role.

Henry came over and gave Christie a hug. She wondered if it would ever stop feeling strange to have her cheek brush against her son's jaw.

"You ready to go?" she asked. "I thought I'd grill some chicken if you're hungry." That line was for Sara's benefit, too.

"Jake, come on, we're late," Sara said, climbing into her car and turning on the engine. She waved as she pulled out of her driveway.

"Are you really making chicken?" Henry asked.

"Sure," Christie said. "We just need to swing by the store to get some." Thank goodness she hadn't gotten too deep into character and said she'd make coq au vin—which she'd eaten once with Simon, the pretentious jerk.

"I wonder what happened to Jamie," Henry said.

She probably forgot you, Christie wanted to say. But she couldn't. Any passive-aggressiveness she felt toward Mike's wife paled in comparison to the love she felt for her son. She couldn't put Jamie down if it meant hurting Henry. There weren't many lines she wouldn't cross in life, but this one was firm.

"Maybe there was some emergency," she said instead.

"I tried calling the house, but no one answered," Henry said. "Should we go by there first?"

Christie thought about it. "Sure," she finally said. She was curious, and she also wanted to see the look on Jamie's face when Jamie realized she'd messed up.

They drove to Jamie and Mike's, arriving a little before 5:00 P.M.

"Looks like they're home," Christie said. "Her minivan's here."

She rang the doorbell and heard the sounds of running feet. "I GOT IT!" Eloise shrieked.

"No, let me," someone was saying—a woman with a deep voice. There was the sound of a brief scuffle, then Jamie's sister, Lou, who quite frankly weirded Christie out, opened the door.

"Yes?" Lou said. Recognition dawned in Lou's eyes a second later. "Oh! It's you. Sorry, I thought—Never mind." She had the door open about six inches, and she looked like a bat peering out of its cave. Lou didn't make a move to let them in.

Seriously, there was something wrong with Jamie's sister.

Eloise was screaming, "I wanna get the door! I wanna get the door!"

"Sorry," Lou said again. "I'm going to shut the door. Can you ring the bell again so Eloise can open it?"

"For real?" Christie asked. The door swung shut. Christie stabbed the bell again.

"Herro?" Eloise said in her little-girl voice. "Henry! Henry! Henry's home!"

"Can we come in?" Christie asked. "It's really hot out here."

"It isn't much better in here," Lou said, but the door finally opened.

The first thing Christie noticed was the mess. Jamie wasn't one of those 1950s-style house-keepers, but her place was generally clean, if not tidy. Today, though, there was a bag with wet bathing suits on the wood floor just inside the entrance, leaking a widening pool of water, and another bag of groceries nearby, slumping over as if it had given up hope of ever being unpacked. Toys were everywhere, and the mail was scattered across the floor, where it must have fallen after being pushed through the slot, and was that . . . ? Christie squinted. Yes. A big old dog turd decorated the middle of the living room rug. She just hoped one of the kids didn't step in it.

"Everything okay?" Christie asked. The yippy little mutt was jumping all over her and barking—probably desperate for someone to take her for a walk, Christie thought. And Lou wasn't kidding; it was stifling in here. Christie lifted her hair off her neck with one hand and fanned herself with the other. "Where's Jamie?"

"I'm here," Jamie said. She came around the corner, and Christie noticed her eyes were swollen and red-rimmed. "Hey, Henry." Jamie reached for the boy and hugged him for a long time, then she let go and turned to Christie. "Thank you so much for coming, Christie," she said. Then she did something remarkable—she hugged Christie, too.

For a moment, shock paralyzed Christie. She couldn't remember if she and Jamie had ever even touched before and now here stood Mike's wife, her arms wrapped around Christie's neck, her face buried in Christie's shoulder. Despite the heat Jamie felt cold. She was trembling, too, and Christie's heart began to pound. Mike worked the seven-to-three shift—he had for years—and his cruiser wasn't out front. He should have been home by now. Had something happened to him?

"What's going on?" Christie asked. Jamie shook her head and held on to Christie tighter.

"Jamie?" Henry asked. "Where's my dad?"

The quaver of fear in Henry's voice was what finally seemed to break through to Jamie.

"Oh, honey," she said. She finally pulled away from Christie and cupped Henry's cheek in her hand. "I'm so glad you're here. Your dad is going to want to see you as soon as he gets home. He'll be here soon. He's fine, everything's going to be fine . . ."

Everything was not fine. The house was an oven and Eloise was wearing shorts but no shirt and holding on to Henry's leg and there was poop on the floor and Jamie was babbling in that way that seemed a thin edge from hysteria.

"Can you go say hi to the other kids?" Lou asked Henry. "They were excited to see me, but you're like a rock star to them."

Lou inched up a bit in Christie's estimation. Henry smiled modestly and went into the living room.

"We should sit down," Jamie said, motioning

toward the dining room. Christie followed the sisters to the big wooden table, feeling anxiety gnaw at her.

"Where's Mike?" she asked. "Did something happen to him?"

"No," Jamie said at the exact same moment Lou replied, "Yes."

"Someone tell me what the hell is going on!"

Before either woman could reply, Henry appeared in the doorway of the room, clutching his cell phone.

"Jamie?" he said. Just a little while ago, when she'd seen him at his friend Jake's house, Christie had been struck by how big her boy was getting. The fuzz above his upper lip, that deepening voice, those broad shoulders—he was teetering on the brink of manhood. But now he looked like a little boy again, all gangly limbs and huge brown eyes.

"One of my friends just texted me," Henry said in a wavering voice. "Did Dad really shoot someone?"

Chapter Six

MIKE DIDN'T COME HOME until nearly seven o'clock that night. Jamie watched as a cruiser pulled up in front of their house and Mike got out of the passenger's seat. She ran to the front door, flinging it open, as the police car pulled away. Her husband's gait dragged as he approached their house. His head was bowed, and he still wore his uniform.

Jamie closed the door behind her, so the kids couldn't hear, and leaned into him. After a moment, she felt his arms rise and encircle her body. They stayed locked together, wordlessly, for a long moment.

"Do you want to talk about it?" she whispered.

She felt his shoulders heave, just once, then he released a sigh. "A bunch of bangers were fighting. I don't know, maybe it was an initiation or some-thing. It was too big to be sponta-neous . . ."

She nodded when he paused. *Tell me,* she thought. *Please don't hold this in, too.*

"We were close by. A car had skidded through an intersection and wrapped around a street-light. Anyway, no one was hurt, so when the call came in we got there first. Jay, the fucking idiot they paired me with, he just starts running into the scene. He doesn't wait for backup, he doesn't stay behind me, he just goes. Maybe he figured they were young-looking so they'd be scared of the cops. What the hell was he thinking?"

"I don't know," Jamie whispered.

"The rain's still pouring down, and Jay's heading straight for two guys fighting. He's screaming, 'Freeze!' like he's on a fucking TV show. And I'm trying to get to him, to cover him, but guys keep running in and out of my line of sight. Someone punches me in the head from behind, and I spin around but he's already gone. When I turn back, I see a guy reaching around behind him. Like to the back waistband of his pants, and I know what he's doing. He's getting his piece. Jay's about twenty feet away and he's got out his pepper spray. How does he think a hot shot versus a gun is going to end?"

Mike's breathing was rougher now.

"The guy started to draw on Jay and I had a shot. I took it."

"You thought he was going to shoot Jay," Jamie said.

Mike nodded. "He *was* going to shoot Jay. Another two, three seconds . . . I see people looking up, like they think maybe the shot is another crack of thunder. Then the sirens come.

Everyone's running around, yelling. Our backup arrives and they secure the scene while I call for an ambulance."

Jamie rubbed his back like she did the kids' when they were hurt or upset.

"I knew it the second I fired. Before I even got close to him and saw his eyes." Mike shook his head, like he was trying to deny his own words. "He was a year older than Henry."

"I know," Jamie said. She kept rubbing Mike's broad back because she couldn't think of anything else to say.

"I play basketball around there sometimes. I might've played with him."

Mike hadn't done it in a few months, but on occasional weekend mornings when he was off duty he joined a pickup game in the community he patrolled. It was a way of showing young men another side to the police. They sweated together, argued over fouls real and imagined, and walked off the courts slapping each other's palms.

"You need to rest," Jamie said. "Come inside."

"Do the kids know?" Mike asked.

"Henry heard something about it from one of his friends," Jamie said. "I told him we'd talk about it when you got home."

Mike pulled away from her and scrubbed his hands over his face. "Yeah."

"Lou's here," Jamie said. "Christie, too."

Mike jerked back. "What's she doing here?"

"She wants to help," Jamie said. "But we can ask her to go if you want."

Mike shook his head again. "I keep seeing him, lying there. You know how the kids like to make snow angels? That's what he looked like. A snow angel bleeding out on a piece of asphalt."

A tremor ran through Mike's body, and Jamie could see his throat working convulsively.

"Honey," Jamie said. "You didn't start the fight. You didn't put the gun in his hand. This wasn't your fault, Mike! You were just doing your job."

Mike nodded, but the expression on his face told Jamie her words hadn't penetrated.

"They didn't find a gun," he said in a low voice.

Jamie felt herself go ice-cold as Mike's words echoed in the space between them. "What do you mean?"

"The union rep came. He told me not to say anything, but that's bullshit. I didn't do anything wrong. I told them what I could tonight and I'm going in tomorrow for a formal statement." Mike shook his head. "Jay told them he didn't see a gun. He thought the guy was just drawing back his fist to punch the kid again. Jay couldn't even look at me."

"He was wrong!" Jamie cried. "He's an idiot. You said so—"

Mike cut her off: "A few of the bangers were

questioned, the ones they could round up, at least. They all said the same thing: No gun."

Mike's voice was a monotone now.

"There wasn't a gun?" Jamie echoed, her throat closing around the words. "Did they look around? Maybe it fell out of his hand."

"They looked," Mike said. "*I* looked. I was the first one to reach the guy."

"No," Jamie said. She felt her insides collapse. "No, Mike."

"I swear to you," Mike said, staring at her, his eyes hard and intent. He gripped her shoulders, his fingers digging into her flesh. "I *saw* it, Jamie."

"We have to think," Jamie said. She was breathing hard now, her mind scrambling. "It was raining! It was hard to see! Anyone could've made that mistake! They can't blame you!"

She felt hysteria rise within her. She saw Mike leading with his SIG Sauer as he walked through their shadowy house, imagining a threat that had never existed. Her eyes went instinctively to the holster on his hip. It was empty. They must've taken his gun as evidence.

Jamie turned to look at their house and the four innocent children who were depending on them. Then she spun back around at the sudden sound of an engine. A white news van was coming down their street.

Mike didn't appear to notice the approaching

van. He was in his own world now. He had been for quite some time. Why had she ever thought he needed to go back to work? He hadn't been ready, not even close, and now a teenager was dead and his family was shattered and all of their lives were wrecked.

Jamie began to tremble. The news van stopped in front of their house.

This can't be happening, she thought.

PART TWO

Chapter Seven

IT WAS THE FIRST time Lou had taken a sick day since she'd begun working at the zoo. The flu, a broken toe (incurred when she'd been assisting with an examination of a hippo who changed his mind about cooperating), a lingering sinus infection . . . none of it could keep Lou from her beloved animals. Being around them felt healing.

She craved the elephants' calming presence even more than usual today, because the scene at Jamie and Mike's was so alarming. By now there were three news vans with big antennas crowding the street, and Lou had glimpsed a reporter she recognized from television standing in front of the house, talking as a cameraman filmed her.

Inside, things were just as disorienting. After Mike had come home last night, he'd changed into shorts and a T-shirt, then slumped on the couch, staring at a Disney movie with the kids. Jamie had stationed herself in the kitchen, making spaghetti and a huge salad and garlic bread and, of all things, an apple pie. An apple pie! As if Jamie had time to be coring and slicing fruit. And the last thing they needed was for the oven to be on, adding a few more degrees of heat to the sweltering house.

"What are you doing?" Lou had asked. "Don't you think you should be with Mike?"

But Jamie's lips had trembled. "It's Mike's favorite."

Lou had understood then: Her sister was trying to find a way to give her husband some small measure of comfort. So Lou had picked up a knife and begun slicing Granny Smiths, too. No one had seemed to notice as the clock ticked later, so at around 9:00 P.M., Lou had cajoled the kids to bed with the promise of a special contest— whoever could pee the longest would win a lollipop.

Lou had realized belatedly that none of the kids had brushed their teeth, and she was pretty sure she'd forgotten at least one other part of Jamie's nighttime routine, but at least they were asleep. She'd finally done one small thing to help her sister, something concrete. Jamie had asked her to spend the night, so she'd borrowed the minivan and hurried home to grab a quick shower and pack up her toothbrush and a nightshirt and change of clothes. Luckily no reporters had followed her. The relief on Donny's and Mary Alice's faces when she told them she'd be gone for a day or two had reminded her that she needed to move out soon, on top of everything else. When she'd returned, Jamie and Mike were talking quietly in the living room, so Lou had gone upstairs to lie down on their bed. Somehow she'd fallen asleep, still wearing her shoes. She'd forgotten to brush her teeth, too.

Lou figured she'd check in after work to see if Jamie needed her to run to the store or something, given that Jamie had used up just about everything in her pantry last night cooking a meal that easily could've served twelve. But this morning, when she'd crept downstairs in the grainy, gray light of dawn, she'd seen Jamie and Mike sitting side by side on the couch, in the same position as the night before. They weren't talking. Lou wondered if they'd even slept. She felt dazed and muddy; it must've been eighty-five degrees in there. It was hard to breathe, let alone think.

"Hi, Lou," Jamie said without turning around, and Lou started. She thought she'd been quiet, but Jamie seemed to have developed supersonic hearing since having children.

"Hi," Lou whispered. She didn't want to interrupt the intimate moment—it seemed like that was all she was doing lately—but Jamie motioned for her to join them. Lou brushed some Legos off a chair and sat down. She looked at her sister and brother-in-law carefully. Jamie was still wearing the same outfit as yesterday, and she was twirling her hair into knots again. Mike hadn't shaved, and his eyes were bleary. They both looked wilted, like flowers whose source of water had run out days earlier.

"Are you going into work today?" Lou asked

Mike. She wondered if the question was too blunt, but Mike didn't seem to mind.

He shook his head. "They told me to stay home for now. Administrative leave."

He put his feet up on the coffee table and crossed his arms. When animals felt threatened, they usually tried to take up more space—puffing up their hair or extending their limbs, Lou thought. Mike was doing the opposite. Did that mean he was accepting defeat?

They sat together in silence, then Lou caught sight of the clock across the room and stood up. "I should probably get going," she said.

Jamie looked at Mike, then back at Lou. "Actually," she said, "would you mind staying today?"

"Yeah, sure," Lou said. She could get someone else to take over her duties at the zoo. She certainly had enough vacation time coming.

"Maybe you could take the kids to a movie," Jamie said. "I don't have any camps or anything lined up this week."

"Sounds good," Lou said.

"Tell her the rest," Mike said. There was a white line around his mouth.

It was only then that Lou noticed the morning's paper spread out on the coffee table under Mike's feet. She looked up to see Jamie's lips trembling. "The press found out about Mike's nickname."

Lou furrowed her brow. She wasn't aware that Mike had one.

"It's Rambo," Jamie said. "Because he's got dark hair and muscles! But the press is turning it into something else . . ."

"How did they find out?" Lou asked.

"Does it matter?" Jamie asked. Tears slid down her cheeks. Mike put his arm around her, and Jamie pressed her face into his chest, her shoulders shaking.

"Mommy?"

They all turned at the sound of Eloise's voice.

"I wet."

That was what she'd forgotten last night—to put a Pull-Up on Eloise, Lou suddenly remembered. Eloise had managed to take off her pajamas, and she was holding a blanket.

"It's okay, baby." Jamie pushed away her tears with her hands and stood up. "I'll clean you up and get you some dry PJs. Do you want to go sleep in my bed?"

Eloise just shook her head and walked around the couch and climbed into her dad's lap. Mike wrapped the blanket more securely around his daughter and rested his cheek against the top of her head. Lou swallowed hard as she watched them.

"I'll go change her sheets," Jamie said. Lou followed her out of the room and up the stairs.

"I can't stand this," Jamie whispered. Part of

her hair was sticking up and her forehead was creased. "Do you think Mike will go to jail?"

Lou shook her head, even though she had no idea. "It's not like he just shot someone in cold blood."

"But I feel partly responsible," Jamie said. "I knew he wasn't himself."

Jamie began stripping the sheets off Eloise's toddler bed as she spoke, bundling them into the laundry hamper in a corner of the room. "He was just a boy, Lou." She dropped her face into her hands and her shoulders shook a few times, then she lifted her head and resumed moving.

"You don't realize how close you are to disaster until it happens," Jamie said, her voice growing shrill. "Do you know what happens to cops in jail? It's worse than you can imagine. And the kids"—her voice broke, but she managed to steady it—"they'll lose their dad if Mike is charged with a crime. Even if they don't charge him, if he ends up losing his job we'll lose the house; we can barely afford the mortgage as it is. I'll go back to work—God, who would even hire me now?—and Christie will probably still try to demand child support. Can you believe Mike pays her five hundred bucks a month? We take care of Henry most of the time!"

"You can't think about this stuff now," Lou blurted. Jamie had a little spittle in the corner of her mouth and her eyes looked as crazy as her hair. The cornerstone in Lou's life was self-destructing.

"I *have* to think about it," Jamie said. "I know you said not to watch the news, but I need to know what we're up against."

Jamie walked over to Eloise's window and pulled back the curtain. She jabbed her finger toward the photographers and news vans staked out in front of the house. "Look at this! Should I just keep the kids in all day? What if a reporter says something to one of them?"

"Um, maybe they should go out, like you said," Lou said. "I can take them to the movie. Keep things normal." Routines were important—at the zoo, animals depended upon them.

"I also think you should take a shower," Lou said. Jamie looked a little surprised, and Lou wondered if she'd hurt her sister's feelings. She tried to soften her words with a joke: "I'm the one people usually say that to."

"I've got to start breakfast—" Jamie began, but Lou cut her off.

"Do you know that by this time I've fed forty thousand pounds of mammal? I think I can handle making some toast."

She'd said the right thing for once. Jamie actually smiled, but a moment later, her lips were curving down again. "I don't know how to do this, Lou. I don't think I can do it. Oh my God . . . that poor boy. His poor mother . . ."

"It's going to be okay," Lou said, and she gently pushed Jamie toward the shower so her sister wouldn't read the lie in her eyes.

Christie pulled her red Miata into the salon's parking lot and chose the most convenient spot. Employees weren't supposed to do that—they'd been instructed to leave their cars in the back, so customers could nab the prime spaces—but it was Christie's last day of work. She'd also begged the best stylist to give her a free cut in between customers. Who cared if the salon's owner objected to any of it? She wasn't ever coming back to this place.

Tonight Christie had her first paid undercover job. The freckle-faced man's wife had given them her husband's daily schedule: what time he usually got to work, what time he left the office, where he routinely ate lunch. Elroy had read through it before crafting a plan. He suggested the wife text her husband and ask him to stop at the Safeway on his way home to pick up diapers and milk. Christie would be in the store, her purse slipping off her shoulder, doing her best to cross paths with the guy. Her outfit was waiting on the passenger's seat: a black minidress with straps that crisscrossed over her back, and red high heels. If everything went as expected, she'd arrange to meet the mark at a hotel in the next day or two. Freckle-face wouldn't know what hit him until he heard the echo of the hotel room door slamming behind her.

She should upgrade her car, Christie thought as she took the keys out of the ignition. Her Miata was cute, but it was seven years old, and now that she had a real job—something thrilling and well paying—she might need to invest in a Mercedes or at least an Audi. Maybe she'd go test-drive some at the dealership tomorrow. It would be a perfect way to celebrate her first case. To kick off her new life.

Christie locked her car, then slung her purse (fake, but a good Chanel copy) over her shoulder and walked toward the salon. It didn't officially open for fifteen minutes, but she could see employees inside, setting up the coffeepot to brew and stocking their stations with hair spray and brushes for the day ahead.

"Hey," she called as she pulled open the heavy glass door.

"Shhh!" someone chided. The flat-screen television toward the back of the room, which was usually turned to music videos, was showing the news. Two stylists stood in front of it, rapt.

"Well, excuse me," Christie said. She walked over to the receptionist's desk and tucked her purse in a lower drawer. Slowly she became aware of the topic of the news report, and without moving her head, she raised her eyes toward the television.

A woman with a helmet of auburn hair and an intense expression was standing outside what looked like—what *was*—Mike and Jamie's house. Christie blinked and took a step closer to the television. The newscaster was saying: ". . . killing an unarmed Hispanic teenager, just a few months after the fatal shooting of Officer Larry Prichard in front of police headquarters. Officer Richard Crawford was also injured in that same shooting and remains on indefinite leave. Officer Crawford was Anderson's longtime partner, and, sources say, Anderson was deeply upset after witnessing the shooting . . . Anderson is currently on paid administrative leave."

One of the stylists flipped the channel to a Christina Aguilera video and moved back to her station, but Christie felt rooted in place.

Mike had killed someone?

Last night, after Henry had come into the dining room with his cell phone containing the text from his friend, Jamie had leapt to her feet to reassure him. Jamie had woven what Christie now understood was a truncated story—Mike had fired at a young man who was holding a gun, it was unclear exactly what had happened, but the details were all being sorted out. Mike was perfectly safe and hadn't done anything wrong, Jamie had repeated at least twice.

"Your dad will explain everything when he gets home," Jamie had said, reaching for the phone and tucking it into her pocket. "Can I hold it for you, honey? It's probably best if you don't talk to anyone until your dad gets here."

Christie had believed the story—and Jamie hadn't bothered to clarify anything to her privately. Did she think Christie was a child, too?

When she'd first arrived at the house, Christie had been shocked by Jamie's hug, but then she'd found her own arms winding back around Jamie's neck. Jamie had seemed so distraught and lost, and Christie had felt proud that she'd been the steady one in the crisis. She'd found a mostly full bottle of Chardonnay in the fridge and had poured them both generous glasses while Lou checked on the kids. They'd talked for a little while, but then Mike had come home, and Jamie had shooed her out of the house, saying she was sure Christie had things to do. Christie had taken the hint; Jamie didn't want her around Mike.

Jamie had also made the decision that Mike should be the one to tell Henry what had happened. But she, Christie, was Henry's mother! Shouldn't she have a say? True, maybe she wouldn't have done anything differently—she probably still would have left Henry in Mike and Jamie's care last night—but it irritated her not to have been given a choice. Not to be included in the family crisis.

Throughout the rest of the day, Christie checked in customers, collected tip envelopes for the stylists, and logged new appointments in the computer, keeping a smile affixed to her face and trying to hide the turmoil brewing within her. How was she supposed to know what to say to Henry, when she didn't even know what Mike had told their son? She was sure everything would blow over in a day or so—the media always tried to dramatize stories, and Mike was a great cop— but it rankled her to be shoved to the outside when all she'd wanted was to help.

At five o'clock, she was packing up her things to go when she heard the sound of a gunshot. She spun around, her heart rate accelerating, but it was just the cork escaping from a bottle of champagne.

"Go get 'em, Charlie's newest angel," said Rita, the stylist who'd given Christie a farewell haircut during her lunch break. Rita filled a bunch of Solo cups and handed them out as the other girls crowded around, touching their cups to Christie's. Everyone seemed in awe of the job Christie had landed, which lifted her mood. She didn't protest when someone upended the last of the champagne into her cup.

"Let me know if you need a sidekick!" Rita offered, and Christie hid a smile. Rita was in her early fifties, with a body that seemed to belong to two different people—a slender top affixed to a huge bottom and chunky legs. She was always complaining about being single. Did she really think she'd be catnip to men with wandering eyes?

But Christie just promised, "I will."

She hugged everyone good-bye, promising to stay in touch, and headed out the door. The moment she climbed into her car and sat down, her worry came rushing back. She couldn't stop hearing the sound of that champagne cork. She wondered what was happening with Mike. She called Henry, but he didn't answer his phone.

She tried to push her unease out of her mind so she could focus on her new job, but instead her anxiety began to spread. What if she blew her first case? Maybe she should've waited to hand in her notice until she was sure the P.I. gig was working out. But planning ahead had never been her forte.

She rapped her fingertips against the dashboard a few times, then checked herself out in the rear-view mirror. Her blue eyes were outlined by smudgy kohl liner and three coats of mascara, and her lips were painted a soft pink. She'd gone into the salon's bathroom to change into the dress before leaving, and her tanned skin showed through the openings in the fabric. Everything was going to be fine, she told herself. She drained the champagne from the cup just as her phone rang.

"He told his wife he's leaving within the hour," Elroy said. "But he's going to stop at the store for her to pick up milk and diapers on his way home."

"Should I head there now?" Christie asked.

"Yep," Elroy said. "Keep your phone close."

"Okay," Christie said. She'd already MapQuested directions—she had a terrible sense of direction and couldn't risk getting lost—and despite the rush-hour traffic, she made it to the supermarket quickly. She parked by the entrance and waited, watching customers disappear through the electronic doors. She tried Henry twice more, leaving bright, upbeat messages, but he didn't pick up the phone. She contemplated phoning Jamie and Mike's house but didn't want to have to end the call abruptly if her mark showed up. Her phone finally rang just as she was regretting drinking the second cup of champagne and debating whether to duck into the store and use the bathroom.

"He's on the move," Elroy said.

Christie felt a little thrill. Even the lingo of her new job was exciting.

"I'm here," she said.

"He drives a 2010 blue Toyota Camry with a dent in the front bumper," Elroy said.

"Sexy," Christie said.

"Can you see the entrance of the parking lot from where you are?"

"Yep," Christie said.

"When you see his car pull in, go into the store."

"I'll put a little extra wiggle in my walk," Christie said.

"Are you sure you can fit any more in there?" Elroy asked.

It took a few seconds to realize that Elroy was making a joke.

She smiled. "I'll call you as soon as I have a date."

She kept vigil, trying to ignore her increasingly full bladder and her worry about Mike's situation, and sure enough, Freckles rolled in exactly eighteen minutes later. Elroy hadn't given her his real name, in case Freckles used an alias for his extracurricular activities, so she wouldn't accidentally slip up.

Christie took a deep breath, doubled-checked that her handbag was unzipped, and strolled toward the supermarket entrance, swaying on her three-inch heels. Milk and diapers, she mused. The dairy section would be better for seduction.

She wondered what would happen if Freckles ignored her spilled purse, or simply handed her a runaway lipstick and went on with his manufactured errand. Sure, guys hit on her all the time—but what if at the moment it mattered most, one didn't? She looked down at her dress. Would pulling the hem up a bit higher be overkill?

Either her heels slowed her down or Freckles was in a rush, because just before she stepped on the mat that signaled a trigger to open the supermarket's doors, Freckles came up behind her. She sensed his presence—she couldn't have said how she knew it was him—but she didn't turn around. Better if he made the first move, she thought.

She scanned the store's layout and moved toward the refrigerated section. She sensed Freckles was still directly behind her; the fine hairs on her arm were standing up. She found the milk and stood there for a moment, studying the selection in the glass case.

"Are you a one percent or a skim girl?"

Seriously? Freckles thought *that* qualified as a pickup line?

Christie made herself smile as if it was the wittiest comment she'd ever heard. She turned to face Freckles, keeping her chin low and looking up at him from under her fringe of eyelashes.

"Skim," she said.

Freckles was sliding his hand into his pocket. His *left* hand. Probably trying to hide a wedding ring, she thought.

"But only in the morning, in my coffee," she said. "At night I'm a champagne girl."

Freckles smiled, as she'd known he would.

"Champagne, huh?" he said. "A woman with classy tastes."

"Only the best," she said. She let her eyes linger as they moved down his body, then rose back up to his face.

"I know a place that serves champagne,"

Freckles said importantly. *Where, Mr. Man-About-Town—every bar in D.C.?* Christie wanted to ask. "I'm Doug, by the way."

"Christine," she said. It was close enough to her name that she wouldn't blow her cover, but it gave her a little layer of protection. Elroy had advised her to give a completely different last name, if asked. But she was counting on the fact that most men wouldn't care enough to ask. They usually didn't.

She grabbed a small carton of milk from the case. "I'm just in town on business for a few days, and there's nothing but powdered creamer in my hotel room," she said. Maybe her sentence was a little clunky, but she'd managed to work the mention of a hotel into the conversation, which might steer Doug in the right direction.

She gave him a final, lingering smile, then began moving toward the checkout aisle. Let him take up the chase, she thought.

"Christine?" He was frowning. "I thought you said you drank skim . . . you just got two percent."

She looked back over her shoulder and gave him a mock angry look. "I blame you for distracting me."

He guffawed then—actually guffawed—and she walked back to switch out the milk cartons. She hoped she didn't have to spend long with him in the hotel room. She could expire from boredom.

"So maybe we should check it out, as long as

you're in town," Doug was saying as he walked her to the cashier station. "The champagne bar."

"Maybe," Christie said, throwing him another flirty glance. She could do this in her sleep—and she might have to, if Doug kept up his corny lines. She put her milk on the conveyor belt.

"Any chance I could get your number?"

She smiled and pulled her phone out of her purse. "Give me yours," she said. He rattled off the digits, and she programmed them into her phone, then hit the "Call" button. A second later, Doug's cell phone rang.

"You've got my number," she said. She'd left her real phone in the car. This was a cheap throwaway cell Elroy had given her. She'd get rid of it, and be given a new one, for the next job. An expense account was a wondrous thing. Maybe she should've picked up some Diet Coke and Lean Cuisines along with her milk, she thought.

"Two forty-nine," the cashier said. Christie started to pull out her credit card, but Doug was faster.

"Allow me," he said, swiping his through the machine with a grandiose gesture, as if he was paying for a diamond. "Next time I'll buy you a real drink."

"I'll look forward to it," she said. "But I'm only in town for a couple days." Elroy wanted to close this deal quickly.

"Then I better call you soon," he said, putting

his gallon of milk on the conveyor belt. He hadn't even picked up the diapers. What a jerk. He deserved everything that was coming to him, Christie thought as she walked away.

This job was almost too easy. Tomorrow or the day after, she'd suggest meeting Doug at the hotel. As soon as the job was done, she'd get paid— probably three or four hundred dollars, when all her hours were tallied up. It would be almost as much as she made in a full week at the salon.

Christie got into her car and turned up her radio, singing along with Adele as she sped toward the nearest public bathroom. There was a Starbucks on the next block; she'd stop there.

At the end of the song, just as Christie turned into the parking lot, the radio announcer began to speak, his voice deep and stern. "Sources say a special Metropolitan Police Department investigative team is collecting evidence in the shooting of a fifteen-year-old boy by veteran police officer Michael Anderson. Sources say several eyewitnesses report the teenager was unarmed when shot by Anderson. The MPD will bring the evidence to the U.S. Attorney's Office, which could decide to take the case to a grand jury for an indictment. We'll have another update on the hour."

Christie slammed on her brakes just in time to avoid hitting a car that was pulling out of a parking spot.

She picked up her phone and dialed Mike. The

media loved to play stuff like this up. Surely once the facts were sorted out, it would blow over. Still, he might welcome a little support. But it was Jamie who answered. "Hey," Christie said. "I just heard the news . . . Wow, what a bummer."

Jamie released a sound that wasn't quite like a laugh. "Yeah," she said. "A bummer."

"Anyway, is Mike around?" Christie asked after a little pause.

"You know, I don't think now's such a good time," Jamie said. "He's resting."

Jamie did this sometimes—acted like the gatekeeper between her and Mike. It never failed to annoy Christie.

Christie felt her spine straighten. "Well, my kid is being affected by all of this, too. Am I allowed to talk to *him?*"

Jamie sighed then, and when she spoke again, she sounded so beaten down that Christie felt bad for snapping. "Of course you can talk to Henry. Let me go get him."

After a minute Henry's voice, which had deepened over the past few months, came on the line.

"Hey, honey," she said. "How are you doing?"

"Okay, I guess," Henry said. "Kind of a weird day."

"Let me know if you want me to come get you," Christie said. Her evenings seemed longer now that Simon was out of the picture. Chinese food and a movie at home wouldn't be pathetic if Henry were there.

"No, I should hang with Dad," Henry said. "Is that okay?"

"Sure," she said. She was all dressed up, her makeup fresh. Surely she could find something to do. But her best friend, Robyn, wasn't speaking to her because she thought Christie had flirted with her boyfriend. And most of the other women Christie knew would be with their husbands tonight.

"I love you," Henry said.

Christie blew a kiss over the phone. She kept her voice light. "You, too, kiddo. See you soon."

Christie wasn't a perfect parent; she knew that. She'd never baked a muffin in her life, let alone hidden pureed vegetables in one. Whenever Henry asked for her help with homework, she told him to Google his questions. She let him fall asleep at night without brushing his teeth—she was pretty sure Jamie and Mike blamed her for Henry's three cavities—and she'd let him watch an R-rated movie when he was seven, mostly because she wanted to see it, too. But somehow, Henry was as close to perfect as it was possible to get.

He wasn't just the most important thing in her life, she thought. He was the only thing she'd ever done right.

• • •

Motherhood had steeped Jamie in stress endurance. She'd once had four kids down with a norovirus, all of them moaning and retching while she ricocheted from room to room with buckets and Pedialyte and fresh towels. Another time—Jamie still shuddered at the memory—Mike had left an open bottle of Drāno on the bathroom sink as he bent over the shower drain, trying to unclog it. Eloise had tottered by, her little fingers reaching out and grazing the plastic bottle. Somehow, Jamie had swooped in and yanked her daughter to safety just as the bottle tumbled down toward her baby's face. (She and Mike had had an epic fight moments later, hurling accusations like spears: "I thought you were watching her!" "Why the hell didn't you take two seconds to put the cap back on!") After so many years of raising children, Jamie had grown accustomed to feeling her heartbeat explode with the intensity of a racehorse pulling away from the gate: a fall from a playground structure, a sudden high fever, a car speeding around the corner just as Sam's ball bounced into the street . . .

She worried every day when Mike left for his job, too. Watching him strap on his gun and baton and pepper spray was a constant reminder of the danger he faced. Jamie dreaded domestic disturbances—those were the scariest calls, the ones proven to be the most deadly—but she also feared the officer-needs-assistance signal, which indicated a situation was spinning out of control fast. She no longer read the police blotter in the newspaper, because it made the scenarios she tried to push out of her imagination even more vivid.

But she'd never experienced anything like the sustained, raw fear that pulsed through her now, as steadily as if it were being infused by IV.

Earlier this morning, Sandy had phoned. "I'm here for you," she'd said. "What can I do? Do you want to bring the kids over?"

An echo of the words she'd spoken to Sandy after Ritchie's shooting.

But Jamie couldn't see Sandy. Not today. Buried beneath the sorrow and anger and pain she'd felt over Ritchie's shooting had always been a kernel of horrible gratitude that Mike had chosen that precise moment to crack a joke and push Ritchie out the door first. She'd always been afraid that Sandy would sense it. But now it was Sandy who pitied *her;* Jamie could hear the emotion infusing Sandy's tone. Ritchie was being hailed as a hero; they were going to put up a plaque in his honor at police headquarters, along with one for the fallen rookie. An entire elementary school had sent notes thanking Ritchie for his service. Ritchie was getting better, and now Mike might go to jail.

Sandy couldn't understand what she was going through. Their sorrows were different species.

"Lou's here," she'd told Sandy, ending the call quickly. "But thank you."

Then she and Mike had left the house to go to the police station so Mike could meet with the lawyer provided by his union and give a statement. Mike hadn't wanted her to come, but she'd insisted. Their minivan had been trailed by news vans as they traveled down their quiet street. Jamie stared out the window, at buildings and intersections that seemed familiar yet changed, as if she were viewing them through the prism of a dream.

After they'd parked at the police station, reporters had leapt out of their vehicles and crowded around her and Mike while they tried to make it into the building. A cameraman had bumped Jamie, and she'd released a little cry of surprise. Mike had whipped around, snarling a warning, as a dozen cameras whirled and snapped. The expression on his face, Jamie was certain, would be the one that appeared on the six o'clock news.

Now they were in the station, and Jamie was sitting on a hard wooden bench in the waiting area while Mike conferred in a private room with his lawyer. After the stifling heat of her home, Jamie felt chilled. She rubbed her hands up and down her arms, wishing she'd put a sweater on top of her simple blue cotton dress. Would Mike actually be arrested? She imagined one of his colleagues rolling the tips of her husband's fingers into black ink before pressing them onto a card, then someone reading Mike the Miranda rights he'd recited to so many suspects.

It was impossible to believe it had been only thirty-six hours since Mike had left for work. She tried to grip on to the memory of that morning, her final taste of normalcy, but time had turned loose and hazy in her mind. She was pretty sure Mike had already been up and showered by the time she'd gotten out of bed around six. She didn't think she'd asked him how he'd slept, maybe because she knew the answer wouldn't be reassuring.

He'd been leaning up against the counter, gulping coffee while she poured cereal into bowls for the kids. She remembered reaching around him to open the refrigerator, and noticing they were almost out of milk. She'd jotted a reminder on the running list she kept on the refrigerator door. Or had that happened the day before? No, it must have been that morning, because she'd been about to put away the milk she'd bought at the store when the phone had rung.

She was certain she recalled the thick, dark clouds hanging low in the sky, blotting out the sun as effectively as an eclipse. "It looks like rain," she'd probably said as she'd kissed Mike good-bye. Had she kissed Mike good-bye that morning? She hoped she had.

Jamie flinched at a sudden touch on her shoulder. She looked up to see an officer named Arun Brahma, a man she'd gotten to know through the years because he and Mike shared a passion for football and sometimes attended games together.

"We're all behind Mike," Brahma said softly. "Is there anything I can do?" Jamie nearly wept with gratitude; Brahma was dark-skinned, and his support meant he didn't believe the horrible accusation that race had played a part in Mike's decision to pull the trigger. If his brothers and sisters in blue had abandoned him, it would've been the end of her husband.

"Thank you," she whispered. "I'll let you know." Brahma nodded and walked away. Jamie wished she'd thought to ask him what was happening with Mike. She visualized her husband sitting across from the lawyer, giving an account of the day. Mike wouldn't break down, that much she knew. He could get emotional about small things, like Eloise learning to ride a two-wheeler, but when it came to a crisis, he never panicked. Sometimes Mike's steadfastness irritated her, like when their kids were babies and they cried in the night. "I let Henry cry it out, and he's a great sleeper now," Mike had said. But Jamie was physically incapable of letting her kids sob in their cribs, which meant she had to get up and rock them and soothe them while Mike rolled over and went back to sleep. She got anxious when their kids ran a fever; he simply reached for the Tylenol. She worried about germs on the handles of supermarket carts; Mike told her kids needed to build up their immunity. Whenever her emotions ran high, he was the tonic that neutralized them. He was the steadiest man she knew.

The steadiest man she knew—but not lately, a traitorous voice whispered in her head.

How had a few seconds erased the thousands of days he'd spent risking his own life to do good? Mike had once talked down a guy who was threatening a woman with a gun. He'd arrested a man who was abusing his dog in public—and had personally taken the little mutt to a no-kill animal shelter so the man would never get it back. He always talked to kids on the street, urging them to avoid gangs, asking them about school and what books they were reading. This wasn't just a job for Mike, it was a calling, as strong as the priesthood.

She wrapped her arms around herself again and looked at her watch. They'd been in the station for only an hour, though it felt like much longer. She could hear the jangling of distant phones, and the front door kept swinging open as police officers walked in and out. A young woman came in and walked to the front desk, her pretty sundress swaying above her knees, saying she'd gotten a call that a Good Samaritan had turned in a wallet she'd lost. The desk sergeant looked at her, then checked her driver's license photo before handing over the wallet. The woman thanked him and turned around, her eyes meeting Jamie's before flickering away. But not before Jamie registered the surprise in them.

No, it doesn't make sense that I'm here, Jamie thought, answering the woman's unspoken question. *I should be driving a carpool, or attending a PTA meeting, or roasting a chicken.* The woman exited the building, and Jamie stared at the door as it shut behind her, wondering if the media were still gathered there, waiting to pounce.

She leaned her head against the hard wall behind the bench, forcing back tears. The door opened again, and an officer carried in a paper bag with the logo of a fast-food restaurant. Burgers, she thought, catching a whiff of grease and cooked meat.

She'd waitressed at a burger joint near Capitol Hill when she was twenty-one. It was how she'd met Mike. Jamie had just graduated from the University of Maryland and had accepted an entry-level job at a D.C. public relations firm. That wouldn't start until August; in the meantime, she was hustling for tips six nights a week. She'd lived in a crowded town house with five other young women, and on weekend nights, the smell of hair spray and perfume and scented candles was overpowering.

That night she'd put on her usual uniform—a black skirt, black T-shirt with an embarrassing restaurant logo of a hamburger with a giant tongue trying to lick itself, red apron, and black sneakers—and headed to her job. The place was a little grimy and the food wasn't anything special, but twenty-somethings flocked there because the burgers and beer were cheap and there were long tables that could be pushed together. On Friday nights there was karaoke and on Saturdays Jell-O shots made with vodka instead of water. It was always rowdy.

It was ninety-nine-cent Jell-O shot night, which usually meant good tips. Capitol Hill staffers didn't earn much money, but drunken ones became more generous when filling in the tip lines on credit card receipts. Jamie was bouncing between five big tables in section three that evening, and she ran back and forth from the kitchen dozens of times, balancing metal trays on her upturned palms, clearing away empty beer pitchers and soiled paper napkins, refilling drinks. One of her tables was especially busy—a group of six or seven guys who cheered each other on as they sucked down shot after shot. At about eleven o'clock, a few of the guys peeled away from the long table, leaving just three. "Can we have another pitcher of Bud?" one of the guys asked. "Sure," Jamie said. She cleared the empty glasses and plates off the table as a new group claimed the unoccupied seats, then went to put in the order with the bartender.

Then she made a mistake. She went to the bathroom.

She was near the end of an eight-hour shift, and it was the first break she'd had. She used the toilet, washed her hands, and splashed cold water on her face. She smelled like grease and stale beer, her hair was coming loose from its ponytail, and her mascara was smeared. She took a moment to fix her hair and wipe away the flecks of black from underneath her eyes. She walked back out and grabbed the full pitcher off the bartop and headed into the dining area.

Almost immediately she spotted the problem. The table of guys, the group responsible for her highest bill of the evening, had walked out.

She ran to it, hoping they'd left some money under a beer stein but knowing she wouldn't find any.

"Did you see where these guys went?" she asked the people seated nearby. They shook their heads.

It had never happened to her before, but it certainly occurred from time to time at the restaurant. It did at every restaurant. The real problem was the owner of the burger place—a middle-aged guy who'd designed the logo and had logged far too many nights hanging out at the bar, drinking steadily and arguing politics with the customers—was an ass. He'd instituted a rule that the waitstaff had to cover the cost of any walkouts, to prevent them from letting their friends escape without paying the check.

The bill was over a hundred dollars—more than Jamie would earn that night in tips.

"Miss?" someone was calling, but she ignored them. She ran out of the restaurant and looked down the street, then swiveled to check the other direction. She could see a big group of people in the distance. Were those the guys? She sprinted toward them, her breath coming faster, her speed increasing along with her anger. Those jerks thought they were so cool, sneaking away. Maybe they didn't realize she'd have to cover the cost of the bill, but that didn't make what they'd done any less infuriating.

They didn't hear her coming—probably because they were too drunk.

"Hey!" she bellowed when she was a few feet away, and one of the guys turned around.

"Oh, shit," he said, leaning against his friend. They exploded with laughter.

"You owe me a hundred and fifty bucks," Jamie said. She wasn't sure of the exact total, but that sounded right, if she gave herself a generous tip.

"Who, us?" one said. His tie was loose and he seemed to be struggling to focus his eyes.

Jamie put her hands on her hips. Most of them probably had trust funds, or good jobs. They had that look—prep school haircuts and blue blazers.

"Pay up or I'm calling the cops," Jamie said. She didn't have a cell phone with her—back then they weren't commonplace—but alcohol had dimmed the guys' reflexes. "Come on, Alexander," she said when the guys hesitated. She'd overheard the name when she'd been serving the guys.

"Shit, she knows you!" one of them said.

"I told you it was a dumb idea," said another, punching his friend in the arm.

"Twenty bucks each," Jamie said. She pointed at the guy who'd absorbed the punch: "Thirty for you."

They still might've turned and run, but then Jamie caught sight of two police officers patrolling the street a half block away.

"Officers!" she called out, waving them over.

It was almost comical, how quickly the guys scrambled for their wallets as the policemen crossed the street. "Everything okay here?" the shorter cop asked. Jamie vaguely registered that he was gorgeous—dark hair, broad shoulders, olive skin—but she was focused on counting the money.

"Everything's great now," Jamie said. The guys had given her an extra twenty, but she decided not to point that out. They were already walking away.

"They try to run out on the bill?" the officer asked.

"It's okay," Jamie said. "I chased them down and got the money."

The officers were grinning now. "I still think we should put a little fear into them. Maybe dissuade them from doing this again," said the second cop.

The two officers turned and began walking briskly down the street. Jamie wanted to watch, but her customers had already waited too long, so she hurried back to the restaurant.

"What happened to you, girl?" another waitress asked. "Your tables kept bugging me for stuff. Now I'm in the weeds."

"Sorry," Jamie said. "Long story, but a table walked out on me."

"That sucks. Bring two pitchers of Michelob to table eighteen, okay? And your corner table wants a jumbo onion rings."

Jamie had just about gotten caught up when she saw a flash of blue in the doorway of the restaurant. The two officers were back.

"Hello, *21 Jump Street*," said her waitress friend, nudging Jamie as they both stared. "Doesn't that cop on the right look a little like a young Johnny Depp?"

Jamie thought he was even more handsome. He was just four inches or so taller than her five foot three, but he seemed imposing. Maybe it was his broad shoulders, or the way he carried himself. As he stood there in the doorway to the restaurant, his hands by his sides, his eyes moving slowly across the room, he exuded calm confidence.

Then his eyes stopped moving. They'd landed on her.

Jamie found herself blushing as she walked over to him, suddenly grateful she'd taken that moment to rub away her mascara smears.

"Hi, Officer," she said. The last name on the brass plate pinned to his shirt read ANDERSON.

"Just wanted to let you know we had a little talk with those guys," he said. "I don't think they'll be back."

"Thank you," she said.

He smiled then, but his eyes stayed serious and watchful. "I don't think you needed our help," he said. "Looked like you were doing just fine on your own."

Jamie grinned. "I'm not sure about that. They were about to run off, and even in my Nikes, I probably wouldn't have caught them."

He glanced down at her sneakers, and she had the impression he was checking out her legs, but maybe she was just flattering herself. She could've stood there all day, but the clatter of the restaurant invaded the moment.

"Can I get you a beer?" she offered. "On the house."

"I can't drink when I'm on duty," he said, and she instantly felt foolish. Here she was, trying to corrupt a cop. "But maybe I'll come in and take you up on that another time." He extended his hand. "I'm Mike, by the way."

"Jamie," she said. His hand felt very warm.

He walked out, then she hurried to get the now-cold onion rings to her corner table.

He didn't come in the next night, or the one after that. Jamie had off the following night, but the other waitresses knew to be on the lookout for Officer Anderson, and they said he hadn't appeared.

A week passed, and she resigned herself to the fact that he'd only been doing his duty. The electricity she'd felt had begun and ended with her, a closed circuit.

But then one evening she'd gone to hand a menu to a guy in jeans and a plain white T-shirt, sitting alone in a corner, and when he'd looked up, the menu had slipped between her fingers and landed on the table.

"Are the cheeseburgers here any good?" he asked.

She shook her head. "They're terrible," she said.

He laughed. "I'll take my chances."

"Brave of you, Officer," she said.

"Call me Mike," he said.

"So what can I get you?" *Me, me, me,* she thought.

"Could I get a Bud on tap and a medium-rare with Swiss?"

"Sure," she said. It was just five-thirty, before the real rush began, so she lingered by his table after delivering his drink. She learned that he'd

185

grown up in New Jersey, that he was twenty-four, and that he knew how to use one of the restaurant's matchbooks to expertly balance the leg on his unsteady table.

But she didn't learn the most important—the defining—thing about him until the following week, when they'd gone out for dinner and he'd driven her home. She thought he was working up the nerve to kiss her good-bye, which was surprising; he didn't seem like the kind of guy who'd struggle with confidence issues. Then he told her about his young son, who was the reason he hadn't come into the restaurant sooner. He had custody of Henry during most of his time off.

When he'd finished talking, he looked straight ahead, instead of at her. Almost as if he expected her to open her front door and run away.

"What's his name?" Jamie asked.

Mike opened his wallet and pulled out a photo of a cute toddler with dark hair and eyes.

"He looks just like you," Jamie said.

"Yeah, except he got his dimples from his mother," Mike said.

"Ah," Jamie said. "And she is . . . ?" Her voice trailed off. She wasn't sure what she'd intended to ask. But Mike seemed to know.

"Not in the picture," he said. "For me, anyway. We share custody of Henry."

"Ah," Jamie said again. She sat there for another moment, and then Mike leaned over to kiss her.

His lips were soft, but the rough stubble around his mouth scratched her chin and she made a small, involuntary noise in the back of her throat as he wrapped a hand around the back of her head, pulling her even closer. She'd had only three real boyfriends, but kissing them hadn't made her feel like this. She felt as if she were dissolving into Mike. When he finally pulled away, she was dizzy.

Jamie had always known she wanted to be a mom. She'd imagined in a vague sort of way that it would happen in her late twenties, and that she'd have three or four kids. But she was fresh out of college, with more than a decade of school loans in front of her. She was barely able to legally drink, and she often slept until ten or eleven in the morning after a late shift at the restaurant. Mike had a real job, an important one, as well as his own town house. When he mowed the lawn, he put Henry in a backpack carrier—at least until Henry was old enough to stand in front of Mike and put his own hands on the handle and pretend to push the mower. Mike changed diapers expertly, hoisted Henry onto his shoulders whenever they had to walk more than a block or two, which always made Henry giggle, and repaired leaky pipes under the sink while Henry lay beside him, banging his plastic Fisher-Price tools against the floor.

How could she have avoided falling in love with both of them?

Summer seeped into fall, and she began working at the public relations firm, which meant her schedule became more aligned with Mike's. She fell into the habit of driving to Mike's place on Friday nights, and he'd cook for the three of them—lasagna or chicken Parmesan or shrimp fajitas. She'd read to Henry while Mike did the dishes, or vice versa. Within a few months, Jamie had memorized the words to *Green Eggs and Ham* and *Chicka Chicka Boom Boom*. After Henry fell asleep, she and Mike would go to the living room and cuddle on the couch. Sometimes he'd rub her feet while they watched a movie.

Her friends teased her for being hopelessly domestic. They were hitting happy hours and dance floors, thinking about joining the Peace Corps or working temp jobs, getting drunk and making out with crushes. But Jamie had always felt older than her peers. She'd been cooking meals for her dad and Lou since she was fifteen, and the day she got her driver's license, she'd begun to do all the grocery shopping and other household errands, too. She'd been an anchor for her family ever since her mother died. Her friends couldn't understand what a deep sense of relief she felt in finally being able to lean on someone else.

She and Mike fought over his propensity to shut down emotionally, over the fact that she got snappish when she was tired, over stupid things like whether to splurge on Thai or Indian food delivery. But they always found their way back to each other. Jamie would finish getting the kids to sleep and come downstairs to discover Mike had built a fire and opened a beer for her. Or Mike would fry up bacon on Sunday mornings and help the kids make a gigantic pancake that he'd cut into wedges for everyone to share.

But now, for the first time, she'd sensed a kind of emptiness in him. The emotional steel running through his core had been chipped away, leaving this gray-faced, slumped stranger. Watching her husband become unmoored was terrifying.

After they'd talked outside their home last night, they'd told the children a simplified version of what had happened. Mike hadn't wanted Christie around, so Jamie had gotten her out of the house quickly. It wasn't until Christie was gone and Jamie had tried to pour herself a second, desperately needed glass of Chardonnay that she'd realized there was only an inch left in the bottle. Christie must've consumed most of it, and that was their last bottle. Jamie had reached for a beer instead and uncapped one for Mike. But she'd ended up pouring his down the drain because he hadn't wanted to touch it.

Now, as the minutes and then hours ticked by and the bench seemed to grow harder beneath her, she realized nothing could have prepared them for this. No amount of stress or training or love.

"Mrs. Anderson?"

She looked up, expecting to see another cop with a sympathetic expression, but a thin guy in a suit with a cowlick in his brown hair stood there instead.

"I'm Davis MacDonald, the attorney for your husband," he said, extending a hand. His wrist slipped out from beneath his jacket cuff and she noticed it was hairless, like a child's. Maybe he was even younger than she'd first thought.

"We're taking a break, so Mike asked me to check in with you and let you know it'll probably be another half hour or so," he said.

"You're from the union?" she asked, and he nodded.

"Do you need anything?" he asked.

Yes, Jamie thought. *I need you to save my husband.*

But she just shook her head, and he started to walk away.

"Wait," Jamie called, and he turned around, his briefcase bumping into his knee. She stood up and hurried close to him.

"Can you tell me anything?" she asked. "Do you think he's going to be indicted?"

The lawyer hesitated.

"Tell me!" she said, her voice too loud in the open space. She saw a few officers turn to look at her, then quickly avert their eyes.

"Look, we're still a long way from that. The FIT team isn't even done investigating," he said.

"FIT?" Jamie echoed.

"It's the Force Investigative Team," he explained. "They've got a special task force for shootings like this so cops aren't accused of tampering with evidence for their friends. Just sit tight for a while. I'll give you new information as soon as I have it."

Jamie slowly walked back to her bench, digging into her purse for her checkbook, wondering how much a more experienced attorney would cost. Their bank account balance was just over six thousand dollars, but they needed to pay the mortgage and credit card bill in a few days. How many mortgage payments could you skip before your house was repossessed? Jamie wondered.

Jamie went to church because it was important to Mike. But she hadn't truly prayed since she was a teenager and her mother had been in the hospital with the staph infection. God hadn't listened to her then.

Now, though, she bowed her head, and began to pray with everything she had.

On the bright side, the fire Lou had started in Jamie's kitchen was a small one. The vent over the stove was going full blast, and all the windows in the house were thrown open now, which didn't matter because the broken air-conditioning meant it was as hot inside as it was outside. Lou had found a can of air freshener in the bathroom and squirted it around, but the combination of floral-scented chemicals and burning plastic might have made things worse.

The day had started off smoothly enough. She'd missed Tabby and the other elephants, so she'd brought the kids to the zoo, and as a special treat, she'd let them sneak in apples and toss them over the fence. Lou had breathed in deeply, filling her nose and throat with the honest smell of hay and dirt and mammal. Being here grounded her, which she'd sorely needed after the tumult of the past few days.

Emily was wearing a pink dress and matching pink sunglasses with lenses shaped like stars. She'd rejected four outfits before settling on the ensemble this morning, and she'd asked Lou to paint her fingernails to match, but Lou had begged off, pretending to be allergic to the chemicals in the polish. She wasn't sure how Jamie felt about nail polish for six-year-olds, and she didn't want to mess up again.

"How can you tell she's pregnant?" Emily had asked as she looked at Tabitha and wrinkled her little nose. "I mean, wasn't she already pretty fat?" Lou had hoped Emily didn't think the same thing about her.

"What we do is take a blood sample from behind her ear," Lou had explained. "The skin is thin there, and when the blood tells us an elephant is ready to get pregnant, we put her with a male. You can kind of tell when the male is ready to . . . to, ah, make a baby."

"What happens?" Sam had asked.

"They get excited," Lou had said. That was generic enough, she'd decided. "Male elephants go through this period called musth, which gets their bodies ready for having a baby."

"Musth," Eloise had repeated, making it sound like "muss."

"Then what happens?" Emily had asked. Her sunglasses had slipped down on her nose and she'd peered over them at Lou, like the world's most adorable librarian.

"Then the female elephant gets pregnant," Lou had said, neatly skipping over the whole description of intercourse. Bad enough to try to describe how humans did it—no way was she talking about elephant sex to this crew. "She stays pregnant for about two years."

"Wow," Sam had said. "That sounds boring."

"She'll probably be happy when she gives birth," Lou had said.

"When is she going to have the baby?" Emily had asked.

"Sometime this summer," Lou had said. "Do you know the crazy part? We've got this thing called an ultrasound. It lets us take pictures of the baby as it grows inside Tabitha's tummy."

"You can see inside her tummy? How?" Sam had wanted to know.

"We have to put the ultrasound wand in her butt."

The kids had exploded with laughter. "In her butt!" Sam had shouted repeatedly, drawing a horrified look from an apple-cheeked grandmother who was holding the hand of a toddler.

They'd stayed at the zoo for hours, visiting the baby cheetahs and eating popcorn and ice cream cones and mimicking the antics of the monkeys. Lou had checked her cell phone as they walked to the minivan in the employee parking lot. No calls from Jamie, which hadn't seemed like a good sign. She'd noticed Sam watching, and she'd erased her frown and tousled his hair.

"Did my mom call?" he'd asked.

"Not yet," she'd said.

He'd just nodded, but Lou thought he looked sad, so she'd stopped at a vending machine and gotten a few bags of M&M's.

Lou wasn't much of a cook, so when they got home, she'd decided to heat up a frozen pizza. She'd turned on the oven, and about five minutes later, the smoke detectors had erupted. That's when she'd realized Jamie stored pots and pans in the oven, including one huge plastic Tupperware bin—probably because the kitchen was so small and cabinet space was at a premium. So much for the pizza.

Lou found a bag of baby carrots and some Granny Smith apples in the refrigerator's bins and cut everything up and arranged it on a big plate, reflecting that she'd made this exact same snack for the elephants countless times. She brought the platter into the living room, where the kids were watching TV.

"It still smells bad in here," Emily said.

"It'll air out soon," Lou promised. She filled Sadie's bowl with fresh water, then let the dog out back. She felt her cell phone buzzing in her pocket as she was calling for the dog to come in.

"We're on our way home," Jamie said in a voice so raw and gravelly Lou almost didn't recognize it.

"Is Mike okay?" Lou asked. Suddenly she had the wild hope that the whole thing had been cleared up. A misunderstanding—it could happen, couldn't it?

"Not really," Jamie said. "There's a DiGiorno pizza in the freezer," she continued. "Can you toss it the oven for the kids? Just take out all the stuff I store there before you preheat it."

"Um," Lou began, then she decided Jamie had enough to deal with. "Sure" was all she said.

"We'll be there in ten minutes."

Lou focused on airing out the house as much as possible, turning on ceiling fans and even opening the chimney flue. But the first thing Mike said when he walked in the house was "Is something burning?"

Then Eloise padded into the hallway and Lou

195

turned to look at her, suddenly realizing her niece had something sticky-looking matting her hair—ice cream, probably—and her white T-shirt was covered with stains. Her face and hands weren't all that clean, either.

"I threw up," Eloise announced.

"Oh, baby," Jamie said, rushing toward her. She buried her head in Eloise's small shoulder, like she was the one seeking comfort. "I'm so sorry I wasn't here when you were sick."

"She seemed okay earlier," Lou offered.

"Her stomach wasn't upset?" Jamie asked.

"I don't know," Lou said. "She didn't mention it."

"Well, did she eat anything?" Jamie asked. She leaned back and brushed Eloise's hair away from her face, then she put the back of her hand against Eloise's forehead.

"Oh, yeah," Lou said. "She had popcorn and ice cream."

"M&M's, too," Sam added.

"Popcorn, ice cream, *and* M&M's?" Jamie said.

"Well, when you put it that way, it doesn't sound like as balanced a meal as I thought," Lou said. She was aiming for a joke, hoping to squeeze a laugh out of Jamie and Mike. She saw the corners of Mike's mouth lift up briefly, but it seemed to take an effort for him.

"It's okay, sweetie," Jamie said. "I'm going to

put you in the bathtub and get you some crackers and juice."

Lou felt a flash of guilt. Jamie's skin was tinged with a violet-blue undertone. She seemed to have sprouted a few lines around her eyes, too.

"I'll check on the other kids," Mike said. He put a hand on Lou's shoulder and gave it a squeeze before walking out of the room.

"Sorry," Lou called after Jamie as she hustled Eloise up the stairs. Maybe she shouldn't have teased her sister about her detailed lists quite so much, she thought.

"Can you come up here a minute?" Jamie called.

Lou followed her into the bathroom, where Jamie was running water into the tub. Lou reached for a washcloth on the rack by the sink, but Jamie grabbed it first and began to clean Eloise's face.

"I should've gotten them a better lunch—" Lou began.

Jamie interrupted her. "Lou, it's fine," she said. But her voice still sounded irritated. Lou didn't blame her; Jamie hadn't asked for much, especially considering all she had done for Lou over the years, and Lou had made one of her children ill and caused the house to smell horrible.

"I can give her a bath," Lou offered.

Jamie shook her head. "Why don't you go talk to Mike? Keep him company."

"Okay," Lou said. She could do that. "Was it . . . pretty awful today?"

"He couldn't even talk about it," Jamie said. "His new partner threw him under the bus!"

Jamie was silent as she worked Eloise's stained shirt over her head, then removed the rest of the little girl's clothes and tested the bathwater with her wrist before helping Eloise climb into the tub.

"I'm worried sick about what's going to happen tomorrow," Jamie said. She reached for the shampoo and squirted a bit in her palm.

"Why?" Lou asked. Jamie didn't meet her eyes when she answered.

"The mother of the teenager who died? She's holding a press conference."

Christie bent over at the waist, reached into her push-up bra, and hefted her breasts another inch higher. They were in danger of spilling out of the top of her blouse now, which was precisely where she wanted them. She sat with her legs crossed on the edge of the bed, nibbling a hangnail. Doug was ten minutes late, and she hoped he was stuck in a terrible traffic jam. Every passing minute meant more money in her pocket.

Doug's wife was paying for a video Elroy would deliver in a manila envelope. Elroy had promised to edit the evidence so that Christie would be unrecognizable, which was a smart strategy. God forbid she bump into the woman at the gynecologist's office.

Christie imagined the scene. Maybe Elroy

would meet Doug's wife at a neutral spot, like a playground. While her kids sat in bucket swings, calling out to be pushed, Doug's wife would reach for the envelope. Her fingers would probably tremble. She'd carry around the evidence until she got home. Maybe she'd wait until the kids were in bed, then she'd pour herself a big glass of wine and slip the DVD into the player. Even better, maybe she'd wait until Doug was home and suggest they watch a new movie together. Christie only hoped the house wasn't just in Doug's name—his wife deserved alimony, child support, and most of his assets. She'd overheard too many stories while working at the salon of women who'd lost everything, because they'd trusted their husbands to be fair. Christie always hid a snort when those sad tales spilled out. Who did these women expect to look after them, if they couldn't even look after themselves?

Someone knocked on the hotel room door, three raps in quick succession. Christie ran her finger over her top teeth to sweep away any lipstick smudges, took a deep breath, and went to pull the door open.

Doug's eyes lit up as he got a glimpse of her: Ka-ching! He'd hit the jackpot, and he didn't even have to pay for the hotel room. That $2.49 he'd spent for her milk was the best investment he'd ever made.

"Nice to see you again," she said, stepping back

to let him in. He gave her a kiss—fortunately not a lingering one—and treated her to a whiff of what smelled like an entire container of Axe body spray.

He wore jeans and a black T-shirt with a blazer over it, and he seemed to be sucking in his gut. Infidelity chic, she thought. Macy's should create a new line.

"You look hot," he said.

She ran her tongue over her lips, slowly. "So do you," she lied.

He took a step toward her, then hesitated. "So, ah, should we . . . um . . ."

Christie smiled. He was making this too easy. She'd been worried he'd launch himself at her—she imagined he'd be all paws and slobby kisses, a human golden retriever—and she'd have to slow him down. She wanted everything to look and sound good on tape. Plus she was making a rather generous hourly rate. Why not draw it out?

"Can I get you something from the minibar?" she asked.

He nodded. "A beer sounds good."

"Sure," she said. She took her time opening the bottle and pouring its contents into a glass, then handed it to him. He nearly dropped the glass, and she saw him wipe his hands on his pants. His palms must be sweating—she could see the droplets of perspiration on his upper lip, too.

"Sit down here," she directed, patting the cushion of a chair. That would put Doug's face directly in line with the video-recording device Elroy had attached to a light fixture. There was another chair opposite Doug's, and she took that one, crossing her legs and allowing the slit in her skirt to fall open, revealing a long expanse of thigh.

"Okay," he said. He sat down, his eyes ricocheting between her thighs and her cleavage.

"Do you know what gets me really hot?" she asked.

He shook his head mutely.

"Hearing you talk about what you want to do to me," Christie said. She leaned back her head and stared at him from under heavy-lidded eyes.

She could see his Adam's apple bobbing as he swallowed.

"I, um, want to kiss you," he said. "Then lick your boobies."

Boobies? She struggled to keep a straight face. "Tell me more, big boy," she breathed.

"Then I want to take off, um, your clothes," he said.

Please don't ever try to get a job working on a phone sex call-in line, she thought.

"Then what?" she prompted.

He frowned, thinking hard.

"Maybe you could walk around for a little bit."

"I'm wearing a black lace G-string," she said. "Should I keep it on? And maybe keep on my high heels, too?"

"Yes! God, yes!" he said.

They were finally getting somewhere, but only because she was steering him, like he was a horse and she had a firm grip on his bridle.

She waited, but he didn't add anything to the scenario she was trying to help him paint.

She leaned forward. "Then what are you going to do with me?"

"Then I'm going to, I'm . . . then I'll take out my . . ."

"Yes?" she breathed.

He burst into tears.

"I can't do it," he sobbed. "I'm married."

"Oh, shit," Christie said.

"I'm sorry," he said, misunderstanding her disappointment. "You're really pretty and everything, it's just . . . I love my wife."

Maybe she could still salvage this.

"But I bet she doesn't understand you, does she?" Christie asked. She leaned forward. *Keep your eyes on the boobies, Doug.*

"No, she does!" Doug protested, wiping his eyes. "She's great. She takes care of the kids and she makes really good buffalo wings and she drives whenever we go on the Beltway because I hate doing it. I just . . . I'm turning thirty-five this year and I feel really old."

"Thirty-five isn't old!" Christie said quickly. "It's actually quite young!"

"I found a gray hair the other day," Doug confessed. "I had to pluck it. It hurt." He began to cry harder.

Jesus, Christie thought.

"Have you ever cheated on your wife before?" she asked.

Doug shook his head. "Never." He sniffed. "Do you have a tissue?"

She tossed him a box from the table by the minibar. Would they still get paid? she wondered. She'd better still get paid for this.

"I should go," Doug said. He stood up.

"Okay," Christie said.

"I'm sorry," Doug said. He walked toward her, clearly intent on giving her a consolation kiss, but Christie sidestepped him and stuck out her hand. When he was finally out of the room, she took a deep breath, inhaling a potentially dangerous amount of Axe, and collapsed onto the bed. A moment later she heard a knock and she sprang back up. Maybe Doug had changed his mind.

"Did someone order champagne?" Elroy asked when Christie opened the door. He was shaking with laughter. She gave him the finger and walked back to the chair Doug had just vacated. He hadn't even taken a sip of his beer, so she gulped some.

"Boobies?" Elroy echoed, and Christie began to laugh, too.

"I still get paid, right?" she asked.

"Of course," Elroy said. "Not the first time a guy has chickened out. His wife is going to be thrilled. She won't dispute the bill. Good thinking on asking if he'd ever cheated on her before, by the way."

"Thanks," Christie said. She began to feel a little better. The Heineken could be helping with that, too, she thought as she had another gulp. "So what now?"

"Now I prepare the file for the wife and you get ready for your next victim," Elroy said. He stood on a chair and peeled away his device from the light fixture.

"Good," Christie said. She tipped back the glass and swallowed the rest of the beer. "You know, I could juggle more than one at a time. I mean, if you've got that many clients."

Elroy appraised her.

"You wanted to see how I'd do on this job first, didn't you?" Christie asked. "Was this a trial run?"

Elroy nodded. "Yep."

Christie wondered, not for the first time, how it was that she could be so cunning about some things and so dumb about others. In high school, she'd known during the first week which teachers were going to ride her ass, giving her Ds on homework assignments and suggesting she sign up for the free tutoring the geeks gave in the library after school, and she'd easily discerned which teachers didn't care if she copied off other kids. And take men—she could be so savvy about certain guys, knowing which ones would be good in the sack but bad about remembering her birthday. Yet when it came to Simon, she'd been a complete fool. It all boiled down to not caring, she thought. Emotions distorted your vision. Maybe those women at the hair salon who'd cried about their divorces hadn't thought about holding on to their assets because they were too busy trying to hold together the shards of their hearts, Christie thought.

"You might've told me this was a test before I quit my job," she said.

"I didn't know you quit your job," he said.

"Well, I did," Christie said. "So you'd better keep me busy."

"Okay," Elroy said. He tossed her two folders. "Take a look at these guys. We can set up meet-and-greets tomorrow if you're free."

"At sixty bucks an hour, you'd better bet I'm free," Christie said. She emptied her beer, then reached into the minibar and took out a few mini-bottles of alcohol. "Let's call these a signing bonus, shall we?" she said. She put them in her shoulder purse along with the two folders.

"I think Doug's wife would want to treat you to them," Elroy said.

Christie grinned, then walked out, her step light.

Chapter Eight

JOSE. THAT WAS THE name of the boy Mike had shot. The teenager had been in trouble a few times before, for fighting and truancy. He'd also gone to church with his mother every Sunday and had sung in the choir. He'd possessed a rich tenor, the newspapers reported. He'd lived with his mother and younger brother in a transitional area of D.C.—not far from the million-dollar row homes or from the run-down ones with cardboard covering broken windows. He was an in-between in other ways, too. Not quite a man, but at five feet, eight inches tall, no longer a boy. The brushes with the law and the church choir were balancing on opposite ends of a scale, too. Eventually Jose would've tipped one way or the other.

The press conference was scheduled for noon today, and Jamie had no idea what Jose's mother was planning to say.

The front page of the Metro section held a photograph of Jose looking off to one side and grinning, his eyes shaded by a sweep of long lashes. Jamie stared down at it, wondering if he had been smiling at his mom. She didn't realize she'd released a whimper until Sam, who was lying across her lap, asked what was wrong. Sam had been extra clingy lately, trailing after her as she worked around the house and waking up in the middle of the night to climb into bed with her and Mike. "Nothing," she said as she bent to kiss his head. Jamie caught a whiff of sweet shampoo and something else, a scent that was uniquely Sam. She wondered if Jose's mother was kneeling in her son's closet, breathing in, despairing at the thought that she might someday forget the sound of her boy's voice. Jamie closed her eyes against the sharp prick of tears and held Sam tighter.

"Are you going to watch?" Jamie asked Mike a few hours later.

Mike shrugged. He was sitting at the little table in the kitchen, an untouched turkey-and-cheese sandwich on a plate in front of him. Three large electric fans had appeared and were blowing air around the house, giving them a little break from the stifling heat. Lou must've bought those, Jamie thought. She vaguely remembered hearing her sister go out last night.

By now the kids were in the living room, watching *Frozen* for the dozenth time. At this point they could probably recite all the dialogue. Jamie had started to set up the sprinkler on the front lawn, but then she'd spotted a guy with a big camera slung around his neck. She'd run back into the house and yanked the curtains shut, her rage swelling. They were trapped. How long were reporters going to be lurking? So far Eloise was mostly unaware of what was happening, but Jamie knew Sam and Emily had figured out some of the details. And Henry had probably read all of the news stories.

So had the neighbors, apparently. When Jamie had driven past an older woman who lived alone at the corner of their block, someone who'd always made a nice fuss over her kids, the woman had deliberately averted her head after Jamie called a hello out her van's window. Jamie's back had stiffened as she pressed harder on the gas.

At least most of their friends were being supportive. The family two doors down had put together a container of fried chicken and a green salad and dropped off the meal along with a kind note, and a number of other people had called or emailed, offering to help in any way possible. Sandy had brought by a giant box of brownies and she'd given Jamie a fast, hard hug.

"I know," Sandy had murmured. But she couldn't. Jamie had sensed Sandy wanted to come inside, but she made up an excuse about Mike being asleep on the couch. If Jamie sat down and looked into Sandy's soft brown eyes and felt Sandy's slim hand grip her own, she might fall apart, and then what would happen to her family?

"Reporters keep trying to interview me," Sandy

had said just before she'd left. "They've been leaving messages."

Jamie's heart had skipped a beat. "Please don't talk to them!" she'd cried.

"Of course I won't," Sandy had said. "I deleted all the messages. I just wanted you to know."

Jamie had held the box of still-warm brownies in her hands as she watched Sandy get into her car and drive off. The casualties kept mounting—Jose, Mike and his reputation, their family's happiness . . . Maybe her friendship with Sandy would be another.

Ritchie had also left a message on the answering machine that morning in his new broken cadence: "Be strong, man . . . this is going to . . . blow over soon. I've still . . . got your back." Jamie had watched Mike bend his head close to the machine. She wondered if he ever wanted to switch places with his best friend, to erase that quick, spon-taneous nudge that had sent Ritchie walking through the doors of police headquarters, into the path of the shooter. She didn't know how to ask him, though. The words that had always flowed steadily between them had dried up like a shallow riverbed in the summer heat. All she could think about was the possibility of the looming indictment, and she knew it was the same for Mike.

Three months ago, the guys had been competing in one-armed push-up contests—Ritchie was the record holder with eight, but Mike had been gaining on him fast—and cruising the streets and giving talks at schools. Their lives had stretched out in two smooth, parallel lines. Now both men were deeply scarred in different ways. But at least Ritchie had a chance of getting better. Hope hadn't deserted him, the way it had Mike.

"Do you want to call Ritchie back?" Jamie had asked when Mike continued to stare at the machine after the message ended.

Mike had shaken his head. "I'll go visit him tomorrow," he'd said. "Drop off a freaking tofu dog." He'd tried for a light tone but couldn't pull it off.

"Good," Jamie had said. She'd reached for him at the same moment he'd turned to walk away. He never even saw her outstretched arms. After he left, she'd stood still for a long moment, feeling so hollow she ached to collapse to the floor.

The previous night she and Mike had been in bed, lying on top of the covers in their underwear because it was so hot, and Mike had suddenly rolled onto his side, kissing her deeply. She'd kissed him back, glad for the connection, and then he'd climbed on top of her and yanked down her underpants and abruptly plunged into her, before she was ready. She'd gasped, but had put her arms around his back, feeling his body grow slick with sweat, grateful for the contact.

But it didn't feel like lovemaking. It felt like he

needed to release something and she was a handy receptacle.

The sad memory fell away as Jamie looked at the clock. The news conference was scheduled to begin in less than half an hour. It would be held at a park near Jose's mother's apartment, where Jose had learned to ride a bike, a reporter had said. Jamie tried to focus on the image of Jose attacking another boy, punching him repeatedly, but the image of him as a little kid, a smile wreathing his face as he learned to pedal, kept intruding.

Jamie could hear the treadmill squeaking in the basement, and the sound of ESPN, and she hoped Mike would keep running and watching baseball instead of tuning in to the press conference. It wouldn't be good for Mike to see the boy's mother on television, to bear witness to her anger and pain.

Jamie went into the kitchen and saw the plate with Mike's sandwich still on the table. He hadn't eaten a single bite.

"I'm bored," Emily called from the living room, drawing the word out to three syllables. "And Eloise spilled her apple juice."

Jamie rushed to clean it up, grateful to have something to do, some small task with a clearly defined outcome. Jamie was just wiping up the last drops when the phone rang. She glanced at the caller ID to make sure it wasn't a reporter, sighed, and answered it.

"Honey?" It was Mike's mother. His parents still lived in New Jersey, in the house where Mike had grown up. Jamie liked them well enough, even though their conversations always circled the same familiar ground. Mike's mother talked about weight—who among her friends had gained or lost a few pounds, who was trying Paleo and who was cheating on the Zone—and Mike's father was obsessed with the weather. He'd spend ten minutes telling you about a storm front gathering over Ohio, then hand the phone to his wife as if you'd had an emotional conversation that had left him drained and unable to carry on.

"Hi, Gloria," Jamie said.

Gloria's voice was always high and anxious, but even more so now. Jamie pictured her pacing around her small living room. Gloria always tried to burn calories while she talked on the phone.

In the week since the shooting, Mike had been checking in frequently with his parents. He'd wanted them to hear about it from him rather than on television, since the story had made the national news, but Jamie worried about how the conversations were affecting him. When he was a kid, his mother had tried to make Mike wear a knitted cap whenever the temperature dropped below sixty. A cold portended pneumonia in her mind, and a stomachache always meant appendicitis. Mike downplayed his job to her, saying he spent a lot of time at his desk doing paperwork and that he always wore a bulletproof vest. Sometimes Gloria's fretting annoyed Jamie. Other times, it made her mourn her own mother, and what might have been.

"I was thinking we should come down there and help," Mike's mother said.

"Oh, no," Jamie said without thinking. "I mean," she quickly qualified, "things are going just fine here, really. I bet this is all going to be cleared up in another couple weeks."

"Are you sure?" Gloria asked. "I've just been so worried."

"I know," Jamie said. She kept her voice light and steady. She had to dissuade Gloria. If she were here, fluttering around Mike and insisting he eat and ferreting out the problems in every situation, like a woodpecker boring into a tree to pull out insects, Mike might snap. He seemed so close to it anyway.

"Gloria, I promise you we're all doing fine," Jamie said. "How about we plan a trip up there later on this summer? We'd love to go to the shore with you."

"I'll make cannoli," Gloria said immediately.

"That sounds wonderful," Jamie said, reaching around with her free hand to rub the back of her neck, where knots seemed to have taken up permanent residence. It was exhausting to have to provide comfort and reassurance to someone when you so badly needed it yourself. Her father had called a few times, and had also offered to come stay with them, which she appreciated, but she knew he wouldn't be much help with the kids—and having more people crowding into the house would add to the stress level.

She eased off the phone a few minutes before the news conference was to begin. She could still hear the sound of the treadmill and Mike's heavy, rhythmic footsteps. She went upstairs, to their bedroom, shutting the door in case one of the kids tried to come in and she had to change the channel quickly.

The news channel was already broadcasting footage of the scene. Dozens of people crowded onto a patch of concrete encircling the park. The playground equipment behind them was out-dated—metal monkey bars and swings and a few slides. One lone, scraggly-looking tree decorated a corner.

In a hushed voice, a reporter holding a micro-phone was narrating what was about to happen: "In just a few minutes Lucia Torres, mother of the teenager shot to death by D.C. Police Officer Michael Anderson, will hold a press conference here at the park where her son loved to play. Gathered together are family, friends, fellow church members, and neighbors of the Torres family, including Roberto Sanchez, who lives next door."

The camera panned back to reveal a fiftyish

man wearing dark glasses and a red T-shirt. He was holding a handmade sign that said: JUSTICE FOR JOSE.

"Mr. Sanchez, can you tell us a little bit about Jose?" the reporter asked.

"He was a good kid," Mr. Sanchez said.

"A good kid," the reporter repeatedly somberly.

Wasn't there going to be any mention of the fact that Jose was fighting? Jamie wondered if anyone had thought to check how bad the other boy's injuries were. Could they get a doctor to testify that the kid might've been killed in the assault? Would that justify Mike's using deadly force? She'd have to mention it to the lawyer.

"Ms. Lucia Torres is approaching the podium," the reporter said, and Jamie leaned forward to get a better look at the woman. She was tall and slim, and wore a simple black dress and sensible black heels. She walked quickly, with determination, flanked by several other women—maybe sisters, or friends. Ms. Torres's head was held high and her expression was restrained, but Jamie could tell turmoil raged within her. In a strange flash of recognition, Jamie saw something of herself in the woman.

Ms. Torres stood at the podium, her large brown eyes passing over the crowd. She nodded a few times to people, then leaned forward and began to speak. Her voice was strong and clear.

"When will it stop?" she asked.

She let the silence gather for a long moment. "Too many of our boys have been killed because of the color of their skin. I ask you this: If my son had been white, would the police officer have drawn his gun so quickly?"

A few people in the crowd shouted, "No!"

"My son liked to watch cartoons," she said. "Jose's favorite foods were pizza and chicken burritos with molé sauce. He went to the grocery store for me every week, because he didn't want me to have to carry the bags home. He watched after his younger brother when I had to work. He was a good boy. I love him."

Her voice broke on the second to last word of her speech, but she kept staring straight into the news camera.

"None of us mothers expect to be here, before news crews, talking about our kids whose only crime was to be brown or black," she said.

It's not like that! Jamie wanted to cry. Where was the mention of Mike's clean record of nearly two decades on the force, his award, the respect he had in the community? Mike had never discharged his weapon in the line of duty before. Mike had once given a boy a ride home late at night after he'd discovered the kid alone in an unsafe area.

"No one can bring my son back," Ms. Torres said, her voice swelling. It seemed to leap out of the television and fill the room. "So now all I can ask is for justice for Jose."

She stepped back from the podium and reporters began shouting questions.

A voice soared above the chorus: "Ms. Torres, the longtime partner of Michael Anderson was shot in front of police headquarters just a few months ago, an attack Anderson witnessed. Do you think emotional trauma could have played a part in the shooting of your son?"

Ms. Torres reached for the microphone. "Perhaps," she said. "But that won't bring back Jose."

Another reporter shouted: "Will you be filing a civil lawsuit?"

A woman who'd been standing just behind Ms. Torres leaned forward and gripped the microphone: "We have no announcement at this time about a civil suit."

At this time. Jamie felt nausea rise in her gut. She thought about their meager assets. The house, the old minivan, a tiny retirement account . . . Could they be held personally liable?

Her stomach heaved. She ran to the bathroom just in time to retch into the toilet.

By the time she made it back into the bedroom, the news conference was over, replaced by a daytime talk show. Fortunately the hosts had moved on to another subject: Fourth of July crafts. Jamie sat there dully, watching a woman demonstrate how to put a candle in a glass vase and layer red, white, and blue sand around it for a festive centerpiece.

At least their children were safe, she thought. She could endure anything, as long as she had Mike and the kids. She thought of Ms. Torres, walking through the park with her head held high, images of her son riding his bike swirling around her like ghosts, and she wiped away tears. No matter what pain she was in, no matter what she would have to endure, it shrank in comparison to Ms. Torres's.

Jamie had to hug her children, to hold them close and feel their soft little hands, to kiss their chubby cheeks. She opened the bedroom door and almost screamed. Mike was standing there.

"Did you see it?" he asked.

She put a hand over her racing heart and nodded. "It wasn't . . . that bad," she lied.

"Oh, come on," he said.

She reared back her head. "You watched?"

"I turned it on in the basement," he said. Their basement wasn't finished, but Mike kept a small television and old sofa down there along with his exercise equipment.

"I'm sorry," she said. She was sorry for lying, sorry for not urging Mike to see that police psychologist after all. Sorry for not recognizing her husband hadn't been ready to go back to work.

He shrugged, a small, defeated gesture. "I need to take a shower," he said.

The doorbell rang, and Jamie felt her pulse quicken. What now? She had the sudden, wild thought that Mike's parents had driven down from New Jersey. But no—it would be impossible for them to get here so quickly. Maybe it was a reporter, or someone serving a subpoena, or a friend of Ms. Torres's who'd been at the press conference today . . .

"I get it!" Eloise shouted, and Jamie began to run down the stairs.

"No! Eloise, please let me—"

It was too late. Eloise had pulled open the door, giving Jamie a clear view of their front stoop from her vantage point midway down the stairs.

Jamie sank down onto a step as men began filing into their house. Five of them, in total. All Mike's good friends from the police force. They weren't wearing their blue uniforms, which meant they'd all arranged to take the day off, which must've been quite a feat. Arun Brahma was with them, holding a huge bag from KFC. Another man carried a few liters of soda.

"Is Mike around?" asked a guy named Shawn. He and Mike had joined the force at the same time. Along with their partners, they sometimes met up for coffee in the morning on slow days. He'd had dinner at their house before.

Jamie nodded, as a tightness filled her chest. She heard Mike coming down the stairs, and she shifted aside to give him room to pass.

"Hey, man," Mike said. He reached out and

slapped Shawn's palm, then Shawn pulled him in for a hug. Suddenly Mike was surrounded, swallowed up by the men.

It was, Jamie thought as she bent her head to hide her tears, as if Mike's fellow officers had heard a silent signal. An officer-needs-assistance call that they'd all rushed to answer.

"Ma'am? Excuse me? Are you deaf?"

Lou blinked and looked up at the guy standing on the other side of the counter. He was young, with a goatee and a Bluetooth phone bud in his ear. Those always confused Lou; she never knew if customers were talking to her or to someone on the line, and sometimes, like today, she guessed wrong.

"Can I help you?" she asked.

"A skinny double latte, extra foam," he said.

When did the word *please* begin to disappear from our vocabulary? Lou wondered. Only about one in every ten people even bothered to thank her for making their coffee. She swallowed a yawn and decided to treat herself to a latte, too. Usually smelling coffee for so many hours put her off it, but today, she desperately needed a jolt. Jamie's house was so hot she hadn't caught more than a few hours' rest. She'd taken to dozing on the living room couch, next to one of the fans she'd bought at Home Depot, but even with the windows open, the air was stifling.

"Hello, miss?" Was the customer actually snapping his fingers at her? Maybe she was moving a little slowly, but come on, she thought.

"Your latte's coming right up, sir," the barista working next to Lou said. He took the cup out of her hand and poured in two shots of espresso before adding milk. "Let me get you a free scone to make up for the wait."

"No carbs," the man said.

"Our apologies, then," the barista said. "Enjoy!"

The customer walked out, and Lou turned to her colleague, a middle-aged guy who'd lost his job in finance a few years earlier and, after six months of filling out applications and with one kid on the cusp of college, had found himself on the other side of the counter. "Thanks," she said. "I'm moving a little slowly today."

"No worries," he said. He winked at Lou. "I gave him decaf and full-fat milk. Do you want to take your break now?"

Lou laughed. "Sure." Normally she walked around the block to soak in the fresh air, but today she felt too exhausted to do anything more than take her latte to a corner table. Unlike restaurants, where there was a clear ebb and flow of customers based around mealtimes, the coffee shop always seemed busy. It wasn't until Lou sat down heavily, releasing an involuntary sigh, that she realized the depth of her sleep deprivation. Her vision was actually a little blurry. She rubbed her eyes and wondered if she could put down her head to steal a catnap.

"Excuse me." The woman standing in front of her was holding an iced tea and smiling. "I just wanted to say I thought that guy was really rude. You handled him well."

"Oh," Lou responded. "Thanks."

The table next to Lou's was empty, and the woman plopped down. "Is it really only five o'clock?" she asked, unwrapping the cellophane from a package of cookies. "I feel like it should already be tomorrow. Want one?"

Lou hadn't realized it, but a cookie was *exactly* what she wanted. Normally she didn't have much of a sweet tooth, but today she craved sugar.

"Thanks," she said again, reaching for the sweet in the woman's outstretched hand.

"Long day for you, too?" the woman asked. She smiled brightly at Lou and didn't wait for an answer. "Hey, are they hiring here?"

"I'm not sure," Lou said. She took a bite of cookie, tasting lemons and sugar. "I could check with the manager."

"Oh, don't get up. I know you probably don't get many breaks. This place is a madhouse," the woman said. "I can ask for myself. Do you mind, though . . . is the job okay?"

"Yeah, usually," Lou said. "The hours are flexible."

The woman nodded. "Oh, I'm Kaitlin by the way."

"Lou."

"Nice to meet you. Here, have another." She passed a second cookie to Lou. "I'm an artist," Kaitlin said. Lou blinked at the sudden turn in conversation, but Kaitlin didn't seem to need any encouragement to keep talking. "But not a real one, I guess. No one pays me for my paintings. I don't know, my older sister keeps nagging me to get a steady job. That's why I asked about this place."

Lou wasn't sure why the woman was revealing all of this, but she nodded to be polite.

"Do you have a sister?" Kaitlin asked.

"Yes," Lou said. She took a sip of her latte.

"Older or younger?"

"She's older," Lou said.

"Ah, so you know what I mean."

Actually, Lou wasn't quite sure. But she was so sleepy, and the woman seemed so certain, that it seemed easier to just sip her latte and nod again.

"Do you get along well with your sister?" Kaitlin asked.

"Sure," Lou said.

"You're lucky," Kaitlin said. "I used to see mine all the time, but she married this jerk of a guy." Kaitlin was ripping open a sugar packet and pouring its contents into her tea and swirling her straw around in her plastic cup, creating a mini-tornado. "He's got a real temper."

"That's too bad," Lou said.

"Is your sister married?" Kaitlin asked.

"Mmm-hmm," Lou said as she covered up another yawn. She only had fifteen minutes off, and she needed every one of them, but she couldn't be rude to a customer. The woman was only trying to be friendly. Besides, she'd given Lou half of her cookies.

"What's her husband like?" Kaitlin said.

"Whose?" Lou asked.

"Your sister's," Kaitlin said, laughing. But not in a mean way, like she thought Lou was dumb. It was more like they were in on the joke together.

"He's great," Lou said.

"You're so lucky," Kaitlin said. "So he's not a yeller, like Joey? That's my brother-in-law's name."

"What? No. I mean, sure, he can get mad sometimes. Once he threw a beer can at the TV when someone messed up a football play."

Kaitlin laughed again, as if it was one of the funniest things she'd ever heard, and Lou found herself sitting up a bit straighter. The sugar and caffeine were coursing through her body now, and her exhaustion was receding. Lou knew she didn't always make a great first impression. She could tell you ten different routes to the Washington Monument and she could multiply double-digit numbers in her head. But people, and the strange, subtle signals they gave off, could be confounding. They cried when they were happy.

They smiled when they were angry, or spoke in especially calm voices instead of yelling. They mixed together their feelings in such a busy way—Lou always thought of it as an emotional stew because it was like walking into a kitchen and inhaling the scent of a stew and being asked to list the ingredients. Who could puzzle out exactly what was cooking, when there were so many different things mingling together?

She looked more closely at Kaitlin, who wore expensive designer jeans and high-heeled shoes with openings at the toes revealing pink-painted nails. She had on a silky tank top and her hair was long and flowing. Her face looked open and friendly. Not the sort of woman who usually tried to befriend Lou, but maybe she was new to town, or lonely.

"Does your sister live nearby?" Lou asked Kaitlin. She was rewarded with a huge smile, as if Kaitlin had been worried Lou would end the conversation.

"Yeah, she's in Virginia," Kaitlin said.

"Mine, too!" Lou said.

"So we've both got older sisters who live in Virginia," Kaitlin said. "But you like your brother-in-law and I don't. Did you like him right away? Because my sister's been married only a year, so I'm thinking maybe it'll get better."

Lou sipped her coffee, thinking back. "The first time I met him it was kind of weird, because his ex was supposed to have his son that day, and she didn't show up. My sister thought it was because she and Mike—that's her husband's name—had tickets to a concert and the ex was trying to mess things up for them."

"Wow!" Kaitlin said. She pulled her chair a bit closer to Lou's, grimacing when it made a screeching noise against the floor. "So Mike was angry?"

"Yeah, I guess," Lou said. "My sister sure was! But then they called me to come over and babysit Henry, and that's how I met Mike."

"So they went to the concert after all," Kaitlin said.

"Yep," Lou said.

"So your sister and Mike's ex don't get along," Kaitlin said. "I guess that's normal, though."

Lou could almost hear Jamie's voice in her ear, telling her to ask Kaitlin something about herself. *People like it when you show interest in them,* Jamie had told Lou countless times. *If you can't think of a question, try to compliment them.*

"So what kind of art do you do?" Lou asked.

"Hmm? Oh, watercolors," Kaitlin said. Lou waited for her to go on, but she didn't.

"Sounds nice," Lou offered.

"Yeah," Kaitlin said flatly.

Lou wondered if she'd done something wrong. Maybe Kaitlin felt her art was private—but then, she'd been the one to bring it up. Her break was over, so Lou finished her latte and stood up. "I need to get back to work," she said.

"Oh, sure," Kaitlin said. She stood up, too.

"Thanks for the cookies," Lou said.

"Anytime," Kaitlin said.

"The manager's here, if you want to talk to him about a job," Lou said.

"What?" Kaitlin said. "Oh, maybe next time. But thanks."

Lou walked behind the counter and began filling a blender with ice to make Frappuccinos. It wasn't until a few minutes later when Lou glanced toward the glass doors that she spotted Kaitlin, still outside but now talking on her phone.

It was strange. Kaitlin was staring straight at her, but once Kaitlin caught Lou's eye, she spun around, as if she hadn't been looking at all.

Christie sat in the driver's seat of a sweet red Mercedes with a tobacco-colored interior and a Bose sound system. She reached for a lever and the sunroof rolled back soundlessly. Classic rock blared from the stereo and the smell of rich leather filled her nose.

It was as if this car had been custom-made for her. Even the seat seemed molded around her body, a perfect fit.

She turned the key in the ignition, feeling the vehicle leap to life. She could turn right and head toward the Eastern Shore, or drive straight and head to New York . . . this car could take her anywhere in style.

"Have fun on your test drive. See you in a week?" the salesman joked.

Christie just revved the engine and drove off, feeling the warm rush of wind through her open window. There wasn't any comparison between this vehicle and her Miata. She loved her sporty little convertible, but the Mercedes was a woman's car, and Christie was turning over a new leaf. For the first time in her life, she had a real job, a sense of direction. She'd been thinking about buying an actual business suit to wear to her meetings with Elroy. Nothing boxy or in navy blue—she hadn't completely gone over to the dark side—but something that represented her new role. Maybe down the line she'd even purchase her own home.

Back in high school, no one had ever expected her to amount to much more than homecoming princess or head cheerleader. She could dance, draw on eyeliner without a single smudge, and expertly forge her mother's handwriting on notes to get her out of school—talents that didn't hold their value during the transition to the real world.

But now things were turning around. She'd pick up her first paycheck from Elroy this week, and she already knew what she wanted to do with some of it. She was going to add to the college account Mike had created for Henry. She didn't want Henry to end up saddled with debt, to have to work the kinds of crap jobs she'd started at sixteen. She imagined popping by Mike's house, a generous check in hand. Jamie would look like she'd swallowed a lemon.

The sleek, purring Mercedes would be her good-luck charm, she decided. She wondered what Simon would think if he saw her pull up to a nice restaurant in this number. Simon would probably be dining with a woman named Beatrice or Kip who had a braying laugh and talked about nothing but dressage. He'd remember what it felt like to be with a real woman when he saw Christie. She'd regard him coolly, thinking of how he'd reacted when she tied his wrists to her bedposts with silk scarves and tickled his bare chest with her hair. The wrist tying wasn't so much a sexual move as it was one born of desperation—Simon had no technique and he pressed her clitoris like he was a teenager and it was a handheld gaming device. The next day a box containing four Hermès scarves had been delivered to her home. She'd never felt such glorious fabric.

She reluctantly turned back down the street to the car dealership. The salesman saw her pull in and was on her the moment she turned off the engine.

"So, do you love it, or do you love it?" he asked. His smile showed all his teeth.

"Not bad," she said.

"Why don't you come in and I'll get you a bottle of water or some coffee?" he offered.

"I have an appointment," she said.

She left quickly, without a backward glance. She'd never before noticed how loud her Miata sounded when it started up, or how low to the ground she felt. Her cell phone rang and she glanced down at the caller ID. Henry.

"Hey, baby," she said.

"Mom?"

ABBA was blaring "Dancing Queen" over the radio so she didn't catch the quaver in his voice until he said, "Can you come pick me up?"

"Where are you?" she asked.

"At Josh's," he said, naming one of his best friends. "I left a message for Dad but he wasn't there."

"Sure," Christie said. "Be there in fifteen."

She wondered if he and Josh had had a fight. Unlikely, since they'd been best friends forever, and Henry was the most even-tempered person on the planet. He didn't get that from her, she thought as an idiot in a Honda tried to cut in front of her and Christie laid on her horn. Still, she pressed her foot a little harder on the gas and made it to Josh's street in just over ten minutes.

She started to turn down the block, then she noticed a tall, thin figure standing on the corner, a good distance away from Josh's house. She pulled over. "Hey, kiddo," she said. "Need a ride?"

She was trying to make Henry smile. But he just climbed into the passenger's seat and slammed the door.

"Are you all right?" she asked.

"Just drive, okay?" he snapped.

She almost gave him a lecture about respecting one's parents—which was pretty funny, considering that by the time she was Henry's age she was sneaking out to meet boyfriends and smoking cigarettes and cursing back at her mother—but the look on his face stopped her.

"Do you want to go home?" she asked.

He shook his head. "I want to see Dad," he said.

"I don't know where he is," Christie said. "Didn't you say you tried to call him?"

"Let's go to his house. I'll wait."

Christie felt the sting of rejection. She wondered why he could talk to Mike but not her. But Henry was acting so uncharacteristically that she decided not to press it. Jamie's minivan was missing when they arrived at the house, but the red ball of sun was sinking low in the sky, pulling some of the heat of the day away with it, so Christie and Henry sat on the front steps. Henry didn't check his phone, like he usually did during life's lulls. When Christie asked if he wanted to use his key to go inside, he shook his head. "Stupid AC's broken," he said. "It's too hot in there."

For some reason, he looked especially like Mike tonight, Christie thought. She'd always been able to see bits of herself in her son—they had the same light skin tone, and his dimples were echoes of her own—but now she could see Mike's features were the ones that would shape his adult face.

Mike had been the one to handle talking to Henry about sex, wet dreams, and drugs. Who better than a cop to drive home the dangers of marijuana use, or drunk driving? Christie had added to the conversation a bit—downplaying her own past flirtation with pot and mushrooms —but Mike was the one who took the reins when it came to hard conversations. She wasn't good at this stuff. Still, she should try.

"Is this about a girl?" she asked.

"Can we just sit here?" Henry snapped.

"Sure," Christie said. She turned away so he couldn't see her face. She knew teenagers could be rough on their parents, but this was the first time it had happened with Henry.

A half hour later, Jamie's minivan came down the street and pulled into the driveway. The side doors slid open, and kids piled out.

"Henry!" Eloise shouted, launching herself at her half brother. Henry picked her up and gave her a hug as the other kids swarmed around him. He was like Harry Styles in this house, Christie thought.

Jamie and Mike got out of the van and went around to the back to get bags of groceries out of the trunk. "Thanks for coming by," Mike said to Henry as he passed by. "Grab a bag on your way in."

Henry didn't respond. Mike didn't seem to notice the tension emanating from his son, but Christie watched as Jamie's eyes flitted between Henry and Mike before landing on Christie. Christie shrugged. "He said he wanted to talk to his dad."

"Okay," Jamie said.

Henry reached out and took the groceries from Jamie's arms and carried them inside without a word.

"What's up?" Jamie asked.

"I have no idea," Christie said. "But he's really upset."

"Is it something about the news conference?"

"What news conference?" Christie asked.

Jamie closed her eyes—actually shut her eyes, like she was dealing with an idiot and gathering her patience—before she spoke.

"How could you have missed it?" Jamie said, like everyone in the world was glued to the news constantly.

"If you'd told me, I would've watched it," Christie said.

"I had a few other things going on," Jamie said. She swallowed and continued in a softer voice. "The mother of the—the teenager held a news conference. She basically called Mike a racist.

She said he shot Jose because her son was dark-skinned."

"Are you serious?" Christie asked. "I mean, isn't this all going to be dropped soon? Maybe she's just trying to keep it in the news."

She heard loud voices from inside the house. Jamie must've heard them, too, because she rushed inside. After a moment's hesitation, Christie followed.

Henry was standing in the middle of the living room, his posture rigid. The house was steaming hot, and Henry's face was red and sweaty.

"I didn't know what she was going to say, okay?" Mike was saying. He wasn't yelling, but just barely.

"She said you shot him on purpose!" Henry shouted. "Josh played it back on YouTube."

Mike and Jamie had really screwed up, Christie thought. Henry shouldn't have heard about this secondhand. She knew the anger on her face reflected her son's.

"You think I did it on purpose? Because he was Hispanic?" Mike roared. He had a look on his face that Christie had never before seen.

"Are you fucking kidding me?" Henry had never spoken that way before—to anyone.

Mike's face was a mottled red now, just like Henry's. For the first time, Christie wondered if Mike was going to hit their son. But before she could scream at them to stop, Jamie stepped forward. Christie thought Jamie would yell, or shove the guys apart. But instead Jamie put a gentle hand on Henry's shoulder and she looked up at Mike.

"I'm so sorry we didn't warn you, Henry," she said, her voice as soft as a caress. "It must've been horrible for you to learn about this from your friends."

"It was!" Henry's voice was still loud, but Jamie's words had drained away the venom from it.

"Your dad has been under so much stress, honey," Jamie said. She was blinking hard now, seeming on the verge of tears. "We all have. You, too. We should have dealt with this better as a family. I'm so sorry you found out this way."

Henry began to cry. "How could she say those things about you, Dad? And then people were writing stuff in the comments, saying they'd like to blow your head off." Henry had morphed into a young boy again, his lips trembling and his shoulders shaking. He'd been scared, not angry, Christie realized belatedly. Just like his dad.

Mike moved closer and folded Henry into his arms. "Don't read that stuff. Look, maybe you should stay at your mom's for a while. Until all this is resolved."

"I don't want to!" Henry said. "I want to be with you!" Christie felt herself flinch.

"They can't just say that stuff about you!" Henry

continued. "It's so unfair! I want to just . . . *hit* them and make them stop."

"Trust me, I know," Mike said.

Jamie moved closer and stroked Henry's hair. "It's going to be okay, honey," she said.

They were a circle of three, linked together physically and emotionally, and they'd all forgotten she was here. They were a family, like snooty Simon surrounded by his mother and brother at the birthday lunch, and she was on the outside again.

Christie didn't even realize she'd walked out of the house until she'd pulled the door shut behind her.

Chapter Nine

IT WAS STRANGE HOW relentlessly life ticked along, demanding your participation without asking for your consent.

Eloise's three-year pediatrician appointment was scheduled for today, and Jamie wanted to cancel it. But the doctor's practice was so busy that she probably wouldn't be able to reschedule for weeks, and who was to say their lives would be any less stressful then? Things could actually be worse. Jamie tried to banish that thought, but it lingered like a dark shadow.

Keeping busy would be a good thing. The photographers and news vans had decamped from the front of her home, but Jamie knew any breaking tidbit would bring them rushing back. So maybe now was the time to get out.

She'd sensed a growing unease in the children. They'd watched way too much television lately, and had fought more often, and their meals hadn't been as regular or healthy. Last night, Eloise had freaked out because there was a tag in the back of her pajamas that itched, even though she'd worn those pajamas dozens of times. When Jamie couldn't find the scissors to cut it out, Eloise had started screaming. Emily had thrown a book at her sister and yelled, "Shut up," Eloise had screamed louder, and Sam had hidden under the covers, plugging his ears with his fingers. Jamie had wanted to join him.

She'd yelled at the girls, and they'd both cried, which had made Jamie feel awful.

She wanted her life back so desperately. She wanted her biggest worries to be about the electricity bill, or the fact that she couldn't button her favorite jeans, or the state of the kitchen floor. She wanted to be annoyed with Mike because he'd gone out with the guys after work and had lost forty bucks in a poker game.

She couldn't push back hard enough against the fear and despair pressing down over their house. In the end, all she could do was this: Take Eloise to the doctor. Make a mental note to pick up a new bathing suit for Emily, since the bottom of her old one had almost rubbed through. Put a load of dirty clothes into the washing machine. Hold together their shredded existence as best she could.

She gave the kids frozen waffles with Mrs. Butterworth's syrup for breakfast and added green grapes on the side to assuage her guilt. Then she piled them all into the minivan, because Mike had disappeared somewhere without telling her he was leaving. He'd probably just gone for a run, and she hadn't mentioned the doctor's appointment to him, but why didn't he consider the fact that she might welcome some help—not to mention his company—this morning?

"Am I going to get a shot?" Sam asked.

"Absolutely not," Jamie said. "You had your checkup a few months ago, remember?"

"Maybe they forgot to give me one then." Sam began biting his nails.

"Definitely not," Jamie said. She tried to keep her voice calm and steady, knowing her son just needed reassurance. They all did.

Her gas tank was almost empty, so she stopped to fill it up, sweating in the strong sun. Her cell phone rang and she pulled it out of her pocket and glanced down. Sandy. She hesitated, then hit the Ignore Call button, telling herself now wasn't a good time to talk.

She lifted her hair off the back of her neck and fanned herself with her other hand. There was a Starbucks next door to the gas station, and she was hit with a deep craving for a Frappuccino with whipped cream and caramel sauce. She could almost taste the icy sweetness. Her mouth watered as she watched a woman come out of the store, clutching a plastic cup with a domed lid, the precise object of Jamie's desire. It would be a bright point in a dismal day, a tiny treat to lift her spirits.

But then she thought about all that would be required: She'd have to find a parking spot and unstrap Eloise and usher all the kids into the coffee shop and negotiate their demands for snacks and drinks. She'd end up spending fifteen bucks and someone would be whining because they got a pink cake pop instead of a yellow one. Eloise would probably have to go potty—she loved investigating new restrooms—and Jamie would have to drag the other kids into the bathroom, because how could she leave them standing in the middle of Starbucks alone? Eloise would insist on doing it "self!" and Jamie would cringe every time her little girl touched the toilet seat or the handle to flush, imagining viruses and plagues attaching themselves to her toddler's fingertips. Jamie would scrub hands and get everyone back out of the restaurant and wrangle them into their car seats . . .

She paid for the gas and drove on to the pediatrician's office. After they checked in, Jamie found a few empty seats in the waiting room. Sam sat down next to a kid who coughed, wetly, directly on him before Jamie gestured for her son to move to another spot.

"Mrs. Anderson?"

She blinked when she heard her name and looked up to see a nurse standing in front of her, holding a chart. Jamie wondered how many times the young woman had called her name.

"I'm sorry," Jamie said. She stood up, took Eloise's hand, and motioned for Emily and Sam to follow the nurse to the exam room, which contained a dog-eared copy of *Highlights* magazine and a few plastic trucks in a bucket under the table. The nurse tucked the chart into a plastic sleeve on the door and exited.

Jamie wanted the Frappuccino. She wanted her husband back. She wanted a Xanax.

"Can I have your phone?" Emily asked.

Jamie handed it over immediately. She didn't have the strength for a battle.

"Can I?" Sam echoed.

"Me!" Eloise demanded.

"Five minutes each," Jamie said, knowing the strategy wouldn't prevent fighting. She knew she should try to engage the kids in a game of I Spy, or tell them a story, but she was too weary. She looked at her watch. Their appointment had been set for twenty minutes ago. If Jamie had showed up twenty minutes late, the receptionist might've told her to reschedule—there was a little engraved brass plate right by the sign-in sheet with that warning. Yet Jamie often waited that long to be seen. She'd switch except for the fact that she liked her pediatrician, and things probably wouldn't be any different at a new practice. She'd read somewhere that doctors were perpetually overbooked, under pressure to hustle as many patients as possible in and out every day.

"My turn!" Eloise grabbed for the phone, and in the ensuing tussle it fell to the floor. Jamie heard a sharp crack, and when she picked it up, there was a spiderweb pattern in the glass.

"It was her fault!" Emily said as Eloise started to cry.

"It's fine," Jamie said. It was only a stupid phone. She handed it to Eloise, who looked suspicious about the lack of a lecture.

"Are you mad?" Sam asked.

She reached out and stroked his hair. "No," she said. He leaned into her and she curved an arm around him. Emily began helping Eloise play a game, being uncharacteristically patient. Jamie listened to their sweet, high voices mingling and she felt Sam's thin body huddling against her own, and a tremble of fear ran through her. Despite everything, the kids were happy. But if Mike was found guilty, they might have to move to another state to escape the backlash. The kids would leave the only home they'd ever known and say good-bye to their friends and school. They'd move to a crappy apartment and she'd have to get a job and she'd never be around. The thought that she might be unable to protect her children from a terrible future made her insides wrench.

Suddenly her fear transformed into anger toward Mike. Why hadn't he been more careful? Didn't he realize his actions would affect all of their lives? He'd obviously had post-traumatic stress disorder, and he'd refused to get help because of his macho stubborn pigheadedness. It was a good thing wives weren't permitted to testify on behalf of their husbands, because if she were called to the witness stand, she'd take the oath, then she'd remove her hand from the Bible and lies would tumble out of her mouth. She'd sell her soul to save her family.

The door to the exam room swung open, and Jamie looked up to see the pediatrician, a woman with gray hair who had a miniature teddy bear clipped to her stethoscope.

"Hi there," she said, and for some reason Jamie's eyes filled. The pediatrician made her think of her mother. It wasn't that the doctor resembled her mom in any way. But being around a kind, older woman who cared about her children's well-being made Jamie imagine how life might've been if her mother had lived. Sometimes Jamie wondered whether her mom might've embraced Jamie's kids in a way she never had her own; she hadn't been a bad mother, just a somewhat distant one. Her primary allegiance was to her husband, not her children, which Jamie now understood wasn't an uncommon family dynamic a few decades ago. Jamie could almost see the ghost of her mother beside her now, looking at her grandchildren with a mixture of love and longing, saying, "Oh, honey, did you see that expression on Emily's face? That's just how you used to look when you were mad." The mother who lived in Jamie's heart made up for all of her past transgressions.

The pediatrician managed to get the iPhone

away from Eloise—Sam triumphantly claimed it—and then she perched on a wheeled stool so she could be at the little girl's eye level. She explained how her stethoscope worked and listened to Eloise's heart before proclaiming it strong and healthy. Jamie was grateful for the chance to blink away the tears in her eyes.

The doctor completed the physical before turning to Jamie.

"So," she said, smiling. "Your little girl is perfect. Do you have any questions for me?"

"I'm perfect," Eloise informed Emily.

"As if," Emily said absently as she watched Sam play Angry Birds.

"There's just one thing," Jamie said. She glanced at her older daughter. "I know we're here for Eloise, but . . . Emily's teacher mentioned something about her fine motor skills in her final report card. She recommended we look into occupational therapy this summer."

The pediatrician nodded. "I can write you a prescription," she said. "Will your insurance cover it?"

"I have no idea," Jamie said.

"It's expensive," the doctor said. "Just so you know."

"How expensive, generally?" Jamie asked.

"About a hundred bucks a session."

Jamie let out her air in a whoosh. "Isn't there something else I can do?"

"You could let her play with Play-Doh more to get her fingers strong, and let her draw as much as possible."

"Okay," Jamie said. "That sounds a lot better."

"Get some scissors and have her practice cutting, too," the doctor said. "I'm not too worried about it. She's still young and some kids just take longer to develop than others. If she's still struggling next year we can talk about OT."

"My dad's in jail," Eloise announced.

"No he isn't, dummy!" Sam yelled.

"He's not! And Sam, don't call her that," Jamie said. "She just got confused . . . I don't know why she said that . . ." She could feel her cheeks turn hot.

"Mrs. Anderson." The doctor put a hand on her shoulder. "I know your family must be under tremendous stress."

So she knew, too.

"How are you holding up?"

Jamie gave the only answer she could in front of her children: "We're okay, thanks."

The doctor reached for a pad and scribbled something down. "In case you need someone to talk to," she said.

That was another hundred-dollar-an-hour extravagance they couldn't afford, but Jamie nodded her appreciation and slipped the note into her pocket.

They left the office, and Jamie corralled the kids

into the van and rolled down the windows, releasing the blistering air. She tried to think of what to do next. The house was a disaster, she had at least three loads of dirty laundry piling up, and breakfast dishes cluttered the sink. Mike would probably be home by now. But he'd be working out, or mowing the lawn, or watching television. Avoiding her again.

Last night he hadn't even come to bed. When she'd crept down the basement stairs in the middle of the night to check on him, she'd seen him sprawled across the couch. He hadn't accidentally fallen asleep there; he'd brought down a sheet and a pillow. The television was on, washing a thin blue light across his face, but Mike was asleep. She'd started to shake his shoulder, then she'd withdrawn her hand. Why bother waking him up? It wouldn't be any less lonely if he was next to her in bed.

For the first time, Jamie was gripped with the feeling of not wanting to go home, despite the fact that it was her favorite place in the world. Their house had scuff marks on the baseboards and magnetic alphabet letters on the refrigerator (the *k* had long since gone missing) and the lower dishwasher rack had a malfunctioning wheel that always got stuck. There was a squeaky floorboard outside of Emily's and Eloise's room that Jamie had to tiptoe around so she didn't wake her daughters at night. The toilet in the kids' bathroom had just started to run—she had to remember to mention that to Mike—and pen marks decorated a kitchen wall, charting the growth of their children. But Jamie had never wanted to live in a show-place. She'd once gone to another family's home for a school function and was awed to see the couches were creamy white, and the tables were glass. On the center of the dining room table was a tall, thin glass vase containing precisely seven lemons (Jamie tried not to think about the jumble of old mail, car keys, notebooks, Happy Meal toys, and tubes of lip balm and sunscreen cluttering her scarred dining room table). Everything was lovely and elegant, but it didn't feel like a home. The marks and imperfections of Jamie's house bore testimony to all it had endured, forming its character. It was much like her marriage in that way—their old battle scars showed in the furrow that had formed between her eyebrows, and in the way either of them could say a single word and an entire history would unspool in both of their minds. She wouldn't want to wipe clean the evidence of all that living, either in her house or in her marriage.

"Mommy? Aren't you going to drive?" Sam asked.

She should put the van in gear and go buy child-size scissors and Play-Doh along with Eloise's bathing suit. But Jamie felt paralyzed, a now-familiar tightness spreading across her chest. Her breath came in shallow gasps.

"Mommy?" Sam asked.

She dropped her head onto the steering wheel. Maybe she should just drive away! She had a credit card and a full tank of gas. They could head to the beach and stay in a cheap motel. They could escape the dishes and laundry and knowing looks. And she could have a break from Mike, because being around him right now felt worse than being apart.

The thought was so tantalizing she was reaching to put the car in drive when her phone rang, startling her. She glanced down and saw it was Lou calling. She snatched up the phone like a lifeline.

"Hi," she whispered. What was she thinking? They couldn't abandon Mike.

Lou didn't seem to notice anything amiss in Jamie's voice. She was packing in preparation for her move, she said. "I can't touch my new roommate's food," Lou said. "Did I tell you that? I'm thinking I might stroke her bottle of orange juice in the morning, though."

The words came out of Jamie's mouth before she knew what she was going to say.

"Come live with us," she said, her throat thick with unshed tears. "Please, Lou. I need help."

Lou hadn't been bullied in high school. She'd mostly been ignored, which she hadn't minded. She'd been like a fourth stringer warming the bench at a football game; she'd never truly expected to get a chance to play.

She knew she could thank Jamie for the fact that she hadn't been teased. Jamie wasn't in the popularity stratosphere, but she was well liked, partly because she was pretty and nice and partly because she wasn't intimidated by anyone. The goodwill surrounding Jamie flowed over to encompass Lou like a puffy cloud. Sometimes Jamie would motion for Lou to join her at her lunch table, if there were empty seats—an honor seniors never bestowed upon lowly sophomores. Jamie's friends always said hi to Lou when they passed her in the hallways, too. Lou knew her high school experience might have been very different were it not for her sister, because Jamie had set the ground rules for how Lou was to be treated early on.

Once when Lou was in ninth grade, she'd stopped in the bathroom between classes. She heard a group of girls come in a moment later, and Lou recognized Jamie's voice. She was about to flush the toilet and come out to say hello; then she heard Jamie say, "Why do you care if my sister comes along?"

"I mean, we might meet some guys there," said another girl.

"So?" Jamie said. "It's just a stupid movie. If you don't want Lou to come, then maybe I'll just hang out at home with her and invite some other people over."

Lou imagined Jamie locking eyes with her opponent, like a wolf defending her territory. There were a few other people in the bathroom, too, but the room felt still, as if everyone was holding their breath.

"Sure, she can come," the other girl finally said. "No big deal."

"Thanks!" Jamie said, her voice gracious in victory. "I like your nail polish, by the way."

Yes, Jamie was sometimes frazzled and bossy and impatient. But Lou never doubted that her sister had her best interests at heart. Jamie invited her over at least once a week for dinner and always made broccoli because she knew it was Lou's favorite vegetable, and she encouraged Lou to attend all of the kids' school events. She was constantly enveloping Lou under their family umbrella, an extension of her inclusiveness in high school.

Jamie had never asked her for anything before, other than to occasionally babysit, which wasn't a real favor since Lou always enjoyed it as much as the kids did. So when Jamie asked her to move in, Lou didn't hesitate. She canceled her lease and forfeited her deposit that same day. Lou could take over Sam's room, Jamie said, and he was going to use the bottom bunk in Henry's room until things settled down.

Now Lou walked to the elephants' enclosure and called for Tabby. The day was already hot and humid, and Lou's khaki shirt was sticking to her back. Funny how she didn't mind the heat a bit when she was outside, but it felt suffocating indoors. Tabby came close enough for Lou to reach out and run a hand over the elephant's big, floppy ear.

"Hey, sweet girl," Lou said. She took out her equipment to draw blood, and Tabby closed her eyes, like she always did when she saw a needle. "It'll be over fast," Lou promised. "Then I've got some apples for you."

She was monitoring Tabitha even more closely these days, because once her progesterone level started to drop, birth would be imminent. When that happened, Lou planned to be here. She'd already set aside a sleeping bag and had packed a small satchel, just like a pregnant woman preparing for labor.

The zoo wanted to capture the birth on videotape and post it online in hopes of drawing more visitors. Lou was sure that marketing move would work, because there wasn't anything cuter than a wrinkly baby elephant with long eyelashes and a curving trunk.

There was a lot that could go wrong during birth, though, and Lou was trying to prepare for any outcome. If the baby was trapped in the amniotic sac and Tabitha couldn't free it so it could breathe, Lou would be ready to intervene. Veterinarians would also be on call in case Tabby fell ill after the birth or started to hemorrhage. There was only one variable that deeply worried Lou. She didn't know if Tabitha had ever seen a baby elephant during the years she'd been in captivity, because Tabby had come to the zoo via a sanctuary and her prior history was unknown. Lou was doing what she could to prepare Tabitha for motherhood. Everything in the elephants' enclosure was jumbo size, which meant the baby might seem even more alien, so Lou had begun introducing smaller objects to the enclosure. She'd put in a plastic ball yesterday, and Tabitha had approached it warily. She hadn't stomped on it, which was a good sign, Lou thought.

Lou just prayed that the gentle elephant's maternal instincts would kick in, trumping the vicious side nature sometimes exhibited. There had been one terrible case at another zoo where an elephant violently rejected her young while the baby cried actual tears. If the worst happened— if Tabby tried to hurt her baby—Lou and the other keepers would need to act instantly. Lou had the closest bond with Tabitha, which meant she was the least likely to be attacked. She hadn't told anyone, but if danger arose, she was fully prepared to get into the enclosure and try to calm Tabby in order to save the baby.

"All over," Lou said, withdrawing the needle. She gave Tabby a few apples, then began her daily head-to-toe inspection. By now Tabby was a pro at the exam, but when she'd first arrived at the zoo, Lou had needed to teach her how to cooperate. The whole process had been broken down into steps. First, Lou let Tabitha use her trunk to investigate a long pole with a pool float attached at the end. When Tabitha was comfortable with the device, Lou tapped Tabitha's foot gently with the float and immediately fed her a yam. Lou repeated that exercise—gentle tap, yam—until Tabitha learned to associate the pole and float with her favorite treat. Like most elephants, she was incredibly smart, so she caught on within a day.

Once Tabby mastered that step, Lou reached the pole into the enclosure while keeping it a few feet in the air above Tabitha's foot. The elephant waited for the tap, but when it didn't come, she initiated contact with the pool float, raising her foot to touch it. "Good girl!" Lou cried, delighted, and she gave Tabby a few extra yams. Maybe this was what it felt like for parents when their kids made the honor roll, or got accepted to Harvard.

Lou began gradually moving the float closer and closer to the exam area, until all Tabby needed was the sight of Lou in a particular place to recognize that it was time for her checkup. The daily exams were critical: Carrying around ten thousand pounds took its toll on an elephant's extremities.

Tabby's feet looked good today. One of her

toenails was cracked, but not too badly, and Lou cleaned it out before feeding the elephant more treats. Her tail was healing nicely, too. Some people might think Lou was in control of the situation—after all, she'd trained Tabitha to lift up her feet—but Lou knew better. The exam would take place only if Tabitha agreed. Otherwise, the massive mammal would simply walk away, leaving Lou pleading with her from behind the barrier.

After all of the elephants were examined, Lou let them out of the enclosure so they could explore. Lou packed up her equipment as Tabitha made her way to the pool and waded in. Lou had heard pregnant women loved to swim because their heavy bodies felt so lightweight in the water, and she sensed Tabs felt the same way. Lou leaned against the fence, smiling, as she settled in to watch.

How could humans do such terrible things to these gorgeous creatures, like hunting them for their ivory? Lou wondered. Animals could be cruel to one another, but at least they had sound reasons for their actions most of the time. Young male elephants were clearly miserable when they were pushed out of their families by their mothers; Lou had seen video footage of them standing around the outskirts of their herds, yearning to be let back in. But only by being ostracized would males seek out new partners and mate. The elephant matriarchs were just ensuring the survival of their species, Lou thought. What excuse did humans have for their actions?

Lou spend the rest of her shift updating charts and feeding and observing the animals. She also led a group of schoolchildren on a tour. "Elephants can poop as much as three hundred pounds a day!" she told them. That was always a crowd-pleaser.

She was wrapping up her shift, mixing vitamins into the elephants' evening meal, when Jamie called.

"Hey, I was about to call to see if you could pick me up at the apartment tomorrow around eight so I can bring my stuff over," Lou said, cradling the phone between her shoulder and ear while she measured out the correct dose of vitamin E. "It should only take me one trip."

"What were you thinking?" Jamie screamed.

Lou fell back, as if Jamie's voice were a punch bursting out of the phone. The vitamin bottle slipped out of Lou's hand and shattered against the floor.

"I don't—what?" Lou asked.

"Mike has a temper? Christie and I don't get along? There's tension in our house? How could you say all that to a reporter? Damn it, Lou!"

"I didn't!" Lou finally managed to get in against the torrent of Jamie's words.

"Yes you did!" Jamie said. "You talked to some

blogger at the coffee shop when you were taking a break! Really, Lou? That empty beer can Mike threw at the TV *five* years ago?"

"I didn't know she was a blogger!" Lou protested. "She said she was thinking about applying for a job! She gave me a cookie."

"A cookie? You sold out our family for a fucking cookie?" Other people had talked to her in this tone, the one that proclaimed they thought Lou was obtuse. But Jamie never had, not until now.

Tears flooded Lou's eyes. She thought about Kaitlin's eager smile, and the way it had dimmed when Lou had turned the conversation away from Jamie's family. Jamie was right; she'd been stupid. She should've figured out what was going on.

"I'm sorry," she said.

Jamie exhaled loudly. "Just don't say *anything* to anyone ever again about my family, okay? If someone brings up Mike, you walk away. Do you understand, Lou?"

"I understand," Lou said. Her nose was running, and she wiped it with the edge of her sleeve.

"Okay," Jamie said. "I've got to go. Eloise is yelling for something."

Jamie hung up before Lou could ask whether she should still move in. This was the sort of situation that paralyzed her. How mad, exactly, was Jamie? Angry enough to cause a permanent shift in their relationship? Maybe Jamie was tired of all the trouble Lou caused, of the broken lamp and burned Tupperware and forgotten Pull-Up and day of junk food that had made Eloise sick. Lou thought about calling Jamie back to ask, but she worried it might make her sister even more upset.

Lou knelt down and began to pick up the shards of the vitamin bottle, putting the glass into a dustpan before reaching for a broom and sweeping up the smaller pieces. She couldn't stop hearing Jamie's words—*Don't say anything to anyone ever again about my family.*

She knew her sister hadn't meant to be cruel. Like the mama elephants who needed to reject their sons so that the species could flourish, Jamie had a good reason for lashing out, for pushing Lou away. But this was the first time Jamie had ever made a distinction that separated Lou from her family.

Lou was on the outside now, yearning to be let back in.

She needed to have a serious talk with Mike and Jamie, Christie decided as she held two shirts up against her black skirt and decided on the gold button-down. First Jamie had forgotten to pick up Henry from a friend's, and while he hadn't been in any danger, what if he'd been waiting at a mall or something? Then, no one had bothered to tell Henry what was going on, so he'd had to learn the details of the shooting via YouTube. YouTube, for God's sakes!

Christie was meeting a new mark tonight at a hotel, then she was planning to go straight home and call Jamie and demand a meeting. Jamie was usually the one who summoned Christie for chats, suggesting they all "get on the same page" when it came to Henry's bedtime (fine, so Christie let him stay up late when something good was on TV) or keeping his study schedule up-to-date (she'd forgotten he had a Spanish final, but she could pretty much guarantee that in another ten years, he'd forget everything except how to say "hola").

But what Jamie and Mike had done was far worse than any of Christie's transgressions. Christie's ire mounted while she dressed for her appointment and freshened her makeup. She picked up her purse and checked to make sure she had the disposable cell phone in the outer pocket and her own zipped inside. She drove the now-familiar route to the hotel and parked in the hourly lot, since it was an expensible fee, then went to the room Elroy had rigged with a camera and audio-recording device. Elroy had kept the same room they'd used the previous night, and Christie expected the same scenario to unfold. She smiled as she remembered how her last client had shown up at the hotel, a CVS bag containing a box of condoms in hand. He'd torn off his pants almost before Christie shut the door behind him. Elroy had knocked a moment later, and Christie had slipped out. She wondered how long the cheating jerk had waited for her to return with the champagne. She hoped his wife had already changed the locks by the time he got home.

Christie stepped out of her Miata and smoothed her skirt, wondering if her mother's exes had known the extent of her cheating. They must've; her mother hadn't exactly been discreet. Once in high school, Christie was crammed in the backseat of a friend's car with a bunch of teenagers and someone had said, "Hey, isn't that your mom's car?" Christie's mother drove a distinctive ancient yellow VW Bug, which had been parked in front of a neighbor's house. The neighbor was a creepy guy who always mowed his lawn shirtless. Rumor had it he'd hit on one of the cheerleaders the previous year after hiring her to babysit.

Christie had just tossed her head and laughed, as if her insides weren't being pierced, while the others in the car went suddenly silent. Funny how certain memories could smack back into you as crisply and powerfully as if they were occurring all over again. She could still feel the warm sun on her face, and hear the echo of the song that had been playing—Bon Jovi's "Always." To this day, she reflexively reached to switch off the radio whenever she heard his voice.

She'd told herself she'd never be like her mother, but had Christie fared any better in relationships? A lot of men had whispered they'd loved her, but none had loved her well. None had ever cupped her face in his hands, or stared deeply into her eyes, the way men in romantic movies did. No one had ever moved past her in the kitchen, putting one hand on her hip to gently steer her aside, the movements so practiced they seemed flawlessly choreographed, the way she'd seen Mike do with Jamie. Mike had good hands; Christie would give him that. They were as strong and well shaped as the rest of him.

Christie turned off her car and headed into the hotel, bypassing the check-in desk since she already had the key to the room. She stepped into the elevator and hit the button for the seventh floor, then stared at the numbers lighting up atop the doors. When she reached her floor, she walked down the long corridor, fit her key into the slot, and stepped in.

She paced the room, feeling unsettled. Something was off, but she couldn't put her finger on it. Maybe the bad energy from last night's cheater still lingered here. She tried to open a window, but they were fastened shut, probably to prevent suicides, she thought. Finally she opened the minibar and took out a small bottle of gin and another of tonic and mixed herself a drink, taking a big swallow. She flopped back on the bed and picked up the remote control and began flicking through channels. Half an hour passed. Her glass was empty, so she got up to make another drink.

Finally, just as she was reduced to reading the card listing the hotel's outrageously priced menu for M&M's and Oreos, she heard a rap on the door.

She stood up, not bothering to put on her shoes, and went to look out the peephole. On the other side was a guy named Jim, whose face was already blending into those of the other losers she'd tricked. He was tall and thin, with graying hair and glasses and an overbite, and he probably didn't deserve his wife.

Scumbag, Christie thought as she pulled open the door.

"Hi there," she said. For some reason she couldn't summon her usual enthusiasm for her job. She tried to shake off her dark mood and smile seductively.

"Hey, baby," Jim said. Did he even remember her fake name?

He walked into the hotel room like he'd paid for it—like he owned it—and when the door shut behind him, he engaged the flip lock that would prevent it from opening, even if someone had a key. "Don't want a maid interrupting us," he said as he leered at her.

Christie tried to smile back, but she knew it looked forced. What was wrong with her today? It seemed impossible that the gloss had worn off her new job so quickly.

Jim strode to the minibar, shedding his coat. "I see you got started without me," he said back over his shoulder.

Something about this guy really chafed her. She rubbed her hands up and down her arms, feeling goose bumps, and not the good kind.

"I couldn't wait," she purred.

He poured vodka into the other cut-crystal glass and didn't add a mixer. He took a healthy swig, sat down on the edge of the bed, and patted the spot next to him.

She walked over, feeling as if she were moving through mud. She had to get in the game. Elroy was watching and listening to everything, and she felt like she might still be on probation.

"So," she said. "Tell me what you like."

"I like you," Jim said. "Come here."

When she'd "bumped into" Jim at the coffee shop he frequented every morning before work, accidentally grabbing his red-eye latte instead of her own cappuccino, the word that came to mind was milquetoast. Why was this guy contemplating extramarital affairs rather than geeking out by playing video games? In high school, she wouldn't have let him give her his lunch money.

Men had all the luck, she reflected. Just because

this guy had a steady job and presumably wasn't wearing fishnet stockings under his Dockers, women were probably lining up to sleep with him. It was D.C.'s fault. All the pencil-necked policy wonks had warped the expectations of single women in the city. Jim clearly thought he was George Clooney's rival. Just look at him, patting the bed again, expecting her to heel like a dog.

She tried again. "Now that you have me here, whatever will you do with me?"

Jim just smiled. How many teeth did he have crammed into that mouth, anyway? It looked like more than the usual number.

He set down his drink on the nightstand, then stretched out a hand toward her. She danced backward. "Tell me," she said. She needed to get him to say it before he got too close.

But suddenly he stood up, reached for her, and crushed her against him. His hands were everywhere, fingers scrabbling up her skirt like roaches.

"Wait!" she yelled. She tried to pull away, but he was surprisingly strong for such a thin guy. His arms gripped her like a vise and he seemed to have sprouted four hands. They poked between her thighs, pulling at her thong and making the elastic cut into her legs. His tongue was wet and thick, jamming its way between her lips when she opened her mouth to yell, as effective as a gag.

He pushed her back onto the bed, her knees buckling as they crashed into the edge of the mattress, and then he was on top of her, reaching for his belt buckle. She couldn't breathe. He was pushing into her lungs and pinning her with his body. Where was Elroy?

The extra lock. He couldn't get in. She was vaguely aware of someone pounding on the door.

She tensed her neck muscles and jammed her head forward, banging Jim's forehead with her own. He cried out and lifted a hand to his forehead, and she wiggled out from beneath him. Her blouse was torn, and she clutched it, trying to cover herself.

"What the fuck are you doing?" she yelled.

"Jesus, I think you gave me a concussion!" he said.

"You had no right," she said. She was shuddering uncontrollably. "No right!"

"Oh, come on." His glasses were askew and there was an ugly red mark forming on his forehead. "You wanted this, you cocktease. You were practically begging for it in the coffee shop."

Christie was struggling to put on her shoes, her own head beginning to throb. She could still feel his insistent fingers running up her thighs and into her panties, taste his stale breath in her mouth.

"You loser," she spat out. She felt tears form in her eyes.

"Oh, I'm the loser," he said. He wasn't coming after her anymore, but his attack wasn't over. He'd just changed his weapons to words. "Listen, you fat bitch, keep loading on the makeup and dyeing your hair because you're probably a dog underneath it all. What's the problem, you want money or something? I'll pay you twenty bucks. That's what you're worth."

"Shut up," Christie said. "Just shut up!" Why wasn't her shoe going on? She twisted her ankle and jammed it on. She ran for the door and flipped the lock, and there was Elroy, his phone raised to his ear.

"Never mind, cancel security," he was saying as she fled down the hallway. He ran after her, calling for her to wait, but she just sprinted faster. She burst out the exit door and tore down seven flights of stairs, her vision blurring.

"Christie!" she could hear him yelling.

"Get away from me!" she yelled back as she ran through the lobby. People were turning to stare at her, well-dressed businessmen and women in nice suits. Respectable people, their mouths forming circles of surprise as they watched the spectacle that was Christie, with her smeared makeup and torn blouse. No one bothered to try to help her, to ask if she was okay. Fuck you, she thought. If she'd had enough breath she would've shouted it. *Fuck you all!*

She found her way to her car and took off

instantly, blaring her horn at someone who was trying to reverse out of a parking spot. She ignored the attendant who was waiting for her ticket in his little booth, and since there wasn't a physical barrier, she sped out of the lot. Let the cops send her a ticket.

She wove through the streets until she pulled up in front of her apartment building. She parked haphazardly and ran inside, shedding her clothes the minute she hit the bathroom. She blasted the hot water and stood under it, shivering, scrubbing at her body with handfuls of body wash. She stayed until the water turned icy, but she couldn't erase the marks the creep had left on her body. They were like tattoos, imprinting her shame and rage, forever staining her.

Christie wrapped herself in a fluffy robe and turbaned her hair into a towel, wincing as it rubbed against the tender spot on her forehead. The woman who looked back at her in the mirror had red-rimmed eyes with fine lines cobwebbing them. All her years of sunbathing, of taking her youth for granted and coating her body with baby oil and putting reflective tinfoil behind her head, were coming back to haunt her now. For the first time, she could see an unmistakable resemblance to her mother.

She turned away abruptly, went downstairs, opened the freezer, and took out a tub of Häagen-Dazs dulce de leche. She let a spoonful dissolve on her tongue, then she ate another, faster this time. She crammed more into her mouth, barely noticing when some dribbled down the front of her robe.

She heard a knock and froze with another spoonful halfway to her mouth. Her first thought was that the creep from the hotel had followed her home and that someone had buzzed him into the apartment building. She looked around wildly, her gaze brushing the knives in the butcher block on the counter. She *wanted* it to be him. She wanted to slice into him, to see the pain on his face, to hear him beg.

But then she recognized Elroy's voice calling her name. She stalked to the door and flung it open.

"Are you okay?" he said.

"I'm fine." She spat out the words.

"Look, I'm really sorry that happened to you," he said. "I've got it on video . . . if you want to go to the cops, I can show them."

"And tell them what?" Christie demanded. "That I lured a guy to a hotel room with the promise of sex and he tried to take me up on it? My ex is a cop. Trust me, no one's going to charge that asshole with anything."

"Hey," Elroy said. He moved closer and reached out. When she shrank back, he withdrew his hand. He stood there, blinking in the sunlight, in his white shirt that stretched over his belly and his ridiculous bolo tie.

"Just go, okay?" Christie said. "Leave me alone."

Elroy looked at her for another few seconds, then nodded. "If that's what you want. I'll call you tomorrow."

"Don't bother," Christie said, in a voice so low she wasn't sure he'd heard.

She pulled her robe tighter around herself, feeling cold again.

Chapter Ten

JAMIE SAT BESIDE MIKE in the second-floor walk-up office of attorney J. H. Brown, looking at surroundings that didn't inspire confidence. The small space was heaped with cardboard boxes that Jamie imagined contained paperwork from other trials. There wasn't a receptionist, and the nameplate on the door was one of those metal slide-in ones, which seemed to suggest J.H. could load his boxes into a truck and disappear tomorrow. The smell of Chinese food from the restaurant one floor below lingered in the air.

The lawyer himself was nondescript—average height and weight, brown hair, pale skin that looked as if it spent too much time under the fluorescent lights in his office. Jamie found herself studying her reaction to him, wondering how a jury might respond. Would his low voice inspire trust, or the opposite? The lawyer wasn't making good eye contact; he kept fiddling with a pen. Jurors might not like that.

But it wasn't as if they had a lot of choice in the matter. He'd called and offered to represent them for a reduced fee, no doubt because of the publicity involved in the case. Their other choice was the union-appointed attorney, the guy who looked barely older than Henry.

"What do you think?" Jamie had asked, covering the phone's mouthpiece with her hand when J.H. called. "Should we meet with him?"

Mike had shrugged. "Dunno."

As if she'd asked him to choose cereal or toast for breakfast. She'd wanted to slap his cheek and snap him out of the daze that seemed to be thickening around him. She needed her husband to be by her side, fighting along with her. Jamie had had a chilling thought: If a second-tier lawyer was offering to represent them for a reduced rate, what kinds of attorneys might be flocking to Jose's mother?

After they were seated and had declined an offer of coffee—Jamie's nerves were stretched far too tight for caffeine—J.H. pulled a fresh legal pad out of his top desk drawer and reached for a pen. He'd said this consultation would be free. Afterward, they'd need to choose which lawyer would represent them if the case went to trial. J.H. had also let them know that if Mike were indicted, he'd lose his paycheck, which meant he would be eligible to be represented by a public defender at no cost.

"But you need me," J.H. had said, more cockily than Jamie thought was warranted.

The lawyer took them through a time line of what would happen. The Metropolitan Police

Department's FIT team had already completed their investigation and given their findings to the U.S. Attorney's Office. That was standard procedure. The next move would be the pivotal one. The U.S. Attorney's Office would review all the evidence, do some investigating of their own, and decide whether to present the case to a grand jury and ask for an indictment.

If that happened and Mike was charged, he'd be arraigned and probably released on his own recognizance, J.H. said, his voice as bland as if he were reading a grocery list.

Jamie forced herself to listen hard as J.H. talked about what would happen when Mike was arraigned. She flinched at the word *when.* She wondered what the lawyer knew that they didn't.

"Do you think he's going to be indicted?" Jamie blurted, interrupting J.H. midsentence.

"Fact is, prosecutors don't need much to get an indictment. A grand jury would indict a ham sandwich for the U.S. Attorney's Office," J.H. said. He must've seen Jamie reach out to grip Mike's hand, because he added, "I mean, look, they're going to try to be fair. The folks in the U.S. Attorney's Office who handle this stuff actually have to go to Quantico and do a simulated training. They get a laser gun and they have to react as if they're a police officer in crisis situations. So they know it isn't easy. The key question for them is whether Mike acted in a reasonable manner in that moment."

J.H. seemed to know what he was talking about. But was he good enough? He'd asked for an eight-thousand-dollar retainer. Jamie had no idea how to amass that kind of cash. Sell her engagement ring, maybe, and remortgage the house. Now she wondered if they shouldn't just sell the house and everything else they owned and use the money to hire the best lawyer possible.

"Do you know what kind of evidence they have?" Mike asked.

J.H. shrugged. "I hear the video surveillance sucks. There was a camera on a public housing unit a hundred yards away, but the angle isn't good. Plus the rain. Crappy visibility; everything's blurry and distorted. So that's a wash. They're going to want to reinterview anyone who was at the scene. They caught three or four guys before everyone scattered, but they all said no gun. So that's working against us. We could make the argument that the bangers don't want to rat out their dead homie, but your partner's the real issue. He was closer to the threat and he didn't even draw. He said the guy wasn't making a move that could indicate he had a gun. That's going to hurt us. I'll be honest with you. It's going to hurt a lot."

J.H. took a sip of coffee that must've been cold, since his cup had been sitting there when they arrived. He leaned back, putting his feet up on his desk. He looked far too relaxed, given the stakes, and Jamie felt the urge to smack his feet to the floor. For him this was routine, like a doctor who read biopsies every day and revealed whether tumors were benign or time bombs. Maybe he was inured to the emotions of his job, but couldn't he at least act as if this was important?

She'd sell the house. She'd sell her minivan and the opal earrings that had belonged to her mother, the ones she'd only ever worn on her wedding day. Nothing mattered but keeping Mike safe.

"We'll offset whatever they come up with at trial, of course," J.H. said. "Call character witnesses. Introduce reasonable doubt—show Mike thought he really did see something. Maybe it was a gun, maybe it was a cell phone. Maybe it was a set of keys."

"It wasn't a set of keys," Mike muttered.

"Look, I'm not saying there couldn't have been a piece, okay? We'll introduce that possibility. But you and your partner both testified that you barely took your eyes off the ki—off Jose. After you fired you were both at his side in maybe thirty seconds, right? For someone to have the presence of mind to assess what happened, get to him, get his gun, and get away without anyone noticing . . . I mean, what's the motivation? Maybe the gun was a sweet piece; we can throw that in there. But this was a brawl. We're talking a lot of guys swarming around. People were busy protecting their own asses. You think someone's going to run *toward* a gunshot, not knowing if there's going to be another one?" J.H. shook his head. "I'm not saying it didn't happen. I'm saying it's going to be a hard sell."

"So that's what it's about?" Mike asked. "What we can sell to the jury instead of the truth?"

J.H. shrugged again, unoffended. "Hey, I didn't create the system," he said. "I just try to work it to your advantage."

"Can someone find the other guys who were at the scene and talk to them?" Mike asked.

"Like I said, they scattered," J.H. said. "I'll try to track down as many as I can, but I won't kid you: It's going to be tough. And hiring an outside investigator is expensive. The U.S. Attorney's Office is probably working on that now, too."

"We should get Ritchie to testify!" Jamie blurted. "Mike's old partner. He's black, you know. The jury needs to see that he believes in Mike, that Mike's no racist."

"I don't think Ritchie's in any shape to testify," Mike said.

"But he would, if we asked!" Jamie said. "We could get an ambulance to bring him to court and he could go right back to rehab after . . . He'd do it for you, Mike."

"Don't you think he's been through enough?" Mike asked. Creases appeared in his forehead, and his dark eyebrows inched lower.

"What about *you?*" she cried. "You're the one that could go to jail!"

"For doing my job?" Mike said. "This is so fucked up."

"Let's all take a deep breath here," J.H. interrupted them. "Okay? We good? Now, we can also explore the idea of PTSD as a defense. Everyone knows you saw your old partner and that young cop get shot a few months ago. Maybe the police department shouldn't have let you come back to work so quickly. How soon after the shooting did you return to work?"

"A couple weeks," Mike said in a clipped voice.

"Any therapy?" the lawyer asked. "Meds?"

Mike shook his head.

"The police counselor offered to put him on medication," Jamie said quietly. "Mike declined."

There was silence for a moment. Mike pulled his hand away from hers and folded his arms across his chest.

"One other thing I need to know," J.H. said. "Is there something in your file that's going to come out and bite us in the ass? Any charges of roughing up a suspect?"

"What? Of course not." Mike shook his head. "I've been late to work a few times. That's it."

J.H. nodded. "Ferguson. George Zimmerman. Too many high-profile cases lately."

Mike exhaled through his teeth and sat back, arms still folded.

"That's the one thing you don't want to do," the lawyer said, pointing at him.

"What?" Mike asked. "Breathe?"

"Show anger," J.H. said. "A jury's going to be looking for that. And you can bet if we go to trial and I put you on the stand, the prosecutor's going to try to provoke you."

Jamie squeezed her eyes shut, thinking of Mike snarling at the cameraman who'd bumped into her, and the way he always yelled at football players on the TV.

"Jay wasn't my partner," Mike said.

"What?" J.H. asked.

"You called him my partner. He isn't," Mike said. "And he's only been on the force for a year. Why are they taking his word over mine?"

J.H. finally put his feet down and leaned forward. "Look," he said. "We want to be very careful about attacking another police officer. We can re-create the scene, point out holes in his vision, get an expert to testify about compromised visibility . . . but you realize those exact same points are going to work against you."

"Are you going to put Mike on the stand?" Jamie asked.

J.H. shrugged. "Haven't decided yet," he said. "It'll depend which way the wind is blowing at the trial. I don't think we're going to look at jail time, if everything you've said checks out. Maybe a little community service, some probation, in the worst case."

Jamie swallowed hard. "The thing is," she said quietly, "you mentioned PTSD . . . there might be something else that could come up."

Mike whipped around to look at her, but she didn't meet his gaze in case he was sending her a visual cue to stop talking. The lawyer had to know everything if he was going to have a chance of helping Mike. If making her husband angry with her could improve his chances, she'd absorb his ire.

"Things have been really difficult for Mike," Jamie continued. "Ritchie is like his brother. Mike couldn't sleep after the attack. He seemed kind of out of it. He blamed himself for not reacting quickly enough, even though of course it wasn't his fault! And a few weeks ago he thought he heard someone breaking into our house. We called the police, but they didn't find any evidence of a break-in."

J.H. nodded slowly.

"What does that have to do with anything?" Mike asked. "You were the one who called nine-one-one, Jamie!"

"But you took out your gun!" she cried. "What if it had been Henry coming in after he'd snuck out to meet some friends or something?" The moment the words left her mouth she deeply regretted them.

When Mike was furious, his eyes were like knives. Now she felt them cutting into her. "So now you're saying I would've shot my own son?"

"No, no!" she cried. "I didn't mean it that way at all! I'm just saying there could have been other explanations for the back door being open, but maybe we can tell the jury PTSD made you assume the worst. I mean, if we can use it as a defense . . ."

She couldn't tell Mike that it was obvious he had PTSD, or that she knew Jose hadn't been holding a gun, or that the old Mike, the one who'd existed before the attack on Ritchie, would never have drawn his weapon and fired. In every marriage, there are lines you don't cross. Things you won't say. She knew she was perilously close to that dangerous place now.

"Sure, tell them I'm crazy," Mike said.

"Mike, please," Jamie said. Her voice sounded tight, a giveaway that she was on the edge of tears. "I know you thought you saw a gun in Jose's hand. I completely understand why you thought that—it was raining hard and everything happened so fast. It was an honest mistake! But you can't keep fixating on that. We've got to start thinking of a way to save you. To save our family!"

Mike jerked up out of his seat, and for a moment Jamie worried he was going to stalk out of the room. But he stayed where he was standing, repeatedly curling his fists into balls and releasing them. Every time he made a fist, Jamie could see his knuckles turn white.

"That nine-one-one call is definitely going to come up at trial," J.H. said. His voice was steady, and he seemed unaffected by the hot emotions coursing through the room. Maybe that was a plus, Jamie thought frantically. Maybe he *was* the right lawyer for them!

"There will be records," J.H. continued. "The AG's office may already have found out about it. I'm surprised a reporter hasn't yet. And speaking of which, that interview your sister gave?"

"She didn't mean to!" Jamie said. "She didn't know it was a reporter. The woman tricked her! She won't do it again."

Mike had been okay with the idea of Lou moving in with them, but he'd gotten upset by the quotes, even though he knew Lou hadn't meant any harm. So Jamie hadn't asked Lou to babysit today. Instead, she'd dropped the kids at Sandy's house, her children's joy at seeing Finn and Daisy adding another layer to Jamie's guilt.

Could her 911 call become the tipping point in a trial? Jamie wondered. Or maybe Lou's quotes would be permitted as evidence, and they would sway the jurors. Out of the corner of her eye, Jamie saw Mike take a step away from her. She couldn't look at his face.

"Let's focus on something else for minute." J.H.

turned over a page in his pad. "I want a basic layout of the scene here," he told Mike. "I know you already did it for the FIT squad, but sketch as much as you can remember. Just put an X for where each main player was standing."

Mike took a deep breath, then walked over and took the pad and a pencil from the mug atop J.H.'s desk and began to draw. He roughed in a few blocky buildings around the perimeter, then a couple of cars.

"Here's where I was standing," Mike said. "And here's Jay, the guy I was partnered with that day." Mike's pencil hesitated, then he drew another X. "Jose was here."

J.H. nodded and accepted the drawing, but not before Jamie saw that Jay was halfway between Mike and Jose. She hadn't realized how much closer Jay had been. Would a jury really believe Mike had seen a gun but Jay had missed it?

"One more thing I want to ask you about," J.H. said. "The papers said you were punched in the head moments before the incident. How hard?"

Mike shrugged. "Nothing I couldn't handle."

"Did your vision get blurry? Any dizziness?"

"No!" Mike almost shouted. "And I said all that in my statement."

J.H. regarded him for a moment. "I think we're done for today," the lawyer finally said. "Let's let everyone have a chance to cool off."

He stood up and offered his hand for Mike to shake. After a moment, Mike did so.

"I'll be in touch," J.H. said.

It took Jamie two tries to get out of her chair. The first time, her legs buckled. As they left the office, Mike began walking rapidly. By the time they reached the street, he was half a dozen yards ahead of her.

"Do you want to go get something to eat?" Jamie called to him. They couldn't go back to the house, not like this.

But Mike just reached into his pocket and tossed her the keys. Her hand automatically came up and caught them.

"What are you doing?" she asked. "Do you want me to drive?"

He was passing their minivan, which was parked at a meter on the street in front of J.H.'s office.

"Mike? Aren't you coming with me?"

He shook his head. "I feel like walking home."

Their house was at least five miles away, it was blazingly hot, and he was in a long-sleeved shirt and dress pants. "Mike, come on. Please!" she called.

She was sure he'd heard her, but he simply walked faster and disappeared around the corner.

Lou finished loading her clothes into a green Hefty bag and stacked it by the door, next to two she'd already filled.

She was leaving behind her IKEA bed, since

Donny said he could use it for guests until Lou wanted to claim it, and the same for her dresser. She'd already taken her prints off the walls and layered her books into a cardboard box. She didn't see the point of knickknacks and shopping was torturous for her, which worked out well, since she didn't have much money. But now she realized how little she'd accumulated in life. She wasn't sure, but she thought she'd brought more than this with her when she'd gone to college. Of course, Jamie had organized things for her then, buying two new sets of sheets and a fluffy bright blue comforter, a bathrobe and plastic caddy for her toiletries, and stacks of notebooks with clean white pages waiting to be filled.

"You don't have to do all this," Lou had protested, but Jamie had continued to load a new pair of flip-flops ("You'll want these for the dorm showers, trust me," she'd said) and a small coffeemaker ("You'll need this during exams") into an old milk crate.

"I don't mind," Jamie had said, and Lou had suddenly wondered who, if anyone, had helped Jamie prepare for college. Lou had used the flip-flops every morning, and at night she'd snuggled gratefully under the warm comforter and sweet-smelling sheets.

Lou wondered what her sister was doing right now, and whether she was still furious at Lou for her indiscretion.

At the sound of a knock on her door, her head jerked up eagerly, but it was only Donny. He looked around, taking in the bare walls and uncovered mattress. Rooms always seemed lonely and vulnerable once you'd stripped away their decorations, Lou thought.

"Need any help?" Donny asked.

"Thanks, but I'm all done," Lou said.

Donny took a step forward, then paused. "Mind if I come in?" he asked.

"Of course not," Lou said. "It's your place."

Donny walked over and sat down beside her on the edge of the mattress. As she looked at him, Lou felt a wave of nostalgia. Donny was a kind, decent man, and she wondered why she hadn't loved him enough. Was it because Donny wasn't the right man for her, or was it because something was broken within her? Maybe the part of her that sometimes missed or misread social cues was responsible for the limits she seemed to hit in her romantic relationships. Or maybe her issues were rooted in the loss of her mother. Baby monkeys who were separated from their mothers had trouble forming attachments later in life.

Of all the memories she was missing, the one that bothered her the most was her mother's funeral service. Lou knew that she and Jamie had worn matching navy-blue dresses, bought for the occasion, and she remembered hers had itched around the neckline and given her a rash. At the reception afterward, a woman Lou didn't know had squeezed her shoulder and whispered into her ear, "You need to be strong for your father." Lou had thought that meant she wasn't supposed to cry, so she didn't. But that didn't mean she didn't grieve.

Lou respected grief, and understood everyone experienced it in his or her own way. Some elephant mothers who gave birth to stillborn babies had frantic reactions and others seemed depressed after the loss. Just because grief didn't always look the same didn't mean its various colors didn't exist.

Lou did know, because Jamie had told her, that their father was the most wounded of the three of them by the loss. He and their mom had been such a pair. They'd met in college, where they'd sat side by side in classrooms, holding hands whenever they weren't taking notes. They'd gone out for dates together on Friday nights, and had slept in on Saturdays while Jamie and Lou rode their bikes to the library to take out stacks of Judy Blume and Nancy Drew books. Once the sisters had found an injured bird in the backyard and had spent the day trying to save it, fashioning a nest from a shoe box and placing a saucer of water and a few plump, wiggling worms inside. The bird hadn't lived, so Jamie had decided they needed to bury it in the backyard. She'd instructed Lou to gather small white stones to mark the grave with a cross, and then she'd led them in the Lord's Prayer, stumbling over a few words. It bothered Lou that she could remember that service so clearly while she'd retained almost nothing of her mother's.

After their mother died, their father ate the simple meals Jamie prepared, even the ones she burned, and he went to his job as an assistant manager of a department store every day, but at night he stared blankly at the television without bothering to change out of his suit. When he remarried, he explained to Jamie and Lou it was a kind of tribute to their mom: He'd had such a wonderful experience being wed that he wanted to re-create it. His new wife was a former college classmate, too, and she'd known their mother. "Was she the one Mom always said had a crush on you?" Jamie had asked their father once.

"Mom said that?" their father had asked, a smile breaking out over his face. In that moment, Lou had known he'd truly moved on. In the past, any mention of their mother had left him with a quivering chin and full eyes. Now his focus had shifted to his new love.

Their stepmother was perfectly fine. She didn't beat them like in the storybooks or try to dress like a teenager and become their best friend, like a character on a television show Lou had once seen. She was petite and talkative, with close-cropped auburn hair, a whirlwind of a woman who was always going for a run or reorganizing the kitchen cabinets. Maybe she would've liked to have been closer to them, but by then the family pattern was firmly established: The parents were one unit, the sisters another.

Right after Lou left for college, her dad and stepmother moved to New York, where her father found another job managing a clothing store and their stepmother taught tap-dancing classes. They lived in a small but conveniently located apartment, saw off-off-Broadway plays nearly every week, and jogged together in Central Park. "Our door is always open if you want to visit," their father had told them when they'd gone by his house before the moving trucks arrived to pick through the attic for the remnants of their childhood that they wanted to keep.

And Jamie and Lou *had* visited, at least until Jamie's kids were born and Lou began working two jobs. Their dad came into town once a year or so, usually just for a single night, and Lou spoke to him on the phone every couple of weeks, but that was the extent of their contact now. He was family, but not like Jamie, who knew all of Lou's flaws and secrets and loved her still.

Did Jamie still love her?

"So," Donny was saying. "I guess this is it."

"Thanks for letting me stay so long," Lou said. "I know you and Mary Alice would've been happier if I'd moved out a while ago."

Donny removed his glasses and massaged the bridge of his nose in the same sort of absent-minded way her father used to. His glasses had left two tiny dents on the sides of his nose. Her dad had sported those parentheses at the end of the day, too. "It's okay," Donny said. "You're easy to have around."

Suddenly she was missing her mother *and* her father—or maybe it was finally hitting her that she was losing one of the few people who truly cared for her.

"She seems nice. Mary Alice, I mean," Lou ventured. They hadn't talked much about Donny's new relationship.

"Yeah," he said. "She really is."

"I'm glad you're happy," Lou said, and meant it.

"How about you?" Donny asked. "Are you going to be okay living at your sister's? I know there's a lot going on for them."

Lou nodded. "Jamie's never needed me before. I want to help her."

Assuming she didn't keep messing things up, Lou thought. She wondered if Donny had seen *The Washington Post*'s gossip column, which had picked up the blogger's report. If so, he was sensitive enough not to mention it.

Instead of continuing their conversation, Donny did something surprising: He leaned over and gave her a gentle kiss on the forehead. Lou closed her eyes, smelling Ivory soap and Crest toothpaste. Donny never used cologne, so those were his signature scents.

"I wish you well," he said, his words oddly formal yet sweet. Lou found herself blinking away tears. When they were a couple, Donny had always driven to pick her up at the coffee shop at the ends of her shifts so she wouldn't have to walk home in the dark, even though she told him she didn't mind. He'd sat through half a dozen elephant documentaries without complaint, and once, when they were short on volunteers at the zoo, he'd helped Lou dole out wheelbarrows of food, despite the fact that he was secretly terrified of elephants. He'd tried to hide it, but he'd leapt a foot into the air when one of them had trumpeted. Donny had a steady job, he loved to cook, and he always put away his clothes in the closet instead of leaving them strewn on the floor. He was a considerate man, which wasn't something you should underestimate.

But it was too late. Mary Alice was moving in, and Donny was moving on. Lou felt panic flood her veins. What if Jamie didn't want her around anymore? Who would she have, other than Tabitha?

"I—" Lou began, but then the buzzer sounded, breaking apart the moment.

"That must be your sister," Donny said, and he got up.

Lou blinked, feeling disoriented. She'd been on

the brink of begging Donny to take her back, but she didn't love Donny. She was just scared. Somehow she'd muddled the two feelings.

Jamie had saved her again, Lou thought. She quickly wiped her eyes and stood up, feeling an intense rush of relief that her sister had shown up. She wondered how Jamie would act. Lou would try to follow her lead; if Jamie was still mad, Lou would keep quiet and out of her way.

But when Jamie came through the door, she hurried straight over to Lou, wrapping her arms around her sister.

"The AC is working! How did you do it?" Jamie asked.

"Oh!" Lou said. She'd momentarily forgotten. "It wasn't any big deal. I called the repair company this morning and asked if they had any cancellations. They did, so the guy was able to come over. You weren't home so I let him in."

"It's a big deal to us," Jamie said. "I just can't tell you what it felt like to walk into air-conditioning. To have something finally go right . . ."

Jamie began to cry, and she leaned her head against Lou's shoulder. Lou had sought comfort from her sister dozens of times when she was small, because of skinned knees or bruises sustained when she'd fallen out of trees, but she didn't think Jamie had ever cried in her arms before. Even on the day of their mother's funeral,

Jamie hadn't broken down. But early the next morning, something had awoken Lou and she'd crept to the bathroom to see Jamie curled up on the cold tile floor, weeping. Lou had quietly shut the door and slipped back into the bedroom. Now Lou did what she wished she'd done on that long-ago morning. She reached out and stroked tentative circles between Jamie's shoulder blades.

"I'm really sorry," Lou said. She needed to tell Jamie this, no matter how hard it was. "I don't know if you saw *The Washington Post* yet . . . but they published some of the things I said today. If you don't want me to move in—"

"Shh . . ." Jamie kept her arms around Lou, and Lou squeezed her eyes shut tight. "Let's not worry about that now, okay? I know you'd never talk to a reporter about us. I was just scared and overwhelmed yesterday. That's why I yelled at you."

"No!" Lou protested. "I'm the one who was wrong. I should have been more careful . . . I thought she was being friendly."

"It was just an accident," Jamie said. "Another accident." She sighed a warm breath of air across Lou's cheek. "Let's not let it become anything more, okay? Mike's angry with me. I can't stand to be fighting with you, too, Lou."

Lou nodded. "I promise I won't do anything like that again. I won't mess up anymore. And I tried to write out a list of the bedtime routine so I could help, but I wanted you to check it to make sure I remembered everything . . ."

"Oh, Lou," Jamie said. "You wrote a bedtime list?" Jamie began laughing and crying, creating an emotional stew.

But that was okay, because suddenly, Lou was doing the same thing.

Christie pulled open her front door and glimpsed the only face in the world she wanted to see: her son's. She pulled him into a hug, ending it long before she wanted to. She still remembered how her mother used to act after a bottle or two of cheap Chablis, all sloppy and overly affectionate. Sometimes her mother would drag Christie to the bathroom mirror and squish their faces so close together that Christie couldn't escape her sour-smelling exhales. "We could be sisters, right?" her mother would demand, pinching Christie's chin in her hand. Christie quickly learned that if she didn't say yes, her mother would cry, then become furious a drink or two later.

Only after Christie released Henry did she realize that Mike was standing to one side of the door. Usually when Mike or Jamie dropped Henry off, they gave a quick wave and headed back to the elevator. Or, more often during the past year or two, they simply dropped Henry off in front of the building.

"Hi," Christie said. She was wearing spandex

shorts and a purple tank top and she'd just finished doing a Jillian Michaels Shred workout video, which had her panting and sweating and yelling right back at the bossy woman on-screen within the first ten minutes. She'd finished it, though, and she'd vowed to do it every day, to offset the word *fat,* which had been knocking around in her mind ever since the jerk had attacked her.

"Hey, do you have a second?" Mike asked.

"Sure," Christie said. She stepped aside to let him come in. Mike was one of the few men she'd let see her in this state. He'd seen her in labor; anything else was an improvement.

Henry went up to his room, muttering something about a summer reading assignment that Christie translated to mean he wanted to be texting with his friends, while Mike followed Christie into the kitchen, where she opened a bottle of Budweiser and slid it down the counter toward him. He took a long sip. "Needed that," he said. "Thanks."

"So what's up?" Christie asked.

"I already talked to Henry," he said. "Thought you should know, too. I'm probably going to be indicted soon."

"What?" Christie gasped. Mike's affect was so calm she thought for a moment she'd misheard.

"Henry seems okay now," Mike said. He wasn't calm, after all. Christie could see the truth in the set of his jaw and his rigid posture. Mike reminded her of a wild animal who'd just been trapped in a net—disoriented and filled with a coiled-up energy. "But if he's upset tonight, will you call me? I can come over and talk to him."

"Yeah, sure," Christie said. She reached for Mike's beer and took a long sip herself. "I mean, what the hell, Mike? Why are they doing this?"

Before he could answer, her doorbell rang again. Christie hurried to open it, and when she caught sight of the familiar Domino's box—dinner for her and Henry—she dug into her purse for a twenty and handed it to delivery guy, then shut the door without waiting for change.

As she walked back toward the kitchen, she saw Mike leaning against the counter. He was still one of the best-looking guys she knew, she thought as she approached the doorway. Mike would probably have that thick head of hair forever, and he was even more ripped than he'd been in his twenties. She felt a wave of gratitude for Mike, for giving her Henry, and for always being there for the two of them. Mike had attended every school conference and every sports event, and he was the one who'd taken Henry for his annual physical at the doctor's. Was it any wonder Henry was turning out so well, given his male role model?

"Whatever they're saying about you is bull-shit," Christie blurted. She walked into the kitchen and set the pizza roughly down on the counter.

"The guy tossed his gun to his friend or something. Or someone else took it and ran."

Mike exhaled and closed his eyes. "Thank you," he said. "You're the first person to—" He cut himself off, and Christie wondered what he'd been about to say. Hadn't Jamie told him she believed him? Was Christie really the first person to do so?

Christie took out a slice of pepperoni and put it on a paper towel, then handed it to Mike.

He took a bite, and she hoisted herself up to sit on the counter.

"I mean, this is going to blow over, isn't it?" she asked. "It's got to."

"I thought so at first," Mike said. "I figured I'd give my statement and that would be it. Maybe desk duty for a week or so, until things got straightened out. I thought—" He shook his head.

"What?" Christie asked.

"I thought I'd be commended for saving the other cop's life," Mike said quietly.

"You should have been," Christie said. She took another sip of beer and pushed the bottle back toward Mike, wondered what her life would have been like if she'd said yes when he proposed. Maybe they'd have had a lot of nights like this. She would've screwed it up eventually, but they could've had a few good years together.

"You okay?" Mike asked. He took a step toward her, frowning.

She reached up and wiped away the wetness on her cheeks. "I'm sorry," she said.

"Thanks," Mike said, and she realized he thought she was crying about the looming indictment. She felt a hot rush of shame for being so self-centered. But then suddenly she *was* crying about the indictment. Mike could go to jail. Henry could lose his father, just as she'd lost hers. At least Henry would know Mike wasn't going away voluntarily.

"Here." Mike handed over a clean paper towel, and Christie blew her nose.

"So what are you going to do?" she asked. "You've got to fight this, Mike! Do it for Henry."

"You're right," he said. "I just kept thinking there was a mistake. That the video would show a gun. That they'd come to me and apologize. I was waiting for that."

"The video didn't show anything?" Christie asked.

"Guess not," Mike said. "They wouldn't be trying to get an indictment otherwise."

Christie reached into the refrigerator and pulled out two more beers. "So what happens now?" she asked.

"The grand jury looks at all the evidence," he said. "Witnesses come in and give statements. It's like a real trial. My lawyer says it'll take maybe two weeks. Then they vote for an indictment."

"And if they get one?" Christie asked.

Mike shrugged, like it didn't matter, but the look on his face revealed the opposite. "Then I show up in superior court to be arraigned. They say I'll probably be released until trial."

"Jesus!" The word exploded from Christie's mouth. "Can I do anything? I'll testify if it'll help, Mike. I'll tell them anything you want."

"I appreciate it," Mike said. "But you weren't there. My lawyer told me that this never would've gone this far if it wasn't for the guy I was partnered with that day. He was closer, and he said there wasn't even any movement to pull out a gun. He just saw the guy gearing up for another punch. Apparently he told the investigators we were talking about the shooting at headquarters right before . . . everything happened."

"Aren't cops supposed to stick together?" Christie demanded to know.

"Yeah," Mike said. "But we're also supposed to uphold the law. He can't lie, Christie. And *he* was the one talking about the shooting, by the way. I was trying to tune him out."

There was a lull in the conversation while Christie tried to think of a loophole, some way for Mike to slide through this mess. But she came up blank.

"Anyway," Mike said. "I better not have this." He slid the beer back over to her. "I'm driving."

Christie felt a stab of disappointment, but she just put it back in the fridge.

"Hey," Mike said. He frowned and reached for Christie's arm, which was spotlighted by the glow from the refrigerator light. She looked down to see a few small bruises running down her biceps, like a tattoo. She hadn't realized they were there.

"What's this?" Mike asked. "Some guy do this to you?"

"Yeah," Christie said. "But it's not what you think."

"Oh, come on, don't give me that—"

"No, I mean, he's not my boyfriend," Christie interrupted. "It was for my job."

"Your job? At the hair place?"

"Salon," Christie corrected. "And no, I quit. I'm working undercover now. Or I was. I kind of quit, but I think I'm going to ask for the job back."

Mike's eyebrows lifted. "Undercover?"

Christie told him about Elroy, and how she'd successfully tricked her first few marks. She left out the details about her last case. She was still trying to erase them from her mind.

"An expense account?" Mike said. "Nice. You're moving up in the world."

Christie smiled. "I was thinking . . . I probably won't need child support any longer."

Mike gestured to her arm again. "And the guy who did this?"

She should have known he wouldn't be so easily distracted. "An overly excited mark," Christie said. Mike studied her face, his expression even.

"You need to get yourself a can of Mace," he said. "And if anyone does anything like that again, tell me."

"It's not like you could arrest him," Christie said. She worried Mike would think she meant it was because he was on administrative leave, so she hastened to clarify herself. "I mean, he didn't do anything illegal. And I'm never going to see him again."

"Doesn't mean a visit from a cop won't scare him," Mike said. "I've still got friends on the force."

Mike wanted to protect her. What a lovely feeling. Christie smiled, feeling a glow that was from more than just the alcohol.

"Hey!" she said suddenly. "The guy I work for—he's a private detective. Maybe he could help you?"

Mike leaned back against the counter and folded his arms. "Yeah?"

"Could the cop who testified against you have it in for you?" Christie asked. She saw something ignite in Mike's eyes, as if he was considering it.

"Maybe, but I don't think so," Mike said. "I mean, I didn't know him well before this."

"But what if he thinks you crossed him somehow?" Christie said. "Or what if the fight was over drugs and he's working with one of the gangs? You're the one who told me drugs sometimes go missing from the evidence room."

"Yeah, but that's different from abetting a gang," Mike said. "You wouldn't think it if you met this guy, Christie. He's practically got a pocket protector. He's the geekiest cop you've ever met."

"But those are the guys who always surprise you," Christie said. A fleeting image of Jim shoving her onto the hotel room bed, his eyes containing something dark and ugly, invaded her mind before she pushed it away.

"You really think your boss would help?" Mike asked.

"Worth a try," Christie said. "I'll call him tonight."

Henry came loping into the kitchen just then. "Do I smell pizza?" he asked.

"Try to get this kid out of bed on a school morning and he plays dead," Mike said. "Set out some food and he comes running from a mile away."

Christie handed Henry a slice. "We saved you most of it," she said.

"He's a growing boy," Mike said. "I can't believe his feet are bigger than mine."

"Where do you think he got his height?" Christie asked.

"I had an uncle who was six three," Mike said.

Christie nodded. "And my mom's father was pretty tall. You can tell from photos."

"Six three?" Henry said. "That'd be cool."

"Do you remember the first time he tried pizza?" Christie asked Mike. The memory was returning to her, a little fuzzy but blooming quickly.

Mike shook his head.

"Oh, come on," Christie said. "His first birthday party?"

"Right," Mike said, and he laughed.

"What'd I do?" Henry asked.

"You grabbed a handful and threw it across the room," Christie said.

"Some of it landed in my mother's hair," Mike said.

"Seriously?" Henry seemed delighted by this. "Grandma's really into her hair."

"I've got it on film somewhere," Mike said. "I'll dig out the videotape and show you."

"But he liked the cake," Christie said.

"What kind was it?" Henry asked.

"Chocolate," Christie said.

"You sure?" Mike said. "I remember carrot cake."

"That was when he turned two," Christie said. "I made him a big chocolate cake for his first birthday." It was from a mix, but still. "Remember, I put little Matchbox cars on top?"

"That's right," Mike said, nodding. "That was a good cake, once we wrestled it away from this pig and got a piece."

"Hey," Henry protested, giving his dad a push.

Mike responded by putting Henry in a playful headlock and ruffling his hair.

Christie smiled as she watched them.

"I should get going," Mike said. He released Henry and gave him a fist bump. "See you tomorrow."

Christie walked Mike to the door, leaning against the frame after he walked out so she could watch him head down the hallway toward the elevator. She reached up and covered the bruises on her arm with her opposite hand, thinking of how Mike had offered to have Jim threatened. Maybe she'd take him up on it, after all.

"Thanks," she called out.

Mike turned around to look at her.

"I was just going to say that to you," he said.

PART THREE

Chapter Eleven

FOR THE WIFE OF a cop, Jamie knew surprisingly little about how someone was indicted. During the long days when the evidence was being presented to the grand jury, Jamie wondered what would happen next. Would a police officer show up at the door with a warrant? Would a process server hand them an official piece of paper?

She kept the kids busy with crafts and videos and trips to the playground and community pool. She drank too much coffee in the morning and too much wine at night. She cleaned toilets and folded laundry and filled the refrigerator, sometimes forgetting bread but buying three cartons of juice when the shelves already contained two full ones. One evening, when the kids were asleep, she raced out to get a flea collar for Sadie, whose itching had kept her awake the previous night, and found herself pulling into a gas station to buy a pack of cigarettes. She sat in the darkness, smoking three Marlboro Lights in a row— something she hadn't done since a brief flirtation with cigarettes in college—then she crumpled up the box and hurled it into a trash can. That was all her kids needed, for her to get lung cancer.

The news cameras were gone for now. But she and Mike were barely speaking to each other. When he'd finally come home, hours after they'd finished the consultation with J.H., it was growing dark outside and his clothes were soaked with sweat. The kids were already asleep by then, and Jamie had asked Lou to go into Sam's room so she and Mike could talk privately.

"Are you angry with me?" she'd asked. He'd grimaced as he sat down on the couch and eased off his hard-soled dress shoes.

He'd leaned his head back against the cushion and she'd waited for a long moment. Then she'd realized his breathing had evened out. He'd fallen asleep, exhausted from his long walk.

He never returned to their bed after that. Instead he brought some clothes and magazines down into the basement, and took the spare quilt from the hall closet. Jamie wondered if he wanted to move out for good. Maybe the only reason he hadn't done so was because he couldn't afford an apartment. She didn't press him to talk anymore— he wasn't the only one who was upset—but every afternoon, J.H. called and updated Mike on the grand jury proceedings. Once after J.H. called, Jamie had sworn she'd heard a muffled barking sound. But when she'd gone down into the base- ment on the pretext of checking the laundry, Mike was dry-eyed, jumping rope in place. She'd watched him whip the rope around his body until she'd felt dizzy.

She lost nine pounds without even trying. A year ago, she would've been jubilant, hailing it as a mini-miracle. Now she just stared at the numbers on the scale as they blurred.

Jamie had seen footage of earthquakes that had left cars teetering on the ragged edges of bridges that had suddenly split apart. She'd wondered what it would feel like to be trapped inside a vehicle that could, at any moment, tilt toward safety or plummet into a crevasse. Now she knew.

When the moment finally arrived, though, their phone simply rang. This was how everything had started, Jamie remembered—with a call from the police letting her know Mike had been involved in a shooting and that he was safe. But the person on the other end of the line had been wrong. Mike wasn't safe.

"They voted to indict for involuntary manslaughter" was all J.H. said after Jamie saw his name on the caller ID and picked up on the second ring.

When she'd imagined this moment, Jamie had seen herself crying or collapsing, but all she did was nod. She'd done her crying in the shower during the preceding weeks, blasting the water to muffle the sounds. She'd allotted herself a few minutes every morning to lean against the tile and sob, her body heaving, her throat raw. Then she'd turn the water spray to icy cold, letting the physical shock dry up her tears and erase the red splotches from her face so she could get dressed and go downstairs to unload the dishwasher or scramble eggs for the kids. She still marveled at the existence of ordinary chores, summoning her attention even in the midst of a crisis.

J.H.'s voice was as bland as ever as he explained they would need to wait a few more days until Mike was scheduled to appear in superior court. That surprised Jamie; she figured Mike would need to go immediately.

"It shouldn't take too long," J.H. said. "He'll be in and out in a couple hours."

Jamie tried to say something, but her voice made a strange cracking sound.

"Do you want me to tell him?" J.H. asked, his tone finally softening.

Handing over the phone would be easier. But Mike deserved better. She cleared her throat.

"I'll tell him," Jamie said.

But when she went to find Mike, she didn't have to say anything. He read the news in her face, just as she'd always imagined she'd be able to discern a tragedy in the expressions of police officers who would come to the door if Mike was killed in the line of duty.

Time seemed to speed up during the next few days. Mike came upstairs more often, to cuddle with the kids on the couch, read books to Eloise, play checkers with Emily, and do Mad Libs with Sam. He built a fort out of sofa cushions and brought in flashlights and sleeping bags and he spent the night there with Sam, who was thrilled to be "camping out" with his dad. Jamie was glad to have him rejoin the family—or at least the kids, since he wasn't seeking out her company—but she sensed a desperation underlying his actions. Once she reached for the video camera to capture him wrestling with the children, then she put it away without filming a single moment. Mike would probably know she was doing it to preserve a memory, in case it had to substitute for the real thing someday.

The day Mike was scheduled to be arraigned dawned sunny and bright. Maybe it was a good omen, Jamie thought as she laid out his only nice suit, the one he wore to weddings and funerals.

He came out of the shower with a towel wrapped around his waist, water droplets rolling down his broad shoulders and disappearing into the dark hair covering his chest.

"You think?" he asked, gesturing to the suit. "I was going to wear my sport coat . . ."

"Hold your head high, Mike," Jamie said. "It was an accident."

She brought him a white button-down shirt and selected a blue-and-red striped tie, then took his dress shoes out of the closet. The shoes were scuffed from Mike's long walk home, so Jamie found a jar of polish and went to work on them until they gleamed. She straightened Mike's tie and smoothed an unruly section of his thick hair, her fingers lingering on him, grateful for an excuse to finally touch him.

"Are you sure you don't want me to come?" she asked. "Lou can watch the kids."

He shook his head. "That's the last thing I want." His rough tone and words stung her. She thought he'd meant that he didn't want her to witness his shame, not that he didn't want to be near her, but she didn't ask.

"I'll have my cell phone on," she said. "I may take the kids out, but if you need anything . . . Or if you change your mind, I can rush down there . . ."

Her words trailed off as she looked at him, remembering how he'd worn this same suit and tie when he and Ritchie were given the commendation for bringing down the armed robbery suspect. Maybe she'd chosen it subconsciously for that reason, to remind everyone else, too.

He'd also worn it when they'd gone to his brother's second wedding in New Jersey a few years ago. They'd brought the kids along but had hired a teenager who lived down the street from Mike's parents' house to watch them during the ceremony and reception. It was a spectacular evening. Jamie had bought a new dress for the first time in years, snapping up a bargain from a deeply discounted rack at Marshalls. It was a silky silver with a neckline that dipped down to skim the tops of her breasts, and she'd felt like a younger version of herself after she blow-dried and curled her hair, put on lip gloss and mascara, and slipped into high heels. The wedding was sweetly traditional, and as soon as it ended, everyone went to the reception at a nearby hotel. A band was playing and the air was soft and warm and drinks were flowing freely.

Mike had pulled her close for a slow dance, and they'd swayed together while Van Morrison sang "Have I Told You Lately That I Love You." Mike had sung along in her ear in his deep voice that was surprisingly on-key: "Fill my heart with gladness, take away my sadness, ease my troubles, that's what you do . . ."

But she couldn't ease his troubles any longer. The only thing she could do was reach for her husband and hold on, feeling desperate to connect with him again. After a long moment, his arms enfolded her. She tried to concentrate on Mike, on his warm skin and his smell, but the thought entered her mind that maybe Ms. Torres had done all these same things on the morning of her son's funeral. Maybe she'd picked out a suit for him to wear. Maybe she'd held what remained of him and had never wanted to let go.

Jamie would probably never meet Jose's mother, but she knew their lives were inexorably twined, like the double helix of a strand of DNA. On days like today, and on the anniversary of the shooting, they'd be brought closer together before spinning off, each into her own private agony.

Mike pulled back, and Jamie felt a desperate, panicky urge to do something else for him—make him a nourishing lunch to bring along, maybe—but she forced herself to let go. She walked him to the door, feeling as if he was heading to an executioner's. She wondered if the press would crowd around him as he entered the courthouse, or if any of his friends would show up.

Mike took his car keys from the hanging wall holder and slipped them into his pocket, then reached for his sunglasses. He patted his back pocket to make sure his wallet was in place, like he always did. She loved that habit of his. Sometimes she patted his behind for him and gave him a wink. "Just checking," she'd say. Those lighthearted moments seemed so long ago. It was like trying to remember your life before you had children, she thought—the experiences were so divergent they were difficult to reconcile.

"I'll see you tonight," Mike said, his posture ramrod-straight.

J.H. had predicted Mike would be released on his own recognizance, but there was a slim chance he'd have to wear an ankle monitor. Jamie wondered what it would feel like, if it would itch and chafe and dig marks into his skin.

"I'll be here," Jamie said. Even though she couldn't see his eyes behind his dark lenses, she tried to let Mike know with hers that no matter what happened, she meant for always.

"I'm sorry I can't give you more notice," Lou said. "Things are just . . . you see, it's a family emergency."

"I understand," the manager of the coffee shop said. Lou could hear the metallic whirl of beans grinding in the background. "No hard feelings."

Lou thanked him and pressed the button on her cell phone to end the call. She'd spent the past few days finding co-workers to cover her shifts, so now all she needed to do was stop in to pick up her final paycheck. Jamie hadn't asked her to quit, but Lou had known it was the right thing to do as soon as she heard about the looming indictment. She'd slipped away during the chaos of breakfast to give her notice.

She'd also left a message for her boss at the zoo asking for a few weeks off. She had plenty of accumulated vacation time, so she didn't think it would be a problem. She was planning to stop by and visit Tabby and the other elephants every day or two, and she still wanted to be there to oversee the birth, but she was hoping the zoo could call in more volunteers and keepers to cover the feedings, exams, paperwork, and tours that Lou usually handled.

Now she went back into the kitchen, where Jamie stood at the sink, scrubbing the big cast-iron frying pan she'd used to cook eggs.

"Are you okay?" Lou asked. She'd heard Mike leave early this morning to meet with his lawyer before heading to superior court, but Lou had stayed upstairs, partly so he and Jamie could have privacy and partly because Eloise was draped across her legs, snoring. Lou had wanted to shift her off, but she knew from experience Eloise would be a terror if she didn't get enough sleep, so she lay still. By the time the other kids began to stir, Lou's back ached and her legs felt numb.

Jamie shook her head, and Lou could see her eyes fill. "It's going to kill him," Jamie said.

Lou put a hand on her shoulder.

"He doesn't want me there," Jamie said, scrubbing the pan harder even though it already looked clean. "I think it'll make him more embarrassed or ashamed or whatever he's feeling. It's like he's angry at me, like it's my fault he's getting indicted. I don't know what he's feeling! He won't talk to me about it! And last night I couldn't sleep, and I kept thinking about the stupid water bill. I forgot to pay it this month. So I got up at three A.M. and went online to pay it and then I made the mistake of doing a Google search about Mike."

"You shouldn't do that," Lou said.

"Yeah, tell me about it," Jamie said. "The

comments section is the worst thing ever invented. A lot of people hate him, Lou. They really hate his guts." She pressed her hand against her stomach and leaned over for a moment. "Then I started looking at apartments in New Jersey."

"New Jersey?" Lou frowned.

"If the worst happens, we might have to move. Mike's parents drive me crazy, but his brothers and sisters are okay, and that way we'd be around a lot of family and maybe we could even live with his parents so we don't have to pay rent. I can't have the kids suffer because of this. Everyone in school is going to be talking about it when they go back. I mean, high school's tough enough without—"

Jamie stopped herself. "Henry," she said. "Of course we can't move. Christie is here. She'd never let us take him. What was I thinking?" She shook her head. "God! We can't leave Henry."

You can't leave me, either, Lou thought, feeling her muscles tense. What would she do without Jamie and Mike and the kids? She wondered if the story written by the blogger had played a role in the prosecutor's decision to try to indict Mike. It would be partly her fault if Jamie and the kids had to leave!

She felt like she was about to cry, so she changed the subject.

"Where is Henry?" she asked.

"Christie's, for now," Jamie said. "I thought it would be better for him to not be around today. And I found a baseball camp we're going to send him to for a few days . . . it's expensive but I think he really needs to get away. I know he's absorbing a lot of stress."

"That's good," Lou said. She tried to think of something concrete she could do to help. "Do you want to take a nap or something?" she asked.

Jamie shook her head. "I can't," she said.

Lou wasn't sure why not—Jamie looked exhausted—but her sister seemed to need to keep moving. She was attacking the counters now, scrubbing them down like she was punishing them for something.

"I'm going to take the kids to the pool," Jamie said, using her wrist to push her bangs off her face. "If I stay in the house I'll go crazy."

"What can I do to help?" Lou asked.

"If you could gather up the bathing suits, that would be great. They might be hanging on the back of the bathroom door, or maybe they're on the floor by the washing machine . . . Shoot, Emily still needs a new suit. I meant to pick one up weeks ago. We'll have to run by the mall on the way."

"Okay," Lou said.

"And we should stop by CVS and get some shampoo, because we're almost out. There's one in the mall." She shook her head. "Mike's going to be arraigned and a boy is dead and I'm going shopping for shampoo. What's happening, Lou?"

Lou took in the rings of blue-black encircling her sister's eyes, and the way her hands trembled. Suddenly Jamie dropped the sponge and put her hand on her stomach again and bolted. A moment later Lou could hear the distant sounds of retching.

"Is Mommy okay?"

Lou looked down to see Emily standing there, her big eyes staring up at Lou.

"Her stomach's just upset," Lou said. She didn't know if Emily bought it; she was a bright kid.

"We should get her some ginger ale," Emily said.

"Yeah," Lou said. "That's a good idea. She mentioned something about going to the store, so we can get some then." She pulled Emily close for a hug, feeling her niece's small, soft arms wrap around her neck.

"C'mon," Lou said. "Let's get ready."

After she'd gathered up the bathing suits and towels, Lou tapped her knuckles gently on the bathroom door. "Meet you outside!" she said brightly. She managed to wrangle all the kids to the minivan and get them strapped in, keeping up a steady stream of chatter about baby cheetahs.

"Even when they grow up they don't roar like the other big cats," Lou said. "They'll just purr when they're bigger. And did you know they only need to drink water once every three or four days? They get liquid from their food."

"I want a baby cheetah," Emily said. "Can we buy one?"

"That's dumb," Sam said. "It would claw you to death."

"I don't want a cheetah to kill me!" Eloise wailed.

"Tell you what," Lou said. "The zoo sells stuffed cheetahs. How about we go visit this week and you can pick one out to sleep with?"

"Me, too?" Eloise asked.

"All of you," Lou promised.

Jamie came out of the house then, glancing around warily. Lou waved at her, hoping Jamie would know it meant there weren't any reporters lurking. Jamie walked toward the minivan before shaking her head and doubling back to lock the front door.

"I can drive," Lou offered. At Jamie's grateful nod, she slipped the minivan's keys out of her sister's purse and started the engine.

"Can we watch a movie?" Eloise asked as Lou backed out of the driveway. "I want *Nemo*."

"*Nemo*'s for babies," Emily said.

Eloise began to cry and tried to hit her sister, but her car seat's restraints prevented her from stretching far enough to connect. Emily leaned closer but still just out of Eloise's reach and stuck out her tongue.

"Emily, that wasn't nice. Say you're sorry," Jamie instructed.

"Sorry," Emily said in a tone completely devoid of sincerity.

"You know we only watch movies on long car rides," Jamie said. "This is a short one. You can listen to music."

Lou reached for the radio dial.

"Just no news," Jamie warned.

"Right." Lou nodded. She found a Josh Groban song, and against all odds, all three kids fell silent and seemed to be listening.

Jamie looked at her watch and sighed. She pulled her cell phone out of her purse and clutched it tightly in her hand.

"You okay?" Lou asked.

"Just . . . wondering," Jamie said. "What's happening now."

Lou didn't know what to say, so she focused on driving. When they reached the mall, the parking lot was crowded, so Lou had to circle up to the second level before finding a spot.

"A bathing suit and shampoo, right?" she asked as she set the parking brake. "Need anything else?"

"Probably," Jamie said. "Let me think . . . Maybe we can get some juice boxes and pretzels at CVS, too—I forgot to pack a picnic for the pool."

"Okay," Lou said. She was going to keep a

mental list so Jamie didn't forget anything. And the next time they went out for the day, she'd pack the picnic. Lou was good at remembering things—she knew the exact amount of nutrients the elephants required every day and she never forgot a single feeding or vitamin. She'd just never had to worry about keeping track around Jamie before, because her sister had always been the one to stay on top of things for both of them.

They corralled the kids toward the entrance to one of the big department stores, with Lou holding Eloise's hand as Jamie led the way through the aisles.

They were approaching the kids' section when Lou noticed the man staring at them.

He was thirty or so, white and with a stocky build. He sported a goatee and a blue baseball cap with a logo Lou didn't recognize. He stood next to a woman who was holding an infant in a chest carrier, and she was looking at them, too. The woman averted her eyes when Lou glanced back at them, but the man kept staring.

"Can we get ice cream?" Sam asked, tugging on Lou's shirt. Clearly he had identified her as the soft touch.

Lou turned away from the couple and looked down at her nephew. "Why don't we hold off for now, okay, little man?" she said, thinking of how the junk-food bonanza at the zoo had ended.

"I think we're in the boys' section," Lou said,

pointing across the aisle. "The girls' stuff is over here."

As they turned to head that way, Lou noticed the guy again. She'd assumed he was with the woman with the baby, but now he seemed to be alone. And he wasn't staring at all of them—he was watching Jamie. Lou looked back as they passed the man. She felt the hair rise on the back of her neck, and she reached for Sam's hand. Physiological reactions were the body's way of alerting itself to danger. Lou knew her pupils were dilating to let in more light, her muscles were tightening, and her blood pressure was rising. That was what happened to some animals if they sensed a threat.

"Let's hurry," Lou said. "We want to get to the pool before it gets too crowded."

Her voice came out louder than she'd intended, and she saw the man shake his head. "The pool," he muttered, barely loudly enough for her to hear. "Must be nice."

Jamie hadn't heard the man's comment. She was flipping through a sale rack, holding bathing suits up for Emily's inspection. They all looked the same to Lou, but Emily kept shaking her head.

"How about this one?" Jamie was asking. "It has sparkles."

"Maybe," Emily allowed.

Lou was still holding Sam and Eloise by their hands, and Emily was right next to Jamie. Lou couldn't see the guy because he'd moved and clothing displays obscured her view. She kept scanning her surroundings, looking for that blue baseball cap.

"This one's pretty," Jamie said. "See the flowers?"

"Yuck," Emily said.

Lou spun around at the sound of a man's voice. She knew it was him before she saw the goatee and baseball cap. "Unbelievable. You're shopping and going to the pool while that kid rots in his grave," the man said.

Jamie froze for an instant, then slowly lifted her head.

For a fleeting moment, Lou wondered how he'd recognized Jamie. Then her instincts trumped her thought process. She stepped up next to her sister, positioning Sam and Eloise behind her and speaking in a calm, low voice, as she'd do if confronted with any other angry mammal. "We have children here," she said.

"Yeah? The guy her husband shot was just a kid, too," the man said.

"Mommy?" Sam's voice was high and wavering.

"Can you get a manager?" Jamie called to a passing salesperson, her voice as desperate as Sam's. "Please?"

"Oh, sure, call a manager," the guy said. "Why don't you just call your husband to come shoot me?"

Emily began to cry, and then so did Sam, their

wails high and thready. Before Lou could do anything, she detected movement out of the corner of her eye. Jamie was stalking toward the man. Hearing her children's cries must have ignited something in her sister.

"Listen to me!" Jamie hissed. She shook her finger in the guy's face. She seemed to have grown physically taller, and her body language was fierce. "You leave us alone!"

Gone was the exhausted woman who'd hunched over her sink this morning. Jamie had transformed into a warrior. Now her arms were outstretched to block the man from getting through her to her children, and her expression made her look like a stranger even to Lou.

Without thinking about it, Lou let go of Sam's and Eloise's hands and stepped forward, too. Jamie had always defended her while they were growing up. Now it was her turn.

"Get away from my sister!" Lou shouted.

She angled herself between Jamie and the man so that if he attacked, he'd have to go through her first. Lou would fight him off as best as she could while Jamie and the kids escaped. She remem-bered the self-defense course she'd taken years ago. She'd go for his eyes, knees, instep, or throat. Lou widened her stance, so he wouldn't be able to easily knock her down, and suddenly she felt grateful for every one of those twenty extra pounds.

The guy made a huffing sound, but he didn't say anything.

"Lou, call the police," Jamie said, without taking her narrowed eyes off him.

Lou pulled her cell phone out of her pocket. Before she could dial a single digit, the guy began to walk away, slowly, as if to convey to them that it was his choice to move on.

Lou poised her finger over the final 1 for the emergency number. "Still want me to call the police?" she asked. The man was twenty yards away by now.

Jamie shook her head. "Let's get out of here," she said. Jamie knelt down and put her arms around her children, drawing them in close, while Lou kept her eyes fixed on that blue baseball cap.

They walked toward the exit. Lou couldn't see the guy any longer, but she checked behind them every few seconds. "You're safe," Jamie told the kids as they passed through the doors and made it to the minivan.

"Was he talking about Daddy?" Sam asked as Jamie unlocked the vehicle.

"Yes," Jamie said. She knelt down to be at eye level with Sam again. "But he was a crazy person. He doesn't know Daddy and he was wrong. That's why he ran away before the police got here."

Sam nodded and sniffled a few times. Jamie patted him on the back, then opened the sliding side door and helped Sam into the vehicle. Lou got Emily and Eloise settled, then shut the door and climbed into the front.

"How did he recognize you?" Lou asked after Jamie started up the engine. Uneasy energy still radiated from her sister, but Jamie's voice was calmer.

Jamie shrugged. "Some of the news stations aired footage of Mike and me leaving the station after he gave his statement. There've been photos in the paper, too."

"Do you want to go home?" Lou asked.

"No way," Jamie said firmly. "We're going to the pool. He is not going to ruin my children's morning. I'll grab a bathing suit out of the lost and found bin for Emily."

"I'm hungry," Sam said.

"How about I buy everyone lunch?" Lou offered.

"Yay!" Sam said. "Can we get Chipotle?"

Lou stole a look at Jamie. The tightness in her sister's face was easing now. "Actually, that sounds kind of good to me, too," she said.

"Chipotle it is," Lou said. "Then the pool. We can get ice cream there, too—my treat."

She didn't think Jamie would mind junk food just this once, especially because at the mention of it, all three kids cheered.

"So you don't have to work today?" Jamie asked.

"Actually, I quit my barista job," Lou said. She cleared her throat. "And I thought I could take a leave of absence from the zoo. I'll have to go back when Tabby gives birth, but other than that, I'll just stop in and visit the elephants."

Jamie pulled up to a red light. She turned to look at Lou.

"You quit?" she asked.

Lou couldn't tell from the expression on her sister's face if the news made her happy or not.

"I just thought . . . that way, I can be around whenever you need me," Lou explained.

Jamie still didn't say anything, so Lou added quickly, "And if you don't, I'll stay in my room or go out for a walk or something to give you privacy—"

She stopped talking when Jamie reached over to give her a brief, hard, one-armed hug.

"Lou, I don't know what I would do without you right now," Jamie said.

The best part was, Lou could tell her sister really meant it.

Chapter Twelve

CHRISTIE AWOKE TO BRIGHT sunlight streaming through her window. She'd forgotten to draw the blinds last night. She buried her face under a pillow, but it was too late. She was awake for good.

She stumbled out of bed and padded into her kitchen to make coffee. Maybe, she thought, she'd start leaving her blinds up deliberately. Her mother usually slept away half the day, and one thing was for sure: Christie was not going to turn into that woman. No way would she end up in a crappy low-rise apartment with water stains on the ceiling and game shows blaring in a continual loop on the television. She had a plan.

Christie poured herself a steaming mug of coffee, added Sweet 'n Low instead of the sugar and cream she really wanted, and leaned against the spot on the counter where Mike had so recently been. She'd made a decision after he left. She was going to keep working with Elroy, after all, but she'd never again let anyone double lock the door to the hotel room. She'd take as many jobs as possible and pay off her credit card debt fast, then she'd start saving for the down payment on a house. Maybe she'd even go back to beauty school, all these years later, and become the manager of a salon, like she'd pretended to be to Simon. And forget shimmying into dresses she bought at Forever 21. From now on, she was going to start purchasing quality pieces, skirts and tops and dresses from Nordstrom. Clothes that fit the woman she was becoming—or hoped to become, anyway.

But first, the car.

Christie took a sip of strong coffee, relishing the memory of how confident she'd felt inside the sleek vehicle. A Mercedes would help erase the feeling of Jim's insistent, scrabbling fingers on her thighs, and the memory of the looks Simon's family had given her at the restaurant.

She was nervous about the price tag, but she'd already called up a calculator on the Internet and figured out that, with interest, she'd owe $620 per monthly payment. That was less than three jobs with Elroy. It didn't seem so bad when you broke it down that way.

She showered, got dressed, and drove to the dealership, arriving a few minutes after it opened. The same salesman saw her coming and met her at the door, holding it open and ushering her inside. "She's been waiting for you," he said, grinning.

Christie tried to make her eyes dull, to avoid letting him see how the car affected her, but she knew it was a lost cause. She ended up paying more than she wanted, but an hour later, she was driving off the lot in the cherry-red Mercedes.

She could have stayed in it all day, she thought as she idled at a stoplight, itching to press the gas again and feel the engine surge. She wanted to roar along the highway, the radio blasting and the wind streaming through her hair. She yearned to drive to the beach and feel the salty air against her cheeks. She heard the toot of a horn and looked over to see a silver-haired man in a BMW checking her out. Christie winked at him, then stepped on the gas pedal and left him behind.

She was born for this car.

She wasn't ready to go home, so she drove to Nordstrom. She parked carefully, in an out-of-the-way location so the Mercedes wouldn't get dinged. She walked purposefully into the store and began looking at dresses. The first few price tags made her blanch, but after a few moments, she began to notice how soft the fabrics felt between her fingers, and how smooth the seams were in comparison to those of the cheap items she usually bought. She selected a few things to try on: an emerald-colored sheath, a crimson sundress, a maxidress in bright blue.

"Can I start a room for you?" Christie looked up to see a bright-eyed young saleswoman stretching out her arm. Christie obligingly handed over the clothes. "Thanks," she said.

"Can I make a suggestion?" the saleswoman

asked. "These bold colors will be nice on you, but have you ever thought about trying something in a neutral?"

"Like . . . beige?" Christie asked, her nose crinkling.

"I was thinking cream," the saleswoman said. Christie refrained from asking what the difference was.

"How about this?" the salesgirl asked, pulling a dress from a rack. "I think the cut will suit you. Size eight, right?"

Maybe eight on a good day, and she hadn't had one of those in a while, but Christie nodded.

"You've got such striking eyes, and hair," the salesgirl said. She was young, maybe twenty or so, with close-cropped hair and flawless skin. "Your clothes shouldn't compete with your best features. They should enhance them. With this dress, people will be looking at you—not your outfit."

"Thanks," Christie said. She looked down at her pink tank top and matching skirt. She wasn't sure if she'd just been delivered a compliment or a backhanded insult (did the salesgirl think she was too flashy?), but the advice seemed spot-on. And when she went into the changing room and put on the dress, which was tight but not so tight she couldn't zip it up, she realized the silk lining made the fabric skim her curves instead of bunching up around the middle. The hem fell to just above her knee, showing less of her leg than she was used to. She'd always dismissed clothes that hit so close to the knee as being frumpy. But as she twisted and turned in front of the mirror, she noticed that because the skirt was so fitted, it hinted at the shape of her thighs. It was sexy without being overtly so. And the salesgirl was right; the color set off not just her eyes, but her skin tone.

She looked at the price tag and blinked: $360. It was more than Christie had ever spent on an item of clothing in her entire life, including her prom dress and the wedding gown she'd worn for her brief marriage to the guy whose name she'd vowed never to utter again.

"Doing all right in there?" the salesgirl chirped. "Need a smaller size?"

She really was earning her commission.

"Doing great," Christie said. She tried on the dresses she'd selected, but they looked too loud next to the beige—no, the *cream*—one. She put the dress on a hanger and walked out.

"Do you need shoes to go with it?" the salesgirl asked.

"What would you suggest?" Christie asked.

The salesgirl held up the dress and narrowed her eyes. "Something in bone," she said. "It'll make your legs look longer. Nothing too structured; I'd go with a simple sandal."

Within an hour, Christie had not only new shoes

but a hammered-gold cuff bracelet. She popped into a few other stores, making an impulsive purchase at a Hallmark card shop and picking up a smoothie for lunch, then she returned to her car and checked her iPhone, which showed two missed calls. Both were from Elroy.

She pressed the Return Call button and waited to hear his gentle voice. He picked up on the first ring.

"Are you okay?" he asked.

"Yeah," Christie said. "I'm fine."

"Look, I don't want you to quit, but if you need to take off a little time—" he began, but she cut him off. What she needed was to start making money before her first car payment arrived.

"I want a can of Mace," she said. "Can you get me one?"

"Of course," he said. "I should've thought of that sooner."

"I'm ready to start again," she said. "But first I have a favor to ask."

She told him about Mike and the shooting—he'd heard about it already, but hadn't known of her relationship to Mike—and Elroy promised to help. "Whatever I can do," he said.

"Really?" Christie asked, a little suspicious. Most guys didn't want to spend effort on you unless they were getting something in return.

"Sure," Elroy said. "You know I used to be a cop, right?"

Christie hadn't, actually.

"I've still got a few contacts in the department. Let me see what's going on and I'll call you back."

After she hung up, Christie checked the dashboard clock. Even the numbers proclaiming it was a few minutes after noon looked elegant. She glanced down at the small Hallmark bag on the passenger's seat and decided to head to Mike and Jamie's house, so she could give it to them in person. It wasn't much—just a hang-in-there card, but along with it she'd be delivering the news that Elroy was going to help Mike's case. Henry was supposed to come over tonight, so maybe she'd save them a trip by picking him up early, if he was home. She couldn't wait to see his face when he glimpsed the Mercedes. He'd be so proud of her.

She put the Mercedes in drive and set up the GPS, even though she knew the way, because she'd never had a GPS before. She preset the radio buttons to her favorite stations, too. She made it to Mike and Jamie's in record time—or maybe it just felt that way because the ride was so pleasant. She pulled up to the curb and listened to the end of John Legend's "All of Me."

She wondered how many times she'd waited in front of this house for Henry to come to her. Thousands, probably. When he'd been a baby, picking him up or dropping him off had also required handing off his diaper bag and ratty stuffed dog and stroller, which was a hassle. Then he'd gone through a phase as a toddler in which he hadn't wanted to leave Mike, which wasn't fun for anyone. Luckily it was short-lived. In a few years, she wouldn't have to pick him up at all. He'd just drive over to her place himself.

As the final, sweet notes of the song faded, Christie saw phantom Henrys running toward her—a little tyke in overalls with sticky hands; a self-conscious nine-year-old with a baseball glove; a tall, lanky teenager who was just a few years from running away from them for good. She shook her head, wondering how the time had evaporated as quickly as wet footprints on the hot pavement.

She picked up the car keys, opened the door, walked to the house, and rang the bell. One of Mike's kids flung it open and ran away without a word.

"Hello?" Christie called.

"Christie?" Jamie came from the direction of the living room, a frown on her face. "Weren't we supposed to drop off Henry tonight?"

"Yeah, but I was in the neighborhood, so I thought I'd stop by and save you the trouble," Christie said. "Hey, you got the AC fixed!"

"What? Oh, yeah," Jamie said. Had she gotten thinner all of a sudden?

"Is Mike here?" Christie asked. She reached

into her purse for the card in the bright yellow envelope.

Jamie started to answer, then she caught sight of the Mercedes.

Christie smiled broadly and stepped aside so Jamie could get a better look. "Do you like it?"

"It's yours?" Jamie asked.

Christie nodded. "Come see," she urged. She tucked the card back into her purse and led the way down the walk.

Jamie followed her without shutting the front door, and the dog escaped and raced down the street.

"Is she going to run away?" Christie asked, but Jamie didn't answer.

"It has leather seats," Christie said. "And a sunroof! Here." Christie opened the door and pulled the Nordstrom bag off the passenger's seat. "You can get in if you want."

Jamie turned to look at her. "Are you fucking kidding me?"

Christie blinked. "What?"

"Mike was just indicted and you bought a Mercedes? He might go to jail and we'll lose everything. And I'm driving a nine-year-old minivan and sitting up at night trying to figure out how to pay the grocery bill and you buy a goddamn Mercedes with the child support money we give you?"

"I didn't—" Christie began, but Jamie cut her

off. Her face was turning bright red and her voice kept getting louder.

"You didn't what? Think? Maybe you're not that bright, Christie, but it shouldn't be hard to figure out!" Jamie said. "You are the most selfish person I've ever met."

Jamie hated her. She'd tried to mask it for years, but now it was so clear. The way she was looking at Christie, her face twisting . . .

Fury and hurt swelled inside of Christie. "Screw you!" she shouted. "You don't think I deserve this car? I'm paying for it! I got a new job, a good one . . ."

"Doing what? Another modeling job?" Scorn seeped into every word.

"No!" Christie bellowed. "Why don't you ask Mike? I told him about it when he came over the other night for pizza and beer."

That hit its mark. Apparently Mike hadn't told his perfect little wife about their visit. Jamie staggered back a step. "What?" she said.

"Oh, I guess he didn't want you to know," Christie said. "Oops!"

Jamie looked like she wanted to hit her. She actually raised her hand, then she dropped it to her side. "Why don't you go back to school, get a real job, and stop mooching off us. I'm sick of it," she said. Her voice dropped, but Christie still caught her last words. "I'm sick of *you*."

Christie got into her car and roared off, her body trembling. *Not that bright. Mooch. Selfish.* So that was what Jamie really thought of her, even though she pretended to pray for Christie.

She made it one block away before the tears came.

Mike had gone to Christie's for beer and pizza?

Jamie's mind cast back over the previous days and nights, wondering when it had happened. The truth was, she and Mike were spending so little time together that she had no idea when he'd done it. What she'd give to have an easy, companionable night like that with her husband. But Christie was the one Mike had chosen to spend time with.

Jamie thought about how she and Mike had wanted to transfer Sam to private school, because he was so bright and anxious, and Jamie knew boys like him sometimes had a tough time in public school. But they couldn't afford it. She'd resented Christie for that. She felt the burn every time she saw Christie in a new outfit. She'd thought she'd pushed it down, but it had just been tamped more tightly into a small space, like explosive powder awaiting a spark.

Jamie dropped her head into her hands. Maybe she'd been too hard on Christie just now—she'd seen pain flash across Christie's face, and she wasn't proud of causing it—but what was she thinking, driving up in that car so soon after Mike had been indicted?

Christie's timing couldn't have been worse. Just this morning, Jamie had had to phone her father to ask if she could borrow money, since Mike was no longer drawing a salary. "I don't know when we can pay you back," Jamie had said, her voice catching. "It might be a while."

"Don't even worry about that," her father had said immediately, and two fat tears had squeezed out from her eyes. He'd probably take it out of his retirement account. "I'll send a check today."

At least they'd be able to pay the mortgage— for now. The indictment meant Mike could be represented for free by a public defender, but Jamie wasn't sure if it would be better to stick with J.H., who seemed to know what he was doing.

The Mercedes probably cost as much as J.H. would charge them. How could Christie be so thoughtless?

Jamie sighed and slumped down to sit on the curb, energy leaching out of her body. She'd felt so righteous and strong after the terrible experience at the mall the other day. After Lou had treated them to lunch, she'd driven to the pool and had searched through the lost and found bin until she'd found a bathing suit that looked newish and would fit Emily. She'd washed it out with hand soap in the bathroom sink, then convinced Emily to wear it, saying the pool kept extra suits on hand for kids who'd forgotten theirs. Lou had taken Eloise into the shallow end while Jamie had gone with Sam and Emily to the slide and diving board.

"Are you going to do it?" Sam had asked when Jamie began climbing the ladder to the slide.

"I sure am," she'd said. She'd forgotten how good it felt to whoosh down the slippery plastic and splash into deliciously cool water.

They'd stayed at the pool for two hours, and Jamie had only gotten out of the water to check her cell phone every fifteen minutes or so in case Mike called. But he didn't, and she found it was surprisingly easy to block out what was happening, to keep her world limited to the narrow confines of games of Marco Polo and diving contests.

Everyone had eaten a Choco Taco or Popsicle from the concession stand, then they'd driven home still in their bathing suits. ("Don't I have to give the suit back?" Emily had asked. "Not for two weeks," Jamie had said. "That's the pool's rule.")

She'd passed a farm stand and had picked up a half dozen ears of fresh corn and a few tomatoes, and she'd pulled out hamburger meat and hot dogs for dinner. She wanted Mike to come home to the smell of good food and the sound of happy children.

He'd walked through the door less than ten minutes after they arrived, as if they'd synchronized it. Jamie had approached him with a question in her eyes, but he'd lifted up a hand like a stop sign. He hadn't said a word; he'd just gone upstairs, changed, and come back down. He'd put on shorts, and Jamie was relieved to see his ankles were bare.

"Smells good," he'd said, watching as Jamie flipped burgers on the small gas grill just outside their kitchen door. That's when she knew he was laying down the ground rules: They weren't to talk about what had happened to him today. Maybe they never would.

She'd thought that it was too painful for him to discuss, but hearing about Mike and Christie together made her wonder. Maybe he was letting other people in.

Maybe he just didn't want to talk to her.

As she stepped out of the bathroom, Lou heard a woman yelling. She looked out the window and saw Jamie standing on the edge of the lawn as a shiny red car peeled away. Lou ran downstairs, through the open front door, calling her sister's name. She wondered if Jamie had had an altercation with a reporter. A few had followed Mike home from superior court after his arraignment the other day, but they'd left after an hour or so.

Jamie was sitting on the curb, her arms wrapped around her knees. "Sadie's gone," she said.

"Which way did she go?" Lou asked.

Jamie pointed.

"I'll go find her," Lou promised. "Was that who you were yelling at? Sadie?"

Jamie gave a half laugh. "No," she said. "Christie."

"She's here?" Lou asked.

Jamie shook her head. "Not any longer."

"I'll find Sadie," Lou promised. She ran to get her flip-flops and the keys to the minivan and her cell phone. "Call me if she comes back," she said, then she headed off in the direction Jamie had indicated, calling Sadie's name through the van's open windows.

She drove slowly, her eyes sweeping both sides of the street. As she pulled up to a stop sign a block away, she noticed a car parked to her right. It was the same fancy car that had peeled away from Jamie's house. Lou saw a flash of familiar blond hair and she squinted, trying to get a better look. Christie was in the driver's seat, her face buried in her hands, her shoulders heaving.

"Are you okay?" Lou called out, and Christie looked up. Her cheeks were streaked with mascara and her eyes were swollen.

"Did you follow me?" Christie asked.

Lou shook her head. "I'm looking for Sadie," she said.

"Well, she's not here," Christie said. She picked up a yellow envelope and began shredding it, letting the pieces fall out her window.

"Littering is illegal," Lou said, in case Christie didn't know.

Christie's face screwed up and she began crying harder. "Just go away!"

Lou sat there, unsure of what to do. Then she caught sight of Sadie in the next yard over. She put the car in park, got out, and crept toward the dog. She grabbed Sadie's collar just as the dog tried to bolt and steered her into the minivan. As she walked around to the driver's side, she looked over at Christie again.

Lou hesitated. Jamie always talked about how important it was for her and Christie to be on friendly terms, for Henry's sake. That was why she invited Christie over for Thanksgiving dinner every year, even though Christie usually didn't come.

"Can I do anything?" Lou asked.

"No," Christie said, but some of the anger had disappeared from her voice and she began to hiccup. She had a funny-sounding hiccup—kind of a gulp followed by a little squeal.

Lou thought of the time a golden-headed lion tamarin monkey had been injured at the zoo—no one was quite sure how, but they suspected its leg had gotten ensnared when it tried to jump from tree limb to tree limb. At first the monkey had bared its teeth at anyone who came close to it, but then one of the keepers had approached it slowly, making soothing sounds, and the monkey had succumbed to treatment. The look in the monkey's eyes—half-threatening, half-wounded —reminded her of Christie's expression right now.

"I'm really sorry you're so sad," Lou said. Christie hiccuped twice more.

"Whatever," Christie said. "I didn't get Henry and I'm not going back there."

"Do you want me to bring him to you?" Lou offered.

Christie looked as if she thought Lou was trying to trick her. "Fine," she finally said. "But he's not supposed to come over until tonight, and I need to get myself together anyway. Bring him around five."

"Okay," Lou said. Christie was being a little bossy, but Lou decided that was okay, because she'd stopped crying.

"And I already told Mike I don't need child support any longer," Christie said. "You can tell your sister!"

Lou nodded. She knew better than to get in the middle of *that* conversation.

Christie stared at her for a moment. "You desperately need a better haircut," she said.

The comment was so unexpected that Lou burst into laughter. "I know," she said. "But I only paid fifteen bucks for this one. Including tip."

"You tipped for that?" Christie said.

Lou laughed again. She wasn't insulted; it was refreshing to hear someone else say exactly what they thought.

"Look," she said. "I'm sure Jamie is sorry you fought."

"I doubt it," Christie said. "Considering she started it."

"She's under a lot of stress right now," Lou said. "I don't think she's sleeping much."

"Whatever," Christie said, her hand flapping away Lou's words. "Do you remember where I live?"

Lou had been there for a few of Henry's birthday parties. She nodded. "Once I go somewhere once, I can always drive there again. By the way, that's a gorgeous car."

Christie narrowed her eyes at Lou.

"So I'll see you soon," Lou said.

She got into the minivan, gave Sadie a pat, and headed back to Jamie's. She'd tell Jamie that Christie had been crying. Maybe that would make Jamie forgive Christie for whatever she'd done.

But she hadn't even finished leading Sadie through Jamie's front door when a text came in on her phone: *Tabby's progesterone just dropped. Baby's coming!*

Chapter Thirteen

JAMIE HAD NEVER FLAT-OUT lied to Mike before.

After her fight with Christie, she'd felt an almost uncontrollable urge to put into place a plan she'd been secretly turning over in her mind. Lou had raced off to the zoo by then, so Jamie told Mike she'd forgotten she had a gynecologist's appointment that afternoon. "Can you watch the children? I'll be back in an hour and a half."

Then she'd gotten into her van and driven in the opposite direction from her doctor's office, to a large red-brick building she'd entered only once before. She parked in the visitors' lot and signed in at the security guard's desk, then took the elevator to the third floor and hurried down the long hallway, inhaling the ammonia smell of disinfectant.

She found the correct room and gently rapped her knuckles against the partly open door before stepping inside. Her palms felt sweaty and her heart throbbed in her chest. What would unfold in the next few minutes was vitally important.

Ritchie was in bed, looking through a photo album, Sandy by his side. Sandy was pointing at a picture and her tone was low and intimate. The twins were sitting on the floor, playing Connect Four.

"Surprise!" Jamie said.

Sandy glanced up, then quickly got to her feet and hurried over to hug Jamie.

"I'm so glad you came!" she said.

Ritchie's smile had always spread the width of his face—it was like a kid's grin, open and unguarded. At least that hadn't changed, Jamie thought as she leaned over to kiss his cheek, then bent down to greet the children.

"Hey," Ritchie said. "You here . . . with Mike?"

"Just me this time," Jamie said. "I was out running a few errands, and I thought I'd stop by."

"I'm so glad you did. It's been a while," Sandy said, her voice containing no judgment. She perched on the edge of Ritchie's bed, by his feet, and gestured for Jamie to take the chair. "We were just looking at pictures from our trip to the beach."

Memories slammed into Jamie. They'd gone to the Delaware shore for a week two years ago. No, a lifetime ago. Ritchie and Mike had taught the older kids to boogie-board, and she and Sandy had brought along pails and shovels so everyone could compete in sand-castle-building contests. They'd eaten steamed crabs with hot melted butter at a restaurant with picnic tables set outside, and stayed in a hotel that gave guests marshmallows to roast by a giant fire pit at night. She and Sandy had woken up early one morning and taken a long sunrise walk on the beach, and she'd talked to Sandy about her mother's death, while Sandy had shared the story of the two miscarriages she'd had before getting pregnant with the twins. One night they'd all gone to a little tiki bar where she and Sandy had gotten tipsy on piña coladas and Mike and Ritchie had gotten tipsier on beer and sung karaoke, badly, with the little paper umbrellas from their wives' drinks tucked behind their ears. Jamie hadn't been able to clean the sand out of the cracks in her minivan for weeks, and her nose had gotten so sunburned it had peeled. It had been the singular vacation of her life.

"We should . . . do it again soon," Ritchie said.

Jamie saw sadness flicker in Sandy's eyes before she erased it. "Sure. Maybe at the end of the summer," Sandy said.

"How's . . . Mike?" Ritchie asked.

"He's, um, well, he's dealing with everything," Jamie said. She forced a smile. "Hanging in there." Another lie. She could tell Sandy saw straight through it, just as she'd known Ritchie wouldn't be in any shape to go to the beach this year. But they were cops' wives, so they were used to putting on a strong front, no matter how much they ached beneath it. For a moment, Jamie felt their old connection flicker.

"If you two need a date night, you can bring the kids over," Sandy offered.

"Thank you," Jamie said, trying to swallow the lump in her throat. How like Sandy to offer help, when she probably could use some herself. Sandy and Ritchie thought she was here as a friend. She needed to let them know she'd come to ask them to save her husband. She hoped they wouldn't be angry when they realized it.

"I was wondering," Jamie began. "When the trial begins . . . would you testify on behalf of Mike?"

Ritchie began nodding even before she'd finished the sentence.

"Thank you," Jamie said. "I just think seeing you up on the stand, and having you tell everyone how close you and Mike are . . . They can't accuse him of being a racist if you're there!"

Sandy got up and moved closer to Jamie and put her hands on Jamie's shoulders. "If you need me, I'll testify, too," she said.

Jamie felt it then, the release of a great boulder of guilt that had been weighing her down. It coursed through her, weakening her knees, making her glad for the chair. She'd pushed Sandy away when the two women should've been supporting each other, and Sandy probably knew exactly why, because she was a smart woman, but somehow Sandy didn't blame her. Maybe Sandy had even experienced some of the same feelings when Ritchie was in the hospital and Mike was whole and healthy, but had been better at hiding them.

"We'll get an ambulance to take you," Jamie said. She'd find a way to pay for it. "And we can have a doctor there, too . . . Whatever you need. We can find out exactly when the lawyer wants you to testify and we can just zip you down there and back."

"Hey, girl, slow down," Sandy said gently. Her hands began to knead Jamie's shoulders. "Your muscles are all tied up."

"I win!" Finn cried triumphantly, sliding a red piece into the board. "Dad, next game?"

"Bring it . . . on," Ritchie said, with that smile again.

Jamie felt a painful knot in her shoulder succumb under Sandy's strong fingertips, and she watched as Finn climbed onto Ritchie's bed and began setting up the game. For the first time, she noticed that along with the family photographs on Ritchie's nightstand was one of him with Mike, the two men in matching uniforms, their arms slung around each other's shoulders. Each was making bunny ears behind the other's head.

I'm sorry, Jamie thought, her eyes filling. Sorry that Mike had nudged Ritchie out the door first, setting off this whole wretched series of events, sorry that neither of the men would probably ever wear those uniforms again, sorry that another mother was grieving, and sorry that she'd with-drawn from her friend.

I missed you, she thought, and her hand reached up to squeeze Sandy's.

It could take hours, or days even, until Tabby gave birth. Lou's bag of supplies, including PowerBars and apples and bottles of water, was stashed under a nearby tree. She didn't want to leave the elephant's side for a moment.

The elephant exhibit had been closed to the public, even though the zoo would still be open for another two hours, and the other members of Tabby's herd were being kept away. A videographer was setting up his equipment, and the zoo's head veterinarian had texted that he was on his way in. A few other keepers and volunteers were milling around, too, clearly excited to watch.

But Lou was focused only on Tabby. Keeping her calm and comfortable was Lou's sole priority.

Tabby was walking around quite a bit, and she wasn't eating much. She wasn't just walking—she was pacing, Lou thought as she leaned against the fence, her eyes moving in tandem with the mammal. It was as if Tabby was searching for something perpetually beyond her reach.

Pacing . . . The word lodged in Lou's brain, forcing her to circle back and reconsider it. Something kept tugging at the corner of her mind, then vanishing, like a firefly that briefly glowed before being swallowed up by the night.

Lou shrugged and gave up on the memory. Her back was a little sore from standing so long, but she didn't feel the slightest bit tired. She'd bought caffeine pills at the drugstore and had packed them just in case, but she doubted she'd need them.

She slid to the ground and settled into a comfortable position, wrapping her arms around her knees. In the wild, animals never showed signs of distress unless they were grievously ill, since doing so could invite attack by a predator. Tabby was camouflaging her discomfort well, but Lou knew it existed, and that it was going to worsen with the passing hours.

"It's okay, Tabby," Lou called out, her voice floating through the soft warm air. "Good girl."

She wanted to remind Tabby that she was here, in case her presence provided comfort. She watched as the elephant walked over to the deep pool and stepped inside. What a smart creature, Lou thought. Jamie had sworn a bath had eased her pain during early labor. Lou hoped it did for Tabby, too.

Dusk would fall in a few hours, but Lou had a flashlight and a sweatshirt in her bag in case it grew chilly. She could hear occasional grunts and screeches, and she smelled earth and sweet, fresh grass and, best of all, the scent of elephant.

"I'm here, Tabby," she called out again. "Don't worry, sweet girl. I won't leave you."

Mike knew going onto the force that he might have to kill people, Christie thought as she began to freshen her makeup. His job was like a soldier's in that way—violence was sometimes necessary to establish peace. Still, knowing you'd taken someone's life . . . She wondered how it felt. It would have to change you in some irrevocable way, wouldn't it?

And yes, she got it that Jamie was under an incredible amount of stress. If Mike went to jail, it would be horrible for Henry, but at least he was old enough to understand. The other kids might not. Did Jamie really think Christie would ask for child support if Mike was convicted? The thought made her seethe, so she tried to temper it with the memory of Jamie's thinness, and the dull look in her eyes—at least until she'd glimpsed the Mercedes.

But it didn't work.

Christie blasted her favorite Rihanna CD to chase away her bad mood, but that didn't help, either. She'd had the Mercedes for less than a day, and somehow Jamie had managed to steal away every bit of its triumph.

It was five o'clock, so Christie poured herself a gin and tonic and took it with her into her bedroom. Her new dress was hanging on her

352

closet door, and she tore away the plastic wrapper so she could admire it. But all she could think about was the fact that she'd spent more than five hundred dollars on an outfit she didn't have anyplace to wear.

She slipped into the dress and shoes, hoping to recapture the magic she'd felt in the store. As she clasped the gold bracelet around her wrist, her doorbell rang. *Perfect,* she thought. She'd wear the dress for Henry. Maybe she'd suggest that they go out for dinner. First, though, she'd slip Lou the card for her old salon and suggest she request an emergency appointment. But when she opened the door, Lou wasn't there.

Instead, it was Mike who'd brought Henry.

"Wow," he said, looking Christie up and down. She felt her skin tingling under his scrutiny.

"Do you like it?" she asked.

"You look great, Mom," Henry said. He kicked off his giant shoes—puppy feet, she always thought when she saw them—and dropped a plastic Sports Authority bag by the closet, then headed straight for the refrigerator.

"I've got turkey and French bread if you want to make a sub," Christie called.

"A little predinner snack?" Mike asked, and she laughed. She was aware he hadn't answered her question, but his double take had revealed enough.

"I thought Lou was going to bring him over?" she asked.

"She had something come up at the zoo," Mike said. "She had to take off."

"Did you want to come in for a second?" she asked. "I actually need to talk to you."

"Yeah, okay," he said.

She led him into the living room, then went to the kitchen and fixed another gin and tonic. Mike didn't like most hard liquors—he was a beer man—but she knew he enjoyed an occasional G and T on a hot summer day.

"That looks like a Dagwood sub," she told Henry, who was piling turkey and cheese and something else—yuck, potato chips—on the French bread.

"Who?" Henry asked.

"This cartoon character who—Never mind, you're making me feel old."

Henry shrugged, picked up his sandwich, seemed to eat a quarter of it in one bite, and headed toward his room.

Christie squeezed lime into Mike's drink, then went into the living room, handed him the glass, and sat down across from him.

"So what's up?" he asked.

"I talked to Elroy," she said. "My boss. And he wants to help with the investigation."

"Really?" Mike said. He leaned back with a sigh and took a sip of his drink. Christie could see his shoulders relax. "That's great."

"He's going to check things out with his police

sources and get back to me," Christie said. "Maybe we can meet up with him to talk about a plan."

"Yeah, sure," Mike said. "Whatever he needs. So he's going to talk to the cops?"

"He wants to see what they have," Christie said.

"Seems like all they've really got is the testimony of Jay—he's the idiot I was paired with that day," Mike said. "Apparently that's the thing that could screw me."

"So we've got to discredit him," Christie said. "Maybe Elroy can dig into his past. Does he have a history of telling lies? If he does, you can be sure ex-girlfriends will be lining up to testify. I mean, maybe he's hoping to get a movie deal out of this or something."

"Yeah," Mike said. "Worth a shot."

"Oh, I just thought of something!" Christie said. "Does he wear glasses?"

Mike nodded.

"Maybe his prescription changed and he didn't know it!" Christie said. "I bet we could subpoena his optometrist."

At Mike's surprised look she confessed: "I watch a lot of *CSI*."

"No, this is good," he said. He leaned forward and put the drink on the table and rested his elbows on his knees. "You're on fire." For the second time that evening, she felt a little thrilled by his reaction to her.

She reached out and clinked her glass against his, then took a sip of her gin and tonic and let an ice cube swirl around in her mouth. It brought forth another memory: When she'd gone into labor (forget pacing and breathing and all the other crap the books said would manage the pain; her labor sent her rushing for the hospital after the first contraction, ready to sue the authors of her pregnancy book) Mike had shown up in his uniform. He'd looked so handsome and strong and solid that she'd almost changed her mind and told him she'd accept his proposal. Of course an hour later, as agony mounted in her body, he'd tried to give her an ice chip and she'd spat it back at him and cursed.

He'd hidden a smile—that had made her even more furious—and had gone to consult with the nurse about getting her epidural turned up.

"It's already pretty high," the nurse had said. She'd shrugged. "Sometimes they just don't take."

"Don't take?" Christie had felt like her head could do an *Exorcist*-style swivel.

"We'll give you a refund after the baby comes," the nurse had joked, and it was only another contraction that kept Christie from lunging out of bed at her.

But Mike had been wonderful. He'd rubbed her lower back with the perfect amount of firm pressure until she decided she couldn't stand to have him touching her, and then he'd distracted her with stupid criminal stories. He'd lied and told her she was almost ready to push a dozen times, and when the doctor had finally come into the room and snapped on gloves, Mike had leaned over and kissed her on the forehead.

"Thank you," he'd said.

"Your fault," she'd muttered at him through clenched teeth. Her hair was sticking to her sweaty face, and the guttural groan that emerged from her mouth seemed to have been loosened from her very soul.

Then the pain was gone, just like that.

"It's a boy!" Mike had shouted, and from the pride in his voice, she knew he'd secretly wanted one, even though he'd insisted he didn't have a preference. She'd heard a reedy, birdlike cry, and she'd fallen back against the pillows, tears of exhaustion streaming from her eyes. Never again, she'd thought.

They'd already decided on Henry for a boy. That was Christie's idea; the name sounded like it would belong to a smart, nice kid, someone who might play a musical instrument and do well in school and get a good job. She didn't have much to give her son, but at least she could give him the best possible start.

Mike had gone with the nurse to give Henry a bath, and Christie had fallen asleep. When she'd awoken, Mike was sitting in a chair next to her bed, staring down at the blanket-wrapped bundle in his arms.

At that moment, she knew she'd made the right decision in turning down his proposal. Mike had never once looked at her the way he was looking at Henry.

"Do you have any other ideas?" Mike asked. She blinked and focused on him again.

"Not yet, but I'll come up with some," she promised. She swallowed the ice chip and smiled. "I was just thinking about the day Henry was born."

"Or the night, since it was two A.M.," Mike said.

"Best and worst night of my life," she said.

"Yeah," Mike said. "You were a trouper."

Another compliment from him, she thought. The alcohol emboldened her to ask a question. "Did you ever resent giving me child support?" she asked.

Mike shook his head so quickly that she knew he was telling the truth. "Nope," he said. "It was our deal. And you had to get a two-bedroom so Henry would have space . . ."

"And I had to drop out of beauty school," she reminded him. "I couldn't stand the smell of the chemicals." She'd been on track to get her aesthetician's certificate two months before Henry would have been born. She would've been able to earn more money with it, maybe even do freelance facials for rich women who tipped well. But once she'd left school and forfeited her tuition, she hadn't felt able to go back. Juggling work with partial custody of Henry and trying to have a life of her own consumed all her energy. There wasn't any room for school and studying.

Christie regarded Mike, knowing she might be about to cross a line. She'd complained about Jamie a few times, and Mike had put on his stoic cop face and nodded and said nothing, which had made the words dry up in her mouth. She'd always felt a little unclean afterward, denied the release she'd been seeking.

"It's just that Jamie said something today," Christie said.

Mike nodded impassively, as she'd expected him to.

"She called me a mooch, actually."

Mike frowned. "You sure about that?"

"Um, yeah," Christie said. "She was screaming at me. It was kind of hard to miss it."

"Huh," Mike said. He lifted his drink to his lips and took a sip.

"I just wanted to make sure you didn't feel that way," Christie said. "We've always had a good relationship"—well, *good* might be a stretch but the glow of the alcohol and their recent camaraderie softened the rough edges of the past—"and I don't want you to resent me."

"I don't," Mike said.

"Okay," Christie said. "And I know I told you I don't need any more child support. I mean it, Mike."

"Yeah," he said. He drained his drink before speaking again. "About that. I'm not getting paid any longer, because of the indictment."

"Assholes," Christie said. "They know how to kick a guy when he's down."

"So if you're sure, it would . . . help," he said.

She knew what it cost him to say those words. His pride was being stripped away in huge swaths, like sheets of old wallpaper.

"Hey," she said softly. She stood up and moved to sit next to him. "They're going to learn they were wrong. I bet you could even sue the city or something."

Mike nodded but didn't look convinced. "One thing I wanted to ask your guy Elroy is for some advice," he said. "I have to choose between a public defender and the lawyer I've got now."

"Do you like the guy you already have?" Christie asked.

"*Like* is a little strong," Mike said. "But he seems like he knows what he's doing. And the public defender would be a crapshoot. Most of them are really good, but what if the one I get isn't? I mean, what do you think?"

"I'll ask Elroy right away," Christie said. "But I'd say if the guy you already have is good, you should stick with him." She was surprised that Mike was asking her advice, since people didn't usually come to her for it.

"He's expensive, though," Mike said. "Maybe it's not worth it."

"Hey!" she said. "You deserve the best, Mike, no matter what it costs!" She reached out and put a hand on his broad shoulder, feeling the hard muscles beneath her touch. He had a heavy five o'clock shadow, and she wondered if he still shaved twice a day, like he used to when they were together. He'd been too macho to use the Calvin Klein cologne she'd given him for his birthday long ago, but whatever drugstore body wash he was using now smelled really good.

"Anyway," he said, getting up, "I should get going."

"Okay," she said. She pushed herself to a standing position, noticing the couch under her hand still felt warm from Mike's body heat. He'd always seemed to run a degree or so hotter than other people. It used to drive her crazy when he slept over; she'd end up kicking off all the covers to compensate.

She walked him to the door, but before he opened it, she impulsively leaned over and kissed his cheek. "Get the best lawyer," she said. "Whatever it costs. You didn't do anything wrong. You're innocent!"

His eyes met hers, and she felt something arc between them. She held his gaze, leaning forward slightly, feeling her lips part.

"Mom?"

Mike turned away from her as Henry called out from his bedroom.

"Could you get me a glass of milk?" Henry asked.

"He's old enough to get it himself," Mike said. He cleared his throat. "Let me know when your boss wants to meet, okay?"

Christie nodded. She felt a little dazed. Had she really been about to kiss Mike?

"And remember David's mom is coming to pick Henry up tomorrow morning," Mike said. "They're going to baseball camp this week. You should remind him to pack tonight. Tell him not to forget his new cleats."

"Right," Christie said absently.

Mike gave her a little wave and stepped out, shutting the door behind him. Christie stayed in place for a moment. She couldn't hear his footsteps going down the hallway and she wondered if he was standing just outside the door, gathering himself. She stayed very still, afraid of disturbing whatever thought process he was in the midst of.

She'd been too young and immature to appreciate him when they'd first met. But you sometimes heard stories about couples reuniting after years or decades apart. It could happen.

She could tell Mike's marriage was in trouble. On the night that they'd shared pizza, Mike had indicated Jamie wasn't supporting him—at least that's what Christie had thought he'd been going to say before he cut himself off. Christie wondered if that was the only reason he'd begun to open up to her, or if there were deeper fault lines in his marriage, a hidden volcano on the verge of eruption. With so many kids running around, it would be tough to ever have sex. And Mike had always liked sex—when they were together, he'd wanted her every time he saw her.

She also suspected Jamie was a little jealous of her. She'd seen the way Jamie looked at her at one of Henry's birthday parties several years back. They'd just cut the cake when one of the balloons tied to Henry's chair popped. At the sudden noise, Christie had clutched Mike's biceps and given a little shriek. Jamie had been pregnant with Eloise, and wearing one of those shapeless shift dresses, while Christie was in a tank top and tight jeans, and Jamie's eyes had run over her from head to toe when Christie walked in.

Jamie had shot her a look, and Christie had let go of Mike's biceps.

A moment later Jamie was fluttering around, cleaning up wrapping paper from the presents Henry had opened and serving ice cream. Jamie sure put on a sweet face in public, but now

Christie knew what she was really like. Jamie had pushed her out of the house the night Mike came home after the shooting, and when Mike and Henry had had their fight, Jamie had wrapped her arms around them, deliberately leaving Christie standing alone. And at the Christmas pageant when Christie had worn the leather skirt, Jamie had probably been gossiping about her with the other snooty wives.

Who knew what Jamie said to Mike when they were alone? Christie thought, feeling her face grow hot. Maybe Jamie was whispering in his ear, poisoning Mike's feelings toward her. Maybe that was why Mike had always kept her at arm's length. Until now.

Christie reached for the phone and called Elroy. He picked up on the first ring.

"Listen, about the case against Mike . . ." she began, but Elroy cut her off.

"I was about to call you," he said.

"Do you have something already?" she asked.

"Maybe," he said. "But first I want to go back to the scene with Mike and have him walk us through it."

"Is tomorrow good?" Christie suggested.

"Sure," Elroy said. "Three o'clock?"

Christie thought for a moment. "How about six?" she countered.

"We just need to wrap up before it gets dark," Elroy said. "But that's fine."

If they met at 6:00 it would be natural to suggest she and Mike grab a beer afterward. They could talk about the case. Henry would be at sleepover camp, so her apartment would be empty. Maybe she'd ask Elroy for a ride downtown and Mike could drive her home.

Jamie's angry, red face flashed in her mind, but Christie thought, *You don't deserve him.*

Chapter Fourteen

WHERE WAS MIKE? HE'D left two hours ago to take Henry out to buy new baseball cleats, since Henry had outgrown his old ones, before dropping him at Christie's. He should have been back by now.

The buzzer on the oven sounded, and Jamie grabbed a pot holder and pulled out the tray of sizzling pork chops, then left the pan to cool on the stovetop. The kids were busy at the kitchen table, pulling apart rolls that came out of a can and arranging them on a baking sheet. And miracle of miracles, they were working in harmony.

"Remember to leave a little space between them," Jamie said.

She put on a pot of water to boil for mac 'n' cheese and pulled a bag of salad out of the refrigerator. Tonight they'd have a real family dinner, their first in a while. A shrink would probably say she was acting like one of those women who compulsively cleaned or exercised as a way of creating a pleasing superficial picture and avoiding dealing with their inner turmoil. But she didn't care. One nice dinner with her family, that was all she wanted. Mike at the head of the table, bowing his head and saying grace in his deep voice. The children pink-cheeked from the sun, their hair combed and hands folded. A basket of hot rolls being passed. An hour of normalcy. Was that too much to ask?

She'd been overly ambitious today. After her fight with Christie and the visit with Ritchie and Sandy, she'd bundled the kids into the minivan and headed to the store. Jamie had always been a careful shopper, clipping coupons and substituting generic for name brands, but today she'd splurged on three perfect pork chops—one for Mike, one for her, and one for the kids to take turns rejecting—from the butcher. At the last minute she'd added a six-pack of Budweiser to the shopping cart, so she and Mike could have a beer or two together. She'd turn on the sprinklers for the kids to run through, and they could catch fireflies. She and Mike could sit on the front steps, and she'd tell him how lonely she'd felt lately. She'd be the one to reach out, to try to break down whatever had arisen between them. Maybe they'd even make love for the first time in weeks, and he'd move out of the basement and back into their bed. She missed looking into Mike's eyes. She missed holding his hand, and dozing in his lap while he watched television.

Henry was leaving for a week of baseball camp tomorrow morning, and Sandy had offered to watch the other kids so Jamie and Mike could have a date. Maybe she'd suggest they do it tomorrow night. They didn't have to go anywhere special—they could even stay home together and watch a movie, like they used to back when they first met.

"Can I put on the frosting?" Eloise asked.

"These are biscuits, honey," Jamie said. "There is no frosting."

Without thinking, she reached to move the metal pan of pork chops with her bare hands. "Ouch!" She rushed to the sink to run her burned thumb and index finger under cold water.

Jamie heard a clatter and turned around to see the tray of biscuits bouncing off the floor. It landed dough side down, naturally.

"You broke it!" Eloise shouted at Sam.

"It's fine," Jamie said. She ran over and picked up the tray. She didn't look at the crumbs and bits of dirt sticking to the dough; she didn't want to think about how long it had been since she'd mopped her kitchen floor. "I'm going to show you a trick."

She took a sharp knife and sliced the very top layer of dough off each biscuit. "They'll be just as good," she promised as she popped the tray into the oven. "Emily, can you make the table look pretty? Maybe pick some flowers from the backyard so we can put them in a vase."

The backyard was a rectangle of grass bordered

with a hodgepodge of flowers, since every year Jamie and the kids picked out an assorted packet, dumped it into a hole, and covered it back up—that was the extent of her gardening—but Jamie hoped Emily would be able to find a zinnia or something.

Mike's beer! She'd put it in the freezer to chill and had nearly forgotten it. She pulled out the six-pack, glad to see no bottles had exploded, and set it in the refrigerator.

What next? She ran into the dining room and searched through the scarred old armoire she'd inherited from her parents' house for a table-cloth. She found a green one they usually used at Christmas and decided it would have to do. She swept the junk off the table and into an old grocery bag and set it in the corner. She laid out plates and silverware and plastic cups for the kids and glass beer steins for herself and Mike. She dumped the salad into a wooden bowl and took a bottle of Kraft ranch out of the refrigerator and put them side by side on the table. She filled a pitcher with ice water and brought it to the table, too. She didn't want to have to be jumping up and down during this meal, constantly fetching things.

She caught sight of the clock on the stove and frowned. It was after six o'clock. She reached for the cordless phone on the counter and dialed Mike's cell, but her call went straight to voice mail.

"It's me," she said, trying to keep her voice light and cheerful. "Dinner's almost ready, so . . . hopefully you're on your way home."

She felt a little light-headed and realized she hadn't eaten anything other than a quick bowl of cereal today. She opened the oven door and checked the biscuits. They looked golden brown and smelled out of this world. She pulled out the tray and took one off, biting into it and savoring the fluffy sweetness.

"I want one!" Eloise cried.

"You'll ruin your dinner," Jamie said, her full mouth taking away her authority.

"You had one!" Eloise protested.

"I just had a bite," Jamie said. "Just to test them and make sure they were good."

"But I'm hungry!" Eloise wailed. Tears rolled down her cheeks.

"I want one, too," Sam said, employing logic as his weapon. "It's not fair for you to try them and not give us any."

Emily came through the back door, her shoes tracking mud all over the mat and floor. She was holding an enormous branch from a hydrangea bush.

"I need a vase," she said.

"I want a cinnamon roll!" Eloise cried. She was gearing up for a full-on tantrum now, her little chest heaving.

"They're not cinnamon rolls, they're biscuits,"

Sam told her, sounding like a miniature professor.

"Just one bite each," Jamie said. She broke the rest of the roll into two pieces and gave one to Sam and one to Eloise.

"Hers is bigger," Sam pointed out.

"Why don't I get one?" Emily cried.

"We're just testing them," Eloise informed her, spitting crumbs across the table.

"She's gross," Emily said. "Don't talk with your mouth full!"

"Fine!" Jamie said. She broke another roll into thirds and gave a chunk to each child. "Everyone happy?"

She heard a sizzle and spun around to see the pot of water bubbling over. She reduced the heat, dumped in the macaroni noodles, and gave them a stir.

"I don't like mac 'n' cheese anymore," Eloise said.

Jamie muttered a curse under her breath. "Can we just have a nice dinner? Please?"

Where was Mike?

She called his cell phone again, but he didn't answer. She didn't leave a message this time.

He didn't show up for another hour. By then, the pork chops were cold, the salad was wilted, and the rolls were all gone. Jamie was on her second beer, her appetite having vanished. The kids were watching TV again; by this point she was beyond feeling guilty.

"Hey," Mike said as he walked through the door. She heard it slam heavily behind him. A moment later he came into the dining room.

"Did you guys already eat?" he asked.

Jamie let silence be her answer.

"I called you," she said. "A couple times."

He took his phone out of his pocket and looked at the screen. "It's dead."

"Where were you?" she asked.

"Driving around," he said.

Why didn't you want to come home to us? Jamie thought. True, he hadn't known about the special dinner, but Mike seemed to be taking every excuse to be away from them lately. No—away from her.

She stood up and began stacking the dirty plates and carrying them to the sink.

"I went to see Ritchie today," she said. She didn't bother to bring up the subject gently, as she'd originally planned. She was too angry. "He wants to testify for you. He'll tell them you're not a racist, and when they see how badly he's hurt they'll get it—the jury will know you were suffering."

Mike didn't react immediately. Then he said, "I told you I didn't want to ask Ritchie to do it."

"We have no idea what's going to happen during the trial!" she cried. "We have to have a strong defense!"

"Did it ever occur to you I might be found

not guilty?" he asked. "Did you ever think, hey, maybe we should get Ritchie to testify that my husband doesn't react unless there's a real threat, instead of trying to trot out my black friend to prove I'm not a racist?"

"I can't afford to think that way, Mike! I don't know what kind of people are going to be on the jury. We've got to save you any way we can!"

He shook his head. "Is that where you were today? Seeing Ritchie? Did you even have to go to the doctor?"

"Yes, I lied to you, okay? Because I knew you'd never ask him!" Why was he being so obtuse? She blasted the sink water, rinsing off the dishes and stacking them in the dishwasher. The wheel got stuck, and when she jerked it the whole rack came out and crashed down onto her bare foot.

"Ouch!" she said. "Why haven't you fixed that?"

"I did," he said. "Twice. You keep pulling it too hard."

He came over, bent down next to her, and picked up the rack, and that's when she saw the pink mark on his cheek. It was very close to the corner of his mouth.

"What is that?" she asked. She reached out a finger and touched it.

"What?" he asked.

"Oh my God," she said, staring down at the sticky smudge on her fingertip. "Christie kissed you." She jerked back, scrambling to her feet. Mike jumped up and reached for her shoulders, forcing her to look at him.

"She kissed me good-bye on the cheek," he said. "After I dropped off Henry."

She could smell alcohol on his breath. "And you had a drink with her!" she cried. "That's why you were so late."

"Just one . . ." Mike said.

His voice was drowned out by the roaring in her head. She was shaking so hard she felt as if she'd implode. She'd done everything possible to hold their family together, while Mike was off with his ex-girlfriend. He'd lied to her, too, even if it was just a lie of omission. Christie had been overly flirtatious with Mike before. Even Mike had agreed that sometimes she tried to cross boundaries. Was that what had happened tonight?

Jamie began to cry and pushed him away.

"Fuck you," she said. "Our family is falling apart and you're out drinking with your ex." Her heart was pounding and her breath felt raggedy. She could still see a hint of pink on his cheek and she wanted to slap it off.

"Why are you so mad?" Mike looked incredulous. "Because of one drink?"

"It wasn't just one," Jamie said. "Was it?"

"What do you mean? I told you—"

"No," she said. "*Christie* told me. You had pizza and beer with her, too."

"Give me a break, Jamie. We talked, okay? That was all. We were talking about the case. Can't I even talk to her?"

Not when you don't talk to me, Jamie thought. A hurricane had swept through her body, leaving it bruised and battered. Her head was so muddled and heavy it was impossible for her to think about anything but the terrible smudge of pink on her finger.

"All you do is sit in the basement," Jamie said. "It's obvious you don't want to be around me. You won't even sleep with me anymore!"

"So everything's my fault," Mike said. His voice was so flat it was almost worse than if he were yelling. At least if he were yelling she'd know he still cared. "I'm guilty of everything, according to you. Good thing you're not on the jury."

He stormed out of the room, and she heard his heavy footsteps going upstairs. Then there was silence until Mike retraced his path downstairs and into the kitchen, where Jamie had slumped onto the dirty floor, next to the stupid broken dishwasher.

He was holding a duffel bag in each hand.

"When did you stop believing in me?" he asked. She blinked and looked up at him. His gaze was steely, but it flickered away a second after she met his eyes. It was as if he could hardly bear to look at her.

"Nothing happened with Christie," he said. "Nothing ever has."

"This isn't just about her," Jamie said. "You're not the only one in trouble. You abandoned me, Mike!"

"You're right," he said. "This isn't about her at all."

Then he took his bags and left the room.

"Where are you going?" she called out, but the only answer she heard was the slamming of the front door.

Chapter Fifteen

THE SKY CYCLED THROUGH darkness, then began to turn light again as Tabby entered her second day of labor. Lou leaned against the fence, her mind drifting. She'd meant to check in with Jamie last night, but she'd been so focused on Tabby she'd forgotten to call. Jamie had probably been too busy to chat anyway. Lou hadn't realized until she'd moved in how exhausting it was to constantly care for small children, and she wondered how Jamie found the strength to do it day after day—to cook meals, clean up endless spills, and referee squabbles, to ease socks onto wiggling little feet and cajole reluctant kids to change into pajamas and brush their teeth and get into bed, to read storybooks and throw in a load of laundry before racing back upstairs to warn the kids to stop talking and go to sleep, to do the hundreds of other things Jamie did every single day, so reflexively she probably didn't even have to think about it. A mother's love could power you better than any race car's motor, Lou thought.

"Doesn't Mike help with this stuff?" Lou had asked Jamie right after she moved in.

"Usually, yeah," Jamie had said. She'd been trying to wash Eloise's hands, which had inspired a shrieking fit in Eloise, who'd had a temporary tattoo applied to her wrist and was worried it would wash off. Jamie had finally rubbed a wet washcloth against Eloise's palms, made a game out of counting her teeth while she brushed them, and picked up and carried Eloise to bed when the little girl thrashed.

"We generally divide and conquer," Jamie had said. "Mike reads to Emily and Sam, or he tidies up downstairs while I do the bedtime routine. I'm just trying to give him a little break now, because of . . . everything."

Now Lou wondered if that was the only reason. It hadn't escaped her notice that Mike had been sleeping in the basement, or that a few days earlier, when Jamie had been entering the kitchen and Mike had been exiting it, he had pulled away abruptly, as if he didn't want to touch her even in passing.

It was obvious Mike was angry with her sister. But why? Lou wondered.

She puzzled over it for a few minutes, then gave up. She certainly was no relationship expert—just look at her history. The thought led her to wonder what Donny was doing at the moment. He and Mary Alice might be enjoying a late dinner, maybe pasta primavera or one of Donny's other specialties. They'd probably opened a nice bottle of Chardonnay, and were talking about the upcoming wedding. She needed to send Donny an email, to see if he wanted to have coffee. She hoped Mary Alice didn't mind if they stayed friends. Now that Lou was gone from the quiet, lovely apartment, she found herself reminiscing about all the things she'd liked most about Donny: the way he turned on classical music when he got ready in the morning and could always name the composer, the way he lined up his shoes when he came home from work, the left always touching the right, like they were a married couple settling in for the night.

She wondered again what had kept her from wanting to stay with him. He didn't have any glaring flaws, so it had to have been her fault. She'd hit a limit with her two previous boy-friends, as well—something that kept her from turning the corner to real commitment. She'd even seen a shrink after Jamie suggested it.

"There isn't anything wrong in talking to someone about things that you're struggling with," Jamie had said. "I think it's kind of heroic, actually. Not many people are willing to do hard work on themselves."

"Heroic?" Lou had said. "You're giving this the hard sell, aren't you?"

Because Lou had returned to college to study zoology, she was eligible for cheap on-campus counseling. It wasn't like she had any pressing social obligation tying up her Thursday nights anyway. She'd made an appointment through the student center and gone in for a session. Lou figured they'd chat for a bit and maybe she'd get some sort of prescription—she wasn't sure for what—but it hadn't happened that way. The shrink had merely smiled at her, taken out a new legal pad and a freshly sharpened pencil, and sat down across from Lou.

Uh-oh, Lou had thought, feeling as if she was in for more than she'd bargained for.

"Tell me about your family when you were growing up," the therapist had begun. She had close-cropped brown hair and slightly slanted brown eyes and perfectly manicured fingernails. She wore a chocolate brown wrap dress and matching heels, and despite her warm smile, she intimidated Lou.

"Growing up?" Lou had echoed.

"Yes," the therapist had said.

So Lou had talked a little bit about Jamie and how they'd shared a room. She'd mentioned how she'd walked to school and had swum the backstroke for the neighborhood pool's swim team for a few years.

"Were you close to your parents?" the shrink had asked.

"Sure," Lou had said.

"What sorts of things did you do together?"

"Oh, you know," Lou had said. "The usual."

The therapist had set her pencil down on her pad, folded her hands, and waited. That was the thing about shrinks, Lou thought. They got paid by the hour, so they were perfectly comfortable with long silences. Silences didn't bother Lou, either, but paying money for nothing did, so she tried to come up with something.

"Cereal," Lou had finally said. "Jamie and I each got to pick a new box of cereal every week. Whatever we wanted—Lucky Charms, Cocoa Puffs. That was breakfast every day."

"Mmm," the therapist had murmured, and Lou had hidden a laugh, wondering if they learned how to make that noise in shrink school or from watching television.

"When something upset you in school, did you talk to your mom or your dad about it?" the therapist had asked after a long pause.

"Um," Lou had said. "Well, I guess I mostly talked to Jamie. But I don't get upset all that easily."

The therapist had scribbled something on the pad. "Was your mother a stay-at-home mom?"

This Lou knew the answer to: "Yes."

"Do you think she enjoyed doing it?"

Lou had frowned. "It's hard to say." She'd realized she was squirming and she tried to be still. The therapist was waiting for her to elaborate, so she might as well.

"I actually don't have a lot of memories of my

mother," she'd said. "She died when I was twelve, so . . ."

The therapist had looked up suddenly. "What do you remember?" she'd asked.

"Almost nothing," Lou had said. The therapist had waited. "Nothing, really."

The therapist had just nodded and written something else in her pad.

"Is that strange?" Lou had asked. That was the thing about therapy; it made you curious about yourself. Which led to more sessions and more money for the therapists. Sneaky, that therapy.

"I wouldn't say strange," the shrink had said. "Sometimes we block out memories that can cause us pain. It's the mind's way of protecting ourselves."

"Like selective amnesia?" Lou had asked.

"In a way," the therapist had said. She seemed to have a Ph.D. in vague answers.

"Anyway, most of my memories are of Jamie," Lou had said. "I have lots of them."

"Your sister sounds special to you," the therapist had said.

"Yeah," Lou had said. "She is."

They'd talked awhile longer, and the therapist had suggested Lou come back next week, and Lou had nodded politely and canceled the appointment the following day. And that was that for her flirtation with therapy.

Tabby climbed out of the pool and came over to

stand near Lou, her muscular trunk stretching through the fence. Lou reached out and stroked it. An elephant's trunk was magical—strong enough to uproot a small tree, and dexterous enough to pluck a single blade of grass. Lou thought Tabby might resume pacing, but instead, she stayed by Lou.

Lou looked into the beautiful creature's eyes, which seemed endlessly wise, and she kept a hand on Tabby's soft, rough trunk.

"Everything is going to be okay," Lou promised, hoping with her whole heart it would be true.

Chapter Sixteen

CHRISTIE WONDERED IF A tiny piece of her had loved Mike all along. Years ago, she'd been having dinner with a friend who was divorced, and her friend had confessed she hated seeing parts of her ex in their children—she cringed when they talked about going to his alma mater for college, and she let her son grow his hair long, because her ex had always worn his in a military cut. But Christie had never minded seeing Mike's expressions cross Henry's face or watching his hair darken until it perfectly matched his father's. Had that been a clue her feelings for Mike had always been murkier than she'd believed? Sure, they'd had their share of arguments through the years, but those differences had tapered away until they'd stopped altogether a couple of years ago. Christie couldn't even remember the last time she'd had a disagreement with Mike.

Early on, of course, there had been many. Immediately after Henry was born, when Christie was still aching and dazed, Mike had infuriated her by asking if she'd breast-feed (his timing so exquisitely bad). When she'd said no, he'd tucked a pro-breast-feeding pamphlet into Henry's diaper bag with a Post-it that said, "Read me, please." Christie had torn the pamphlet in two and returned it to the diaper bag, and it had eventually disappeared. But Christie had conceded to some of Mike's wishes. She'd let Mike have Henry baptized, and she'd gone to the ceremony, even though she typically never set foot in churches except for weddings, and even then she sometimes skipped the ceremony and headed straight to the reception. The service was the first time she'd met Mike's parents and siblings, and she'd breathed a sigh of relief that she wouldn't have to sit around with them at holiday meals—his mother was a ninny, the brothers talked over one another in a nonstop game of one-upmanship, and the whole group seemed loud and larger than life, except for the father, who kept sneaking out to his car to turn on the radio and listen to, inexplicably, weather updates.

Christie glanced at the kitchen clock. She'd texted Mike that morning to let him know Henry had gotten safely off to sleepaway camp and to confirm the meeting with Elroy. Mike had responded immediately, saying he'd be at the spot of the shooting at the appointed time.

Now only an hour remained until she'd see him again. She felt a tingle in her lower belly and she went to get dressed in the outfit she'd chosen after some deliberation—her most flattering jeans and a simple pink cotton top. She didn't go overboard with her makeup, either. She wanted to connect with Mike honestly. If he was having serious issues with Jamie, as she suspected, she'd be a friend for him. And, someday, maybe more. She wondered how Mike felt about her now. Maybe that was why Jamie had been so awful to her; maybe she felt threatened. Christie felt the ire rise inside her as she thought again about how Jamie had degraded her.

From now on, she was going to interact with Mike directly. That's how it should have been all along. How had Jamie managed to worm her way between them, with her tight-lipped, superior smiles?

Christie looked in the mirror as she applied a clear lip gloss. There definitely were lines around her eyes, spreading outward like cracks in a mirror, and her lips seemed a little thinner, too. Aging was like climbing aboard a train—it started gradually, the scenery outside your window changing so slowly you weren't sure if everything else around you was shifting or if it was you that was moving, then it accelerated suddenly, catching you off guard. Maybe that was part of the reason most of the things she'd wanted a decade ago had lost their luster. Trips to Vegas and Cancún were expensive, partying even more than two nights a week left her exhausted and haggard, and living in a crummy apartment no longer seemed as if it was a stepping-stone to something better; it was pathetic. The truth was, she'd been scarred by Simon and Jim, and by the guys before them, too, like the one she'd married who'd had a dozen texts from other women on his iPhone when she scrolled through it a week after their wedding. Then there were the guys who'd had sex with her, given a satisfied grunt, rolled over, and gone to sleep without a word. Their faces blended together, all of the men who'd taken her for granted or used or mistreated her.

She applied a single squirt of Bobbi Brown's Beach perfume to the hollow of her throat and went downstairs to wait for Elroy in the lobby. He pulled up a few minutes later in his ancient Volvo, and she got in the passenger's side, brushing fast-food wrappers off the seat and hoping there weren't any lingering ketchup smears before sitting down.

"Mike meeting us there?" he asked.

Christie nodded.

"I got that Mace you wanted," Elroy said. He gestured to the glove compartment, and Christie opened it. Inside was a small canister with a nozzle. Christie took off the cap, and Elroy nearly drove off the road. "Mind not aiming that thing at me? I got you industrial strength."

"Sorry," Christie said, replacing the cap.

It would be intensely satisfying to wait in the darkness outside Jim's house, biding her time until he took out the trash. Bam! She'd squirt the entire canister into his face. She pictured him in his boxers and bare feet—they were probably stark white and hairy—writhing helplessly on the ground, tears streaming from his eyes. She'd never asked Elroy what happened to the video, but she hoped Jim's wife had seen it, and had run far away from him.

"Got a few new cases," Elroy said. "Up for starting again tomorrow?"

"Sure," Christie said. She ran her fingers over the cool metal of the can. It would never be out of her reach.

Elroy cut down a side street, then took a sharp right, following a path to downtown that Christie had never before taken. "Is this a shortcut?" she asked.

Elroy nodded. "At this time of day, with traffic, it's usually the quickest. If it wasn't rush hour, I'd take the bridge."

"Are you one of those people who can drive anywhere if you've been there once?" Christie asked, thinking of Lou.

"Guess you could say that," Elroy said.

Christie pulled down the passenger's-side visor to check herself in the mirror, suddenly feeling nervous about seeing Mike again, which was equal parts silly and thrilling. A picture of a woman was clipped to the visor. She had curly blond hair and a big smile.

"Who's this?" Christie asked.

Elroy kept his eyes on the road. "My wife," he said.

"You're married?" Christie asked. Somehow it surprised her; would a married guy drive a car full of fast-food wrappers and dress like that?

"Ex-wife," Elroy mumbled.

"Sorry," Christie said. Something clicked into place; she thought she knew why Elroy had taken on this job. "Did she cheat on you?" Christie blurted.

"No." He shook his head.

Christie frowned; she would've bet money that she was right. They drove another mile, with Elroy expertly weaving in and out of traffic, then he broke the silence.

"I cheated on her," Elroy said. He cleared his throat. "And I lost her."

Christie sensed the pain contained in those simple words, and she reached out and touched his hand. Sweet Elroy, with his courtly manners and cowboy hat, had probably messed up the best thing that had ever happened to him.

"Anyway," Elroy said, his voice businesslike now, "this week we've got a wife who found a pair of panties in her husband's car. He tried to blame it on the parking lot attendant at his office, said he must've been having a little fun during his break, but she knows. He's in a bowling league on Thursday nights, so you can catch him there."

"Is she sure he really bowls?" Christie asked.

Elroy nodded. "She followed him once. She did as much as she could on her own before calling us. Then we've got a bride-to-be who's worried about what went on at the bachelor party. The wedding's in six days, so we need to move fast. In this case we'll need you to try to get the story out of the groom if he doesn't come on to you."

"I'm ready," Christie said. She closed the visor, sealing away the photo of Elroy's ex-wife. She wondered if he regretted telling her.

They rode in silence until they reached the scene of the shooting and she saw Mike. Elroy pulled into the parking lot and turned off the ignition. Mike didn't seem to notice their arrival; he was standing with his hands in his pockets, staring at the ground, at a memorial of dying flowers, a teddy bear, and a spray-painted RIP JOSE across the pavement.

Christie opened the car door and hurried toward him. "Hi," she said. She turned around and waited for Elroy to approach. "This is Elroy. Elroy, this is Mike, my—" She paused. In the past, she'd introduced Mike as "my son's father." But today, something made her say "my good friend."

She saw Mike smile at her, as if he understood the shift in the relationship.

"Thanks for coming," Mike said. He reached out and shook Elroy's hand.

Elroy nodded. "Can you walk me through what

happened?" he said. "Then maybe we can go talk."

Mike nodded. "Sure," he said, although Christie saw a white line form around his lips, vivid against his tan skin. She hadn't thought about how difficult this would be for him. She wondered whether Mike had returned to this spot since the shooting.

"We, ah, entered from this angle," Mike said. He took a few steps away from them and twisted to the right. "Jay was ahead of me." Mike pointed. "And the, ah, the teenager was over there. When it happened, I mean. About where the flowers are."

"Okay," Elroy said. "Just take me through it, nice and slow, from the beginning." He didn't write anything down or videotape it, but Christie saw how carefully he was watching. He was motionless, his eyes fixed on Mike.

"We got the call and pulled in. We left the cruiser there." Mike gestured to a spot near Elroy's battered Volvo. "Jay, the guy I was partnered with, he started running," Mike said. "He pulled out his pepper spray and held it up." Mike's hand went to his belt and he demonstrated. Mike seemed almost in a trance now, his words a soft monotone. "That's about when I got hit. I spun around. When I turned back, Jay was ahead of me. He's yelling for the guy to freeze, then I see the motion to grab a weapon. I see the gun come up and I draw and shoot."

Elroy nodded. Christie held her breath. Mike

was staring straight ahead, to where Jose had fallen. She watched as Mike slowly approached that spot, then got down on his knees and touched a finger to one of the dying red roses. Christie thought she saw his lips move.

Elroy gave him a moment. "Let's go through it again," he said. "Christie, can you take Jay's spot?"

Elroy went over and stood next to the memorial. He looked around, and Christie saw him taking in the parked cars nearby, the building behind them, the road running parallel. Elroy was odd, but something in his expression told Christie he was brilliant.

While Christie walked over to where Jay had been standing, an old car that needed a new muffler slowed down as it cruised by the parking lot. The young guy at the wheel wore reflective sunglasses, but Christie thought he was staring at them. When she looked back, though, the car turned the corner and disappeared.

"Okay," Elroy said. "Let's do it."

He took them through the scene three more times, like they were actors preparing for a play.

"Why isn't he saying anything?" Mike asked Christie at one point while Elroy squatted down in the position Jose had held at the time of the shooting, shielding his eyes as he stared in the direction Mike and Jay had come from.

"He's busy thinking," Christie said.

Finally Elroy straightened up and came toward

them, his gait in his old cowboy boots as unhurried as ever. "You guys know Jay worked in California before coming here, right?" Elroy asked.

"No," Mike said. "Actually I didn't. I barely talked to the guy. He couldn't shut up, so I always tried to tune him out."

"Well, it's not like the prosecutor is going to volunteer any information to you," Elroy said. "Anyway, he put in three years on the force. I talked to his old partner. He couldn't say enough good about the man."

Christie stared at Elroy. By now she knew him well enough to know more was coming.

"Then I talked to another guy on the force. Off the record, of course," Elroy said. "He wasn't so keen on Jay."

Mike's expression transformed; his eyes turned bright and his face grew alert. "What'd he say? You've got something, don't you?"

"They pulled over a car once and Jay missed seeing a bag of coke on the passenger's floor," Elroy said. "Guy had a piece in the glove compartment, too. He didn't reach for it, but they never would've found it if the other officer hadn't spotted the coke. Thing was, Jay was standing on that side of the car. He was closer."

Christie felt a flush of excitement. "I'm telling you, there could be something wrong with his eyes!"

Elroy quashed that hope. "He would've undergone a vision test regularly to be a cop."

"But he missed seeing something important," Mike said.

"That he did," Elroy agreed.

Mike closed his eyes for a second and swallowed hard. "You don't know what this means to me."

"Hey, it's not going to win you the case," Elroy said. "There's still the issue of the missing gun."

Christie caught motion out of the corner of her eye and saw the same old car driving past the parking lot again. She reached into her purse for her Mace and closed her fingers around the cool metal.

"Maybe we should go somewhere else to talk?" she suggested.

She saw Mike follow her eyes and take in the car. "Yeah," he said. "Probably a good idea."

"You want to follow us?" Elroy suggested.

"Actually," Mike said, "I took the Metro here. I, ah, had to turn in my cruiser a while ago."

"So hop in," Elroy said. Christie felt as if she couldn't get into Elroy's Volvo quickly enough. The old car was still there, idling at the stop sign. There were three guys in it now. She couldn't be sure, but she thought there had been only one previously.

Maybe the guys had known Jose. Maybe they'd recognized Mike.

She and Mike and Elroy all climbed into the car without another word, and Christie locked her door.

"So where to?" Elroy asked, starting the engine and pulling out the exit that would put them farthest away from the idling car.

"Why don't we head back toward my place?" Christie said. "We can get a drink around there."

Mike kept twisting around to look out the back window, and Elroy's eyes flicked to the rearview mirror every minute or so. "Are they behind us?" Christie asked.

"Nope," Elroy said, and she released the breath she didn't realize she'd been holding.

They were all quiet for the rest of the drive. They found a pub in Arlington and got a table for three. Elroy ordered a vanilla milk shake along with French fries—Christie didn't want to think about his cholesterol—and Mike asked for a Coke.

"No beer?" Christie asked. She'd imagined them having a cocktail together, then maybe moving on to dinner. The table was a disappointment, too; she'd been hoping for a booth.

Mike shook his head. "I'm not drinking any-more."

"Since when?" Christie asked.

"Since now," he said. "I want my head to be clear."

He turned to Elroy. "So what happens next?"

Mike asked. "And man, I can't tell you how much I appreciate this. I don't know what your hourly rate is—"

Elroy held up a hand. "You're not paying me anything," he said. "Truth is, I kind of like being back on a real case. So, the next step is I want you to write everything down. I know you've done it already, but you were probably defensive before, right?"

"Yeah, but I told the truth," Mike said.

"That's not what I meant," Elroy said. "You were probably just focusing on your actions related to the shooting—what you saw, what happened to you. I need you to look at things with a wider lens. Take time to really go through it all like a movie, frame by frame. Look at things in the corners of the picture. Write down every single detail, even things that don't seem important."

"Okay," Mike said. "I can do that." He hung his head, and Christie barely heard his next words: "I've been doing that every night, pretty much."

Christie's cell phone buzzed in her purse, but she ignored it.

"I'm going to do some more checking in the meantime," Elroy said.

"Are you going to look more deeply into Jay's background?" Christie said.

"Yup," Elroy said. "That's top on the list."

396

Mike's cell phone rang a moment after Christie's stopped.

Jamie, Christie thought. Did she know they were together?

"I better get this," Mike said. He answered and listened for a moment. His forehead creased, and he looked up at Christie. Something in his expression made her heart drop.

"When did this happen? Can I talk to him?"

Not Jamie, Christie thought. It was worse. It was Henry.

"That's ridic—You know what? Fine. I'll be there as soon as I can," Mike said.

He hung up and got to his feet in one fluid motion. "Henry got in a fight at baseball camp," he said.

"Is he okay?" Christie cried. She'd kill anyone who'd hurt her baby.

"He's the one who started the fight," Mike said. He reached into his wallet, extracted a twenty, and put it down on the table. "He's getting thrown out of camp. We need to go pick him up."

"What? He's only been there a day. What could have happened?" Christie slung her purse over her shoulder. "We can take my car. It's in the lot at my apartment building."

Elroy stood up, reaching for his cowboy hat. "I'll drive you there."

"Thank you," Christie said. She impulsively reached out and gave him a hug. He was such an odd, dear man. The thought came to her that he was perhaps the only man in her life who could become a friend. Other than Mike, of course.

"Did they tell you anything else?" Christie asked.

Mike shook his head. "Henry wouldn't have done this unless someone provoked him. It had to have been about me," he said.

"Not necessarily," Christie said. "It could have been about a girl. It could have been about anything!"

Mike just shook his head again.

"Hey," Christie said. "We're going to get through this together, okay? We'll go help our son now, and then Elroy's going to get these stupid charges dropped."

"Okay," Mike said, looking at her with such gratitude that her heart seemed to swell inside her chest.

Ever since the previous evening, when Mike had packed his bags and left, Jamie had felt numb, unable to eat or think clearly. Shock, she thought, looking down at the slim gold band on her left hand. When Mike had slipped it onto her finger all those years ago, staring at her with his intense eyes, so handsome her knees had gone rubbery, she'd decided she'd never remove it. And she hadn't, even when her fingers had swelled during pregnancy and it had bitten into her flesh.

Six months ago—no, three!—she would've said she had a great marriage. Not a perfect one, but a solid union, something that would endure through the years, weathering bumps, growing sweeter when one of their kids got married and she and Mike danced cheek to cheek at the wedding, and when they looked down at the face of their first grandchild.

Now she had no idea where Mike had gone, or if their marriage was shattered beyond repair.

Jamie walked over to the kitchen table and sat down, her eyes gritty and her limbs heavy. She should have fed the children dinner at least an hour ago, but instead she'd opened the snack drawer and told them to have at the granola bars and Pirate's Booty. On a normal evening, the kids would be taking baths now, or changing into pajamas. But Jamie no longer cared about bedtimes or nutrition. The routines that had given shape to their days had been blasted apart.

She wondered what Jose's mother was doing at this exact moment, if she was also fighting to stay upright when everything in her begged to collapse to the floor. Lucia had another son to care for, and maybe that was the only thing keeping her going. Jamie thought about what she'd read in the papers, that Lucia was a single mother who worked as a receptionist at a doctor's office. Church was a constant in her life.

Lucia Torres sounded like a good person, Jamie

thought. Maybe she talked to patients who'd gotten scary diagnoses, promising to pray for them and bringing them glasses of water as they waited to be seen. She might give them a reassuring pat on the arm as she murmured words of comfort.

Church was probably even more important to her now, Jamie thought. She wondered if Lucia was going to services every day, lighting candles and taking communion. Praying for her lost boy.

Maybe Jamie should start going to church more often, too. Wasn't it supposed to be a place filled with forgiveness and love? She could desperately use some of that.

Forgiveness.

Jamie was on her feet before she realized she'd had the intent to move, her fatigue falling away.

"Kids?" she called, and for once, they appeared in the kitchen on cue. All three of them.

"We have to get in the minivan, now," Jamie said. She couldn't believe she hadn't thought of this before. It was a way out, maybe the only way out. She grabbed her iPhone from the charger on the counter and Googled the Whitepages website. Luck was with her; she found the address she needed quickly.

She wondered briefly if driving was safe, since she still felt strange—outside of herself, almost, as if she was a bystander watching a Jamie clone in action—but a sudden surge of energy was overpowering her sleeplessness, more than compensating for her recent insomnia.

Eloise was struggling to strap on her sandals, so Jamie just scooped her up, shoes and all, and ran to the minivan and deposited her in her seat. When Sam and Emily came outside the dog followed them, so Jamie just motioned for everyone to get into the vehicle, even Sadie.

"Hurry!" she called, adrenaline thrumming through her veins. The sky was turning a dusky purple; she had to rush before it got too late. "Let's go!"

The kids were remarkably obedient; they climbed into the van, strapped themselves in, and sat without fighting or demanding the radio. In fact, they were quieter than Jamie could ever remember them being. Either they'd sensed the urgency brewing in their mother or too much television had left them in a semipermanent daze.

"Are we going to McDonald's?" Eloise asked.

"Maybe later," Jamie said. "We just have to do something first. Something really important."

Remarkably, everything went her way: traffic wasn't heavy, and lights turned green as she approached. The kids stayed quiet. No pedestrians cut in front of her car. Though she knew it wasn't possible, the whole city seemed poised, waiting for what would unfold. She reached her destination within twenty minutes. It was a minor miracle, a sign that her plan was the right one.

"You guys need to stay in the van while I go talk to someone," Jamie said. "It's really important. Maybe the most important thing I've ever asked you to do."

"Where are we?" Sam asked, looking out his window. They were parked by a curb in front of a three-story, industrial-looking, gray building.

"We're doing something to help Daddy," Jamie said. "Here." She handed her iPhone to Eloise to ward off any potential problems. "You guys watch her, okay? You'll be able to see me the whole time. I'm going to be standing right at that door. Just don't get out."

She stepped out of the minivan and hurried to the building's doorway. She ran her finger down the listing of apartment numbers behind Plexiglas and found the right one. She pushed the corresponding button. Her luck held: Someone answered, the voice coming through the intercom garbled and fuzzy, but Jamie could tell it belonged to a woman: "Hello?"

"This is Jamie Anderson," she said. "Michael Anderson's wife. Please, can you just come down here for a moment? I'd like to talk."

She waited, but there wasn't a reply. She stood in the twilight, wondering what would happen next. *Please,* she thought, clasping her hands together. There were some dents and scuff marks near the bottom of the door, as if someone had tried to kick their way in, and the lower windows were protected by metal bars. But someone had planted yellow petunias in a window box, and an American flag hung off a nearby balcony, billowing in the gentle breeze. An in-between place, she thought.

She turned around to check on the children, and when she glanced back, the door was opening to reveal a tall, thin woman.

"What is it?" asked Lucia Torres. The skin on her face looked haggard, and her eyes were puffy, as if she'd been crying recently.

"Thank you," Jamie said. She meant to say more—thank you for listening, maybe—but when she glimpsed the deep sorrow on Jose's mother's face, her throat turned dry and her eyes wet.

Ms. Torres wore a simple blue dress, not unlike one Jamie owned. Her expression was shifting, becoming more wary.

"I wanted to tell you how sorry I am," Jamie finally said. "I'm so sorry about Jose." The tears in her eyes spilled over, but she pushed on. "I know I'm asking for something I have no right to ask for."

Ms. Torres folded her arms. "*You* want something from *me?*"

"My husband . . . he's a good man. He has always looked out for kids from this neighborhood. He wouldn't have—He never would have hurt your son intentionally. It has ruined his life, too. He'll never be the same."

"Neither will me or my son," said Lucia evenly.

Jamie thought she meant Jose, but then she saw a head peeking around from Lucia's back and realized it must be Lucia's younger boy. A pair of big brown eyes stared up at her. Seeing that little face, so similar to his brother's, shredded Jamie. Jose had liked chicken with molé sauce. He'd carried home groceries for his mother. How could Lucia endure losing him?

Jamie forced herself to press on, knowing this would be her only chance. "I came to ask if you would just consider forgiveness," she said, her voice breaking. Tears were streaming down her cheeks now, her torrent of words matching their pace. "Maybe if the jury sees you don't want an eye for an eye, they won't punish Mike severely. There isn't anything more they could do to him—he's going to be in a kind of prison for the rest of his life no matter what. But my children"—Jamie's voice caught on a sob as she gestured toward the minivan just a dozen yards behind her, and she saw Lucia's eyes flick to the vehicle—"you see, they need their father. Please."

She thought she saw something soften in Lucia's face at the mention of the children, at the sight of her old minivan with the dented fender parked out front, Sam's small face peering out of one window, and Sadie in the passenger's seat with her furry head extended through another.

Jamie reached out and touched Lucia's hand.

"I'm begging you," she sobbed. "Mother to mother."

Lucia's face closed and she withdrew her hand. "Do you know my son was stopped and threatened by a cop when he was walking in his own neighborhood? Told to get home and stop causing trouble or the cop would give him real trouble? Tell me that didn't happen for any reason other than the color of his skin. Jose was ten years old. He cried that night and asked me why the policeman thought he was bad."

"I know those things still happen, and it's horrible," Jamie began. "But—"

Lucia cut her off. "You don't know. Not the way I do." She folded her arms. "Do you have a boy?"

"Yes," Jamie said.

"His experience growing up will be nothing like my son's. He won't be afraid of policemen, like Jose was. He won't have store clerks following him around, watching with angry eyes to see if he tries to slip something in his pocket when all he wants is to buy milk for our morning cereal. He won't have people cross to the other side of the street when they see him coming. You have no idea what life is like for our brown boys. Your son lives in a different world, one that doesn't automatically treat him with disrespect."

"You're right," Jamie said. "But my husband—I promise you—he isn't like that."

"There's nothing I can do," Lucia said in a flat voice. "Justice must be served."

She stepped back, and without looking at Jamie, she clicked the door shut.

"No!" Jamie cried. She wanted to bang on the door until her hands bled, to shout and beg and drop to her knees, but the children were watching. She gulped air as her body trembled compulsively. She'd hoped so desperately this would work. She'd imagined forging a connection with Jose's mother. She'd thought if Lucia could just see her as a woman, she would no longer view Mike as a villain. The prosecutor might even drop the charges. Mike would come home. Maybe the three of them could work together on some sort of task force, a way to pair at-risk youth with police mentors. They could try to honor Jose's memory.

But now, in the sudden stillness of the evening, she had no hope left. She had never felt so empty and alone.

"Mom?" Sam called out the window.

She did the only thing left to her. She wiped away her tears and turned and began walking back to her children.

"Okay if I film here?" the videographer asked, coming over to stand next to Lou with his tripod.

"Sure," she said. "I'll get out of your way."

"It's okay," he said, but Lou moved anyway. He might want to chat, to while away the time, and she wanted to focus exclusively on Tabby. She made sure the elephant saw her new position in case she wanted to come over again for reassurance.

It was growing dark now, on the second night of Tabby's labor, and when the videographer turned on his camera, a piercing white light shone on Tabby. Lou was on her feet in an instant.

"Turn that off! Now!" she demanded, catching herself just before she yelled. Tabby might be scared if Lou raised her voice; she'd never before heard anger coming from her keeper.

"The quality won't be as good if we don't have light," the videographer protested. "I can barely see her."

Lou strode over and ripped the power cord from his camera.

"Hey!" he said. "Careful! That's expensive!"

"Listen to me," Lou said. "No lights. No loud sounds. If you do anything to disturb her, I'm throwing you out of here."

Now she had a sense of how Jamie had felt that day at the mall.

"Sheesh," the videographer said. "Sorry." He reattached the cord and turned off the light.

Lou settled back down, a little closer to the videographer this time. Her stomach growled and she realized she hadn't eaten in hours. She reached into her pack for a PowerBar and a bottle of water.

Tabby had slept for a while this afternoon, and Lou had dozed along with her, but now the elephant was pacing again.

"It's okay," Lou called. "Good girl."

She was vaguely aware of the videographer turning his camera in her direction. Tabby came over to the fence again, and Lou reached into a basket for a sweet potato. Tabby took it from her open palm.

"Plenty more where that came from," Lou whispered. She hoped Tabby wasn't afraid.

The elephant tossed her trunk and began circling the enclosure again. Lou wanted to let her out so she could roam the miles of trail, but all the medical equipment was here. It would be too tough for everyone to follow her and get to her quickly in case of an emergency. Besides, the vet was napping on a cot a dozen yards away, so he'd be fresh if he was needed.

Lou took a sip of water and kept her eyes fixed on Tabby. Lou knew the birth would be sudden, almost violently so. They'd have very little warning before the baby slipped out and fell to the earth. Maybe Tabby would make a sound, or suddenly become very still. Lou wasn't sure what the signal would be, but she felt confident she'd recognize it when the moment arrived.

The elephant took long strides around the

perimeter of her enclosure, her tail swinging, her movement the only sign of her discomfort. Pacing . . . there was that word again, the one tickling at the edges of her mind.

Lou closed her eyes and tried to hold on to it.

Pacing was the only thing that helped. Someone had spoken those words to Lou. She could hear their echo, a tinny, faraway sound. Had it been Jamie, recounting the story of one of her kids' births? The memory fluttered away again.

"You got another PowerBar?" the videographer asked, his voice too loud. He was just a kid, maybe twenty-two, with a pimply chin and long hair. But Lou didn't regret being so hard on him; she'd do it again if she needed to.

Lou reached into her pack, grabbing a bottle of water, too, and walked over to hand the snacks to him.

"She needs quiet," Lou said, gesturing to Tabby. "If you want anything else, you come to me and whisper. But only if it's an emergency."

Instead of sitting down again, Lou began to walk, too, trying to keep up with Tabitha. Together they went back and forth, back and forth, Lou wishing she could absorb some of Tabby's discomfort.

Pacing was the only thing that helped.

Lou felt her eyes widen and her heartbeat stutter. It wasn't Jamie who had said that about labor.

Lou could hear the voice, low and soft and faintly musical, so clearly now. Suddenly the memory snapped into place.

The voice belonged to her mother.

Henry was waiting in the camp director's office, his T-shirt torn and his right eye swollen.

Christie wanted to run to him and throw her arms around his thin shoulders, but she knew it would embarrass him. Despite his defiant expression, she could tell from the quiver in his lips that he was struggling to hold himself together.

"Hey, buddy," Mike said. He reached out and tilted up Henry's chin. "You're going to have a serious shiner. Didn't they give you some ice for that?"

"I don't need ice," Henry said, jerking his chin out of Mike's hand. There was blood on the front of his shirt, too. It pained Christie just to look at it.

Suzanne, the camp director, cleared her throat. She was thirtyish, broad-shouldered and pink-cheeked, with khaki shorts and wheat-colored hair pulled into a ponytail—exactly the type of person you'd expect to be running a camp.

"As I said on the phone," Suzanne told them, "Henry was in a fight. I saw it myself. He threw the first punch."

"Henry wouldn't do it without a good

reason," Christie said. Of that she was certain.

"I'm all ears," Suzanne said. She squatted down next to Henry so she could look him in the eye, but Henry just shook his head.

"If he won't talk about what happened, we have no choice but to dismiss him immediately," Suzanne said. Christie had been prepared to yell at her, to call her on bureaucratic bullshit, but it was clear from her expression Suzanne didn't relish the thought of making Henry leave.

"I have a feeling this is probably unusual for Henry," Suzanne said as she straightened up. "He's only been here a day, but I saw him helping the younger kids with batting practice while the rest of his group was swimming."

Suzanne walked to the door and hesitated. "He won't tell me, but maybe he'll tell you," she said as she left, closing the door behind them.

Christie had no idea what to say. She wondered whether the onset of puberty was responsible for the changes in Henry, or if it was something more. She'd hidden so much from her mother—boyfriends, joints, cleavage-baring tops (though she'd hidden those only so her mother wouldn't borrow them). Maybe she'd been foolish to think that because Henry was kind and polite and a good student he'd be immune from the typical pressures of adolescence.

"Did someone say something to you about me?" Mike asked.

"Why do you think everything's about you?" Henry asked.

"Henry!" Christie was shocked.

"Look, it had nothing to do with that stuff," Henry said. "The guy was just a dickhead."

"Okay," Mike said calmly. "But you usually don't go around punching dickheads, which makes me think there's something more to it than that."

"Maybe," Henry said. "Can we just go already?" His duffel bag was near his feet. He probably hadn't even had a chance to unpack it.

Christie looked at Mike, who shrugged. "Sure," she said.

They opened the door, and Christie shook her head at Suzanne. "He wants to leave," she said.

"I understand," Suzanne said. "Henry, if you change your mind and want to talk about it, I'd still like to hear your side. You can call me anytime. Even after the session ends."

Henry nodded. "Okay," he said.

Suzanne touched Mike's forearm. "Usually we don't give refunds if kids are asked to leave, but in this case . . . Well, please call me," she said.

Mike nodded his thanks and shouldered Henry's bag, despite Henry's protest that he could carry it, and the three of them walked down the dirt path toward the parking lot. There were a half dozen wooden cabins nestled in the woods to the right, and a little farther off, Christie could see the sun setting low over the cool blue sheen of a lake. A few sailboats with bright masts were docked by the edge and a big tire swing dangled from the limb of a tall tree.

"How'd you find this camp?" she asked Mike. Despite whatever had happened to Henry here, it looked like a really nice place. Henry lived in the suburbs and certainly had access to parks and other green spaces, but there was nothing like this in Mike's neighborhood or in Christie's. Even though the camp was just sixty miles away, it was like something out of a storybook, an enchanted spot for kids.

"I didn't," he said. "Jamie did."

"Oh," Christie said. She thought about how Jamie had complained about paying child support, yet willingly put up money to send Henry here without even asking Christie to chip in. She wrestled with an unwelcome feeling of gratitude toward Mike's wife.

"I think we should go get something to eat," Christie said. "Are you hungry, Henry?"

"Do you even need to ask?" Mike joked.

Christie could tell they were on the same page; they'd silently agreed not to bring up whatever was troubling Henry for now, to keep the mood light and safe.

"Let's go find someplace with man food," Mike said. "No stinking salads for us." They reached the car, and Henry climbed into the backseat. The sky was completely dark now, and the Mercedes thrummed comfortably as they headed down the paved road.

After a few miles, the street widened into two lanes and they began seeing neon signs for gas stations and fast-food outlets.

"Is Wendy's okay? Or wait—how about Subway?" Mike asked. "There's one up ahead."

"Subway's good," Christie said at the same moment Henry said, "Okay."

They pulled into the parking lot and found a spot near the entrance. The place was deserted, so their food and sodas arrived quickly.

"I was thinking we could throw the ball around tomorrow," Mike said. "Just you and me."

Henry nodded and took a bite of his foot-long sub.

"Do you want to stay with your mom tonight?" Mike asked.

Henry shrugged. "Whatever."

"We'll figure it out later," Mike said. "Still got a ways to go before we get home."

They ate quietly for another minute, then Henry's voice erupted in the stillness. "I'm not going to apologize!"

"Okay," Mike said, again in that calm cop voice.

Christie didn't respond. She hoped Henry

would keep talking if they didn't bombard him with questions.

"There was this jerk who kept cheating!" Henry said. "He kept insisting he got on base when it was so obvious he was out. Then we played hoops and he was fouling this short guy nonstop. And I kept calling him on it, but he just gave me this stupid smile, like he knew exactly what he was doing. And then I see him trip the short guy when everyone was running out to the fields to practice getting fly balls before dinner. He did it on purpose. Just stuck out his foot, watched the guy go down, and then he kept running like he had nothing to do with it."

"Did you tell one of the counselors?" Christie asked.

Henry shook his head. "What's the point?"

"They're there to help you, buddy," Mike said. "They would've done something to the guy. Talked to him, or watched him more closely."

Henry shrugged. "He's the kind of guy who sucks up to adults. It would've been his word against mine."

Christie saw something flicker across Mike's face. He pushed away the rest of his sub.

"Listen to me," Mike said. "Never stop doing the right thing. It doesn't matter if they believe you or not."

Henry slumped back in his seat. He was still wearing his baseball cap, and the brim cast a shadow over his eyes. "Look where it got you," he said.

Mike closed his eyes, and Christie could see pain washing over his face.

"I get it," Mike said, opening his eyes again. "I messed up."

"But you said the guy had a gun—" Henry began to protest.

"That's not what I meant," Mike said. "But yeah, I thought he did. Every bit of training I've had, every instinct—Look, that doesn't matter. I did what I thought was right."

Mike leaned closer to Henry. "But then you saw people on the Internet attacking me, and your friends were saying stuff, and I was just sitting around the house doing nothing."

Henry began to cry then. "Are you and Jamie going to get divorced?" he asked.

Christie's eyes widened.

"What? Why do you say that?" Mike asked.

"Because you've been sleeping in the basement!" Henry said. He swiped his hand across his nose. His voice rose and cracked with his next sentence. "You think I didn't notice?"

Christie tried to hide her shock. Things were that bad between Jamie and Mike?

"Look, I've had insomnia, okay?" Mike said, his voice low. "That's why I started staying down there." He was lying, Christie thought. She wondered if Henry picked it up, too.

"Henry, we should talk about this privately later," Mike said. Christie looked down at the table and didn't say a word.

"I didn't know you felt this way . . . I guess I've been wrapped up in my own stuff. Seeing my best friend like that, knowing I might've been able to stop it if I'd only been faster . . . It killed me," Mike said.

"It wasn't your fault!" Henry blurted.

Mike reached across the table and grabbed Henry's hand. "Partners are supposed to protect each other."

Mike's eyes were nearly as red as Henry's now, and Christie could see a muscle in his jaw tensing. "After I went back to my beat, and—and everything happened and they said there wasn't a gun . . . I was first at the scene and even *I* couldn't find a gun . . . it did stuff to my mind. Made me wonder if I was going crazy. Sometimes I thought you guys might all be better off without me."

"Dad!" Henry burst out, his voice panicked.

"Don't worry," he said. "I'm not going to do anything. But maybe I should've talked to you."

He let go of his son's hand and took a sip of soda, then continued. "Your mom has been helping me. She and the detective she works with, that guy Elroy."

"You are?" Henry asked, turning to Christie. She nodded, feeling oddly shy.

"I don't think I'm going to be found guilty of anything, Henry," Mike said. "I thought I saw a gun, so I did the right thing in that moment. That's what I keep trying to tell myself, anyway."

"Was it weird?" Henry asked. "To kill someone?"

Christie saw Mike swallow hard. He didn't directly answer Henry's question, but in a way, he did. "I think about it all the time," Mike said. "All the time."

"I'm almost his age," Henry said, looking down at the napkin he was shredding.

Mike closed his eyes briefly. "That's the worst part," he said.

They were quiet for a moment, then Mike released a tired-sounding sigh. "Look, maybe I wanted to be punished. Maybe that's why I didn't fight back. Because even though I did what I thought I had to, he was just a kid . . ."

His voice trailed off.

Henry's tears had dried up, but Christie noticed his usually neat fingernails were chewed off. How had they missed the signs that Henry was suffering so? She'd been buying a Mercedes while her son was floundering. She wondered if Jamie had seen it and had come up with the money for camp because she sensed Henry desperately needed an escape.

"I felt like you never talked about it," Henry

said. "And it was all anybody else was talking about."

"You mean your friends?" Mike asked.

"And sometimes when I was at someone's house, I'd hear a mother on the phone say my name. Once I went into Brian's kitchen and his dad and mom were there. They got quiet and looked all guilty when they saw me," Henry said.

"I'm sorry you had to go through all that," Mike said.

Henry nodded and sniffed a few times. Then he looked down at his father's half-eaten sub. "Can I have that if you're not going to finish it?"

Christie laughed. Mike didn't join in, but at least he smiled, even though his face still looked sad. "I'll buy you another one," Christie said. "As many as you want."

"Look, why don't you go to your mom's tonight," Mike said. "I'll come for a while, too, if that's okay, and we can talk more. Christie can tell you what the private detective found." He looked at Christie.

She felt as if the three of them were ensconced in something as fragile and shimmering as a bubble. Whatever was unfolding now—she wasn't exactly sure what it was—felt beautiful and true.

"That would be really nice," she said, and she was rewarded by matching smiles from her son and his father.

Chapter Seventeen

MIKE'S ABSENCE WAS EVERYWHERE: in his blue toothbrush standing in a cup by the bathroom sink, in the empty running shoes by the front door, in the T-shirt in the basket of still-warm laundry Jamie was folding. She held the shirt against her front and folded down its arms, realizing her movements mimicked a hug.

It was nearly ten o'clock on the second evening after he'd left. As darkness had fallen, her regrets had begun to mount: the anger she'd flung at Mike, the way her effort to save him had led to an even bigger gulf, and her disastrous visit to Ms. Torres. She should have known what had happened would forever be unfixable. She couldn't get Jose's mother's haunted brown eyes out of her mind. She wondered if Mike ever saw them, or if it was only Jose's face he pictured.

But one emotion had risen above the others swirling within her, like a bright buoy bobbing in dark, turbulent waters. She still loved her husband.

She finished folding the T-shirt, laying it atop the stack in the laundry basket. Maybe she shouldn't have blamed Mike for withdrawing, because she'd done plenty wrong lately, too. She should have told Mike about the incident at the mall instead of shielding him, and she never should have blown up at Christie. She probably should have pulled Mike back into the family by asking him to help more with the kids, instead of letting him retreat. And she'd known exactly what the strange barking noise she'd heard in the basement had been; she'd just been too scared to acknowledge it, because if Mike was breaking down, where would that leave her?

She stood up, the heavy basket of laundry digging into her hip as she carried it into her bedroom and set it atop the dresser. She went back into the living room, tossing plastic Barbies and metal trucks into toy bins and retrieving a sticky sippy cup of apple juice from beneath a pillow on the couch. She straightened a pile of books on the coffee table and picked up the small, handheld vacuum to get the crumbs off the rug. Every time a car drove past the house, its headlights flashing, her heart leapt, then fell as she realized it wasn't a taxi bringing Mike back home.

She finished tidying the room, then went into the kitchen with the thought of having another of the Budweisers she'd bought for Mike. She froze, the unopened bottle in her hand, when she heard a sound that could've been Mike's key scraping in the front door's lock, but the door never opened. She looked at the beer, wondering if she should skip it and go to bed. But she felt wide awake, her nerves tingling, and she knew her bed would feel too empty tonight, even though she was used to sleeping alone by now. She set down the unopened drink and picked up her phone, her finger hovering over the button that would connect her to Mike.

Jamie hesitated, then slid the screen of her phone over to the next page and found the app they'd installed a few months earlier, after they'd—well, actually Christie had—gotten confused about whose turn it was to pick Henry up from baseball practice. It had been Jamie's turn, but Eloise had had a potty-training accident just as Jamie was about to leave. By the time she'd gotten her daughter cleaned up and changed and made it to the field, it was empty. An hour later, Jamie was in a full-blown panic and Mike was rushing home. Henry wasn't answering his phone. None of his teammates had seen him leave. She finally reached Christie, who blithely informed her they were at a bowling alley and hadn't heard their phones ring over all the noise. A few days later Mike had suggested they install the app, which used satellites to track the location of every phone in their family plan.

Which meant Jamie could use it to see Mike's current whereabouts. She pressed the button to activate the app and watched as it zoomed in on Mike's location. She recognized the address immediately: Christie's place.

The room spun as she gulped air. Mike had known how upset she was about the shift in his relationship with Christie. And yet his ex was the one he'd turned to! Jamie wondered if they were having drinks together again, if Christie was leaning forward, her fingernails gently scraping the skin on Mike's forearm.

She started to call Mike, then hung up before being connected. She couldn't bear to talk to him, knowing Christie would probably be listening in the background. She began to pace, hot currents roaring through her.

Even though she couldn't believe Mike would cross the line into cheating with Christie, his presence at her apartment was betrayal enough. He couldn't be planning to spend the night in Henry's room, which would be empty since Henry was at overnight camp. Could he?

Whatever was happening between Mike and Christie needed to stop—now. Jamie gripped her head in her hands, trying to think of what to do next. She had to find someone to come watch the kids. Lou was still at the zoo, and it was too late to call a friend. But there was a college kid named Rob who lived around the corner who'd occasionally babysat for them last summer. He was in school somewhere on the West Coast. Maybe he'd come home for the summer and hadn't yet heard about the shooting. Jamie found his number in her contacts, then texted him, asking if he was around and free to watch the kids for an hour or two while she ran an errand. *They're asleep so it'll be easy!* she typed, hoping her desperation didn't show.

She waited, wondering if he even had the same number. Maybe he'd joined the Peace Corps, or had decided to stay in California for the summer. Maybe he knew about the shooting and didn't want to return her message. But a moment later, a reply pinged back: *No prob. Be there in 10.*

Okay, she thought, feeling the clamp in her chest ease a tiny bit. She went upstairs and changed into a clean shirt, then loosened her hair from its ponytail and brushed it out around her shoulders. Her heart was pounding and her throat felt thick and dry. She cupped water from the sink in her hand and sipped at it greedily despite the metallic taste.

She went back downstairs and waited by the open front door until she saw Rob approaching, his stride loping and his shaggy hair falling into his eyes, whistling a tune she didn't recognize. She suddenly felt as if she'd never been that young and carefree; Rob existed in a different universe, one Jamie had departed so long ago she couldn't even remember its contours.

"Thanks for coming on such short notice," she said. "You can hang out and watch TV or whatever. I'll be back as soon as I can. Just call me on my cell if one of the kids wakes up, but they should be good."

"No worries," he said.

I wish, she thought.

She waited until he shut and locked the door, then she hurried down the front path and got into her minivan and turned on the ignition. She pulled into Christie's apartment complex fifteen minutes later with no memory of driving there. She parked in a guest spot near the entrance and got out, staring up at the squares of light streaming from windows in the brick structure, wondering which one Mike was behind.

Now that she'd arrived, she felt unsure of her plan. She'd have to be buzzed into the building, unless she waited for a resident to enter and slipped in behind them, which seemed like the better choice. Then she'd knock on the door and wait for one of them to open it . . . and then what?

A feeling of déjà vu washed over her, heavy and foreboding: For the second time this evening, Jamie was standing outside an apartment building, unsure of her welcome, desperate to salvage something vitally important.

She sat down on a decorative rock wall, wondering if there was a chance Mike could sense she was here. She'd always felt as if an invisible current was binding them together. When they were in conversation with other people, she knew without even looking at him the precise moment when he became bored or impatient (the room mother for Sam's class usually inspired those feelings in him within thirty seconds; if the conversation revolved around football, that moment would never occur). And sometimes, when she was waiting for him to come home from work, she'd be drawn to the window seconds before his car turned into their driveway. She'd always wondered whether there was an extra-sensory element that grew in happy marriages over time, similar to the phenomenon that caused longtime couples to resemble each other.

But Mike didn't come out. Maybe the current had finally snapped.

It was a warm night, and soon her T-shirt grew wilted and damp, and her hair felt sticky against the back of her neck. She was tired now, and more scared than angry. What would she say when she saw Mike? *Come home,* maybe. But those words might not be enough. He could shut the door in her face, as Ms. Torres had done.

She wasn't sure how long she'd been sitting on the rock wall before a couple finally approached the building. Jamie blended in behind them as they entered. They were young and wrapped up in each other and barely noticed her as she followed them onto the elevator and pushed the button for Christie's floor.

She exited and walked down the hallway, treading the familiar path to Christie's apartment.

She'd brought Henry here countless times, but she hadn't been inside in at least a year.

She stood before the door, staring at it as she gathered her courage and rapped twice. After a moment it opened to reveal Christie wearing a short, silky bathrobe. Jamie felt as if she'd been rammed in the stomach with something sharp and hard.

"Oh," Christie said in a flat voice. "It's you."

"I'd like to see my husband," Jamie said.

Christie opened the door wider and stepped back. Jamie walked in, her eyes glancing off Mike's flip-flops by the front door. She couldn't help picturing him kicking them off, just like he did at home. When did he become so comfortable here?

Christie led Jamie down the hallway toward the bedrooms and hesitated at the one with the closed door. She pushed it open and gave a little wave with her hand that Jamie took to mean she should look inside. Jamie sucked in a breath as she walked across the threshold. The light was dim, but she could see Mike sleeping in Henry's queen-size bed. For a moment her eyes blurred, which was why she didn't immediately notice the lump beside him in the bed.

She moved closer and saw a second thatch of dark hair against the light pillowcase. Why was Henry here instead of at camp?

Jamie reached out to shake Mike's shoulder,

but seeing him sleeping so peacefully, his right arm flung over his head, his son by his side, made her hesitate. Instead she pulled the covers higher over them both, then bent down and kissed Mike on the cheek. She straightened up and walked out of the room, quietly closing the door behind her.

"You're not going to wake him?" Christie asked.

Jamie shook her head. The anguish had drained out of her at the sight of Mike, and now she felt only a deep exhaustion, her stress and sleepless nights piling up and crashing into her. She took a step forward and stumbled, regaining her balance just before she fell.

"He should rest," Jamie said. That was what she needed, too. She closed her eyes and rubbed a hand against her forehead as a wave of dizziness washed over her. She hadn't eaten anything today, and the intense emotions roiling through her had left her feeling gutted. She wasn't even angry with Christie any longer. Maybe Mike had come to see Henry, not Christie.

"You don't look so good," Christie said.

Jamie's throat felt parched again. "Could I have some water?" she asked, her tongue thick and heavy. "Then I'll go."

Christie shrugged and led the way to the kitchen. She filled a glass from the tap and handed it to Jamie.

Jamie started to lift the glass to her mouth,

but it slipped through her hand and smashed against the floor, shattering into dozens of pieces.

"I'm sorry," she said. She crouched down and began to pick up the bigger shards. "Shit!" She'd knelt on a piece of glass, and it had bitten into her skin.

"It's just a stupid glass," Christie said, misunderstanding the reason for Jamie's curse.

Jamie stood up, grabbed a paper towel from the dispenser by the sink, and pressed it against her knee. "Do you have a broom?"

"Forget it," Christie said.

"No, I can't let you clean it up," Jamie said.

"It's fine," Christie said. "I'll—Are you crying?"

"No," Jamie sobbed.

"Oh, Jesus," Christie said.

"I'm sorry," Jamie repeated. She couldn't stem the tears flowing down her face. She was gulping air and making weird, squeaking sounds. Ugly crying, that's what it was called. She bent over and wrapped her arms around herself.

"Do you want a Valium?" Christie offered.

Jamie began to laugh through her tears, despite herself. "You mean you've had Valium all this time and I'm only now finding out about it?" She gripped the counter and pulled herself to a standing position.

"I need to go," she said.

Christie squinted at Jamie. "Have you been

drinking? I don't think you should drive. I'll take you."

Christie walked to the hall closet and pulled on a trench coat.

"Are you coming?" She was already at the door. "I'm rethinking my offer."

Jamie looked at Christie and nodded. "I'm coming," she said.

She forced herself not to look at Mike's shoes as she left.

It was happening. Lou ran to the fence and watched as Tabby stood motionless except for a slight flicking of her tail. Her sudden stillness was the giveaway.

"Good girl," Lou said, just loudly enough for Tabby to hear. Her heart pounded but her voice stayed calm.

Tabby's body began to quiver. Lou shot a warning glare at the videographer, then turned her entire focus back to Tabby.

"It's okay," Lou whispered, wishing more than anything that she could be with Tabitha, stroking her and providing comfort. She was tempted to do it, to ignore the rules and scale the fence and leap down onto the soft earth on the other side, but she'd probably lose her job. She was more scared of that than of being accidentally injured by the elephant.

Tabitha didn't make a sound, but she shifted

from side to side a few times and then squatted slightly. Lou held her breath and gripped the fence so tightly her hands ached.

The calf's rear legs, encased in the milky-looking embryonic sac, appeared first, sliding out of Tabby's body agonizingly slowly. Lou's eyes flitted from the emerging baby to Tabby, whose trunk was now curled around a fence post, as if for balance.

Tabby wasn't looking back at her any longer. She seemed lost in a world of her own. Lou wanted to speak words of encouragement but worried it would distract the elephant. Tabby squatted lower and opened her mouth wide, as if in a silent scream, but she didn't make a sound.

Suddenly, the baby slid completely out of Tabby, still in its opaque embryonic sac. It crashed to the ground, and the sac burst, releasing a torrent of fluids.

Lou glanced quickly at her watch to mark the time, then looked back at Tabby because she already sensed something was wrong. The calf wasn't moving. It was curled on its side, looking impossibly small next to its mother. Lou could make out the chunky outlines of the baby's toenails, and the fuzzy hair on its head. It was perfect.

"It's not breathing!" a zoo volunteer cried, her voice high and frightened.

Tabby walked in a circle around her baby, her

trunk reaching out to explore it. Then she lifted her front leg and kicked it—hard.

Lou heard someone gasp.

Tabby kicked her calf again and again, jerking it along the ground. The baby's body flopped helplessly with each blow.

"Oh no!" the same volunteer cried.

Tabby reached down with her trunk, scooping up the baby's head and letting it bang back down. Lou glanced at her watch. Forty-five seconds. The little elephant remained still.

Tabby stepped over her baby—for a moment Lou worried she would step *on* it—and struck it with her front foot again, this time even harder.

"Lou, shouldn't you call Tabby over here?" someone asked. "We need to get in there!"

Another kick rocked the calf's limp body back and forth. One minute.

The volunteer ran over and tugged on Lou's arm. "Make her stop!" she said. "She's killing it!"

"No." Lou shook her head. "She's saving it."

Tabby was in great distress now, circling her baby, pawing at it, trying to lift it with her trunk, trumpeting loudly near its ear.

"Come on," Lou said urgently.

And then the calf's mouth opened, and it took its first breath.

Tabby's foot had been poised for another kick, but she stilled the motion and stepped back.

"Oh, Tabs," Lou said, her voice trembling. "You

got your baby to breathe. Good girl. You're such a good girl. You did it."

Tabby gently explored her calf with her trunk while it lay on its side, its mouth opening and closing as it gasped in air. Its wide, inky black eyes were finally visible. The volunteer who had been so panicked squeezed Lou's arm, and she could hear murmurs of relief from the other workers.

After a moment, Tabby reached down with her trunk and encircled her baby's head again, trying to lift it up. The calf seemed too weak to move, but Tabby was determined. Again and again she used her trunk and foreleg to jab at it, trying to get it on its feet. Lou knew why: In the wild, an animal might be attacked if it looked helpless. Its survival would depend on it being upright. Tabby was still trying to save her baby.

The little elephant protested mightily, releasing a kind of yelp that Lou thought sounded not unlike that of a human kid who didn't want to wake up for school.

Tabby kept at it, relentlessly, and with her help, the baby finally found its way to its feet. It wobbled a bit, then fell back down when it tried to take a step. But Tabby was there by its side, helping it stand up again, more gently this time, and soon the small elephant found its footing. Lou's eyes roved over its wrinkly gray body, its gently curved back and fuzzy forehead and wide feet. She'd never seen anything so beautiful.

Tabby took a step forward, and her calf followed, struggling to move its front and hind legs in synchronicity. With every passing minute, it seemed to grow more confident.

Lou slid back to the ground, her legs as weak as the baby elephant's had been. Someone pressed a paper cup into her hand, and she took a sip of something dry and fizzy. Champagne. She didn't usually drink alcohol, but if ever an exception was called for, this was it.

She lifted her cup toward Tabby in a silent salute. "Congratulations, Mama," she said.

"I've never seen anything like that," the young videographer said. "Usually I do weddings."

His voice was still a bit louder than she would've liked, but Lou let it go. "I've never seen anything like it, either," she said.

She rested her head against the fence. Tomorrow—or actually, later today—Lou would open the gate to let the little elephant explore miles of trails with Tabby. She'd hide extra sweet potatoes and greens and apples along the way. She'd give Tabby a thorough examination, then she and the vet would carefully look over the calf, although Lou already knew it was healthy. They'd learn the gender, too. The other elephants were being kept away for now, but elephant herds were famously protective and nurturing of their young. Soon they'd get to meet little

Masego—whose name meant blessing in Setswana.

Lou smiled as she watched the baby unfurl his or her trunk, then curl it back up, like a kid with a paper blower at a party. The tiny elephant's gray coat was saggy, as if he or she was wearing a too-big suit.

I can't wait to watch you grow up, Lou thought.

She took another sip of champagne as Masego gave a trumpet, testing out its voice. Lou's limbs felt as loose and heavy as honey and she didn't think she could get up even if she wanted to.

Tabby walked over to her water supply and took a long drink, but she kept her eyes on her baby the whole time.

"You're a natural," Lou told her. "I always knew you would be."

Lou could see the videographer beginning to pack up, and the volunteers and veterinarian doing the same. She was going to stay straight through for another day or two, to keep watch. She welcomed the sweet solitude, not just so she could enjoy the new elephant but because she was holding close a remembrance that had been buried deeply for decades and had loosened only with Tabby's pacing. She wanted time to replay it again and again, to imprint every word and inflection on her memory, so she'd never lose it.

On the eve of Lou's birthday, her mother had always told her the story of her birth. It was their tradition. The story had always begun the same way: *Pacing was the only thing that helped . . .*

Lou sipped champagne and watched Tabby and her baby make slow progress around the enclosure and felt her cheeks grow wet as she remembered.

I thought I'd have plenty of time to get to the hospital, but I barely made it there before you decided to come out! her mother had said. *They had a resident deliver you because my doctor couldn't get there fast enough—I swear, the resident looked about twelve—but you didn't make things difficult. Out you came, with just three pushes. And then they put you into my arms and you gave this little bleat, like a sheep, and fell fast asleep. You had Daddy's eyes and my chin. I held you for hours.*

Lou could hear the voice so clearly now, the memory as true as the summer-blue sky of her mother's eyes.

"Thank you," Lou whispered to her beloved elephant.

"Isn't Henry supposed to be at camp?" Jamie asked. She was sitting in the passenger's seat of Christie's Mercedes as they drove through darkened streets.

"He got in a fight," Christie said. "Mike and I had to go pick him up."

"What?" Jamie didn't seem as surprised as Christie had expected.

"Yeah, he punched some other kid in the dining hall. Mike talked to him about it. He's okay now, I think," Christie said. "Henry, I mean. I hope the other kid has a broken nose."

Jamie shook her head, then turned to stare out the window. They rode in silence for another few minutes, with Christie sneaking glances at Jamie. Was this how a nervous breakdown began? Jamie seemed completely unaware that blood from her knee was running down her leg, but at least she wasn't crying any longer. It was unlike her not to ask more questions about the incident at camp, though. Jamie always wanted "open lines of communication"—a reference that Christie used to think sounded annoyingly New Agey. But the absence of Jamie's chatter made Christie realize she missed it.

"This other kid was being a jerk to a smaller boy," Christie said. "Henry was trying to protect the littler kid . . . Well, there's more to it than that."

Jamie just rubbed her eyes, leaving Christie unsure if she'd even heard. Jamie's hair was slightly matted and her shirt wrinkled, but that wasn't what made Christie nervous. She'd glimpsed something when Jamie was kneeling on the kitchen floor, looking small and vulnerable, surrounded by shattered glass. There had been this awful expression in Jamie's eyes—or maybe it was an absence of expression. Her eyes were so . . . bleak.

"Oh, no," Jamie said.

"What?" Christie asked, nervous about what Jamie might do next.

"I got a little blood on your car seat," Jamie said. "It's leather, though, so it should come right off. Do you have a napkin?"

Christie reached into her purse and gave Jamie a tissue. Yesterday she might've been upset at the thought of something marring her Mercedes. But now all she could think about was Henry's raw, bitten nails, and that emptiness in Jamie's red-rimmed eyes . . .

"I'm returning the car tomorrow," Christie said. She wasn't sure if she'd be able to—who ever read the fine print in contracts?—but she was going to try.

"Why?" Jamie frowned. "Because of what I said?"

Christie pulled up to a stoplight and turned to look directly at Jamie. "You mean when you called me a mooch?"

Jamie sighed. "I'm sorry, okay?" she said.

"You were right," Christie said. "Not the part about me being a mooch. But I shouldn't have bought this car. I don't really need it. And just so you know, I already told Mike I don't want any more child support."

Jamie nodded, and Christie felt a little deflated. A thank you would've been nice.

Jamie didn't say anything else as Christie made

a few turns and eventually reached Jamie and Mike's street. She pulled up in front of their house and waited for Jamie to step out, but Jamie didn't move.

"Can you, um, tell Mike I stopped by?" Jamie finally asked.

Christie nodded. "Sure," she said. It felt strange, Jamie asking her to convey a message to Mike.

"I left the minivan there, so if he wants to bring it home when he wakes up tomorrow . . . he can," Jamie said.

"Okay," Christie said.

"If you talk to him, could you just let him know . . ." Jamie gulped in some air and her face crumpled. "Would you tell him . . ." Again Jamie's voice trailed off, then she reached for the door handle and exited the car.

Christie stared after her as Jamie made slow progress to her front door in the darkness. She was limping, and the strap on one of her cheap-looking sandals was broken and flapping with every step. She'd trip if she weren't careful.

Christie put the Mercedes in drive and made it a few feet away before stopping again and looking back. Jamie still hadn't reached her front stoop. She was shuffling along like someone who was sick, or very old. Her head was bowed, and every line in her body seemed steeped in misery.

Christie flung open her door and ran after Jamie.

"Listen, Mike's at the apartment because of Henry," she said.

Jamie stopped walking and looked up at her. "That's the only reason," Christie continued. "Henry really needed him tonight. That stuff I said to you earlier about Mike and I—all we did was go over the case. The private detective I'm working for is trying to help him. That's why we've been talking so much."

Jamie nodded slowly. "Oh," she said.

How many times had she communicated with Jamie through the years? Christie wondered. Hundreds. No, thousands. They'd talked about Henry and the other kids, about immunizations and diaper rashes, about music recitals and grades and cyberbullying. Jamie knew Henry intimately, maybe even as well as Christie did.

"But you don't know me!" Christie blurted. "You've never once tried to know me!"

Jamie looked up at Christie, her forehead creasing. Christie hadn't meant for her private thoughts to spill out, but before she could back-pedal, Jamie spoke up.

"Maybe that's true," she said.

"Well," Christie said. She cleared her throat. "It's probably a little late now. I mean, Henry's going off to college in a few years, so . . ."

"Yeah," Jamie said.

"Anyway, maybe I didn't notice what was going on with Henry, or how upset he was . . . and fine, so I shouldn't have gotten that car . . . but I'm still a good mother!" The words erupted from Christie with a force that surprised her.

Maybe this was what it came down to, she thought as Jamie blinked up at her. The discomfort that had always underlain her relationship with Jamie could be rooted in the times she'd messed up and Jamie had rushed to cover for her, in the way Henry had asked long ago why Christie never made green trees for dinner like Jamie did (trust Jamie to find a way to turn broccoli into a treat), and in the moment when a waitress had mistaken Christie for just another guest at Henry's birthday party a few years back. The waitress had caught Christie's eye and said, "What a beautiful family"—meaning Jamie and Mike and Henry and the other kids. Christie had felt a kind of rage toward Jamie then. She'd watched Jamie rub her big, pregnant belly, Mike's hand resting possessively on her lower back, and Christie had walked to the bar and ordered a tequila shot and downed it quickly. Only then was she able to rejoin the party. When the balloon had popped a moment later, she'd hung on to Mike's arm and hadn't let go until Jamie noticed and glared at her.

Jamie looked confused. "I mean, our styles are different. But you're a good mother. Of course you are. Anyone can see how much you love Henry."

Christie felt her throat tighten and she shook her head. She wanted to say that wasn't what she'd meant, but she was unsure of what she did mean. So she walked back to her car before she did something ridiculous, like burst into tears. There had been far too much crying tonight anyway. She had no idea what had gotten into her; maybe Jamie's crazy mood was contagious.

She put her Mercedes in drive but waited to pull away from the curb until Jamie made it safely inside her house.

You're a good mother, Jamie had said, sincerity threading through her voice.

As Christie headed home, back to her son, she knew in her heart it was true.

Chapter Eighteen

MIKE STOOD IN THE doorway, wearing a T-shirt Jamie had picked up last year at a discount outlet because she knew the mossy green color would complement his olive skin. His hair curled down around his ears and stubble coated his jawline, a look she loved.

"Are the kids ready?" he asked. "I'm gonna take them to the park."

It had been two weeks since she'd gone to find him at Christie's. When she'd awoken the next morning, the minivan was in the driveway and Mike was sitting at the kitchen table, his hands cupping a steaming mug of coffee. She'd begun to hurry toward him. Then she'd glimpsed the expression on his face and she'd stopped short.

"Christie told me you came by when I was asleep," he'd said. "I want you to know I wasn't there the whole time. I crashed on Shawn's couch the first night."

She'd eased into the seat across from him. "Okay," she'd said, her voice coming out as a whisper.

Mike's two duffel bags were at his feet. He hadn't unpacked them.

"I'm going back to stay at Shawn's," he'd said.

His words had felt like a hard pinch. "For how long?" she'd asked.

He'd shaken his head. "I don't know."

"A night? Two?"

"Look, I just—I've got to get away for a little while."

From me, Jamie had thought.

Shawn was one of the guys who'd brought over fried chicken after Ms. Torres's press conference. If Mike was sleeping there, it meant he would have to watch his friend leave for work in his blue uniform, a painful reminder of the life Mike used to have.

How could staying with her be worse than that?

"I'll tell the kids it's because of all the reporters hanging around the house," he'd continued, not meeting her eyes. "The press is going to be all over me now that we're going to trial. I'll say I want to draw them away. Henry's having a rough time, so when he's here I'll be around as much as possible. I'll probably stay in the basement some of those nights. And I want to come by and see the kids every day."

"Why even leave, then?" Jamie had asked, wondering when he'd planned this all out and how long he'd been thinking about it. "You can keep sleeping in the basement. Or I'll stay there if you want!"

But he'd just shaken his head and stood up and

put his barely touched mug of coffee into the sink. She'd bought that mug for the kids to give him last Christmas. It was the kind you could write on with a special pen, and all the children had signed their names, with Jamie's hand helping guide Eloise's as she printed shaky but still recognizable letters. Henry had sketched a baseball next to his signature, and Sam had drawn a paw print for Sadie. After he'd torn away the gift wrap, Mike had said he'd never use anything else for his morning coffee.

"Wait!" Jamie had cried as Mike picked up his bags and began walking toward the front door. "Don't just—Let's talk this out! Go to marriage counseling or something!"

"I need to get through the trial," he'd said.

She'd hurried after him. "I know things haven't been good between us," she'd said. "But I still love you, Mike. Why are you so angry with me? It can't only be because I went to see Ritchie!"

He'd sighed, one hand on the doorknob. "Look, I'm not even sure I can explain it," he'd said. "All I know is I need a break, okay?"

"No, it's not okay!" she'd cried. "I've been furious with you, too. Don't you think I haven't wanted to walk away once or twice? But I didn't. And you can't, either! Talk to me, Mike. You can't just leave . . ."

But he had.

Now she gestured for him to come inside,

feeling a mixture of anger and sorrow that she was inviting her husband into their house. "The kids are in the kitchen," she said. "They're finishing up breakfast."

Sadie ran to Mike, her nails scrabbling against the wood floors, and he squatted down and rubbed her neck. Then he followed Jamie to the kitchen, where Lou was flipping a pancake high into the air. Lou tried to catch it in the pan, but missed and it landed on the floor.

"Oops," Lou said as Sadie gobbled it up. "You weren't supposed to see that."

"Hey, elephant girl," Mike said, giving Lou a quick hug.

"Hey, Thor," she replied, hugging him back.

"Sadie's eating the pancake!" Eloise said, laughing. "Do it again!"

"Want one?" Lou asked Mike.

"Sure," he said, taking the empty seat next to Emily.

"I'll get their shoes," Jamie said. "Oh, and sunscreen. Do you want me to pack some snacks?" Talking about logistics helped fill the empty space between her and Mike.

"Nah," Mike said, stealing a strawberry off Emily's plate and popping it into his mouth. "We'll pick something up if they get hungry."

Twenty minutes later, they were all clustered by the door and Jamie was rubbing sunscreen on Sam's arms over his protests while Mike helped

Eloise strap on her sandals. Above the din came the sound of Mike's cell phone ringing.

He reached into his pocket and glanced at the caller ID.

"Better take this," he said. "It's J.H."

He stepped away, toward the family room, but Jamie could still hear his side of the conversation.

"When is it going to happen?" Mike was asking. His tone revealed it wasn't good news. Jamie felt a clutch of fear.

"Okay. Talk to you after."

He slid his phone back into his pocket and stood there, staring into space.

Jamie handed the tube of sunscreen to Lou and walked over to him. "What is it?" she asked softly, not wanting the kids to overhear.

"Lucia Torres is holding another press conference," he said.

Jamie gasped. A few days after Mike had left, Jamie had called and told him about her visit to Jose's mother, knowing she needed to be honest with him. She'd been worried Mike would feel betrayed again, but he'd only said he appreciated her effort. Now Jamie wondered if she'd violated some sort of law.

"What's she going to say?"

"He doesn't know," Mike said. "But she's starting it in half an hour. He said it's so rushed that a lot of reporters probably won't get there in time."

"That's good, right?" Jamie asked.

Mike shrugged.

"Do you want to watch it here?" she offered.

Lou stepped toward them. "How about I take the kids to the park?" she suggested. "I can bring them back in an hour."

Mike hesitated. "Yeah, okay," he finally said.

He was probably going to watch it with her only because he didn't have time to get to another television, Jamie thought, feeling stung. They saw Lou and the kids off, then Jamie busied herself cleaning the kitchen. Mike sat on the living room couch, flipping through the newspaper so quickly he couldn't be reading a word.

"Seven minutes," he said, looking at his watch. He flicked on the television and switched the channel to a local news station.

"Can I get you anything?" Jamie asked, sitting down a few feet away from him.

"No thanks." Mike began drumming his fingers against his leg.

They stared at a commercial for a retirement community, then another for English muffins.

They should've watched the earlier press conference together, Jamie thought as she remembered how she'd stayed upstairs instead of going into the basement with Mike. She'd thought she'd been shielding him. Now it was just another regret.

A young male reporter appeared on the screen,

holding a microphone and recapping the facts of the case. The press conference was taking place at Ms. Torres's lawyer's office, the reporter said. He wrapped up, and the camera cut to a podium positioned next to the doorway of a large room.

In a voice-over, the reporter narrated what was happening on-screen: "Ms. Lucia Torres is approaching the podium. She called this press conference unexpectedly and has not released any statement about its contents."

Only when she began to feel light-headed did Jamie realize she was holding her breath. She exhaled and leaned forward, trying to glean clues from Ms. Torres's appearance. Jose's mother wore the same black dress she'd had on for the last press conference, and her expression was somber. She seemed to have aged since Jamie had seen her just a few weeks ago. She reached the microphone and stood there for so long that Jamie wondered if she was going to speak after all.

"I have always told the truth, all my life," Lucia Torres finally began in a low voice. "And I have tried to teach my children to do the same."

Jamie gripped her hands together, wishing she could hold Mike's instead.

"My younger son, Alejandro, is not here today, and I ask that none of you try to contact him in the future. My lawyer or myself will answer your questions. He is to be left alone. He is a little boy, eleven years old." Her voice faltered on the word *little* and her mouth twisted. But then she straightened up and lifted her chin higher. "He made a mistake because he was trying to protect me from something he knew would break my heart."

She stepped back, and the woman standing behind her—the lawyer? Jamie wondered—leaned toward the microphone. "Ms. Torres wants to let you all know that she received a gun from her younger son last night. The boy took it from where it had fallen near his brother Jose's body just after Jose was shot by Police Officer Michael Anderson. Alejandro had followed Jose to the scene of the fight and was hiding under a nearby parked car during the time of his brother's shooting."

The room was silent for a moment, then it exploded with shouted questions.

"The gun was turned over to the district attorney early this morning," the lawyer said, waving her hand for quiet. "That's all the information I have at the moment. Please respect the fact that this is a grieving mother who tried to do the right thing. And Alejandro, too. Until recently he didn't understand the extent of the repercussions of his actions. Once he did, he took the courageous step of telling the truth." She took Ms. Torres by the forearm and led her from the room.

Jamie struggled to process the words. She stared at the television, remembering the pair of big brown eyes peeking out at her from behind Ms.

Torres. Alejandro—Jose's little brother. He'd listened as Jamie begged on behalf of her husband and talked about how her children needed their father. He'd seen her cry.

The male reporter appeared on the screen again, his voice tense and his words spilling out rapidly. "We have just heard from Lucia Torres that her—that a gun was recovered from near her older son, Jose Torres's body immediately following his shooting death. The gun—Ms. Torres said—was picked up by her younger son and brought home, where presumably it has remained this whole time. We'll, ah, we're going to bring you an update on the case as soon as we have more information. Right now we are—we are confirming that Lucia Torres has just said there was a gun a few feet away from her teenage son, Jose's body immediately after he was shot by Police Officer Michael Anderson."

The phone erupted upstairs.

Jamie turned to Mike. His mouth had fallen open. He was still staring at the television, even though a weatherman was now on, predicting another scorcher.

The phone stopped ringing, then started up again. Jamie could hear her cell phone buzzing frantically.

Mike's breathing turned ragged. "They found a gun?" he asked. "I knew—I thought—but then when there wasn't any evidence—"

"Mike, he had a gun, just like you said." Jamie felt dazed and muddy, as if everything was happening in slow motion. "You were right all along."

"I saw it in his hand. There wasn't any doubt— but then after I got to him so fast, and nothing was there—" Mike said.

Mike's cell phone was ringing now, too, but he ignored it. He was a cop again, intent on puzzling out the clues.

"That was why I couldn't find it. It must have fallen behind him, toward the cars," Mike said, his voice gaining confidence. "Someone had to have cut in between me and Alejandro right when he bent down to get the gun. Otherwise I would've seen him."

Mike was very still. He squeezed his eyes shut, something he only did when he was concentrating intently.

"But something still doesn't add up," he said. "Jose was a good kid. Everyone said so. He'd never been in any real trouble before. People don't just turn on a dime like that. So why'd he have a gun? Why'd he aim it at Jay? It doesn't make any sense."

Jamie reached a hand toward Mike's leg, then withdrew it without touching him.

"I gotta figure this out," Mike said. "There's another piece I'm not seeing yet." He opened his eyes.

452

"You will," Jamie said. "But Mike, we've got to tell the kids!"

She still felt numb, but she leapt to her feet. "And your parents!"

"Yeah," he said, but he didn't move.

"They'll have to drop the charges!" she cried.

Why was Mike just sitting there?

She knelt down so they were face-to-face. "I know this has been horrible for you. We haven't even really had any time to think about what you had to do. But I want to help. We can get through this."

"Yeah," Mike said again, leaning back. Away from her. "I just wish . . ."

"What is it?" she asked. She reached for his hand, but his fingers didn't close around hers.

Fear clamped her body like a vise. It wasn't over, not yet, she thought.

"I wish you'd believed me," Mike said, and he dropped his hand from hers.

The knowledge of what she'd done slammed into her. "I'm sorry—I was just trying to help!" she cried. "I was scared!"

He didn't respond.

"Mike, I didn't mean—I wasn't even focused on if there was a gun or not, I was just trying to protect us!" she continued. "To save our family!"

Why hadn't she believed him? She thought back to right after the shooting, when Mike had come up their front walk, his head low, his gun missing from its holster. He'd gripped her shoulders and looked at her intently. *I swear to you,* he'd said. *I saw it, Jamie.*

And she'd responded: *It was raining! It was hard to see! Anyone could've made that mistake!*

"It made me doubt myself," Mike was saying. "When you didn't even pretend to believe me. You're the person who knows me best, so if you thought I really did it . . . that was the worst part. Wondering if I'd killed a boy for no reason."

"You have to understand," she said, her voice frantic and choppy. "It was like J.H. said, it was about what the jury would believe! And it was raining, and you were so stressed, and—Mike, I'm not saying this well, but don't you see that I couldn't even think that much about what actually happened?"

"But it meant everything," Mike said. His dark eyes were wet. "I see Jose on the pavement everywhere I look. I dream about him all the time. And I began to think it was all my fault again. Just like with Ritchie."

"Oh, Mike, no, it wasn't your fault! Neither of them," Jamie said. She was crying hard now. "I was just—Mike, I was so afraid for you, for our family . . ."

Her voice trailed off as he stood up, leaving her kneeling on the floor. "I should call my parents, like you said. And J.H. But Henry first."

"Do you want to do it from here?" she asked.

He shook his head. "I'll go meet Lou and the kids at the park. I can phone everyone on my cell there."

"Mike, I know you're still so angry with me," she said. She tried to catch her breath, to find the words to make him understand. "You deserve to be angry with me! But I did what I had to. Can you try to see that? It wasn't just me—J.H. talked about PTSD, and—"

Mike cut her off. "Christie believed me," he said.

Jamie went still. "I was wrong, Mike," she said.

He nodded, just one quick up-and-down movement of his head. Then his phone rang again, and this time he looked at it. "Henry," he said.

He answered and began walking away as he talked to his son. "I know," Jamie could hear him saying. "Me, too. Yeah, I'll come get you right now. I want to see you, too . . ."

Mike left without even saying good-bye. Without looking back at her.

Chapter Nineteen

A PUFFY WHITE CLOUD drifted in front of the sun, providing temporary relief from the relentless heat. Dozens of parents and siblings packed the bleachers of a local community center for the final game in the summer youth league baseball tournament, but it was so quiet that Christie could hear a breeze rustling the leaves of the tree behind her.

Her eyes were fixed on Henry, who was leading off second base. In the bottom of the final inning, the game was tied six-all, with one out.

Henry was in position to score, and his team's other best player was up at bat. "He's got this," Christie announced to no one in particular, then began gnawing her thumbnail.

The pitcher wound up and let the ball fly. At the crack of the bat, Christie jumped to her feet, screaming, "Go, Henry!" Next to her Jamie and Lou leapt up, too.

Henry sprinted toward third base as the ball hung in the sky, then it began arcing down as two outfielders ran to make the catch. But Henry's teammate had hit it into the sweet spot, the no-man's-land between first and second base, and the ball bounced against the turf before being scooped up by one of the opposing team's players.

Henry rounded third hard, never hesitating as he headed for home plate.

"Gogogogogo!" Christie shrieked.

"The play's at home! The play's at home!" the opposing team's coach bellowed, his voice soaring over the noise of the crowd.

The ball smacked into the glove of the cutoff man, who pivoted and hurled it toward the catcher. Henry's arms were pumping, and his feet kicked up puffs of brown dirt with every step. He ran so fast the batting helmet flew off his head and bounced behind him. But the ball was faster.

Just after it slammed into the catcher's mitt, Henry threw his head and shoulders backward, sliding in feetfirst.

"He made it under the catch, didn't he?" Jamie asked, grabbing Christie's arm. "The ball didn't touch him, right?"

"Of course it didn't!" Christie said, although she wasn't sure.

The umpire extended his arms straight out, and half of the people in the stands erupted in applause. Lou reached over and stung Christie's palm with a high five.

"Did Henry win?" Eloise asked. She was eating a snow cone and her lips were the color of blueberries.

"He sure did," Jamie said. "Him and the rest of his team. Aren't you proud of your big brother?"

Christie squinted and caught sight of Mike running toward Henry, pumping his fists over his head. Even though he'd never played baseball, Mike had signed up as an assistant coach for the summer league, saying he wanted to spend more time with Henry.

Christie had been with Henry at the time of Ms. Torres's second press conference. She'd been getting ready to take him out for breakfast when Henry had pounded on the door of her bathroom, yelling for her to come quick. She'd stood there with him, her hair damp on her shoulders and mascara coating only her right lashes, staring at the television screen while everything changed.

Immediately after that Mike had picked Henry up, but this time, he hadn't come upstairs. Instead, Henry had waited outside the apartment building, eager to see his father the moment he arrived. Christie had thought about going downstairs to wait with him, but in the end, she'd thought Henry deserved to be alone with Mike.

"What a game," Christie said now, watching Henry's teammates dog-pile on top of him at home plate.

"It was amazing," Jamie said. Christie was surprised to hear a catch in Jamie's voice. But then, Jamie understood how badly Henry had needed this moment.

Christie reached for her purse and started to follow Lou and the kids as they exited the bleachers, but Jamie put a hand on her arm, drawing her back.

"There's something I've been wanting to ask you," Jamie said, her voice low. "How did you know all along there really was a gun?"

Christie looked at her, surprised. "Because it was Mike," she said without even having to think about her answer. "He never would've made that kind of mistake."

"Oh," Jamie said. She nodded slowly. "You're right . . . Well, thank you for helping him. Mike told me about Elroy."

"Hey, it was nothing," Christie said quickly. Jamie's face was a little scrunched, which was a tad alarming, given what had happened the last time Christie had seen her.

"Come on," Christie said, heading toward the dugout. "Let's go see Henry."

They had to wait a few minutes, but finally Henry pulled away from his team and ran over to them.

"Did you see it?" he asked.

"Are you kidding?" Christie said, throwing her arms around her sweaty boy. "You were awesome!"

"I caught it all," Lou said, holding up a video camera. "I'll make you a copy so you can watch the highlights."

Henry grinned. "Thanks," he said.

"Congrats, sweetheart," Jamie said. She gave Henry a quick hug, then released him as Mike walked over to them.

"So what's the plan, champ?" Mike asked, slinging an arm around Henry's shoulders.

"The guys are going out for pizza," he said. "Can we go?"

"You bet," Mike said.

"I'll get my stuff," Henry said and ran off toward the dugout again.

There was a pause, then Mike said to Jamie, "Are you guys coming tonight?"

"No, I think Eloise is too tired," Jamie said. "But thank you."

"I can take the kids swimming tomorrow," Mike said. "Should I pick them up around eleven?"

"Sure," Jamie said.

Whoa, Christie thought, watching as Mike gave the younger kids hugs and swung Sam around a few times before ruffling his hair. She shot Lou a questioning look, but Jamie's sister was fixated on some sort of bug that had flown onto her arm, pointing it out to Emily, who was making a disgusted face, as they walked toward the parking lot with Jamie and the other kids.

"Man, do I need a Gatorade," Mike said, pulling off his baseball cap and running a hand through his hair.

"It sounded like you and Jamie aren't even living together," Christie blurted.

"Yeah," Mike said. "I guess it did."

"Oh, don't give me one of your cryptic cop nonanswers," Christie said. "What's going on?"

Mike glanced around—probably hoping Henry would save him—but Henry was posing for a team picture.

"Are you separated?" Christie pressed.

"More like a break," Mike said.

"Does Henry know?" she asked.

"Sort of," Mike said. "I stay at the house when he's there. I told him we're working things out."

"Are you?" Christie asked.

Mike looked at her for a moment. "I don't know," he said.

"Oh," she said. She looked down at the ground.

"Anyway, can I catch a ride to the pizza place with you?" Mike asked. "I don't have my cruiser, since I'm not officially back at work yet."

"What have you been doing for a car?" Christie asked.

"My friend Shawn loaned me his," Mike said. "But he needed it today."

"Sure, I'll drive you," Christie said. She walked a few steps away to lean against the chain-link fence surrounding the field, needing a moment to think. This was what she'd wanted only a month or so ago—not for Jamie and Mike to separate, exactly, but for her to have another chance with

Mike. But the two events were entwined. One was impossible without the other.

Henry was still posing for photos, near one end of the line of players, his red socks pulled up to the knees of his gray uniform, the number 8 boldly stamped on the back of his shirt. As a little boy, Henry had dressed up as a baseball player one Halloween, back when he'd first become interested in the game. Jamie had even bought him a tiny Rawlings glove, which had instantly become Henry's favorite possession. Christie had gone trick-or-treating with them for an hour or so, then she'd peeled away, because she had a sexy cat costume and a party of her own to go to. She'd walked back to her car parked next to the white picket fence Mike had built, passing a wooden swing hanging over a branch of the maple tree in a corner of the yard.

The brown lines of the baseball field bisecting the grass reminded Christie of something. Henry had adored that swing. And Jamie had spent so much time pushing him on it that a patch of grass had been worn away by her footsteps, leaving a streak of brown earth cutting through the green.

Christie glanced at Mike again. He was staring off toward the place where Jamie and the kids had been.

Oh, who was she kidding? Mike had never truly wanted her, not when they'd first been dating and not now. He'd only been grateful for her help.

She'd tried to imagine Mike kissing her that night in her apartment, when they'd been interrupted by Henry. But he'd leaned away ever so slightly at the precise moment she leaned in. She'd tried to block out that part of the memory, but there was no unseeing his quick, reflexive action.

She thought of the money Jamie had spent to send Henry to camp, while the broken strap on her sandal flapped with every step. That bit of earth woven through the rich green grass under the swing. The catch in Jamie's voice when Henry had scored the winning run.

She walked back over to Mike. "You're a big old idiot," she said.

"Say what you really think," he countered, but he was smiling. "Don't hold back. You need to get over your shyness."

"You and Jamie were meant for each other," she said. "Don't you dare get divorced."

"Look, it isn't—"

"Yeah, yeah, it's none of my business," she finished for him. "Who cares? I'm your friend and I'm telling you to go home to your wife, who loves you."

Mike was looking at her strangely. "Since when are you such a fan of Jamie's?" he asked.

"So she didn't believe you about the gun," Christie said. "People make mistakes. Don't tell me you've never made one in your life."

"It isn't that easy—How are we talking about this?" Mike asked.

"She's sorry, Mike. Really sorry," Christie said. "I can tell. And she loves you. She loves Henry. Jamie loves your family more than anything in the world. That's got to count for something."

She let it go then and walked back to the fence, suddenly remembering something she'd meant to do at the game. She picked up her phone and began to type in a text message.

"Who are you calling?" Mike asked.

"Not Jamie, so calm down," she said. "I'm texting Lou. I forgot I'm staging an intervention with her tomorrow."

"An intervention?" Mike furrowed his brow.

"Have you seen her haircut?" Christie asked.

Before Mike could answer, Henry came back to them.

"Ready to go?" he asked.

"Let's hit it," Christie said, putting away her phone.

The three of them left the field, with Henry walking between her and Mike, which, Christie thought, was exactly as it should be.

Chapter Twenty

Two months later

JAMIE WAS STARING AT the dry-erase board they'd attached to the kitchen wall to use as a family calendar when Lou walked into the room, yawning hugely.

"Sleep okay?" Jamie asked.

"Like a sloth on a fat branch," Lou said. She grabbed a Honeycrisp apple from the fruit bowl on the counter and crunched into it. "You?"

"Fine," Jamie lied. She walked over to the coffeemaker and poured herself another cup. She would've offered one to Lou, but Lou had sworn off coffee after quitting her barista job, saying it made her feel like she was at work. Jamie added a spoonful of sugar and a dash of cream to her mug—her appetite had resurfaced recently, beckoning back six of the nine pounds she'd lost—then she began taking out the ingredients for waffles. The kids would be hungry when they woke up. They'd all shot up like crocuses over the summer, and Sam had become a really good swimmer, while Emily had lost two more of her baby teeth. Eloise had begun preschool the previous month, and Jamie had worried the transition might be difficult, but Eloise had marched right in on the first day, her new Dora the Explorer backpack firmly in place.

None of the kids seemed to bear scars from that horrible stretch of time in early summer and all that had followed. Jamie only wished she shared her children's resilience.

"I'm heading out," Lou called softly. Jamie walked to the front door to see her sister off.

"Dinner at six, right?" Jamie said.

"Yup," Lou said.

"I can't wait to meet him," Jamie said. "He sounds really great."

Was Lou blushing?

Jamie leaned against the doorframe, watching Lou head toward the secondhand Honda Accord she'd leased. A cool breeze nipped at Jamie's bare arms and she shivered. Soon the rising sun would burn off the chill, but right now, the promise of fall had encroached upon the day.

As Lou climbed into her car, Jamie reflected that she still wouldn't recognize her sister from behind. Christie and Lou had formed a completely unexpected friendship—Jamie still had no idea how it had happened—and Christie had whisked Lou away to the salon where she used to work. Jamie, feeling protective of her younger sister, had almost intervened in Christie's intervention, but Lou had just laughed and said she didn't mind. Lou had returned home three hours later, looking dazed, her hair shaped into a layered bob with highlights framing her face.

"It's crucial that you keep up the highlights," Christie had instructed Lou. "Go back every four weeks."

Lou had just nodded, her eyes wide and round— Jamie noticed her eyebrows had been waxed and wondered if other, more delicate parts of her had been, too—and Lou hadn't ventured anywhere near the salon again.

Christie had given a deep sigh when she'd seen the highlights growing out. "I did my best," she'd said, then she'd asked Lou if she could set her up on a blind date. That, at least, had gone well, and Lou was bringing Elroy by for dinner tonight, so he could meet the family.

Jamie had sent Christie an email, asking if she'd come, too. *Sure,* Christie had written back. *I'll bring the wine.*

A friendly toot sounded from a car horn, and Jamie waved at the neighbor driving past. It was the elderly woman down the street who'd ignored them after Mike had been indicted. A week ago, the neighbor had shown up with a casserole, lingering on their doorstep and chatting away as if she'd been in their corner all along.

Mike had brought the kids to visit his parents right after the charges were dropped, partly to escape the reporters who'd returned to camp out in front of the house. He hadn't asked Jamie to come with them. Knowing her husband needed to escape from her, too, was one of the most painful things she'd endured, along with her father telling her that her mother had died.

Jamie had planned to immerse herself in activity while the kids were gone, to try to distract herself by getting caught up for once—the refrigerator was desperate for a good scrubbing, the kids' toys begged to be organized, and the attic needed to be cleared out before the floor collapsed under it—but she'd ended up staying in bed, not even bothering to shower or change out of her nightshirt. The quiet and solitude she'd used to fantasize about felt like a form of torture, and the sleep she'd long craved eluded her. The kids phoned every evening, their bright voices bubbling over as they talked about body surfing, picnics on the beach, and a trip with Grandma to a candy store to load up on saltwater taffy. Jamie made sure her voice was equally cheerful, even though she felt as if something heavy was crushing her. Mike came on the line only to say a quick hello, which was almost worse than him not talking to her at all.

On the fourth morning after they'd left, Lou stood at the foot of her bed like an apparition.

"Come on," her sister had said, yanking back the covers. "Get up."

"Why?" Jamie had muttered.

"Because you need to," Lou had said, opening the blinds and flooding the room with sunlight. Lou's voice was so determined it seemed as if it would take more energy for Jamie to fight her than to succumb, so she'd crawled out of bed and headed for the hot shower Lou had already turned on. It was odd to think their roles had somehow been reversed while she'd been resting.

Lou had driven her to the zoo and directed Jamie to muck out the elephant enclosures and weigh food. At first Jamie had moved slowly, her limbs aching and her eyes gritty, wanting nothing more than to be in the dark nest of her bed. But gradually she'd become aware of her sister. Jamie had brought the kids to visit Lou at the zoo dozens of times, but she'd never spent the whole day here, watching Lou give directions to volunteers and work with the animals. This was her sister's habitat, Jamie realized with a sense of wonder. She watched how the elephants responded to her sister, and listened as Lou talked to baby Masego in a gentle voice, her movements swift and assured as she examined him, and Jamie was filled with pride.

"How did you know this was exactly what I needed?" she asked Lou as they drove home that night, her muscles pleasantly sore.

"I guess," Lou said slowly, "because it always helps me."

Mike had returned to work, too, and he'd been

paid for the weeks of salary he'd lost. Gradually, the story had emerged: Jose was supposed to stay home that afternoon and watch his younger brother, but instead he'd turned on the television and slipped out to meet up with a new group of friends—several of whom were gang members. Alejandro had secretly followed his brother, and when the brawl broke out, he'd become frightened and crawled under a parked car. He'd seen the blood blooming on his brother's chest, and had watched Jose collapse.

Jamie could see it happening: Jose falling onto his back like a snow angel. The gun—which turned out to be a Beretta with a filed-off serial number—following the arc of his arm as it was thrown backward. The gun clacking against the pavement behind Jose, bouncing and sliding to land within ten feet of Alejandro's hiding place. The boy slipping out from beneath the car, unnoticed in the melee. Alejandro closing his hand around the weapon and running home.

After they'd retrieved the gun, investigators determined that Jose's fingerprints were still on the handle. They also learned Jose had been given the gun the previous day by a leader of the gang. Apparently Jose wanted to join it so he could begin selling drugs—but one of his friends said Jose told him he'd do it only temporarily, to help his family. He knew his mother worked long hours, and dreamed of someday owning a house.

Jose had wanted more than anything to give her one.

Jamie closed the front door and went to start making waffle batter, her eyes flitting to the calendar once more. The day's activities were listed: a dentist appointment for Eloise, Sam's soccer practice at three-thirty, and Henry's baseball practice at five.

One previously scheduled item was missing, though. Mike's trial was supposed to have begun this morning.

Jamie shivered again.

"Cold?"

Mike walked up behind her and enveloped her in his thick arms. She leaned back against his chest, tears pricking her eyes. He *had* forgiven her, eventually.

"If you hadn't gone to Ms. Torres, Alejandro might not have come forward," Mike had said during one of their marriage counseling sessions. He'd looked at her then—really looked at her for the first time in weeks—and she'd felt a glimmer of hope. "You saved me. I need to thank you for that."

Now she had to find a way to forgive herself.

"Do you want to finish making the waffles and I'll go wake up the kids?" she asked Mike.

"Sure," he said. She gave him a kiss—she found herself kissing him all the time now, and constantly touching him—and headed upstairs.

Mike had started to renovate the basement in the time he'd taken off before going back to work, roughing out a tiny bedroom and bathroom for Lou, so Sam could have his old room back until Lou found a place of her own. *No rush,* Jamie had told her. She liked having her sister around.

Mike hadn't returned to his patrolman's job, even though he'd been offered it back. Instead, he'd taken the detective promotion he'd once turned down. Jamie had also heard through the grapevine that no officer in the entire force would agree to be partnered with Jay. He'd quit and had apparently moved to North Carolina.

Jamie had asked Mike whether he thought he'd ever go back to working a foot patrol, and Mike had shaken his head. "Doesn't feel right without Ritchie," he'd said. It made Jamie sad to think that part of his life was over, at least for the foreseeable future.

But they were going to visit Ritchie, who was back at home now, too, this weekend. Jamie was planning to make a couple of giant lasagnas—one spinach and mushroom instead of meat, because that was Ritchie's favorite—and Mike and some of the other officers were going to tear down the wheelchair ramp. Ritchie had made swift progress to a walker, and his speech was improving, too. Jamie could almost hear the teasing that would go on. The guys would joke about signing Ritchie up for a marathon next year, and they'd pretend to eat a bite of the veggie lasagna and gag. Before they tore down the ramp, they'd probably hold races down it in the wheelchair. She and Sandy would make a big salad in the kitchen, chatting as they sliced cucumbers and washed lettuce side by side. The officers would pick up Ritchie's kids and toss them around, and they might notice a sticky door hinge or a leaking pipe and they'd make a mental note to come back and fix it. And in the thick of it all would be Mike, clinking beer bottles with his pals, reminiscing about old cases, making plans to get together for a football game. Because he was one of them again.

Jamie walked upstairs, into Sam's room, and saw that he'd kicked off the covers. Sadie was curled up in the curve behind his knees, and she opened her eyes, looked sleepily at Jamie, and then closed them again.

"Thanks for keeping my boy warm," Jamie whispered.

She sat down at the edge of Sam's bed, watching him sleep. The once-soft curves of his face were turning angular, and his feet looked too big for his body. In another few years, he'd be a mini-Henry.

The buttery smell of cooking waffles drifted upstairs, and Jamie knew she should wake up her son and then her daughters, prod them all to get dressed and come downstairs, but she wanted to stay like this, for just a little longer, listening to the peaceful sound of Sam breathing.

Jamie thought about what they were going to do today.

After they took the kids to school, they were going to drive to Ms. Torres's apartment. Mike had already phoned to ask if he and Jamie could visit. At first he'd suggested a neutral spot, like a diner, but she'd said she preferred that they come to her home. They were going to bring donuts and coffee, and Mike was going to ask if he could talk to Alejandro sometime, to tell him how proud he was of the boy for doing the right thing.

And Mike needed to tell Ms. Torres about the missing piece of the puzzle. Maybe the most important piece.

He'd finally figured it out in the middle of the night, while he'd been lying in bed. He'd sat up so abruptly that he'd awoken Jamie.

"Are you okay?" she'd asked.

"I can't stop thinking about how that idiot Jay was running toward Jose with that can of pepper spray," Mike had said, his voice hoarse. "What if . . ."

Jamie had sat up, too, suddenly feeling wide awake.

"Jose wasn't the kind of kid who joins a gang," Mike had said. "He had no idea what he was getting into. He probably thought he could move some pot and buy his mom a house and get out in a couple of months. He was fifteen. Kids that age—they don't think through stuff."

Jamie had remained silent, sensing Mike was on the cusp of something vitally important.

"So he's in the fight, and he's probably scared out of his mind because he's in way over his head. Maybe he was thrown in as a type of initiation. Maybe it would've scared him enough so he would've tried to have gotten out." Mike had massaged his forehead with his thumb and index finger. "Then he hears someone yell, 'Freeze!' and he looks up to see a cop charging him. The cop is lifting his hand with something metallic and gray in it. Pointing it at him."

"Oh my God," Jamie had gasped. "You think—"

Mike had nodded slowly.

"All along, everyone assumed I was the one who'd imagined I'd seen a gun. But I think it was Jose who did."

"It was raining," Jamie had said. "Maybe he couldn't see clearly . . ."

"Exactly what they said about me. You just gotta flip it," Mike had said.

"Mike, Ms. Torres told me a police officer harassed Jose when he was just a boy," Jamie had blurted. "The officer told Jose to get home and stop causing trouble or the officer would give him real trouble. He made Jose cry."

"Might not have been the only time something

like that happened. Maybe that officer was the regular one on the beat," Mike said.

"So Jose drew the gun because he thought he had to defend himself?" Jamie had asked.

"Yeah," Mike had said. "That makes . . . what happened . . . even worse."

He'd fallen back against his pillow and exhaled.

"He was like Henry," Mike had said softly. "He loved his mom. He took care of his younger brother. He didn't have a violent record. You heard what one of his teachers said—he was a smart kid. He started out life like Henry."

Your son lives in a different world, one that doesn't automatically treat him with disrespect, Ms. Torres had said. *You have no idea what life is like for our brown boys.*

You're right, Jamie had thought. She'd closed her eyes, feeling herself begin to tremble.

"Henry started a fight at camp when he was under pressure for the first time in his life," Mike had said. "If he'd been feeling desperate, and wanted to help Christie—if he didn't have us around—you can't tell me he wouldn't be tempted by the idea of moving pot."

Jamie had rolled over and put her head on Mike's chest, feeling his heart thudding.

"Do you still dream about him?" she'd whispered.

"Not as much," Mike had said after a moment. "Not every single night."

476

But she knew Mike thought about Jose every single day, as did she. She saw it in the way the expression in her husband's eyes changed sometimes when he was with their children, in the way he stayed kneeling at church, praying, after everyone else had risen to their feet.

Today they would tell Ms. Torres everything. Mike had said if she wanted to hold another press conference, to reveal the whole story, he'd stand beside her.

Now Jamie stared at Sam, seeing the sweep of long eyelashes against his cheek, remembering the photograph of Jose in the paper. She wasn't sure how long she'd been sitting there when Sam lifted his head and stared at her sleepily.

"Do I have school today?" he asked.

She reached out and stroked his soft, thick hair. "Yes," she said.

He groaned and flopped his head back onto the pillow.

"Daddy's downstairs," she said. "He's making waffles."

The bedroom window was cracked open, and she could hear a squirrel chattering in a nearby tree. Sam's laundry basket was overflowing, so Jamie picked it up as she began to walk out of the room. She'd try to throw in a load after breakfast.

She could hear the sounds of Eloise stirring in the next room now, and Mike was calling from downstairs that everybody should come eat while it was hot, and Sadie was giving a little whine that meant she needed to go outside, fast, or there would be an accident to clean up.

"Come on, honey," Jamie said to Sam. "It's morning."

Acknowledgments

Things You Won't Say was born during a conversation with my extraordinary editor, Greer Hendricks. Greer helped me pinpoint exactly what I wanted to write about—and because of her probing questions and creative contributions, this novel was in good shape even before I sat down to type a single word. A good editor can improve a manuscript. A great editor can help inspire an entire book. I'm honored to get to work with Greer, and I'm grateful beyond measure for her friendship, her faith in me, her talent, and her generosity.

My literary agent, Victoria Sanders, is fiercely protective, brilliant, boundlessly kind and loyal. Victoria's careful reading of *Things You Won't Say*—and her subsequent suggestions—made this book better. In good times or bad, Victoria is the kind of agent, and friend, an author needs by her side.

I suspect Sarah Cantin cloned herself a few years ago, because there's no way one woman can do so much, so well. I'm immensely grateful for her constant help.

Marcy Engelman is one of the best dinner companions you could ever hope to have in New York City, and I'm so thankful she continues to sprinkle publicity magic dust over my novels.

My thanks to Chandler Crawford for her many years of hard work and dedication in selling foreign rights to my books, and to Lisa Keim at Atria for the same. Bernadette Baker Baughman is a joy to work with, as is Chris Kepner, and I look forward to many more years and books together. My heartfelt appreciation also to Emily Gambir in Marcy's office.

My gratitude to everyone at the amazing publishing house Atria Books: Judith Curr, Ben Lee, Lisa Sciambra, Carly Sommerstein, Hillary Tisman, Jackie Jou, Yona Deshommes, and Paul Oleswski. And a special thanks to the very funny, very smart Ariele Fredman.

My sincere appreciation to my film agent, Angela Cheng Caplan, and to Kim Yau in her office, for all they have done. And thanks also to Caroline Leavitt for an insightful early read, and to Judge Jennifer Anderson and Robert Seasonwein for providing legal expertise.

More than a decade ago, while working as a features reporter for the *Baltimore Sun*, I wrote an article about police officers in crisis. Recalling that story helped inspire this book. I was incredibly fortunate to work with editors Bill Marimow, John Carroll, and Jan Winburn on "Officer Down!" And I will always be grateful to Officers Lavon'De Alston and Keith Owens for speaking with me at such a difficult time. Officer

Harold Carey Jr., a hero who died in the line of duty in Baltimore, Maryland, in 1998, was the subject of that story.

My gratitude also to the incomparable Kathy Nolan, for her friendship and her incredible support. I'd also like to thank the elephant keepers at the Seattle Zoo for sharing their experience.

Finally, a gigantic hug to my sometimes chaotic, occasionally nutty, usually messy, and always beautiful family.

Discussion Questions

1. Early on in the novel, Jamie feels her husband Mike slipping away: "No matter how hard he tried to exhaust himself, though, the nightmares persisted, and with every passing day, Jamie felt as if her husband was withdrawing a bit more, an invisible casualty of the shooting" (page 15). How does Jamie try to get Mike to open up to her? What did you think of her strategies? As a group, discuss what you think she could have done differently.

2. Jamie, Lou, and Christie are three very different women. Which of them do you identify with the most? The least? Are there any personality traits exhibited by any of these women that you wish you had—or are grateful you don't have?

3. Parenting is a major theme in the novel. At one point, Christie says of Henry: "He wasn't just the most important thing in her life, she thought. He was the only thing she'd ever done right" (page 169). Do you think Christie, Jamie, and Mike work well together in co-parenting Henry? Do you think it's ever

stressful for Henry to split his time between two very different households, with two sets of rules and expectations, or do you believe most children are adaptable?

4. Henry learns about the shooting via text messages, YouTube, and other forms of social media. Discuss how you would handle interference by the media if this were your family. What could Mike and Jamie have done differently to help the kids, especially Henry, cope with the situation?

5. Communication, or lack thereof, is a major issue among the family members. On page 159, Christie expresses that she's hurt to not have been "included in the family crisis." Discuss the communication issues between Jamie and Christie, Christie and Mike, Jamie and Mike, and Lou and Jamie. Is there someone in your life you find it especially difficult to communicate with? Is there anyone in your family who seems to be the "designated communicator"? Why do you think they are in that role?

6. Compare Lou's breakup with Donny to Christie's breakup with Mike. Do you think either relationship could have worked out, had the circumstances been different? Do

you think Christie truly fell back in love with Mike, or was he more appealing to her because she didn't think she could have him?

7. Discuss the scene in the mall with the stranger who verbally harasses Jamie on pages 318–23. Do you agree with how Jamie and Lou handled it, or do you think they risked making the man more upset and angry and possibly escalating the incident? Do you tend to fight back when challenged, or do you prefer to walk away?

8. Christie and Jamie have a relatively strained relationship. Did you find yourself sympathizing with one woman more than the other? Who do you think was more at fault for the issues in their relationship, or do you believe that both women were doing the best they could?

9. During her press conference, Lucia Torres says, "None of us mothers expect to be here, before news crews, talking about our kids whose only crime was to be brown or black" (page 214). Do you agree with Jamie's reaction? If you were to read this scene through Lucia Torres's eyes instead of Jamie's, what do you think she would have

gone through emotionally during her press conference as the mother of the slain boy?

10. Discuss this interaction between Mike and Jamie on page 373: " 'When did you stop believing in me?' he asked. She blinked and looked up at him. His gaze was steely, but it flickered away a second after she met his eyes. It was as if he could hardly bear to look at her." Why is it hard for Jamie to believe there was a gun? Would you have believed your spouse in this case? Why is Christie so quick to believe Mike?

11. Is Mike and Jamie's relationship weaker or stronger by the end of the book?

Scientists in the Legal System

Tolerated Meddlers or Essential Contributors?

edited by
WILLIAM A. THOMAS, PhD, JD

ann arbor science PUBLISHERS INC.
POST OFFICE BOX 1425 ● ANN ARBOR, MICHIGAN 48106

CI

Preface

The objective of this book is to encourage scientists and other technically trained individuals to become more actively involved in our legal system. It originated when the American Association for the Advancement of Science sponsored a symposium entitled "Scientists in the Legal System: Tolerated Meddlers or Essential Contributors?" at its annual meeting in Washington, D.C., in December 1972. All the speakers were lawyers experienced in working with scientists on a variety of legal issues, and their short, provocative presentations elicited spirited debate. Papers presented at that meeting are assembled here with two additional ones to broaden even more the volume's scope. All activities related to the publication of this book occurred while I was affiliated with the Environmental Program at Oak Ridge National Laboratory, where a grant from the RANN Program of the National Science Foundation supported my work.

At the symposium we first examined the interface between science and law as competing or cooperating social forces and how the two should work together to fulfill their responsibilities to the public that supports them. We then examined specific instances of how scientists contribute their knowledge and ideas to help courts reach sound decisions, legislators enact scientifically defensible laws, regulatory agencies function competently, citizen groups serve society better, and other institutions organize their affairs more efficiently. Scientists who attended received not only an overview of how the legal system functions but also an appreciation of how essential science is to its operation. We hope readers of this book will gain the same insights.

This volume is not meant to provide encyclopedic coverage, but rather to present an overview of ways in which scientists and lawyers interact to resolve issues. The spectrum is broad and diverse indeed, as reflected by the range of subjects covered by the authors.

We have endeavored to make the book useful to both scientists and lawyers in an attempt to encourage cooperation between two professions that has been hindered in the past by mutual misunderstandings. These must be overcome if we are to respond to the increasing demands of society. Scientists and lawyers share an obligation to work together within the legal system for the mutual benefit of all concerned, and we shall consider this book a success if it facilitates that cooperation.

American Bar Foundation   William A. Thomas
Chicago, Illinois   *Editor*
January 1974

Contents

Scientists and Lawyers: Their Obligation
to Cooperate, *William A. Thomas* 1

Jurimetrics: Science in Law, *Lee Loevinger* 7

Reception of Science by the Legal System,
Ralph Norvell 26

Law, Science, and Public Policy: A Problem in
Communication, *James W. Curlin* 35

Obligation of Scientists to Respond to
Society's Needs, *Ralph Nader* 46

The Legal System: Can It Be Analyzed to
Suit the Scientist? *James P. Vanyo* 55

Exchange of Ideas Between Scientists and
Lawyers: A Benefit/Cost Analysis,
Roderick A. Cameron 67

Courts as Institutions for Assessing Technology,
Philip L. Bereano 73

Scientists as Suppliers of Facts: Do Lawyers
Listen? *Donald R. Moore* 97

Scientists in the Courtroom, *David Sive* 103

The Time Lag Between Medicine and Law,
Edwin J. Holman 109

The Scientists' Role in Citizen Environmental
Advocacy, *John S. Winder, Jr.* 118

Who Stole Scientism from Science and Law?
George S. Robinson 123

Science and Society in the Environment Age,
Maurice F. Strong 130

Scientists and Lawyers:
Their Obligation to Cooperate

WILLIAM A. THOMAS*
Environmental Program
Oak Ridge National Laboratory†
Oak Ridge, Tennessee

SOCIETY'S INCREASING DEPENDENCE ON SCIENCE AND ITS CONTINUING RE-
liance on law to resolve the inevitable conflicts require an examination
of how scientists contribute to the legal system and how the incorpora-
tion of science and scientists' viewpoints can be facilitated. Although
these two professions appear to be dissimilar, they actually share many
attributes and are working together now more than ever before.

The legal system interprets and utilizes science in four somewhat
distinct yet complementary ways.[1]

1. As a reference to the scientific method whereby knowledge is
   categorized in an orderly manner. This is the emphasis given
   science in such classics as "Law in Science and Science in Law"
   by Oliver Wendell Holmes[2] and *The Paradoxes of Legal Science* by Benjamin N. Cardozo.[3]
2. As a necessary component of the adjudication process involving
   knowledge related to specific factual issues. The technical nature of much evidence today and the scientific issues in question indicate an increasing demand for scientists in the courtroom.[4]
3. As an impetus for change that often advances faster than the
   law. That is, science's purposes of understanding the universe

* Current address: American Bar Foundation, 1155 East 60th Street, Chicago,
Illinois 60637.

† Operated by Union Carbide Corporation for the U.S. Atomic Energy
Commission.

1

and promulgating organized knowledge are being realized faster than is the law's purpose of assuring an ordered society.[5] The Industrial Revolution required 150 years to fashion the Industrial State, thus allowing time for our legal system to accommodate new developments. Now, technological advances all too often outpace the law.[6]

4. As an important consideration in establishing policy at local, state, national, and international levels. The growth and influence of science and technology simply cannot be overlooked when establishing priorities and grand designs within the social system.[7]

The scientific and legal systems both stem from a common historical purpose—ascertaining the truth—but the conceptual approach differs markedly between them. Science seeks truth with impartial objectivity; law seeks a truth tempered with justice.

Law serves to ensure a stable social order, and lawyers generally search for the truth on a case-by-case basis in which the fact finding often cannot wait for elaborate testing of theories, models, and ideas; the scope of factual issues is circumscribed by the situation. On the other hand, science seeks an understanding of our surroundings, and scientists search for universal truths that often defy rapid elucidation; there is no predetermined limit to the significance of a particular investigation. The work of one scientist is based upon the accumulated works of his predecessors, but in law the search for specific facts usually ends when the trial concludes, although the evolution of legal principles runs throughout the entire chronological series of similar cases.

Simply stated, lawyers need answers as soon as possible, or at least the best possible answers, whereas scientists generally do not work under a deadline for finality. Scientists and lawyers frequently work together on specific cases as individuals, but as professions the degree of cooperation is not so encouraging. The subtitle of this book is intended to reflect some uncertainty about the relationship.

Most lawyers feel at ease in an adversary proceeding, but scientists generally shun this as a method for fact finding, preferring cooperation with fellow investigators in working toward a common goal. As more scientists become involved in the political process, they no doubt will accept the adversary procedure as a workable one when the issues involve social decisions that cannot be resolved by the familiar scientific regimens.[8] Perhaps this transition would be eased if scientists were not so willing to be categorized into professional subdisciplines. Lawyers traditionally resist classification, and most tend to think of themselves more as generalists than as specialists.

Lawyers often appear surprised to learn that all scientists are not equally conversant in oceanography, genetics, and high energy physics, and many scientists have trouble understanding why every lawyer cannot describe the inner workings of the United Nations, explain the federal licensing procedures for nuclear power plants, and offer an instant analysis of a newly discovered deed executed in 1850. Not unexpectedly, inadequate communication between scientists and lawyers accounts for these unfulfilled expectations.[9] Neither profession should place the responsibility on the other for initiating the needed exchange of information that will increase understanding of the capabilities and limitations of each.

For an idea of the existing opportunities to introduce scientists' viewpoints into the legal process, consider the scientific activities generated by only two federal statutes, the National Environmental Policy Act of 1969[10] and the Occupational Safety and Health Act of 1970,[11] let alone all the others that create and support the myriad of activities within the executive branch.[12] As a result, courts are called upon to resolve more and more issues of an increasingly technical nature.[13]

Due to relatively modern events, lawyers need to become more familiar with the scientific philosophy. Of course, lawyers frequently need to know something about science in order to establish facts to which they can apply law in resolving specific issues, but a more fundamental reason exists. Science now is an integral component of our culture and, in fact, dominates many of the current local, national, and international political questions that will be decided almost exclusively by nonscientists. It is imperative that lawyers understand more about science and how scientists approach problems because most of our laws are created by lawyers and the majority of governmental and similar social institutions are governed by persons trained in the legal tradition.

The authors in this volume emphasize primarily the physical sciences, including the biological and chemical, rather than the social ones because the latter are so entwined with the legal system that they often are indistinguishable. Examples of social sciences within the legal system abound: anthropologists study the coordinated evolution of cultures and legal systems; economists compare efficiencies of operations within different systems; psychologists look into lawyer–client relationships, jury selection, and courtroom behavior; political scientists evaluate the various institutions of government; and sociologists compare legislation in various jurisdictions and the different judicial interpretations of laws among geographical areas. As these few examples demonstrate, social sciences are inherent within the legal system. In fact, law itself often is classified as a social science.

Scientists seem to be awakening to the realization that a need exists for their talents within the legal system,[14] if for no other reason than the upsurge in citizen involvement in governmental operations at all levels. However, scientists cannot expect to influence society through law without some knowledge of how that system utilizes science and of how scientists can respond to society's need in this manner. Scientists who accept the challenge fulfill an obligation they share with lawyers as citizens and as professionals to further the causes of our democracy. Without question, lawyers recognize the contributions of scientists. Equally without question, the legal system does not operate as effectively as it could if it had the benefit of more active participation by scientists.

REFERENCES

1. For a similar classification under five headings, see Cavers, "Law and Science: Some Points of Confrontation," in *Law and the Social Role of Science* 5 (H. Jones ed.), Rockefeller University Press (1966).
2. 12 Harvard Law Review 443 (1899).
3. Columbia University Press (1928).
4. *See, e.g.,* A. Moenssens, R. Moses & F. Inbau, *Scientific Evidence in Criminal Cases,* Foundation Press (1973); Bazelon, "Justice Stumbles on Science," 1 Irish Jurist 273 (1966); Korn, "Law, Fact, and Science in the Courts," 66 Columbia Law Review 1080 (1966); Sive, "Securing, Examining, and Cross-Examining Expert Witnesses in Environmental Cases," 68 Michigan Law Review 1175 (1970); and Wolder, Halpern & Gerver, "Finding Scientific Fact" (Editorial), 1 Lex et Scientia 61 (1964).
5. About a decade ago, Chief Justice Warren reminded us that "In 1692 in Massachusetts, only a few miles from Cambridge where Harvard University had been advancing the sciences for more than a half century, they were burning innocent women at the stake for witchcraft under the law in Salem." Warren, "Science and the Law: Change and the Constitution," 12 Journal of Public Law 3, 5 (1963). Perhaps we too readily assume that such contradictions are limited to centuries past.
6. For discussion see Curlin, "Saving Us from Ourselves: The Interaction of

Law and Science-Technology," 47 Denver Law Journal 651 (1971); Katz, "The Function of Tort Liability in Technology Assessment," 38 Cincinnati Law Review 587 (1969); Miller, "Science vs. Law: Some Legal Problems Raised by 'Big Science,'" 17 Buffalo Law Review 591 (1968); and Note, "The Role of the Courts in Technology Assessment," 55 Cornell Law Review 861 (1970).

7. *See* E. Patterson, *Law in a Scientific Age*, Columbia University Press (1963).

A quick review of United Nations or U.S. Congressional publications will dispel any doubts about the need for more cooperation by scientists in policy-making. Charles A. Mosher, U.S. Congressman from Ohio, concluded a discussion of how Congress reaches decisions as follows:

> There is abundant room and a very real need in the political policy-making system for more participation by you business, academic, scientific, and engineering people who are here today. We politicians need your help. I do invite you—urge you—to become much more politically "concerned," "relevant," "activist"—in all the more positive, affirmative meanings of those somewhat hackneyed phrases.
>
> *I suggest that in the past, too often you have been shy, timid, or diffident, sometimes too disdainful* [emphasis in original].

Mosher, "Needs and Trends in Congressional Decision-Making," 178 Science 134, 138 (1972).

The Technology Assessment Act of 1972, 2 U.S.C. §§ 471 *et seq.* (Supp. II, 1972) created an Office of Technology Assessment to provide early analyses of probable beneficial and detrimental effects associated with applications of technology.

8. As crystallized by Weinberg:

> If the question is unambiguously scientific, then the procedures of science rather than the procedures of law are required for arriving at the truth. Where the questions raised cannot be answered from existing scientific knowledge or from research which could be carried out reasonably rapidly and without disproportionate expense, then the answers must be trans-scientific and the adversary procedure seems therefore to be the best alternative.

Weinberg, "Science and Trans-Science," 10 Minerva 210, 215 (1972).

9. Curlin, "Fostering Understanding Between Science and Law," 59 American Bar Association Journal 157 (1973); Huard, "Law and Science: Marriage, Divorce or Meretricious Relationship?," 5 Santa Clara Law Review 1 (1964).

Perhaps basic educational policies in the United States contribute to the problem. Miller, "Science and Legal Education," 19 Case Western Law

Review 29 (1967); Morris, "Future Lawyers, Science and Innovations in Grading," 58 American Bar Association Journal 43 (1972).

10. 42 U.S.C. §§ 4321 et seq. (1970). For an account of progress to date see F. Anderson (assisted by R. Daniels), *NEPA in the Courts*, Resources for the Future (1973).

11. 29 U.S.C. §§ 651 et seq. (1970).

12. Even the Internal Revenue Service found the services of expert entomologists useful. Rev. Rul. 63–232, 1963–2 Cum. Bull. 97, commented upon by Pinkerton, "The Turmoil Over Termites," 42 Taxes 713 (1964).

13. *See, e.g.*, International Harvester Co. vs. Ruckelshaus, 478 F.2d 615 (1973), in which the court considered technological, economic, and ecological arguments concerning a proposed suspension of federal regulations for automobile exhausts.

14. "There is a whole web of issues on which advancing medical, technological, sociological, or psychological knowledge does, should, or perhaps will argue for legal changes." Wolfle, "Law and Science" (Editorial), 166 Science 457 (1969).

Jurimetrics: *Science in Law*

LEE LOEVINGER*
Hogan & Hartson
Washington, D.C.

THE EFFORT TO MAKE LAW SCIENTIFIC IS, IN A SENSE, OLDER THAN SCIENCE itself. The essence of science is the use of reason to seek objective answers to specific questions. From the time of earliest recorded history, man has sought to make legal inquiry more rational. By contemporary standards, the efforts have often been mistaken, misguided, and inadequate; but, by their own standards, ancient societies were far more rational than modern man usually assumes or is willing to believe.

The great legal historian, Maine, says:

> It is now clearly seen by all trustworthy observers of the primitive condition of mankind that, in the infancy of the race, men could only account for sustained or periodically recurring action by supposing a personal agent. Thus, the wind blowing was a person and of course a divine person; the sun rising, culminating, and setting was a person and a divine person; the earth yielding her increase was a person and divine. As, then, in the physical world, so in the moral. When a king decided a dispute by a sentence, the judgment was assumed to be the result of direct inspiration. . . . The only authoritative statement of right and wrong is a judicial sentence after the facts, not one presupposing a law which has been violated, but one which is breathed for the first time by a higher power into the judge's mind at the moment of adjudication.[1]

Throughout most of the history of mankind such factual issues as the law undertook to determine were settled by submission to the wager of law (or compurgation), the wager of battle, ordeal, or torture.[2] These barbaric practices were not the result of sadistic impulse but rather were methods of appealing to some supernatural or divine power for a decision because of the "natural tendency in the human mind to cast the

---

* Mailing address: Hogan & Hartson, 815 Connecticut Avenue NW, Washington, D.C. 20006.

burden of its doubts upon a higher power, and to relieve itself from the effort of decision by seeking in the unknown the solution of its difficulties."[3] The ordeal as a mode of trial began to decline in 1215 when Pope Innocent III forbade the participation of priests in ordeals, thus depriving them of their divine sanction.[4] However, the ordeal persisted in one form or another into the 19th century and appeared in its most vulgar and abhorrent form in the episode of sorcery and witchcraft trials in the 16th and 17th centuries.[5] Trial by compurgation and accusatorial conjurators was maintained until the 16th century,[6] the use of torture persisted in England into the 17th century[7] and in Scotland until the 18th century,[8] and trial by battle survived until finally abolished by law in England in the early 19th century.[9]

In English law there were no rules of evidence at least until the 13th century, since under the primitive practices of trial by compurgation, battle, and ordeal, proof was accomplished by appeal to God.[10] During the period from the 13th to the 16th centuries there was a gradual change to trial by jury with a differentiation of the process of pleading and procedure from that of proof; and the foundation for the rules of evidence was not laid until the 16th century when this process had taken place.[11] The principle that a verdict must be reached solely on evidence presented in court was not established until the end of the 17th century; and it was not until Bushell's Case in 1670 that English courts accepted the principle that jurors may not be punished for acquitting a defendant.[12] Right of cross-examination by counsel was established at the beginning of the 18th century.[13] The rules of evidence were developed during the 18th century, and the first treatise on the law of evidence was published in 1726.[14] The rules of evidence were fully developed into a system by the early 19th century.[15]

In the early 19th century the primitive modes of trial or truth-seeking were formally abolished, and the two basic evidentiary principles of modern legal procedure were established: first, none but facts having rational probative value are admissible;[16] and, second, all facts having rational probative value are admissible unless some specific rule excludes them.[17]

Ancient science, like ancient law, was taught by priests and was not a distinct or separate subject of its own.[18] While primitive man sought to study and to control nature, he employed magic based on superstitious belief in rite and spell and a faith that superhuman powers would intervene directly in response to such rituals, as in the case of legal battle and ordeal.[19] Science as an organized discipline with recognized tactics and strategy involving rigorous modes of observation and experiment has been developed only since the early 17th century.²⁰

James Conant has observed:

As one skims the histories of the natural sciences, it seems clear that in the embryonic stages of each of the modern disciplines, violent polemics rather than reasoned opinion often flowed most easily from the pen. . . . But if I read the history of science in the Seventeenth and Eighteenth centuries rightly, it was only gradually that there evolved the idea that a scientific investigator must impose on himself a rigorous self-discipline the moment he enters his laboratory.²¹

The beginning of the modern scientific era is sometimes dated from the time of Nicolaus Copernicus (1473–1543), but the astronomical theories of Copernicus, which were not published until the last year of his life, were largely speculative and inaccurate until refined and supported by the observation of Tycho Brahe (1546–1601), Galileo Galilei (1564–1642), and Johannes Kepler (1571–1630).

It is probably more than coincidence that Francis Bacon (1561–1626), who is mentioned as an important figure in the early development of modern law, is better known as the author of an essay on a new method (*Novum Organum*) in the early history of modern science. It was Bacon who perceived the vices of the scholastic method and set forth clearly the widening breach which separated the men of his day from the Middle Ages.²² The writings of Bacon were an impetus of the foundation of the Royal Society, and he is thought by some to be one of the founders of the empiric method in science.

Even a casual survey of the pioneering work in the major fields of science will show the concomitance in the development of modern science and modern law. Modern medicine began with the anatomical observations of Andreas Vesalius (1514–1564) and the physiological observations of William Harvey (1578–1657). The modern study of optics began with Christian Huygens (1629–1695). The systematic study of botany began with Carl Linnaeus (1707–1778). The foundations of modern biology were laid by Charles Darwin (1809–1882). Antoine Lavoisier (1743–1794) destroyed the old idea of phlogiston, established the law of conservation of matter, together with Joseph Priestley (1733–1804) discovered oxygen, and laid the foundation of modern chemistry. Sir Isaac Newton (1642–1727) established the laws of motion and gravitation and laid the foundations of modern physics. The founder of the modern scientific study of electricity is William Gilbert (1544–1603), but the basic theory of contemporary work in the field was laid by James Clark Maxwell (1831–1879), and modern work in the field of electricity did not really begin until the discovery of electrical waves or cycles in 1887 by Heinrich Hertz (1857–1894).

Thus, science and law both had their origins in the superstitions of primitive religion, and both developed their modern intellectual outlooks during the 17th, 18th, and 19th centuries as a reaction against and rejection of medieval scholasticism and superstition. The common elements in both have been an effort to be wholly rational, to organize and institutionalize the search for truthful data, and, above all, to seek truthful data as the basis for judgments. Science can equally well accept the basic principles of the legal system of evidence: to accept only rationally probative evidence and to examine all relevant evidence unless there is some overriding reason for disregarding it.

Nevertheless, it is clear that the legal and the scientific methods of inquiry are, despite those similarities, quite different. The legal method of inquiry relies primarily on the testimony of human observers, tested by examination and cross-examination, and subjectively weighed by a judge or jury. Essentially this is the method of inquiry by interrogation which may appropriately be called "dialectic." The dialectic method is most organized and formalized in the evidentiary and procedural rules for the conduct of legal trials. However, essentially the same method is employed throughout the ramifications of government in all but the most undeveloped countries. In the legislative process, as in litigation, information is sought in hearings which employ the dialectic method, although the more formal and rigorous rules of the evidentiary system are not commonly employed. It is fair to say that, taking law in its largest sense as encompassing all aspects of government, the predominant mode of securing legal data is the dialectic method.

The scientific method is clearly a different and distinguishable approach to data gathering, although it is not nearly so certain, as was once thought, that there is any specific and unique technique that is entitled to be known as "the scientific method."[23] Science is like law in that it is a mode of securing agreement among different individuals with respect to certain kinds of questions and problems.[24] The strength of science derives from its objective and demonstrative, and therefore highly persuasive, techniques. The limitation of science is that it is not applicable to all kinds of questions and problems. Essentially the scientific method is applicable only to questions of the kind commonly characterized as those involving issues of "fact."

The basic methods of science are experimental, statistical, and clinical.[25] The experimental method is to control the variation of one or a few elements in a series of phenomena while observing the concomitant variation of other elements. The statistical method involves observation of a relatively large number of cases, either directly or by a representative sample of the universe, to ascertain the concomitant variation of specific elements within the universe. The clinical method involves the observation and analysis of individual cases to determine causal, necessary, or influential relationships among the elements of a given class of phenomena. Although scientific inquiry may thus be experimental, statistical, clinical, or possibly taxonomic or something else, it is always empiric. Science recognizes no meaning that is not empirically definable and accepts no significance that is not empirically demonstrable.

This does not mean that the scientific method is inapplicable to legal problems. Much of the activity of government, including that of legislators, judges, administrators, and other lawyers, consists of investigating and ascertaining facts. The facts sometimes concern a single instance, as in investigating the circumstances of a particular lawsuit, and other times involve ascertaining data concerning a class or universe, as in a legislative investigation to determine the need for a new law and the abuses to be cured by it. However, "facts" never exist in isolation; even when an inquiry appears to be directed at a single set of circumstances, it necessarily involves either data or assumptions regarding the universe in which those circumstances occurred. Implicit in the whole legal system of seeking and accepting evidence in particular cases are a host of assumptions concerning the reliability of observation, retention, and recall by human witnesses and the effectiveness of examination and cross-examination as a means of eliciting and testing recollection. These assumptions are themselves not subject either to falsification or corroboration by the dialectic method and are precisely the kind which can be investigated and tested by the empiric method.[26] The law has to date made no systematic effort either to investigate the validity and reliability of testimonial evidence or to utilize the scientific data available on this subject, and the subject seems to have received little attention from scientists in recent years.

However, the use of science in seeking answers to social and legal problems has long been urged by eminent scientists and lawyers. The great scientist, Karl Pearson, writing in 1892, expressed the spirit of his age when he said:

The classification of facts and the formation of absolute judgments upon the basis of this classification—judgments independent of the idiosyncracies of the individual mind—essentially sum up the aim and method of modern science. The scientific man has above all things to strive at self-elimination in his judgments, to provide an argument which is as true for each individual mind as for his own. The classification of facts, the recognition of their sequence and relative significance is the function of science, and the habit of forming a judgment upon these facts unbiased by personal feeling is characteristic of what may be termed the scientific frame of mind. The scientific method of examining facts is not peculiar to one class of phenomena and to one class of workers; it is applicable to social as well as to physical problems, and we must carefully guard ourselves against supposing that the scientific frame of mind is a peculiarity of the professional scientist.[27]

The same views were expressed by the great lawyer and jurist, Oliver Wendell Holmes, in 1895 when he said:

An ideal system of law should draw its postulates and legislative justifications from science. As it is now, we rely upon tradition, or vague sentiment, or the fact that we never thought of any other way of doing things, as our only warrant for rules which we enforce with as much confidence as if they embodied revealed wisdom.[28]

Holmes reiterated this theme more than once; and he spoke for a school and a generation of legal realists when he declared:

For the rational study of the law the black-letter man may be the man of the present, but the man of the future is the man of statistics and the master of economics.[29]

. . . The growth of education is an increase in the knowledge of measure. To use words familiar to logic and to science, it is a substitution of quantitative for qualitative judgments. . . . In the law we only occasionally can reach an absolutely final and quantitative determination, because the worth of the competing social ends which respectively solicit a judgment for the plaintiff or the defendant cannot be reduced to number and accurately fixed. The worth, that is, the intensity of the competing desires, varies with the varying ideal of the time, and, if the desires were constant, we could not get beyond a relative decision that one was greater and one was less. But it is of the essence of improvement that we should be as accurate as we can.

. . . I have had in mind an ultimate dependence upon science because it is finally for science to determine, so far as it can, the relative worth of our different social ends, and, as I have tried to hint, it is our estimate of the proportion between these, now often blind and unconscious, that leads us to insist upon and to enlarge the sphere of one principle and to allow another gradually to dwindle into atrophy. Very likely it may be that with all the help that statistics and every modern appliance can bring us, there never will be a commonwealth in which science is everywhere supreme. But it is an ideal, and without ideals what is life worth?[30]

The 20th century has seen the most spectacular advances in the achievements of science and its products as well as in the proliferation of legal rules and precedents. If, then, the foresight of those who spoke for the 19th century was sound, it would be reasonable to expect that science should by now have made at least some substantial contributions to the solution of basic legal problems. However, realism compels the conclusion that science has contributed little, if anything, to the solution of legal or social problems. Indeed, it may well have exacerbated latent problems or created new ones.

This immediately poses a challenge to seek the reason for this failure. Has science failed to live up to its promise? Have we failed to recognize or utilize the answers provided by science? Or was the insight of earlier thinkers in error, and is science necessarily concerned only with physical phenomena and inapplicable to social fields?

Certainly there are no clear and unqualified answers to any of these questions. However, at least part of the failure stems from the fact that those who invoke science have asked the wrong questions and set it the wrong tasks. They have expected science to distill social policies from a test tube or a retort, much as Aladdin summoned a genie by rubbing a magic lamp. They have imagined that social scientists could produce tables that would permit us to read the numerical value of competing interests and desires much as the mathematicians have produced tables of logarithms, sines, and cosines. Justice Cardozo sighed for a "table of logarithms" to produce the "formula of justice."[31] With the recent advent of electronic computers, some now have the impression that scientists may be able to produce or construct a machine that will by itself give the answers to legal questions or give reliable predictions as to the actual decision of legal cases or issues. The fulfillment of such expections is obviously not imminent and probably not possible. An analysis of the problems of law and the functions of science may suggest why.

The difference in the legal and scientific modes of securing data is, as has often been observed, at least partially a function of the different tasks performed by law and science. While science seeks to analyze and predict phenomena, law seeks to classify and control conduct. In the most simple and elementary terms it may be said that the function of science is descriptive and that of law is prescriptive. The task of law is normative—to provide standards for conduct and living; the job of science is explicative—to provide data and principles that permit understanding and predicting observable phenomena. The two are related, for control is based on understanding and prediction. But the two functions are not the same, as will be observed by more detailed analysis of the legal job.

Law operates on two levels, often characterized as the public and the private. What the lawyers call "public law," and scientists would call "macrolaw," has to do with the making of public policy—things like the relations between countries, the construction of social security and welfare systems, the formulation of broad policies for the protection of consumers, ethnic minorities, and the like. What is called "private law," or what scientists would call "microlaw," is the law as it is applied to individuals and businesses in particular cases. The distinction is not absolute, since individual cases are sometimes the vehicle for promulgating broad public policies, but the distinction is a practical one that differentiates the great mass of legal work.

The principal interest of those who are concerned with contributing to law usually is in the making of policy, or the public, or macrolaw, sector. The principal interest of most lawyers and other professionals in the field is in the private, or microlaw, sector. To varying degrees in both there are at least half a dozen distinguishable aspects of the legal task. When confronted with any problem, the law must, first, adopt an objective or goal. Second, it must establish its method of inquiry. Third, it must secure factual data. Fourth, it must organize its concepts or logical framework. Fifth, it must analyze the data. Sixth, it must formulate a rule or decision.

The contribution that scientists have been able to make to law up to the present time has been mainly by way of offering evidence in specific cases, that is, by providing factual data in the microlaw field. There has been a substantial amount of this, particularly in personal injury and criminal cases. Most of the seminars for lawyers offered in past years under the title of "Science and Law" had to do with the use of medical science in ascertaining the extent of personal injuries in accident cases. In the field of criminal detection, apprehension, and identification, law has used fingerprints, blood and hair identification, ballistics, microscopic and chemical analysis, radar, devices to test blood, breath, and urine alcohol, psychiatric testimony as to responsibility, and will undoubtedly use such things as voiceprints when their reliability is established. The polygraph, or lie detector, and other means of detecting testimonial deception are still struggling for legal recognition; they are used to some extent at the present time, and they will probably be accepted by lawyers when they have become more generally accepted by scientists.

In the fields of regulation of such subjects as communication, power, and transportation, scientific data are regularly sought and relied upon with respect to such matters as transmission and interference in the electromagnetic spectrum, modes of transmitting and interconnecting electric power, resources of petroleum and natural gas, and, of course, all aspects of atomic energy. Psychologists, sociologists, and survey research experts testify in cases involving consumer habits and attitudes. A variety of scientists are employed to provide evidence in cases involving asserted liability for unsafe or defective products. Finally, the computer is beginning to be utilized in what must be termed limited and experimental attempts to record and retrieve legal data.[32] Although the potential impact of computers on the law has been hailed and denounced as basic and far-reaching, a more realistic appraisal would appear to be that computer retrieval may enable lawyers to discover more quickly and completely the same kind of legal data they now use. This application will be mostly on the microlaw level, although computers are also being used to record and retrieve data in the process of drafting and compiling statutes and ordinances. Computers are also being used in law, as in business, to improve the efficiency of bookkeeping processes both in law offices and in courts. This is important but hardly revolutionary.

The major obstacle to an even greater use of science and scientific evidence in microlaw, or individual cases, is undoubtedly the ignorance of lawyers and judges about science. Few lawyers have even a vague impression of the basic principles of statistics, sampling methods, or probability theory, much less of more specific scientific matters such as the conservation principles. Nevertheless, lawyers will learn about areas of science that appear relevant to their jobs, as is demonstrated by specialists in personal injury, communications, and other fields, who become quite expert in the narrow areas of science and technology that have practical application to their specialties.

The obvious method of making science more useful in the legal process, at least on the microlaw level, is to require all law school graduates to have a basic knowledge of science. Demonstration of the relevance to law, and exploration of the nexus between science and law, will probably require that the subject be taught in law schools rather than as a more generalized course at the undergraduate level. At a minimum, law school graduation should require a general knowledge of the elements of scientific method, including operational definitions, reliance on empirical evidence, quantification and indeterminacy, testing by multiple hypotheses, replicability, and the concept of disclosure and peer review. The relationship between statistics, sampling, and probability theory as used in science, and weight of evidence and burden of proof as used in law should be explored. Lawyers should understand that conservation principles are highly relevant to what happens in automobile accidents and similar events. Lawyers should learn that there is a substantial body of scientific data to establish the unreliability of testimonial evidence and to show that no two individuals perceive any complex occurrence quite the same; that the ability of individuals to retain, recall, and relate memory differs greatly; and that there is no wholly reliable witness since observation, retention, and recall of all witnesses are faulty in some degree and some situations.[33] Practical applications of sampling procedures and statistical analysis of probability can be illustrated by cases involving charges of employment discrimination, issues regarding fair jury selection, and equal protection cases involving inequality of sentences and other objective or quantitative indicia of treatment. As lawyers and judges become more familiar with scientific principles and attitudes, it seems likely that they will be more inclined to employ such principles and attitudes and to seek scientific data in dealing with issues of public or macrolaw.

The real crux of the subject is this: What influence shall science have on public law and public policy? The faith of many enlightened thinkers during the first half of the 20th century was that science could not only offer data and methodology but that it could also choose goals and make decisions. Those who take this view, and there still are some of them, are not satisfied to have science merely offer evidence in particular lawsuits; they believe social salvation requires a much broader role. Sociologist George A. Lundberg, writing shortly after World War II, was stating the case most strongly when he said:

Can science save us? Yes, but we must not expect physical science to solve social problems. . . . If we want results in improved human relations we must direct research to the solution of these problems. . . . It comes down, then, to this: Shall we put our faith in science or in something else? We have already answered that question as regards our physical problems. Once we make up our minds to do likewise regarding our social predicaments, the path before us is clear. . . . When we give our undivided faith to science, we shall possess a faith more worthy of allegiance than many we have vainly followed in the past, and we shall also accelerate the translation of our faith into actuality.[34]

"Science" in this context, of course, means "scientists," and the faith is that right decisions are more likely to be made by scientists, or on the basis of their advice, than by others. Nearly a quarter of a century later, C. P. Snow writes:

I want scientists active in all levels of government. By "scientists" here I mean people trained in the natural sciences, not only engineers, though I want them too. I make a special requirement for the scientists proper, because, partly by training, partly by self-selection, they include a number of speculative and socially imaginative minds.[35]

It is noteworthy that sociologist Lundberg puts his faith in social scientists, while physicist Snow demands natural scientists in government.

Without being explicitly adopted publicly, these views have been influential with government. In this country there is an Office of Science and Technology in the Executive Office of the President, there are scientists in many major departments and agencies, and there are some fifteen hundred committees set up to provide advice to government agencies specifically in areas of science and technology.[36]

The difficulty is that, from the viewpoint of the average citizen, it is not at all apparent that science has solved, or significantly contributed to the solution of, any social problem, while it appears to have created or exacerbated a number of problems. It is readily admitted that science has nearly wiped out many diseases that used to scourge mankind and has considerably improved the health and comfort of the average person. Against this many see as problems created or exacerbated by science the mounting threat of environmental pollution; the risks of radiation from atomic energy use and atomic wastes; the whole complexus of problems involving human sex and arising from newly developed methods of sterilization and birth control, artificial insemination, and genetic engineering; organ transplants; electronic snooping and invasion of privacy; computer record keeping (which has victimized almost everyone in one way or another); weather modification; the threat of atomic bombs and of the many other new and devastating weapons science has helped to create; and even the ubiquitous daily problem of urban transportation. Even when presented with a specific, limited social question, scientists cannot provide an unequivocal answer, as the Surgeon General has recently demonstrated in his report on the effects of television violence on the behavior of children.[37] In 1954 the Supreme Court thought that it was echoing the conclusions of social science in declaring that segregated education is unequal and therefore unconstitutional.[38] Now at least a few scientists challenge that premise.[39] The problem is, as C. P. Snow admits, "it is not always easy to know which scientists to trust."[40]

This has inevitably produced a protest and reaction against the use of science, which has been articulated by Jacques Barzun in these terms:

During the past thirty years the articulate have unceasingly cried out against the tyranny of scientific thought, the oppression of machinery, the hegemony of things, the dehumanization brought about by the sway of number and quantity.

. . . [O]ur scientific culture often expects behavioral science answers to the question What Ought to Be, and the answer often given is a composite report that conceals under figures subjective impressions and shifting measurements of What Is. Leaning on the normal distribution curve we try to compute the greatest good of the greatest number, a response to perplexity which is now a habit, and one strengthened by every extension of the behavioral search for causes. The determinism that warrants this search rests on the axiom that man is kin with the animals and functions like a machine. The problem is to find the physical facts and social forces that drive it. It is by this kind of study that the general public is alternately alarmed and reassured, while the philosophical are alienated. . . . The much more dangerous superstition abroad today is that if behavioral science did progress our problems could be solved. This plausible proposition is fraught with calamity.[41]

Unfortunately, there are those in science who lend plausibility to the charges and fears of Barzun and those who agree with him. The editor of a popular social science journal celebrates its tenth anniversary by writing:

Social science is more than a business, and it is even more than a series of findings and methods: it is an ideology. It has needs and makes representations of its own. It demands the same passions, the same sense of commitment, the same driving series of beliefs that any other ideology requires. It is not enough to speak of ideology as some kind of hybrid of science and theology. It is much more than that. It is the driving passion for a world of peace and reason to which all social science must ultimately dedicate itself, despite the absence of any logical, formal mandate to do so.[42]

As scientists become more committed they become more shrill and more adversary—and less scientific.[43] Scientific meetings are interrupted by heckling and rowdyism.[44] Scientists announce themselves as adversaries and advocates,[45] and an administrative law judge says that scientific witnesses spoke "words that were not those of a free mind. Nor did they express a proper respect for the discipline of a free science."[46]

Unfortunately, a scientist who is a zealot is no different than anyone else who is a zealot. Both are possessed by a burning conviction of self-righteousness and an intolerance for opposition or difference of opinion. It is presumptuous arrogance to suggest that a passion for a world of peace and reason is the special possession of social scientists or in any way the particular domain of social science.

The fact seems to be that many who have the proper academic credentials and labor in fields denominated "scientific" do not, themselves, understand science. As the editor of *Science News* has put it:

Until recently many segments of the scientific community tended to adopt a stance of self-righteous High Priestism toward the general public. One was not to understand how scientists arrived at their answers, one was only to receive their pronouncements with thanks and a measure of awe. Scientists allowed the misconception to grow that science was the source of final answers rather than merely a continual process of asking questions and searching for answers.[47]

A committee of the National Academy of Sciences reports that the typical science teacher does not understand that

science is more than a collection of facts to be memorized or techniques to be mastered but is instead an inquiry carried on by people who raise questions for which answers are unknown and who have gained confidence in their ability to reach conclusions, albeit tentative ones, through experiment and careful thought sharpened by the open criticism of others.[48]

Many of the professionals working in fields of science and calling themselves "scientists" are merely highly trained and educated technicians who do not truly understand the history, the methods, or the philosophy of science.

There is no basis for a claim that scientists as such are entitled to speak in the realm of law or policy with any more authority than any one else. There is no evidence that the study or practice of science makes men wise, objective, or ethical, or even scientific outside their own fields of specialization. Certainly not everything uttered by a scientist is necessarily science—any more than everything uttered by a lawyer is necessarily the law. Scientists speak as scientists only when they speak of science and within their own fields of expertise and labor. Discussing topics other than their professional fields, scientists speak only as ordinary citizens, sharing all the faults and fallibility of normal humans. Don K. Price has observed:

It is obvious on the record that scientists who are highly sophisticated in their own disciplines are quite capable of supporting authoritarian political theories on either the right or the left, or at least passively accepting them—and this seems to be as true in the social as in the physical and biological sciences.[49]

Another difficulty is that there is a fundamental incompatibility between the role of scientist and the role of lawgiver. Science is, and by its nature must be, completely nonauthoritarian and dedicated to the proposition that every rule and datum is open to challenge and testing. Government, on the other hand, is, by its nature, necessarily authoritative and even somewhat authoritarian. Science is committed to theorizing and to seeking and accepting answers which are perpetually tentative. Government is in the business of deciding controversies and terminating debates by declaring one side to be right, or prevailing, and the other wrong, despite the fact that there may be much merit on both sides. Science is an activity that is interested only in the pursuit of knowledge, that is disinterested in power and other practical considerations, and that is attached only to intellectual ideals. Government is in the business of managing power and is primarily, if not solely, concerned with practical considerations. Government has no institutional concern with intellectual ideals, but is, or should be, guided by ethical ideals which may be quite different.

When science becomes a part of government, it is the science that is corrupted, not the government that is ennobled. As a speaker at the 1971 AAAS annual meeting pointed out:

To the extent that the scientific enterprise becomes enmeshed in this [governmental] network, its critical distance is diminished. Independent, critical work is dampened and impeded where there exist obligations or close connections to those in power. What this means is that one cannot serve two masters—at least, not at the same time. A commitment to theorizing, for example, precludes involvement in the practical world of policy-making.[50]

In the words of Don K. Price,

wherever science tries to become a unified and authoritative system of thought that pretends to explain all types of knowledge and to guide all types of actions, it becomes more a rationalization of a will to power than a valid intellectual discipline.[51]

Nevertheless, we see a continually increasing need for scientific knowledge in policy-making institutions. Scientific data are clearly not only relevant but crucial to the consideration of many of our most pressing contemporary social problems. If scientists cannot become governors and remain scientists, how then are we to secure the input of science in government?

In a democracy the most appropriate and promising method for incorporating scientific knowledge into public law is public dialogue. This is the method by which other disciplines, religion, economics, and politics itself in the partisan sense, all make their contribution to government and exert their influence on public policy. There is no reason to claim a preferred position for science.

Public discussion, education, and persuasion are inevitably slow and uncertain. Even where scientific data are clear and voluminous, as in the case for fluoridation of drinking water, the process of public education and persuasion may be so gradual as to seem immobile or negative.[52] But speed and certainty of action are not characteristics of policy-making in a democratic society. They can be secured only by abandoning democracy and imposing strong authoritarian rule.

Our preference for democracy rather than authoritarianism illustrates as well as anything the nature of public policy choices. We prefer democracy because it serves the basic values we cherish, not because of any scientific demonstration that it is, by some abstract or theoretical scale, better or worse than another system. No argument by scientists, no purported demonstration of benefits to be secured by another system, will shake our faith in and adherence to a democratic society with its implicit valuation of individualism, freedom, and personal dignity. Beguiling as the prospect may seem to some, society will—and should—reject the notion that men of science and technology have a more legitimate claim to rule by natural right than contemporary politicians or than the ancient monarchs whose claim of divine right has long since been expunged by blood.

This means, too, that society will—and should—reject the vision of a unique, scientifically validated solution to social problems as well as hope for a scientific calculus applicable to society. It is the part of wisdom and maturity to recognize social problems as conflicts of interests and values to which science can contribute data and methodology, but which science cannot claim special authority to resolve. Scientists can show the public the means of defining the parameters of problems, the methods of investigating possible solutions, and the data that are relevant to the choice of solutions. Beyond this, scientists can offer interpretations, inferences, and implications from their data for the enlightenment of the public. However, their data and arguments will be accepted as scientific only if it is apparent that they were sought and offered in a truly scientific manner—that is, in a spirit of objective inquiry and not of advocacy. To put the matter most simply, scientists can best influence law and government by working as scientists.

Scientists in their work must clearly reject the mod-god of ideology. Science and ideology are fundamentally incompatible. Ideology starts with a conclusion, accepted on faith, and demands that all data and subsidiary propositions be molded to support or be reconciled with the conclusion. Science starts with a question and demands that all subsidiary propositions be considered as tentative hypotheses, that data be gathered objectively (i.e., regardless of whether they corroborate or falsify the hypothesis or conclusion), and that the conclusion then be derived from the data thus gathered. Ideology is based on faith and science is based on skepticism; and the two are intellectual and philosophical antipodes. Ideology, ethics, and law do constrain science, in some respects, as they constrain all human activity in civilized society, but they are not part of the same discipline. Modern ideology may be more humane than ancient religion, but it is no more scientific. You cannot make science out of religion by calling it ideology any more than the ancients could make science out of religion by calling on divine intervention. To call for the interjection of ideology into science is a throwback to the medieval era of superstition and polemic rather than reasoned inquiry. It is a subversion or abandonment of science as we know it.

In an age dominated by the works of science and technology, law and science must and will interact and work together. The issue is not "whether" but "how." One approach is jurimetrics: the use of scientific methodology and data in seeking the solution of legal problems. Its use and application have been very limited but only partly because of resistance by the law. Equally or more important has been the paucity of contributions by science. Few truly significant and proved scientific contributions have been spurned by lawyers and policy makers. If scientists are to make a significant contribution to law, on the level of either microlaw or macrolaw, they must first produce relevant and significant scientific data and conclusions. To do this they must work as scientists and maintain their separation and distance from the apparatus of law and government.

REFERENCES

1. H. Maine, *Ancient Law* 4, 7 (3d ed. 1888).
2. H. Lea, *Superstition and Force* (1878).
3. *Id.* at 94.
4. 13 *Encyclopaedia Britannica* 159 (1966).
5. H. Lea, *Superstition and Force* 217–370 (1878).
6. *Id.* at 13–91.
7. *Id.* at 506.
8. *Id.* at 510.
9. *Id.* at 176–216.
10. 1 Wigmore, *Evidence* § 8 (3d ed. 1940).
11. *Id.*
12. 13 *Encyclopaedia Britannica* 160 (1966).
13. 1 Wigmore, *Evidence* § 8 (3d ed. 1940).
14. *Id.*
15. *Id.*
16. 1 Wigmore *Evidence* § 9 (3d ed. 1940).
17. *Id.* at § 10.
18. 1 Forbes & Dijksterhuis, *A History of Science and Technology* (1963).
19. Malinowski, "Magic, Science and Religion," in *Science, Religion and Reality* 19 (Needham ed. 1925); Singer, "Historical Relations of Religion and Science," in *Science, Religion and Reality* 85 (Needham ed. 1925).
20. J. Conant, *On Understanding Science* (1947).
21. *Id.* at 6–7.
22. 2 *Encyclopaedia Britannica* 993 (1966).
23. *See* P. Bridgman, *The Logic of Modern Physics* (1927); C. Churchman, *Theory of Experimental Inference* (1948); J. Conant, *On Understanding Science* (1947); T. Kuhn, *The Structure of Scientific Revolutions* (1962); and K. Popper, *The Logic of Scientific Discovery* (1959).
24. *See* T. Kuhn, *The Structure of Scientific Revolutions* (1962); *see also* other material cited in note 23.
25. The proposition stated is my own formulation from work in the field and study of literature, including particularly the references cited herein. For an illuminating analysis, see P. Meehl, *Clinical Versus Statistical Prediction* (1954).
26. J. Marshall, *Law and Psychology in Conflict* (1966); McGauch, "*Time-Dependent Processes in Memory Storage*," 153 Science 1351 (1966).
27. K. Pearson, *The Grammar of Science* 6–7 (1892).
28. O. W. Holmes, "Learning and Science," in *Collected Legal Papers* 139 (1920).
29. O. W. Holmes, "The Path of the Law," in *Collected Legal Papers* 187 (1920).

30. O. W. Holmes, "Law in Science and Science in Law," in *Collected Legal Papers* 231, 242 (1920).
31. B. Cardozo, *The Paradoxes of Legal Science* 1 (1928).
32. *See* Loevinger, "Jurimetrics: The Methodology of Legal Inquiry," 28 Law and Contemporary Problems 5 (1963); Loevinger, "The Computer Revolution and the Law," 2 Juris Doctor 6 (Dec. 1971); Hamilton, "Computer-Assisted Legal Research," 51 Oregon L. Rev. 665 (1972). A vast body of literature on the subject of computer use in legal research is being built up. The subject is currently reported in *Jurimetrics Journal*, a quarterly publication of the American Bar Association. *Computer Law Service*, edited by Robert P. Bigelow and published by Callaghan & Co., provides an up-to-date loose-leaf report of developments in the field of law and computers. Prof. Michael Duggan of the University of Texas has prepared a bibliography on the subject that contains thousands of entries.
33. H. Munsterberg, *On the Witness Stand* (1908); Loevinger, "Facts, Evidence, and Legal Proof," 9 Western Reserve Law Review 154 (1958). *See also* R. Henson, *Landmarks of Law* 422 (1960) and J. Marshall, *Law and Psychology in Conflict* (1966).
34. G. Lundberg, *Can Science Save Us?* 104, 114–15 (1947).
35. C. Snow, *Science and Government* 71 (1962).
36. 102 Science News 3 (July 1, 1972).
37. *See, e.g.*, Efron, "A Million-Dollar Misunderstanding," TV Guide, Nov. 11, 1972, at 8, and Nov. 18, 1972, at 36.
38. Brown v. Board of Education of Topeka, 347 U.S. 483 (1954).
39. C. Jencks, *Inequality—A Reassessment of the Effect of Family and Schooling in America* (1972).
40. C. Snow, *Science and Government* 82 (1962).
41. J. Barzun, *Science: The Glorious Entertainment* 1, 173–74, 186 (1964). In the same vein see F. Matson, *The Broken Image* (1964) and Wade, "Theodore Roszak: Visionary Critic of Science," 178 Science 960 (1972) and compare Frankel, "The Nature and Sources of Irrationalism," 180 Science 927 (1973).
42. 10 Society (formerly TransAction) 78 (Nov.-Dec. 1972).
43. *See, e.g.*, Anon., "Beyond the Ehrlich-Commoner Dispute," 102 Science News 99 (Aug. 12, 1972) and Shapley, "Nobelists: Piccioni Lawsuit Raises Questions About the 1950 Prize," 176 Science 1405 (1972).
44. Walsh, "AAAS Meeting: Pro Forma Protest and Constitutional Reform," 175 Science 42 (1972).
45. *See* Denniston, "Gestation of 'Adversary Science,'" Washington Star-News, Aug. 11, 1972, at A–14.
46. Anon., "A Defeat for Scientific Integrity," Business Week, July 8, 1972, at 60.
47. Frazier, "What is Science?," 102 Science News 131 (Aug. 26, 1972).

48. *Id.*
49. D. Price, *The Scientific Estate* 270 (1965).
50. Habarer, "Politicalization in Science," 178 Science 713 (1972).
51. D. Price, *The Scientific Estate* 271 (1965).
52. Sapolsky, "Science, Voters and the Fluoridation Controversy," 162 Science 427 (1968).

Reception of Science by the Legal System

RALPH NORVELL*
Professor, School of Law
University of South Carolina
Columbia, South Carolina

HISTORICALLY, THE RELUCTANCE TO ASSIGN SCIENTIFIC FINDINGS A DOMinant role in decision making has frustrated scientists and raised suspicion that the resistance stems from bias. Doubtless bias and inertia impede reception. However, at times society simply places higher values on nonscientific objectives than on scientific truth.

Different reasons for rejection and modifications of scientific inputs appear in three categories of illustrations. (1) In a few instances circumstances render the scientific elements irrelevant to policy formulation. (2) There are occasions when the utilization of science and technology infringes individual choice, action, and privacy; in such cases science and technology take a secondary role in decision making. (3) Finally, a large number of situations involve nonscientific objectives which are coequal in importance with scientific inputs for policy making.

There is a shocking example in the first category. A court decided that a couple over the age of seventy could have born to them another daughter. This assumption was made to reach the conclusion that an attempted gift, to take effect upon a remote contingency, violated the technical doctrine known as the Rule Against Perpetuities. The inclusion of the potential offspring as an eligible recipient produced the violation and resulting invalidity.[1]

Why would a court ignore so plain a biological fact? That a woman over seventy will have no more children is clear; however, another factor dictates the result. One legal policy aims at keeping facts which do not appear in the written documents of title from affecting ownership of

---

* Mailing address: School of Law, University of South Carolina, Columbia, South Carolina 29208.

property. Reducing the chance of unknown claimants appearing to upset or encumber what was thought to be a clear and certain title is one objective. Another is to keep down the costs of title investigations and of title insurance. Reducing the number of facts, including extrinsic documents of title which are permitted legal effect, has similar objectives in probate and in the administration of trusts.

Some extrinsic facts are admitted. Those relating to marriage, death, and family circumstances bearing on heirship, for example, are so intertwined with the normal holding and disposition of property that they are considered along with the written documents. The facts admitted are relatively easy to ascertain and require little testing by either legal or scientific standards.

The reforms put forward in recent years to modify the Rule Against Perpetuities, known as the "wait and see" legislation, do not radically depart from protecting the written record of title from inquiry into extrinsic facts. These reforms generally aim at having the test for remoteness of a gift done after all of the events have occurred which could affect vesting rather than testing at the time of the creation of the gift for possibilities which might cause a vesting at too remote a time.[2] As long as the inquiries relate only to easily ascertained facts, no great harm will result unless the holding open of final determination of validity proves to cause more expense than the saving of a small number of poorly drafted provisions warrants.

The wisdom of the holding reached in the example depends upon the accuracy of the judgment that the inquiry into the extrinsic facts produced too great a practical burden upon property ownership. The scientific truth was not helpful in assessing the wisdom; it was irrelevant. If the issue were whether Biblical accounts of miracles should control, the scientific data would have a predominant role. However, the issue is not of that nature.

The reactions to eavesdropping afford an excellent illustration for the second category. Both the scientific reliability of the electronic devices which aid eavesdropping and their usefulness in criminal investigations are open to little doubt. Nevertheless, there are severe limitations imposed on their use[3] to safeguard privacy for the individual. Science and technology have played a secondary role in reaching the decision to restrict.

The public reaction to the Watergate incident of the 1972 presidential campaign dramatically demonstrates that concerns are broader and deeper than an interest in protecting the civil rights of those accused of crime. The reaction also indicates that the values which block a full utilization of technology have been generated by society generally. The values are not the product simply of the applied expertise of judges, legislators, and lawyers any more than that of scientists. Society looks with great suspicion upon electronic intrusions into the private lives of citizens.

The serious reservation proceeds from more than the vague, unfavorable reaction to the tattle-tale. For example, the "bugging" of an agent to permit the conversations others had with him to be overheard and recorded did not offend the federal statutory regulations. The reasoning was that those who engaged in conversations with the unidentified agent gave up their protection when they decided to confide.[4]

The ban on eavesdropping is incomplete in another respect. The statutes permit electronic surveillance under court order when law enforcement officials meet carefully drafted procedures.[5] These constrain use of the devices to situations in which officials can demonstrate probability of criminal conduct. There are additional requirements designed to prevent invasions of privacy beyond the minimum necessary for effective investigation.

Here the science and technology are not irrelevant, as was the biological knowledge in the Rule Against Perpetuities case. Rather, science and technology have a secondary role in determining the policies which should govern eavesdropping.

The saga of the polygraph affords another illustration in the category. The reason usually stated for excluding evidence of lie-detector tests is that the scientific reliability of test results is insufficient to support admissibility. Two elements are emphasized. The physiological and mental conditions of some individuals give false indications. The reliability of tests rests critically upon the skill of the operator.[6] Very likely much more is involved.

Doubt as to scientific reliability normally would result in having both the polygraph test and the evidence relating to reliability submitted to the fact finder with instructions. The fact finder would be instructed to consider the evidence of reliability in assessing weight to the test results.[7] It is probable that the scientific reliability of the lie detector is at least equal to the reliability of opinions given as evidence by scientific experts. The judicial hostility to admitting polygraph evidence must rest on additional factors.

This conclusion is reinforced by legal reservations found in circumstances which do not involve admissibility of evidence. Strong indications in the labor cases disclose legal disfavor toward employers' use of the polygraph to screen employees.[8] Although much of the disapproving language refers to the scientific unreliability issue, at least one arbitrator rationalized that the time has not yet come when management can substitute a machine for persons in the function of supervision.[9] It is clear that scientific probing by machine is viewed as an unwarranted intrusion and that it should be left to the actions and reactions of people to work out conditions of employment.

The polygraph has not been proscribed; its use has been circumscribed. The policy decisions establishing the restrictions have relegated the scientific inputs to a secondary role. Society's values in individual freedom of choice and of action are the primary force shaping the policy.

The tort and workmen's compensation claims for harm produced by exposure to low-level radiation afford an illustration in the third category. The cases present an interesting interface of law and science in respect to the determination of standards of conduct which should be imposed on industry. In addition the litigation process includes a difficult resolution of the standards by which the causal connection between exposure and harm should be judged.

The crux is the unwillingness of courts to accept as determinative the standards established by the Atomic Energy Commission for the maximum permitted dose of radiation. The most rigid adherence to the guidelines does not insure that industry has met the legally required standard of care. In both tort and workmen's compensation cases the Commission's standards are not determinative of the causation issue. Pursuit of the judicial treatment of the causation cases will develop the illustration of an application of legal rules which relies heavily upon scientific knowledge; yet, science takes coequal billing with other bodies of knowledge in shaping the controlling policy.

The basic law is simple. A claimant must prove that his injury was caused by exposure to low-level radiation. The injury usually is cancer or radiation-related disease or a physiological condition (such as premature aging) which could have a relationship with exposure. The claimant's evidence must establish that the exposure probably caused the harm for which compensation is claimed. Proof that disease or injury could have resulted from exposure is not enough.[10]

For example, an employee claimed compensation for disability caused by cancer. He claimed that the cancer was caused by exposure to low-level radiation in the course of his employment. Since he had worn the film strip monitor beneath lead gloves there was no direct evidence of the amount of radiation absorbed. His expert medical testimony went no further that that his cancer could have been caused by his exposure. The court concluded that the evidence did not support the jury's finding that the exposure caused the cancer.[11]

The other side of the coin is the case where the evidence indicates that the cumulative exposure is below the maximum permitted dose allowed under the standards established by the Atomic Energy Commission. Courts will let the issue of causation go to the jury and uphold its finding of causation if the evidence includes the opinion of a scientific expert that exposure "probably" caused the disease or injury.[12]

The irony is that more determinative consequence is given the opinion evidence than is given the more carefully constructed scientific standards of maximum permitted dose.

Two elements of potential unfairness result. The first is illustrated by an employee who develops cancer while employed in circumstances exposing him to radiation. The combination of proof of infinitesimal doses of radiation with the opinion testimony of an expert can produce a substantial award. Another employee who suffers a heart attack while employed goes uncompensated for his disability. Scientifically, there may be little to choose between the two cases in regard to a causal connection between employment and disease.[13]

The second element is that many cases turn on the happenstance of a litigant finding an expert willing to testify that the disease was caused by exposure. The potential unfairness is sharpened by the fact that the expert must be willing to testify that the disease was "probably" caused by radiation. The more careful scientific assessment of the same facts that the disease "could" result is not enough.

There are two divergent suggestions which have been put forward to remove the potential unfairness. One is to remove the requirement of proof of causation in its traditional form.[14] The other is to give determinative effect to the scientifically designed standards for maximum permitted dose.[15]

The probability of a favorable fact finding for the claimant is high. Hence, in practical terms the prescribed legal minimum for an element in the cause of action tends to set the standard for recovery.

If the element of causation in its traditional form is removed, liability of industry to its employees in workmen's compensation and to others in tort will be judged by whether there is a consequence which can be connected with radiation exposure. There will be much less differentiation for amounts of radiation involved and for standards of safety practiced in the specific case. The affected industries will tend to become insurers against diseases and physiological conditions which can be produced by exposure. However, only those conditions which can be connected will be included. In addition only those of the population who are employed in these particular industries can claim compensation. The result is not responsive to a broad policy determination allocating industrial risks and allocating costs of disease incurred by the working population.

Since the same probability of favorable fact finding applies, adoption of the maximum permitted dose standards as determinative of the minimum proof required would make proof of receiving such dose practically the equivalent of recovery. In practical results, policy considerations relating to risk allocations would be subsumed to be solved by scientific evaluation of biological data.

The adoption of either suggestion will truncate the process of policy determination. In the one case policy largely will be determined by the observations of legal specialists with attention focused on anomalies in the litigation process—that is, upon the potential for unfairness. In the other case policy will be preempted by the dictates of scientific findings which consider only the physiological responses to radiation. The work of both types of specialists is indispensable. However, neither should be given a determinative role in policy decision because neither marshals all of the relevant considerations.

Before final policy conclusions are reached a number of factors need attention. Broader inquiries into economic consequences to the consumers of goods and services produced by the affected industries should be made.[16] More empirical experience would aid assessment of the magnitude of the risk of radiation disease and its consequences. Impact on the incentive of industry to lower hazards should be considered. Information produced by experimentation with risk shifting and risk sharing through insurance, governmental guarantees, and collective bargaining would be helpful.

Adoption of either of the suggestions would tend to lower the sensitivity of both the legal system and of industry to economic and other factors through restricting the determinative factors to such narrow compass as each entails. Encouragement of further study and experimentation is more important than finding a formula to remove some anomalies in the litigation process. It matters little whether the formula be that of the scientist or that of the legal specialist.

There are important problems at the interface of law and science for which controlling policy is being evolved in the legal system. The reception of the scientific factors, along with the narrow legalistic projections, will be qualified as indicated in the illustrations.

Those working to improve consumer protection will experience the frustration of resistance to modification of product and lessening of personal convenience which, in some instances, will be indicated by scientific studies. For example, it is likely that attempts to compel automobile drivers to wear shoulder harness and other constraints will be viewed as a substantial invasion of individual freedom of choice. There will be those consumers who will prefer to take risks with health and with safety as an alternative to increased prices. Attempts to improve nutrition will conflict with tastes and choices in diet.

Dealing with the environment is even more difficult. Most obvious are the costs of cleaning the streams and the air. The costs will be funded by increased prices, decreased real wages and profits, increased taxes, or a combination of these means. Society probably will weigh the economic impact as well as the credibility of scientific suggestions in arriving at decisions.

Some of the studies will impact on so fundamental a matter as jobs. Rearrangement of sites for and methods of industrial production will raise questions of whether the total number of jobs will eventually be the same as before rearrangement. Such suggestions must raise anxiety concerning job dislocation both in the geographic sense and in the sense of requirements for retraining for new jobs which will replace older ones being phased out. Ultimate policy decisions must take such fundamental impact into account along with the guidance from legal specialists and scientists.

Attempts to maintain ecological balance and an adequate power supply will raise sharp questions. Currently disputes concerning the types of plants to build and the desirable sites for them have slowed the provision for additional generating capacity to the point that there is a real prospect of a near-term shortage of power that will slow economic growth and produce personal inconvenience. The not-too-distant future holds promise of more difficult choices. We shall face the issue of individual curtailment of use of basic convenience electrical appliances (including such things as air conditioning) with the concomitant effects upon quality of life. Even architecture may be affected. The mounting evidence of power requirements entailed by glass-curtain-wall construction indicates that a serious consideration whether such type of architecture must give way to other types is an immediate prospect.

The ultimate policy decisions will require more than the inputs of scientists and legal specialists. The decisions affect too much individual freedom and too many basic economic concerns for such narrowly based elements to dictate them.

There are three observations which should be considered together. The three relate to different forces which operate simultaneously and shape the policy-making processes of the legal system.

First, history teaches that the individual prizes freedom of choice to the point of taking chances with safety, longevity, and rational order. Cigarette smoking in the teeth of the scientific findings is an obvious illustration. The continued popularity of the automobile despite the record of death and injury affords another. Revolutions constitute dramatic examples.

Second, the illustrations discussed earlier indicate the complexities of problems when viewed from the policy-forming point of view. Ultimate resolution involves the testing of a selected, tentative conclusion for impact upon a variety of social and economic goals[17] of a society and for impact upon individual freedom of choice and personal privacy.

Third, a basic method of the legal system is a deliberate avoidance of broad and conclusive commitments until a period of experimentation and observation has occurred. There is a great reluctance to commit to a determinant which is based upon or produced by one segment of expertise. Operations are attuned to the gathering of information empirically while the process of deciding and disposing of discreet cases or particular problems is in progress.

The sum amounts to a system which eschews the commitment of decision making to an oligarchy, whether that oligarchy be composed of legal specialists or of scientists. Society expects and demands more than such commitment would afford. It demands leeway for experimentation in economic endeavors and in the resolution of other social problems. It expects more reserved space for individual expression and action.

The great stress comes when a society moves to the level of technological development that ours currently enjoys. Legal problems, along with the others, require large scientific inputs. However, the inputs are received under conditions and with modifications to insure efficiency of nonscientific aspects of operations, to safeguard primary societal values, and to provide room for empirical examinations and observations beyond those considered by the scientist.

References

1. Jee v. Audley, 1 Cox Eq. Cas. 324, 29 Eng. Rep. 1186 (1787).
2. *See* 5 *American Law of Property* § 24.11 (J. Casner ed. 1952); Simes & Smith, *The Law of Future Interests* § 1230 (2d ed. 1956); and Leach, "Perpetuities in Perspective: Ending the Rule's Reign of Terror," 65 Harvard Law Review 721 (1952).
3. *See, e.g.,* 18 U.S.C. §§ 2510–20 and 47 U.S.C. § 605 (1970). State statutes on the subject also exist.
4. United States v. White, 401 U.S. 745 (1971).
5. 18 U.S.C. §§ 2516–18 (1970).
6. *See* McCormick, *Law of Evidence* § 207 (2d ed. 1972).
7. Keyes & Howarth, "Approaches to Liability for Remote Causes: The Low-Level Radiation Example," 56 Iowa Law Review 531 (1971) [Hereinafter cited as Keyes & Howarth].
8. *See* Burkey, "Privacy, Property and the Polygraph," 18 Labor Law Journal 79 (1967).
9. General American Transportation Corp., 31 Labor Arbitration 355 (1958).
10. Prosser, *Law of Torts* 241 (4th ed. 1971).
11. Parker v. Employees Mutual Liability Insurance Co., 440 S.W.2d 43 (Texas 1969).
12. *See* Keyes & Howarth.
13. *See* Keyes & Howarth at 561.
14. *See* O'Toole, "Radiation, Causation, and Compensation," 54 Georgetown Law Journal 751 (1966).
15. *See* Keyes & Howarth.
16. *Id.*
17. *See* Korn, "Law, Fact, and Science in the Courts," 66 Columbia Law Review 1080 (1966).

Law, Science, and Public Policy:
A Problem in Communication

JAMES W. CURLIN*
Congressional Research Service
Library of Congress
Washington, D.C.

INTERPERSONAL ATTITUDE IS A STRONG FORCE IN EFFECTIVE COMMUNICA-
tion. The importance of personal attitudes in social intercourse is obvious
in the context of everyday living. Less obvious is the role of attitudes in
professional life. Interprofessional relationships represent a microcosm
of society which is hidden from the casual observer, and attitudes play
as important a part in professional communication as they do in general
society.

One of the most interesting areas of professional interaction is that
between law and science. There are both striking similarities and sharp
disparities between legal process and scientific method. On the one hand
law is normative while science is objective. On the other hand the processes are similar with regard to relying on precedence, assuming the
burden of proof, and to some extent the evolution of evidence. The
differences between the professions may best be reflected in the personal
traits embodied in the practitioners of law and science. Neither can be
categorized absolutely, yet scientists in general show an aversion to the
adversary process.

Solutions to current problems are being sought through a marriage
of science and law. The resolution of social conflict is the *raison d'être*
of law. Technology's disquieting advances have resulted in an increase
in legal activities in environmental protection, consumer affairs, and
rights of the disadvantaged. Failure of our social and political institutions to deal effectively with these issues has resulted in numerous legal
actions, notwithstanding ample evidence that courts are ill equipped to
resolve these conflicts in an effective and lasting way. Science is the

---

* Mailing address: Environmental Policy Division, Congressional Research
Service, Library of Congress, Washington, D.C. 20540.

source of knowledge upon which long-term solutions must be based. The infusion of scientific information into legal and legislative process offers an interesting challenge to lawyer and scientist alike.

Communication problems are of particular concern to the legal profession because lawyers must synthesize the knowledge of specialists into a usable and understandable body of general knowledge to solve problems. Likewise, the scientist who wishes his work to have an impact on social institutions must be capable of communicating his knowledge in an understandable and usable form.

A lawyer dealing with environmental and technological problems is beset with a confusing mixture of scientific facts, conflicting expert opinion, and value judgments. Yet professional academic training woefully fails to prepare either the scientist or lawyer for the close interdisciplinary cooperation demanded by modern problems. Scientists and lawyers have not yet established efficient lines for transferring information. This problem was discussed at the Airlie House Conference on environmental law in September 1969:

... Open lines of communication not just in one direction, but make sure the feedback is fed back where it can be meaningfully acted upon. Unless the ... law schools ... that can afford it and the major scientific organizations and the trial bar agree that each has something to tell the others, and, more important, that each has something to ask the others, we will get nowhere.[1]

A survey conducted by the Oak Ridge National Laboratory in 1971 under the sponsorship of the National Science Foundation attempted to evaluate the extent of the communication gap between law and science. The Natural Resources Law Section of the American Bar Association cooperated in the survey. Its membership of 2,300 lawyers active in the area of natural resources and environmental management law served as an experimental population.[2]

A questionnaire was designed to (1) identify the professional activities and characteristics of the respondents, (2) identify the sources of scientific information used by the bar, (3) evaluate possible options to improve communications between scientist and lawyer, and (4) solicit opinions, criticisms, and suggestions concerning improvement of the transfer of information and professional relationships. The questionnaire was mailed to the entire section membership, and 25% responded—an excellent response for mailed questionnaires.

A majority of the 575 respondents who replied were associated with law firms primarily involved with general practice (see Table 1). Ap-

TABLE 1. Respondents and Percentage of Respondents by Function in Organization

Organization	General practice	Distribution	Extractory	Regulation	Electrical generation	Primary manufacturing	Secondary manufacturing
Law firms	277 (73%)	5 (14%)	23 (22%)	10 (22%)	3 (>12%)	4 (19%)	1 (10%)
Corporations	9 (3%)	25 (72%)	71 (68%)	4 (9%)	18 (75%)	10 (48%)	8 (80%)
Self	77 (21%)	3 (9%)	8 (8%)	3 (7%)	3 (>12%)	0	1 (10%)
Federal agencies	3 (<1%)	0	0	9 (20%)	0	1 (5%)	0
Universities	5 (1%)	0	0	2 (4%)	0	0	0
Local government	5 (1%)	2 (5%)	1 (<1%)	14 (31%)	0	0	0
Industrial associations	0	0	2 (1%)	3 (7%)	0	6 (29%)	0
Private conservation organizations	2 (<1%)	0	0	0	0	0	0
TOTAL	378	35	105	45	24	21	10

proximately one-fourth were employed by corporations or businesses, the majority of which are in the distributive or extractive industries (fossil fuels or minerals). Of all respondents, 65% were in the general practice of the law. Few considered themselves specialists in environmental or natural resources law. Of those in general practice, 18% represented organizations within the extractive industries; the remainder were equally divided among distribution, regulation, electrical generation, and manufacturing.

Individually, lawyers associated with law firms or classified as self-employed general practitioners dealt primarily with real property matters, fossil fuels, minerals, and water problems—in that order of frequency. Corporate practitioners were primarily involved with fossil fuels and minerals. The respondents who actually engaged in trial practice reported the highest frequency of litigation in oil and gas, followed by water pollution, water rights, zoning, air pollution, and minerals.

Respondents were asked to identify the literature they read for technical information. The ten most frequently mentioned popular, scientific, and legal periodicals are shown in Table 2. News weeklies and newspapers with wide national circulation were most frequently mentioned among the popular tracts. The predominance of oil and gas interest among the respondents was reflected by the frequency with which the *Oil and Gas Journal* and *Oil Daily* were listed in the scientific and specialty category. A significant number read *Scientific American*, a monthly magazine featuring popularized articles of broad scientific interest. Several periodicals that feature conservation and natural history are also widely read.

The *American Bar Association Journal* and *Natural Resources Lawyer* were the most frequently listed legal publications—not surprising considering the survey population. The *Environment Reporter* followed the Association's publications in popularity. Numerous other periodicals, newsletters, and law reviews were mentioned by the respondents, but none stood out prominently. From the number of titles listed by the respondents, it is evident that information about natural resources and the environment is being widely read in many general sources.

Nine specific yes-no questions dealing with improvement in the exchange of information were posed. Questions and responses are shown in Table 3. The consensus of responses may be summarized thus:

1. Communication between scientists and lawyers is inadequate.

TABLE 2. Ten Most Read Periodicals as Sources of Scientific Information

Rank	Popular	Scientific/Specialty	Legal
1	Wall Street Journal	Oil & Gas Journal	ABA Journal
2	Business Week	Scientific American	Natural Resources Lawyer
3	Time	Oil Daily	BNA Environment Reporter
4	National Geographic	Air & Water News	Texas Bar Journal
5	U.S. News and World Report	Science News	Harvard Law Review
6	Fortune	Sierra Club Bulletin	Land & Water Law Review
7	Newsweek	National Wildlife	Rocky Mountain Mineral Law Review
8	Life*	Natural History	Business Lawyer
9	Kiplinger Report	Audubon Magazine	Texas Law Review
10	New York Times	Science	American Judicature Society

* Ceased publication in 1973.

2. Scientists and lawyers should cross-publish in each others' journals.
3. There is no consensus on the need for new interdisciplinary journals.
4. Briefings and workshops should be held at universities and laboratories to familiarize lawyers with current developments in science and technology.
5. Scientists should participate in American Bar Association programs and meetings.
6. Special sessions should be organized for lawyers at national and regional meetings of scientific associations.
7. Scientists should write and communicate more clearly to enhance understanding by lawyers and laymen.
8. A system of environmental indexes is needed to describe the state of the environment in readily understandable terms.

TABLE 3. Close Ended Questions and Responses

	Percent	
	Yes	No
1. Communications adequate	14	86
2. Scientists should publish in legal periodicals	85	15
3. Lawyers should publish in science periodicals	79	21
4. New periodicals should be created	59	41
5. Special briefings at universities and laboratories	77	23
6. Scientists on programs of ABA and other legal associations	88	12
7. Scientists should develop special sessions at national and regional meetings for lawyers	77	23
8. Scientists should write to be better understood by lawyers	75	25
9. Environmental indices needed	84	16

Respondents were invited to comment on the subject of interdisciplinary communication. Almost every respondent contributed. The comments fell into three general categories: criticisms of scientists; criticisms of lawyers; and suggestions for improving communications. Of the three categories, a majority of the comments dealt critically with science and scientists.

Many respondents perceived scientists and engineers to be narrow in their social outlook and provincial in their approach to problems:

Scientists tend to specialize in professional subareas and the positions they advocate fail to recognize the broader general implications.

Most scientists remain academicians, aloof from the community.

Scientists tend to disregard the human factors and respect the "truth" of only those things which can be enumerated and quantified . . . [they] tend to measure human responses by slide rules.

. . . their political notions are absurd.

The veracity and objectivity of scientists and engineers were questioned by a large proportion of the respondents:

Scientists are often arbitrary about matters, believing they have the only set answers . . . [the] information is inaccurate, based on individual opinion rather than fact.

Scientists' attitudes are influenced by the propensities of their employers.

Scientists are too dogmatic, visionary and impractical in their discussion of ecological problems . . . [those] who are environmentalists are too emotional to provide the practical ideas needed.

Many scientists currently giving public utterances [regarding protection of the environment] appear more interested in creating a sensation rather than giving objective analyses and suggestions for practical solutions.

Scientists tend to extend their *expertise* in environmental matters into areas of politics and society which are beyond their competence.

There was also criticism of the peer approval system of science and a general feeling that scientists should be more vocal in public debate.

Legal theories and opinions are constantly being validated (and invalidated) in courts; there appear to be no comparable activities by which scientific opinions on ecological problems may be weighed.

There is an understandable but frustrating unwillingness to stake reputation when *risk* of harm becomes apparent, preferring more research.

There is a concern about failure of scientists to publicly rebut unfounded assertions by politicians and pressure groups.

One significant barrier in communicating scientific information seemed to be the publication and distribution policies of scientific literature:

The abundance or rather overabundance of scientific articles created under pressure of publish or perish creates a confusion of too many articles with too little content—a result thereof being none are read or the few significant articles are buried.

Scientific writing and speaking is unnecessarily technical and assumes too much knowledge on part of general public.

Scientific articles are difficult to understand and are not readily available to the general public.

... both professions use jargon too much.

In the opinion of many of the respondents, scientists do not understand the role of the law or the nature of law in resolving societal problems.

There is a general lack of understanding of the role of the law and lawyers on the part of environmental scientists. . . . They do not realize that the law is not an exact science and that you cannot put a legal problem into a computer and receive a precise answer.

Many scientists have a basic and rather indefinable distrust of lawyers. . . . [P]articularly academicians tend to be intolerant of apparent obstacles which law and administrative process seem to place before . . . their ideas.

On the other hand, there was some, but much less, criticism of lawyers. Several of the respondents felt that blame for poor communications must be shared equally among the disciplines:

. . . Only problems come when individuals are unwilling to take time and effort to learn to communicate. . . . Semantics is a problem.

Both professions use jargon too much. . . . Lawyers write for lawyers, scientists write for other scientists . . . scientists know more about law than lawyers know about science. . . . Lawyers should learn some science.

There is not enough contact between scientists and attorneys.

Suggestions for improving communications favored interdisciplinary studies and ventures under the auspices of the legal and scientific associations:

Joint studies of a scientific-legal nature . . . should be fostered. . . . Interdisciplinary study would help overcome communication problems.

Communications can only be improved by a progressive program initiated by professional associations in both fields. . . . [The] legal profession could bring influential and representative members of the scientific community into their functions.

There should be established within the ABA a law-science academy or institution to serve all sections of related organizations . . . that may share some interdependence on each other as a result of the developing problems of law and science that go hand in hand.

Bibliographies, indexes, and glossaries are most difficult to find. . . . Scientific documents should be "paraphrased" not only for lawyers but also for other interested people—and vice versa.

Co-authored articles in present journals . . . on which legal and scientific professions may cooperate [should be promoted].

Given the opinions that many of the respondents expressed about scientists and engineers, it is not surprising that there is a lack of effective communication among the professionals. The commentary shows a serious credibility gap based on a perceived lack of veracity and objectivity on the part of scientists and engineers. This is contrary to what is considered to be the foundation of science.

Whether or not the impressions of the respondents are well founded is unimportant. That they exist at all is destructive of the communication process. Are scientists equally distrustful of lawyers? I fear they are and hope to test this hypothesis with a similar survey in the scientific community. Lawyers and scientists are unaccustomed to talking with one another. Their professional life styles have kept them apart, academically and in the commercial world. Often the only contact between the professions is through adversary proceedings. Within the corporate structure a lawyer is cloistered in a legal division, and the only substantial contact others may have with him is in his role as counselor. Lawyers are seldom integrated into the research process.[3] The professional life styles must change if we are to overcome our communication problems.

The blame for ineffective communication lies at the feet of both professional groups. The legal profession has been negligent by failing to inform the general public, including scientists, of the nature of the legal process. Television programs about fictional lawyers have done more to acquaint the public with our legal system, albeit in a distorted manner, than has the legal profession. Scientists also have shown little proclivity for enhancing public understanding. The only "respectable" mode of publication still remains the disciplinary journal. While the peer review system assures a homogeneity of thought, style, and philosophy, publication in popular media may subject one to criticism by his colleagues for "grandstanding" or for being a "purveyor of simplistic nonscientific pap." Only those of the highest scientific bearing dare risk the ire which may result from popularization. I have heard my scientist colleagues refer to *Time* and *Newsweek* as "law journals" because they are the only sources of understandable information available to non-lawyers. The results of our survey at Oak Ridge National Laboratory indicate a similar reliance on the weeklies by lawyers for scientific information. It is paradoxical that both professions must rely on third parties not skilled in either discipline to translate for each other.

If we are to improve communications, we must provide ways for lawyers and scientists to come together. We have learned from experiments in interdisciplinary organization that effective communication is learned and developed through personal contacts. In 1970 the American Association for the Advancement of Science collaborated with the Association of American Law Schools by sponsoring joint sessions to discuss environmental problems at their annual meetings held in Chicago. These sessions provided a useful prototype for similar symposia. It is clear that professional societies must assume the leadership in developing interprofessional communications. Toward this end, the American Bar Association and the American Association for the Advancement of Science have begun negotiations to establish a joint conference on science and law. A standing conference of this kind may lead to the development of joint programs to deal with interdisciplinary issues; but their outstanding contribution may be the development of interprofessional understanding which could make interdisciplinary communication second nature rather than formal and contrived.

Our universities are also recognizing the value of interdisciplinary research and are establishing interdisciplinary curricula. Today's students seem to realize that satisfactory solutions to the most important problems facing society can come only from coordinating the resources of the natural sciences, behavioral sciences, and the law. Several innovative programs that integrate law and the sciences have been developed in universities. Cornell's Science, Technology, and Society Program, the Center for Law and the Health Sciences at Boston University, and the Science and Technology Program at George Washington Law School are a few. *Ad hoc* student societies organized to deal with environmental and social problems provide an extracurricular source for interdisciplinary experience.

Many research institutions and quasi-academic organizations have shifted toward interdisciplinary programs. Credit for the institutional changes taking place in the universities and research groups must be given to the RANN program at the National Science Foundation which has insisted on interdisciplinary approaches as a condition precedent to funding projects. In addition, RANN has initiated a program on public briefings and summaries to discuss the policy aspects of projects of national interest. These have proven most useful for transferring knowledge to those interested in policy implementation. Within the federal government one may also detect a shift toward interdisciplinary cooperation on matters concerning the environment. This has resulted largely from the mandates of the National Environmental Policy Act of 1969, which in statutory language recognized the need for interdisciplinary environmental assessments.

The magnitude and severity of our social problems will force us to abandon the myopic professional perspectives we have cherished in the past. We will be forced by necessity to adopt an interdisciplinary work style. Communication is one of the most important elements for developing the mutual understanding needed to accomplish this task. We must speed up the learning process so that we can get on with the work ahead.

REFERENCES

1. M. Baldwin & J. Page (eds.), *Law and the Environment* 366, Walker & Co. (1970).
2. Curlin, "Fostering Understanding Between Science and Law," 59 American Bar Association Journal 157 (1973).
3. Curlin, "Saving Us from Ourselves: The Interaction of Law and Science-Technology," 47 Denver Law Journal 651 (1971).

Obligation of Scientists to Respond to Society's Needs

RALPH NADER*
Public Interest Research Group
Washington, D.C.

BEFORE DISCUSSING THE FUNCTION OF SCIENTISTS IN OUR SOCIETY, I WOULD like to make a few preliminary remarks. It is an unfortunate attribute of many specialized roles such as those of scientists to be accompanied by a commensurate narrowing of their range of accountability and their perceived duty. This is particularly the case when these roles are performed within bureaucratic structures of power, governmental or corporate, which command the resources and the priorities for their use. On occasion the use or misuse of influence displays the catastrophic realities or risks, as in the harnessing of the atom; then the issues of duty and morality prey more heavily on the minds of scientists. A prime example is the great moral and philosophical debates following the bombing of Hiroshima.

But, such a response occurs only occasionally and especially when the causes and effects can be easily perceived. This is a cardinal point that we need to focus on much more strenuously than we do. Today, of course, the risks come thickly and are imperceptible to the average individual. Indeed, these come in the form of silent violence over time, affecting the individual and future generations. By and large, they escape the immediate sensory perception of the victims, whether the risks be radiation levels, cadmium in water, carbon monoxide in air, asbestos, or hormones. This mounting silent assault upon human beings, whatever its motivation or negligence, has underlined the physiological obsolescence of human beings to detect for themselves the dangers that result from evasive or preventive action.

The management of such potentially violent substances as chemicals, gases, radiation, particulates, etc., rests initially upon scientists who dis-

---

* Mailing address: P.O. Box 19367, Washington, D.C. 20036.

cover and shape the sources of these risks as well as upon those who ultimately decide their use. By their knowledge these scientists possess the early alert capacity; but by their being citizens they define their broader range of responsibility to society. This is another way of saying that any subject that deals with the obligation of scientists must start with their obligation as citizens.

The legal system through which policies are made and administered and through which conflicts are resolved or extended has established little by way of affirmative duties of citizenship by scientists. As a matter of fact, the legal system has established little by way of affirmative duties of citizens at all. For example, citizens don't have to vote, although they have to pay taxes and obey thousands of laws. Yet as it was said in the days of ancient Rome, so it is true today: "Out of the fact comes the law." The more facts that were disclosed about the parameters of automobile safety, the more the courts began to recognize certain product liability standards imposed upon the manufacturers. The same is true with flammable fabrics, pharmaceuticals, unsafe household appliances, and the whole diversity of consumer products. Out of the fact comes the law. Yet the law does not generally require scientists to disclose the fact apart from the narrow regions of the subpoena or the contract, and those narrow regions are no longer sufficient to serve the pressing needs of the present and future of an interdependent society.

No matter what we insist on or how the scientists respond, these challenges foreseen and unforeseen by the scientists still rest mainly on voluntary ethics. Alfred North Whitehead characterizes professional ethics when he says, "Duty arises from the power to alter the course of events." Whether in matters of peace, or ecology, or energy, or consumerism, or communication, or population, or transportation, or housing, or health care, or genetics, the blossoming of independent scientific judgment will rely on many, many full-time scientists working in public interest roles as well as rigorous legal defenders and practitioners to free the conscience and open the scientific judgment and advocacy from the authoritarian strictures of organizational edicts and pressures. As has so often been true in the past, the horizon of human liberty is focused by the extent to which the conscientious individual can successfully combat the constricting organization.

Let me now focus briefly on the scientific adviser and his participatory role in policy making, then examine a few illustrations. We do not have to debate the proposition that scientists are essential contributors to the democratic process, but their contributions have been heavily weighted by the corporate and governmental shaping of their contributions. That is why so many discussions of scientific ethics dwell on the realm of spectacular examples. This situation exists because we have considered such a subject as one that should be separated from the very hard realities of what corporate, government, and other large institutions observe. The concern for the environment and consumer safety makes it imperative that the risks and benefits of new technology, federal land-use, power, and water projects be weighed more carefully than before. Such a concern has yet to develop the kind of institutional support outside government and large corporations that is so necessary to meet the goals of society. Instead we have a kind of no man's land, a complex scientific advisory system with few guidelines and little disclosure.

This complex scientific advisory system is often part of a massive buddy system that restricts access. It has developed to assist federal regulatory officials and the courts in these technical decision-making processes. Formerly these were limited to primarily defense issues, but scientists are now playing an expanded role in federal decision making in food additives, pesticides, drugs, cosmetics, pollution control, and nuclear power—to mention only a few. *Science* magazine estimated recently that these public and semipublic advisory groups involve more than fifteen thousand scientists and engineers. The new vogue of "technology assessment," about the dullest phrase in the English language other than "citizenship," leads to the establishment of centers of technology assessment in both federal and state governments and at universities like the Massachusetts Institute of Technology. Fortunately these activities may in the long run create new opportunities and pressures for scientists to apply their expertise to public policy issues—that is, instances where the first question to be answered is "What is the impact on the public?" rather than "What is the impact on some entrenched bureaucratic commission?"

Unfortunately, the fruits of this expensive and informed scientific advice in the past often have not reached the level of public debate but have instead supported narrow bureaucratic viewpoints formed in advance. The evaluation of scientific advice has been greatly impeded by the confidentiality of the advisory procedure. Often the advice given to government officials, which may be extremely controversial indeed from a public policy viewpoint, is given without any intention that it ever be considered other than confidential by the government. The Executive branch of our government has often used the science advisory establishment to legitimate its decision in the eyes of Congress and the public, while invoking the confidential relationship as an excuse to conceal the technical bases for their decisions.

One form of this advisory establishment, the "Think Tank" industry, has attained a powerful function within government agencies as well as a public policy role. This needs to be more thoroughly examined because that is where a great many scientists work who are called upon for advice. For example, in 1969 President Nixon appointed a committee to evaluate the environmental, technological, and economic aspects of the supersonic transport. In March 1969 the committee presented a report that was almost entirely unfavorable to the SST. Despite this advice the administration continued to give the SST its enthusiastic support. To keep the report from being used by the plane's opponents, the administration kept the report confidential even though there was nothing in it having to do with national security or military matters. Not even Congress, which had to pass on future SST appropriations, was allowed to see it. Finally, in October 1969 Congressman Yates of Illinois obtained partial release of the report for Congressional inspection. Concealment, then, is not just against the public; it is against the elected Congress, and it is rigorously engaged in by most administrations.

Recent efforts by public interest groups to widen the application of the Freedom of Information Act and a decision by the White House to open some advisory committees to the public have increased the data available to outside scientists on policy issues. Pressure is now on the National Academy of Sciences and the National Academy of Engineering to open the selection procedures for these advisory panels to public inspection and to provide meeting records and transcripts of the advisory panels to interested citizens, not only to themselves. I once tried to learn about a National Academy of Sciences advisory committee and was referred to a prominent Washington law firm which handles the Academy's affairs. There is still a question of whether the Academy is or is not under the Freedom of Information Act. This has not yet been formally adjudicated, although the Justice Department leans in the direction of saying that it is not. Of course, this takes away an essential tool that we all need to gain greater disclosure.

The Federal Reports Act, although little known, is of tremendous importance in that it requires governmental agencies to refer any questionnaires that are going out to more than nine respondents to be cleared by the Office of Management and Budget. This has been going on for some thirty years and is a very effective Kyber Pass, blocking the attempts by many governmental agencies to obtain the kind of corporate information that is necessary for public policy making. Not only is this an unreasonable denial of information flow in itself, but in effect it allows the Office of Management and Budget to refuse an agency's request to issue a questionnaire on the alleged grounds that it will be harassing to the industries or that it will intrude upon undefined trade secrets or the like. Because the Office of Management and Budget has few people working on this, they have delegated routinely the actual decision-making power to its apparatus of industrial advisory committees. These powerful committees actually decided what questions they would permit governmental regulatory agencies to ask them. They operated in near total secrecy until about three years ago when Senator Metcalf and some public interest groups began to pry open this process, at least in terms of more direct consumer-related questionnaires. Little has changed in this private industrial government, however.

Recent efforts to modify the Freedom of Information Act are gaining in strength, and perhaps in the next two years we will see some amendments to this effect pass. While the climate has improved somewhat for the involvement of unaffiliated scientists in public policy making, the fact remains that the number of independent scientists outside the network of government and corporate consultantships who are willing to intervene in legal administrative or Congressional efforts to reassess the impacts of official policy making is very small. The rationale for involvement by independent scientists should be clear. Where the government agencies or corporations are unwilling to inform the Congress and the public of potentially deleterious consequences of their decision, the scientists must fill the gap. They enjoy the luxury of freedom of expression which scientists who are employed by corporations or appointed by the government to give confidential advice usually feel that they do not have. The executive often is forced to listen and respond to scientific arguments presented at public hearings which it would not have to do if they were produced to be heard in private. Unfortunately the independent scientists are outnumbered by a factor of several hundred!

When independent scientists make the effort to intervene in public policy issues, they are expanding the benefits of work by a few truly dedicated scientists over the years toward expanding this role. In 1970 Dr. Matthew Meselson, after fruitless requests to the government to study the ecological human impact of the United States' chemical warfare program aimed at the "defoliation" of Vietnam (which added a new word to our lexicon of hypocrisy), took this case to the American Association for the Advancement of Science. The AAAS took the unprecedented step of funding a small Vietnam study group with its own resources. The findings of this group, known as the Herbicide Assessment Committee, were made public in 1971 and were said to be instrumental in convincing the White House to phase out some portion of this chemical warfare. In most cases, however, it is not enough for scientists to contribute to the debate on issues of public policy through academic media alone. They must be willing to act as consultants to public interest groups who are dealing with these issues in administrative, judicial, and Congressional forums. This is where the decisions are going to be made.

Unlike corporations with scientists on their payrolls, these public interest groups cannot demand that scientists in universities drop their other duties to make presentations on a certain date or at a certain place to meet the convenience of the requester. As a result, their capability to make a timely response to technical material presented by scientists is severely curtailed. On the other hand, when scientists have provided public interest groups with the needed technical information, their contribution has made a significant difference, as in the cases of Dr. Samuel Epstein in the areas of food additives and occupational diseases and of Dr. Karl Morgan in the area of unnecessary radiation exposure from medical and dental x-rays.

Another illustration is a little more limited. When the Environmental Protection Agency asked for public comments on its proposal to ban the use of the herbicide 2,4,5-T in food crops, the agency was deluged with replies from chemical companies, public utilities, timber companies, paper mills, and from other representatives of vested interests who presented several hundred lengthy papers prepared by staff scientists to support the alleged safety and beneficial consequences of 2,4,5-T. If scientists think lawyers can present one-sided cases, they may wish to rediscover themselves! There was not a single submission by an independent scientist or by a public health specialist or by any representative of the insurance industry. The independent scientist who acts as a consultant to public interest groups in these proceedings is not simply a directed person. He can refuse to get involved, or he can carefully define the limits of his involvement. All he is doing is presenting the insight of his research analysis in a nonacademic form. In doing so this scientist performs a public service while making certain that the technical and scientific data considered by the decision makers are balanced and reasonably comprehensive. Both the public interest groups and the scientists lack the resources, however, to respond rapidly to regulatory issues which require the application of scientific expertise.

But the problem goes deeper than that; it goes to the basic education of the young scientist as a student. Among the professional schools, the law schools appear to have encouraged faculty members and students to participate in public policy issues more than have any of the other professional schools. Traditionally a law student or lawyer can function as an independent citizen without fearing the subtle ostracism of professional retaliation. If the scientific community continues to lag behind, the Executive branch and corporations, when challenged by citizen groups, will also continue to reply as they did in frequent past instances: "Here are our experts; where are yours?"

Sufficient disclosure resulted from the recent Atomic Energy Commission hearings to indicate that rather traditional restraints on free speech operate to curtail many scientists from articulating publicly their fears about the unanswered questions related to the technology that they are working on. We have heard for over fifteen years about the claims of fantastic safety of nuclear power plants, but one was dismayed to learn in the past two or three years about such unresolved issues as emergency core cooling systems; the collection, transportation, and storage of high-level radioactive wastes; and a number of perhaps less momentous risks that have been documented recently. I think we have to look at scientists at least in some fashion as similar to other human beings; that is, they are subject to cowardice, they are subject to career advancement temptations, they are subject to pettiness, and they are subject to enormous inertia when stressing the benefits of the technology that they are working on, while assuring present and future generations that the risks indeed are minimal. One recalls in this respect the two nuclear submarines resting at the bottom of the ocean.

The problem, of course, also extends to the role of the universities in terms of the type of education that they provide. In the last two years there has been an interesting development of students organizing their own public interest groups, which we have encouraged and helped. The process goes like this. The students themselves petition, either on a state-wide or regional basis, the various schools' Boards of Trustees or Regents, or whatever, to assess themselves three or four dollars a year to develop a fund which the students will control. This fund and its management are independent of the university itself. The students hire their own lawyers, scientists, community organizers, and other professionals. At present there are about four hundred thousand students who are assessing themselves in fourteen student public interest research groups throughout the United States. Once these groups get underway and are expanded, they are obviously going into public issues that require scientific and legal input, not because of some inner interdisciplinary desire, but because of the demands of the public policy issue itself. There is a difference in the kind of response that comes from these two stimuli, and with the enormous opportunities for students to work on these projects supported by their own public interest groups, there may be a beneficial temptation of these individuals to enter a more noninstitutional career in science research and social participation.

It is also important to raise the question of how the law defends the scientists who get embroiled in controversy and who are exposed to a lack of due process by their university or by their corporation or by their governmental agency, and who are either demoted, ostracized, penalized, or fired. Perhaps it comes as a surprise to many people to learn that blue-collar workers in corporations, because of their union contracts, have far greater due process protection than do members of management. As a result responsible scientists, lawyers, engineers, and other professionals in the same company can be shown the door at 5:00 P.M. without any due process and without any grievance procedures. This obviously has a great inhibiting effect because there is an extremely effective grapevine among companies and among governmental agencies that labels "trouble makers" very quickly, thus reducing the prospects of their employment to near zero. In short, the scientist has a skill right, and when that skill right is subjected to that kind of expulsion or administrative laceration, there is not much that the scientist can do because this skill right is not really considered as property by the courts. The field is littered with the bones of scientists who spoke out bravely about controversial issues and were then forced to be at the mercy of a totally unresponsive and uncharitable society. For details, see *Whistleblowing* by Nader, Petkas, and Blackwell (Grossman Publishers 1972).

The approach here is clear, but the mechanics of how to get it implemented are much more difficult. We have to extend basically the Constitutional Bill of Rights to individuals as employees of private corporations or government agencies. As we all know, the Bill of Rights was primarily directed against governmental abuse of citizens, particularly those belonging to any minority classification, and in the intervening hundred and fifty years or so there has been obviously an enormous growth of governmental employment and an enormous growth of corporate employment which didn't exist in the days of our Founding Fathers. As a result we have not extended adequately these freedoms of speech, protection against search and seizure, invasion of privacy, and many others to the relationship between individuals and these two massive organizational systems. What is needed is legislation that will define these rights, define the grievance procedures, and give effective remedies as well as provide the kinds of legal assistance that would make these rights realistic and not just paper rights. Although these rights should be enforced, the courts have not done much in this area. They have a few cases before them now involving professional individuals who have spoken out and, having allegedly been discharged arbitrarily, are suing their former corporate or government employers. These are malicious discharge cases, but the courts are not likely to go very far without some kind of statutory authority to pinpoint the legal terrain more specifically.

The professional societies have long forsaken their role in this area. The professional societies of engineers and scientists need to establish standing grievance committees that really have some sort of backing or authority, or they need to provide an ombudsman who investigates the issues on appeal by the aggrieved individual and who can perhaps develop a process of exposing companies who put unfair pressure or unconscionable influence on these scientists.

In conclusion, the problem of getting some of these things underway does not include lack of interest nor lack of problems nor, certainly, lack of solutions. Rather, the obstacle is the lack of the most fundamental and mundane requirement—money. Financial support is not available for this kind of new and independent career role for scientists who want to work in the public policy area. Scientists could be the initiators, the interpreters, and the advocates in many public policy issues. I think it is certainly not too early for the scientific community to realize that they have got to find the answers of how to support such roles for themselves and to realize that it is important to begin considering the ethical imposition of tithes upon scientific and professional people. There is an important need for self-assessment of dues to establish funds for these types of groups for all professions so that they can get underway as soon as possible. The prospects for societies without public-interest scientists are not encouraging.

The Legal System:
Can It Be Analyzed to Suit the Scientist?

JAMES P. VANYO*
Attorney at Law and Associate Professor
College of Engineering, University of California
Santa Barbara, California

AFTER I HAD AGREED TO PREPARE A PAPER WITH THIS TITLE, I BEGAN TO consider how best to prepare for it. I began to wonder how I would explain the words "legal system" to a scientist. I also began to wonder what I would mean by the word "scientist." I was afraid to think what it would take to suit a scientist. In fact, I started thinking about Ralph Nader's book, *Unsafe at Any Speed*, and I began to wonder if I would be unsafe on any grounds.

As a starting point I decided to look up the concepts "legal system," "legal method," and "jurimetrics" in a dictionary. First I consulted my desk dictionary, not really expecting to find them there; they weren't. Next I consulted an unabridged edition of the *Random House Dictionary of the English Usage* and also the *Dictionary of American Slang*. I did find "legal eagle" and "legal beagle" in the slang dictionary. Bouvier's and Black's law dictionaries also offered no help, nor did *Corpus Juris Secundum*. Finally in Ballentine's *Law Dictionary* (1969), I found this definition of the legal system: "The historic and traditional system including the legislative and judicial process as contrasted with the emergent or lately adopted system which includes the legislative, administrative and judicial process."

People sometimes accuse lawyers of talking in circles. That definition proves that at least part of the time the people are right. But the real problem, of course, is that no one can agree exactly on what the legal system is. Also no one agrees on what jurisprudence or a system of jurisprudence means or on what the legal process is.

* Mailing address: College of Engineering, University of California, Santa Barbara, California 93106.

I decided to enlarge my research considerably by going to the library and thumbing through almost every volume of every law journal written in English that I could find. I also included a select list of books and journals from related fields. The library of the University of California, Santa Barbara, has roughly a hundred ten journals in this category. In each journal I first researched back through 1969 and summarized the articles that related to law and technology in a broad sense or that talked about computers and their application to the legislative, judicial, or administrative processes. I also looked for articles that applied quantitative methods to or developed mathematical models of what I regarded as the legal process or any of its components. I especially looked for articles that applied techniques of systems analysis to the legal system as defined in the most general sense. If I found material I considered to be relevant, I continued the search for another four years—back to 1965. If the journal was especially relevant, I researched it back to about 1960.

Obviously the search would have been much easier and more complete if some of the advanced computer search techniques now being proposed had been available. It is to be hoped that symposiums like this one will help to arouse interest and support for such projects.

Before 1960 there were very few references to this type of material. There are several reasons for this: (1) computers were just beginning to come into wide acceptance; (2) the mathematical formulations that make up systems analysis and operations research had only recently begun to be applied to problems other than those of the military; and (3) there were only a few pioneers in the field who, like Lee Loevinger (see pages 7–25), had foresight to predict that such an interdisciplinary study as this would emerge in the future.

When discussing this interdisciplinary field of science and law, I often wonder if I'm speaking to scientists or to lawyers. You know, of course, that communication appropriate to a scientist is not appropriate to a lawyer, and vice versa. In a recent article in the *Michigan Law Review*, Lozowick, Steiner, and Miller[1] say that a lawyer would rather face a page of fine print than a single algebraic formula—and that agrees with my experience. At the other extreme, when you write for most scientists and you fail to use complex mathematical expressions, you stand the risk of being criticized for publishing narrative nonsense.

I want to examine this difference between scientists and lawyers for just a moment. Every scientist in his school days is exposed to the scientific method. Every lawyer in his school days is exposed to the legal method. There are very strong similarities between the two. Scriven[2] lists side by side the resources and practices of the lawyer and the scientist and shows that they do indeed have strong parallels. They both involve rules of some sort; they both involve data or facts of some sort; and they both reach conclusions based on analytical reasoning. Rosenberg[3] comments on Scriven's article and specifically compares the legal method and the scientific method. He shows that while there are many similarities there are also some subtle but important differences.

Once the lawyer leaves his law school, he gets into a different world. He gets into the world of people and compromise and negotiation where the formal legal method gets lost in the exigencies of day-to-day problems. The practice of the formal legal method is reserved for law school professors, students, some attorneys in appellate practice, and some judges. The scientists also, especially the physical scientists, the engineers, and the mathematicians, quickly leave the philosophical narrative world of the scientific method far behind in their quest for higher mathematics and precisely quantified data.

The similarities in their basic approaches indicate a potential for cross-communication, but their specializations severely limit it. Interesting articles by Shapiro[4] in *Law and Society Review* and by Savoy[5] in *The Yale Law Journal* discuss this problem. Shapiro traces the historical development of science and law and observes that law did not autonomously march through history in that law and science were considered a natural combination in at least the 17th century. Savoy discusses some of the current problems associated with interdisciplinary research and traces the typical path of failures. He quotes a statement by Campbell[6] that "Interdisciplinary integration has to take place within single minds."

This concept of interdisciplinary integration is critical in attempting to analyze the legal system as a scientific pursuit. Only a handful of lawyers are concerned with attempts at quantifying the legal process. The great body of lawyers are indifferent or even hostile to the attempts. Also there are very few physical scientists, mathematicians, or engineers who would be interested in trying to apply their knowledge to the solution of something as vague as the legal system. What they know and what they do might have great impact on society, but their kinds of knowledge cannot be used directly in attempts at understanding the legal system.

There is a third group, independent of the lawyers and the physical scientists. In this group I want to lump social scientists, systems analysts, systems engineers, operations researchers, and in fact almost anyone who has potential interest in this general area and who doesn't think of himself as a pure lawyer or as a pure physical scientist.

Now I can go back to the title of my paper and answer the question of whether the legal system can be analyzed to suit a scientist. When one is speaking of physical scientists or most mathematicians and engineers, the answer is *no*. The reasons are first, the concept "legal system" can't be defined rigorously; and second, even if it could, it would not come out looking like the Schroedinger Equation, Maxwell's Equations, or maybe even Hamilton's Principle. But one equation from the hard sciences that would almost certainly relate to an analysis of the legal system is Heisenberg's Uncertainty Principle—although with a much larger constant, of course. Now if one asked the question whether the legal system could be analyzed to suit the soft scientists, the systems analysts, or anyone from that group of people, the answer would probably be *yes*. At least it's *yes* for those who are endeavoring to apply quantitative methods to situations that involve people. Whether the legal system can be analyzed to suit a lawyer is a different question!

One of the things I discovered in this interdisciplinary area is that there are strong controversies raging in almost every discipline between those who are doing quantitative studies and those who are doing narrative studies. This is true in the field of law, it's true in the field of sociology, it's true in the field of psychology, and it's true in the field of political science. In these disciplines the establishment espouses the narrative approach, while the quantizers are the radicals.

In the harder sciences, mathematics and engineering, the same type of controversy exists, except that the establishment consists of those who mathematically model physical variables capable of precise definition and measurement. The radicals in this field are trying to extend some of their ideas and measurement techniques to variables that are less well defined and that can be only crudely approximated at the present, or perhaps ever.

I'm going to assume that anyone who is interested enough in this paper to read it through probably falls within the group of radicals. I cautiously add "radicals" in a professional sense, maybe not in the political sense. Now that I've decided what my audience is, let me briefly review the results of my literature research. Out of the hundred ten journals, I collected approximately two hundred articles that are related in some way to the idea of doing a systems analysis of the legal process.

By now I'm using the concept *systems analysis* to include any of the mathematical techniques by which people have tried to analyze systems, whether they be physical or nonphysical systems. This certainly includes all of the mathematics applied to analyzing physical systems, all of symbolic logic, and all of the area of operations research. Also by now I'm using the concept *legal system* to include any and all of the mechanisms by which a society rules or regulates itself. However, I prefer the concept *legal process* somewhat over the concept *legal system* because a legal system implies, at least to me, a static relationship and legal process implies a dynamic process. This would include the transition from one type of a legal system to another—it might be a smooth continuous transition, or it might occur fairly rapidly and with discontinuities.

I arranged the papers I collected into subgroups. The first subgroup was for narrative discussions of the legal process, or jurisprudence. The second subgroup included papers that discussed specific components of the overall legal system or legal process. This group also included studies that looked at particular mathematical techniques that might have utility in understanding the legal system or some of its components. The third group was those papers that discussed the application of quantized systems concepts to understanding a legal system or the legal process in the broadest terms.

A good bit of the material did not fit into any of these three groups but fell in allied areas such as legal education, nonspecific discussions of law and technology, data banks, and economic analyses related to law and technology. Relative to the economic analyses, there seems to be a tendency for economists to equate the concept *systems analysis* with the concept *cost-benefit analysis*. I question this identification; cost-benefit analysis is only one part of systems analysis, and it tends to place an undue emphasis on monetary values.

As an example, the people of Santa Barbara had fought off the freeway people (and sometimes their own City Council) for a decade or so on whether a freeway should extend through the downtown area. Last year the controversy recurred, and I discussed with a group of students the possibility of doing a linear programming analysis to seek an optimum solution. Had they, as one of them suggested, used cost as the objective function, the analysis could have only yielded an estimate of the least cost. That the freeway should be built would have been assumed in the statement of the problem. A better analysis would use a variable like "desirability to the community" as the objective function. This permits, as a possible solution, that the freeway should not be built regardless of cost.

The obvious objection is "How do you quantify a variable like desirability to the community?" It is admittedly difficult; however, it is no more difficult than the basic question of whether the freeway should be built. If one cannot really define and quantify that variable, he cannot rationally resolve the question. One can ignore a problem, or he can even make a decision in some undefined way; but if he cannot define and quantify the variables in the problem, he cannot rationally resolve it. In the same manner if one cannot define and quantify variables appropriate to the legal system, he cannot rationally resolve the complex issues that the legal system is facing.

Forrester,[7] working in the area of large-scale computer simulations, speaks of "counter-intuitive" systems. By this he means that so long as a problem is small (a relative term), it is within the capacity of a human mind to comprehend all the facts and all the relationships. Therefore, a human is able to solve the problem—like a bar exam question or a homework problem. For much larger problems with very large amounts of data and with many complex relationships, the problem becomes too large to solve without a computer. This is especially true if the situation extends over a long period of time: "How will what you do now effect the situation many years in the future?"

Campbell[8] states that most reforms are advocated as though they were certain to be successful. He stresses a need to evaluate the effectiveness of legal reform. The next step of course is to learn to predict, with at least some accuracy, what the short- and long-term effects of legal reform will be during the design stage.

This brings me back to my three groupings: (1) narrative discussions of the legal process (jurisprudence); (2) specific components of the legal process and mathematical techniques; and (3) mathematical models of a legal system or the legal process.

The number of published papers appropriate for the group one category is very large. I selected only typical papers that might be especially relevant for nonlawyers who desire to try their hand in this field. The second group was fairly complete and has, as far as I could tell, most of the references available in the recent legal literature and some of the material in associated literature. Group two did not purport to be a survey of the mathematical literature of systems analysis or operations research.

The third group is small, and to my knowledge essentially complete. All of this group (ten papers) are discussed here and included in the references. None of the papers in group three actually model an entire legal system or even a large part of it. Like the saying about the weather, these papers talk about modeling the legal system, but they don't do . . . Well, perhaps they do represent some very modest beginnings.

The first of the papers I selected for group three was written in 1968 by Navarro and Taylor,[9] who constructed a simulation model of a court system and its operations to examine the effect of changes in the system. It was applied to the District of Columbia court system for processing felony cases. In the same year Lawlor[10] gave an excellent description, both narrative and mathematical, of decision theory applied to judicial decisions. He briefly updated it in a more recent article.[11] Later Blumstein and Larson[12] presented a detailed model of the criminal justice system which has as its components police, prosecution, courts, correction agencies, and individuals. It includes feedback effects of offenders released at various stages in the system. Test results were developed on California data.

Sheldon[13] presented the need to construct narrative and/or mathematical models as a necessary part of social research. Although he correctly noted that "a model of the judicial process that is to simulate the real properties and actions of the actual process must also be dynamic and in motion," his understanding of the mathematics of systems analysis is limited in that he assumes that it is limited to static situations. This leads to an erroneous conclusion: "The system model may not be an adequate tool." His descriptive understanding of the judicial process as a dynamic system is, however, very useful. Birmingham[14] constructed a model of the criminal process by setting up a game theory matrix with associated strategies available to the individual and the state. He optimizes utility of licit behavior. Goldman and Jahnige[15] discussed Eastonian systems analysis as applied to the judicial system and included the role of feedback responses.

The more recent papers depart from modeling the judicial system to include more general applications of systems analysis to the legal system. An article written by Reimers and Hamilton[16] discussed the concepts of systems analysis in a narrative form without application. Two of my own papers[17, 18] discussed the possibility of using operations research and systems analysis to mathematically model the legal process. The legal process is treated symbolically as a feedback situation in which, first, unacceptable situations in society result in litigation. In response to these situations and litigation, there is social reaction, court revision of precedent, and law review articles. These three factors combine and ultimately result in new laws and revised governmental structure. As a result of the new laws and revised governmental structure, a new set of substantive and procedural rights are created. These, in turn, combine with other factors from society to yield new social values. The new social values combine with random interactions between people, resulting in new unacceptable situations that eventually end in litigation completing the feedback loop. It certainly is not a complete description of the legal process, but it does provide a simplified block diagram as a skeleton approach. I also briefly discussed the possibility of applying other techniques of operations research to the problem of understanding the legal process and some of its components.

The most recent paper is by Drobak.[19] Drobak's paper considered understanding legal problems in terms of simulation and game theory. It included a brief survey of the uses of simulation in management, economics, social science, and psychology, and the use of computer gaming as a research and educational tool.

Let me add one caution about the completeness of the research. The time I had available did not permit me to make a search of political science journals, but I was able to review approximately thirty books from the field of political science that deal with quantified methods. Although several of the authors are apologetic of their efforts, I feel it is the political scientists who have done much of the work in advancing quantified methods of the political and legal process. Anyone entering this field should carefully review the political science literature—especially for contributions that would fit in my group two.

Let me quickly give a prognosis of where I think the field is and where it may be headed. People in science are actually beginning to do something about the weather. I think in this field of applying systems analysis to the legal system, some people are actually on the verge of doing something about it also. Computers of necessary complexity exist; appropriate mathematical and computer programming techniques exist; a significant number of components of the legal process have already been modeled in at least some preliminary ways; and even the philosophical concepts of jurisprudence are beginning to be placed into paradigms with the potential of leading to mathematical models.

I think that in ten years' time (1984) people will have modeled the legal system with a considerable degree of accuracy. Use of computers to retrieve legal data will be very advanced; great banks of data on society and even individuals will exist and will be used for better or worse. Researchers already have acquired the ability to predict the outcome of specific judicial decisions with a surprising degree of accuracy. This work will continue, and some time during the next ten years people are going to ask: "Well, if a computer can do as well, why not use the computer?" And the question is going to deserve more than a flip answer. As James Thurber[20] said: "Skepticism is a useful tool of the inquisitive mind, but it is scarcely a method of investigation."

Incidentally, one of the better satires in this field is the article by Rohner:[21] "Jurimetrics, No!" in the *American Bar Association Journal*. He has a President Reagan use John Marshall's axiom, "This is a government of laws and not of men," to justify replacing the entire federal judiciary in 1984 with late-model JUDIVAC computers. More seriously Dennis[22] asks why "lawyers did not find it reassuring to know that judges are sufficiently consistent in their thinking so that their decisions could be predicted."

Certainly if you went into your local prison and took a poll of the people there, most of whom are poor and/or nonwhite, you would find a group of people who would vote overwhelmingly in favor of a legal system that lacked some of the emotional and prejudicial factors that might have been imposed on them. Further, when a client picks an attorney for himself or his firm with the knowledge that sophisticated computer techniques are available, is he going to select an attorney who can represent him to the fullest and best degree by making use of computerized techniques? The answer is probably *yes*. In fact, some agencies of the federal government are today using computerized techniques in the preparation of litigation.

I guess the next question that could be asked is: "Should the calendar year 1984 be identified with George Orwell's year 1984?" I can't avoid the suspicion that at least to some degree these computerized techniques will be misused and that at least a part of society will have a somewhat Orwellian character. Barry Commoner,[23] in a recent article about the environment, had this to say: "Clearly we have compiled a record of serious failures in recent technological encounters with the environment. In each case the new technology was brought into use before the ultimate hazards were known. We have been quick to reap the benefits and slow to comprehend the costs." What has happened with the hard technologies and their impact on the environment will, I think, be paralleled by the soft technologies and their impact on society. Hopefully, both of the processes are reversible.

Back in the late 1950s when computers were beginning to come into general use in the business world, many companies saw, or were talked into seeing, the computer as a cure-all for all their business problems.

They were quick to reap the benefits and slow to comprehend the costs. In some cases the costs were so high that the companies went bankrupt. In other cases they were able to recover. There must have been many company presidents who swore "I'll never see a computer in this company again" and who then made the decision to return to conventional, precomputer methods of doing business. They must have gone home that night and tossed and turned in their sleep and then awakened in the morning with a sick realization that they could not go back to the old techniques for the simple reason that the old techniques were failing and that that was the reason they considered the use of a computer in the first place. And so what did they do? They went back to work the next day and used the computer more cautiously, and the next week, and the next month, and the next year, and gradually worked out an appropriate man–machine relationship that would permit them to reap many of the benefits of a computer while paying only a limited amount of cost.

There are very few companies or organizations today that could exist without a computer. If you ever have had trouble with flight reservations, think what the chaos would have been had the airline tried to keep track of its airplanes and its passengers without the use of a computer. It would be totally unthinkable in that case to consider going back to precomputer times.

The analogy I'm trying to make here is that when quantified methods and computers are first brought into the legal system, there will indeed be some hard times, and many voices will be raised to the effect: "Get these computers and scientists out of here!" But they, like the businessmen who threw their computers out, will remember that the system was failing without the computers and that's why people began to look at them in the first place. It's like the old saying about the lover that you can't live with and can't live without.

That the legal system and especially the courts are in trouble is common knowledge to those active in the area. Judge Frank[24] in his book, *Courts on Trial*, discusses the critical problems facing the legal system and states the need for reform. Senator Tydings[25] states, "The mills of justice are not only grinding slowly, they are grinding to a halt." Perlov[26] in *Soviet Law and Government* critiques Soviet law procedures and cites the need for reform, including the application of scientific techniques for improving justice.

The application of analytic techniques to improve on the components of the legal system and even to analyze the dynamics of the legal process itself are necessary parts of the administration of justice and the application of humanitarian principles. They can and inevitably will be misused. As Harrington[27] notes, while speaking about the need for bureaucracy in implementing government: "Bureaucracy . . . is also an enormous potential source of arbitrary, impersonal power which folds, bends, spindles, and mutilates individuals but keeps IBM cards immaculate."

The increased use of mathematical models, quantified data, and computers may often tend to strengthen bureaucracy and its impersonality, but it need not be so. If used properly, these analytic and computer techniques have the potential for reducing the need for bureaucracy and ultimately the achievement of timely, effective, and even personal governmental action. These new techniques most certainly will be used. The critical need is for humanists to keep informed and to stay active in these developments so that humanitarian principles will be given sufficient consideration.

REFERENCES

1. Lozowick, Steiner & Miller, "Law and Quantitative Multivariate Analysis: An Encounter," 66 Michigan Law Review 1641 (1968).
2. Scriven, "Methods of Reasoning and Justification in Social Science and Law," 23 Journal of Legal Education 189 (1970).
3. Rosenberg, "Comments," 23 Journal of Legal Education 199 (1970) (Comments on article by Scriven cited here at note 2).
4. Shapiro, "Law and Science in Seventeenth Century England," 21 Law and Society Review 727 (1969).
5. Savoy, "Toward a New Politics of Legal Education," 79 Yale Law Journal 444 (1970).
6. Campbell, "Ethnocentrism of Disciplines and the Fish-Scale Model of Omniscience," in *Interdisciplinary Relationships in the Social Sciences* 328 (M. Sherif & C. Sherif eds.), Aldine Publishing Co. (1969).
7. Forrester, "Counterintuitive Behavior of Social Systems," 73 Technology Review 52 (1971).
8. Campbell, "Legal Reforms as Experiments," 23 Journal of Legal Education 217 (1970).
9. Navarro & Taylor, "Data Analyses and Simulation of a Court System for the Processing of Criminal Cases," 9 Jurimetrics Journal 101 (1968).
10. Lawlor, "Personal Stare Decisis," 41 Southern California Law Review 73 (1968).

11. Lawlor, "Analysis of Disagreements," 1970 Rutgers Journal of Computers and Law 70 (1970).
12. Blumstein & Larson, "Models of a Total Criminal Justice System," 17 Operations Research 199 (1969).
13. Sheldon, "Structuring a Model of the Judicial Process," 58 Georgetown Law Journal 1153 (1970).
14. Birmingham, "A Model of Criminal Process: Game Theory and Law," 56 Cornell Law Review 57 (1970).
15. Goldman & Jahnige, "Eastonian Systems Analysis and Legal Research," 2 Rutgers Camden Law Journal 285 (1970).
16. Reimers & Hamilton, "Systems Analysis and the Law," 64 Law Library Journal 137 (1971).
17. Vanyo, "Law, Operations Research, and the Environment," 1 Journal of Environmental Systems 213 (1971).
18. Vanyo, "Dynamics of the Legal Process and Environmental Law," 10 California Trial Lawyers Journal 44 (1971).
19. Drobak, "Computer Simulation and Gaming: An Interdisciplinary Survey with a View toward Legal Applications," 24 Stanford Law Review 712 (1972).
20. J. Thurber, "Look Homeward, Jeannie," in *The Beast in Me and Other Animals* 114 (1928).
21. Rohner, "Jurimetrics, No!," 54 American Bar Association Journal 896 (1968).
22. Dennis, "Shall We Put the Law into the Computer?," 73 Case and Comment 28 (1968).
23. Commoner, "Evaluating the Biosphere," in *Man's Impact on Environment* 50 (T. Detwyler ed.), McGraw-Hill (1971).
24. J. Frank, *Courts on Trial*, Princeton University Press (1950).
25. Tydings, "Court of the Future," 13 St. Louis University Law Journal 601 (1969).
26. Perlov, "The Science of Soviet Criminal Procedure and Improvement of Legislation," 6 Soviet Law and Government 11 (1967).
27. M. Harrington, *Toward a Democratic Left* 144, Macmillan (1968).

Exchange of Ideas Between Scientists and Lawyers: A Benefit/Cost Analysis

RODERICK A. CAMERON*
Executive Director, Environmental Defense Fund
East Setauket, New York

WHAT HAS TROUBLED ME MOST ABOUT PREPARING THIS PAPER HAS BEEN the title I selected for it. I cannot imagine now what euphoric vision I must have had when I conceived the notion of providing a benefit/cost analysis of the relationship between scientists and lawyers who join together for a noncommercial broad social purpose. Molding my vague flounderings around in this trackless field into the precise sounding format of a benefit/cost analysis is carrying presumption into the realm of sublime fantasy—something the Corps of Engineers, of course, does all the time in its benefit/cost calculations. I think what I had in mind was to look at some of the practical opportunities and problems which present themselves to lawyer-scientist teams as they work toward a public interest goal.

Incidentally, I will be using the term "public interest" throughout. There is a considerable arrogance implicit in the use of this term by "public interest" groups such as the Environmental Defense Fund. Nevertheless, the term has come to have some currency and has no good substitute. So I will be using the term "public interest," recognizing its limitations.

The greatest problem lies in defining a suitable goal. Our task of finding suitable means to accomplish our end is complicated because we do not know what that end is. When a scientist leaves his laboratory or a lawyer cuts free of the conventional attorney–client relationship, he enters an area which is truly bewildering. A scientific experiment usually has a clear research objective; a client usually has an identifiable

---

* Mailing address: Environmental Defense Fund, 162 Old Town Road, East Setauket, New York 11733.

interest he wants his lawyer to protect. But when one addresses broad social needs, like environmental degradation or consumer welfare, the problem often begins with finding a suitable goal.

This is not always true, of course. It is clear that we need safer cars. It is clear that we need to replace total reliance on broad-spectrum, persistent pesticides with integrated biological and chemical pest control techniques. It is clear that we need more reliance on mass transportation and less reliance on the individual automobile. But what is it that this nation needs in the way of an energy policy? What kind of land-use patterns should emerge from the present controversy over wetlands, open spaces, crowded cities?

The National Science Foundation's Research Applied to National Needs program is finding that these questions are just as perplexing after an extensive inquiry into them as they were before. The National Academy of Engineering's Committee on Public Engineering Policy, in a recent review of RANN's energy policy activities, stated: "The major problem with energy is clear: *as with most important policy questions, we don't know what we want as a nation. . . .*"

When a scientist and a lawyer form a team to work in the public interest on a problem, each tends to respond to the tracklessness of their situation by hoping that the other will give the venture its directionality. The lawyer tends to regard himself in his traditional role as a "hired gun." The scientist seems to suffer from a more complex set of problems. The scientific community tends to equate one's objectivity or standard of accuracy with an unemotional state of mind. Part of the emotional gestalt of this objective state of mind seems to require an indifference or valuelessness concerning the data about which the scientist is expert. It even includes a passivity toward the issues surrounding the data. The unconscious assumption is that activism precludes high standards of accuracy and objectivity. Activism seems to be bad form in parts of the scientific community. The concepts of the citizen and of the scientist seem to be considered immiscible by the scientific establishment. I think this is a false assumption, but it is true that deep involvement may pose an obstacle to objectivity. But an obstacle is not a barrier. In my view, the benefit is worth the risk. The thin line which the scientist must tread between objectivity and indifference was touched upon in the 1972 article "Public Interest Science" by Frank von Hipple and Joel Primack (177 *Science* 1166).

The most sensible way for me to deal with my topic is to relate the experiences of the only practicing, functioning, long-term example of an action-oriented science-law experiment with which I am familiar. The Environmental Defense Fund was established in October 1967. It considers itself a coalition of scientists and lawyers. It likes to think of itself as a legal action arm for the environmentally concerned scientific community. (It also, by the way, does considerable work in related consumer welfare areas.)

The Environmental Defense Fund's guiding conceptualization of the relationship between scientists and lawyers has scientists delineating substantive policy, determining goals and priorities. Because the law is essentially a procedural discipline, the lawyer is expected to find ways to implement the policies laid down by the scientists. As conceived, the relationship is like that of an investor and a broker. The lawyer, acting as a broker, finds ways to put the scientists' data and conclusions into public policy.

In reality, of course, the conceptualization is only that. The lines of demarcation are not clear. Since both scientist and lawyer are operating interdependently, productive relationships result from a yeasty interplay of personalities.

Both the lawyer and the scientist must be expected to be policy activists. By this I do not mean activists in terms of the politics of Capitol Hill, the White House, state governors' mansions, or state legislatures. Partisan or party politics command national and local attention far out of proportion to their importance. By policy activism for public interest law–science teams, I refer to the much more important politics of the big regulatory and developmental bureaucracies. These agencies command little attention, and their politics are characterized by inertia and internal jurisdictional squabbles. Nevertheless, the bulk of governmental policies and decisions germinate and are implemented in these bureaucracies. It is in that political milieu that effective public interest activism must occur.

By policy activism I also mean that the lawyer and the scientist must be skillful in dealing with the press, with local organizations, and in raising funds to support their activities. The scientists must be skilled diplomats in obtaining the involvement of experts in those diverse disciplines which apply to nearly every major social problem.

Public policy work requires much activity outside of one's professional training. I cannot overemphasize the importance of a scientist-lawyer team functioning in this "political" way. They are relatively impotent when they do not take their case to the public and to sympathetic people in a position to help them. The reason for this is that the legal process in our democratized society has always been subordinated to the political process. Indeed, one of the difficult realizations for the scientist to make is the degree to which the legal process is hemmed in to avoid conflict with political processes. The most important of these restrictions is the "arbitrary and capricious" standard for judicial review of administrative action. To put the matter inelegantly, judges will not overrule a bureaucrat if they decide he is simply wrong in a decision to register a pesticide or to permit a laxer automobile emission standard test. The judge will not overrule the bureaucrat unless the bureaucrat is so wrong that his action can be characterized as arbitrary and capricious. Thus it is not enough to merely win, you must win big.

Another important restriction, which has been diminishing in recent decades, bears on the interest which is being vindicated. If it is a broad public interest not having particular effect on the organization or individual challenging the bureaucrats' action, then a question is raised whether the issue is really any of the plaintiffs' business. This consideration goes under the legal name of "standing to sue." The scientist must learn the limitations of his lawyer partner and why it is not enough to "sue the bastards." As an old, anonymous English verse has it:

> The law locks up both man and woman
> Who steals the goose from off the common.
> But lets the greater felon loose
> Who steals the common from the goose.

Similarly, the lawyer must realize the diversity and limitations of science. A biologist is not an automotive engineer, a traffic projection engineer, a flood control expert, a meteorologist, a nuclear engineer, or a systems analyst. Yet the lawyer is prone to think that once he has allied himself with a technically trained person, his "expert problem" is done. He should learn that his scientific partner must develop liaisons with a broad spectrum of applied scientists whose expertise will bear directly on the problem. As an expert, a scientist has a narrow input into any broad problem. But when he serves in a liaison capacity he has a broad, almost administrative input which depends on his judgment and sense of perspective.

The Environmental Defense Fund has given much thought to the career implications for scientists when they either volunteer their services to EDF or join its paid staff for a period of years. The fear, of course, is that public service will diminish their professional marketability. Scientists are not practicing their profession, as such, when they work with public interest lawyers on a case concerning environmental or consumer welfare. Whether they are acquiring skills of equal importance is unclear, at least in the minds of university department heads who would employ them.

Some scientists, particularly those in the applied sciences, may be tainted by public policy activity. They may find it difficult to work for consulting or engineering firms whose usual clientele consists of industry or government agencies which the scientist has challenged. Indeed, in some disciplines such as entomology, water resource engineering, and oil geology, it is nearly impossible to hire a consulting firm even on a straight-fee basis if the work you wish it to do may antagonize their clients or imperil lucrative consulting arrangements. Imagine the plight of a consulting sanitary engineer being asked to testify to the optimality of his local county sewage board's proposed multimillion dollar plant. It can be next to impossible to obtain certain kinds of necessary expertise to deal with important public issues. The expertise which is most needed is that which is least available: applied and engineering sciences. Not surprisingly, these disciplines tend to play an important part in the functioning of the economic status quo that public interest groups seek to change.

There is nothing new in scientists and lawyers meshing together to change public policy. Over the last three-quarters of a century such teams have been an important, if unrecognized, force for national policy formulation. In the past, however, these teams have nearly always been assembled by industry. They have gotten registration for drugs and pesticides, licenses to dredge and fill wetlands, and permission to use chemicals in our foods. They have served industry's needs admirably. And they have not done so with the handicap of the bewildering lack of clear goals which plague the public policy scientist-lawyer teams.

Industry representatives always have a clear goal. Profit orders their universe and renders their world susceptible of understanding. It is ironic to note that, despite such a simplified prospective, they often make mistakes and create situations which are to their long-term financial detriment. It is important here to point out a compensating factor which benefits public interest science-lawyer teams. They do not represent an economic interest; consequently, they are free to "run to the highest factual ground." By that I mean that they are free to adopt whatever position is supported by the strongest scientific evidence. They are not required, as industry so often is, to sit helplessly in defense of a position which is not supported by scientific fact but which is dictated by the need to preserve a profitable market or avoid an expense industry has hitherto been able to pass on to the public. This freedom to "run to the highest factual ground" places great responsibility on public interest policy activists and requires them to exercise extraordinary care to obtain the best judgment that the scientific community can provide on their issues.

It is important for scientists to understand what is meant by the legal process. The stereotypic image is that of court proceedings. But the time spent in court plus the time preparing to be in court is perhaps less than 20% of a scientist-lawyer team's total work. By far the largest portion is directed toward administrative hearings within agencies such as the Food and Drug Administration, the Environmental Protection Agency, and the Federal Aviation Administration, among many others. Amending regulations, obtaining rulings on how regulations apply to given situations, arguing over standards, implementation procedures, and numerous similar activities are the great bulk of a scientist-lawyer team's effort to reform institutions and public policy.

One further thought is pertinent: a team consisting of a scientist and a lawyer is incomplete. The raw data from the scientist need to be processed in a form suitable for decision makers. The language of decision makers seems to be an amalgam of law and economics. It is thus necessary to have the data and the technological options which the scientist proposes analyzed by an economist. This is perhaps the most significant step of all. If our options are grossly uneconomic or if they are successfully characterized by the opposition as being so, the chances of getting them implemented are virtually nil.

The Environmental Defense Fund has thus sought to provide economic analysis for as many of its contentions as is feasible. Recently a very important organization called the Public Interest Economics Center was created in Washington which will, it is hoped, supply a vital element to the public interest presentation of issues that until now has too often been missing.

Courts as Institutions for Assessing Technology

PHILIP L. BEREANO*
Department of Environmental Engineering
Cornell University
Ithaca, New York

A LAWSUIT IS NOT ONLY AN ATTEMPT TO RESOLVE A PROBLEM, IT IS ALSO A means of calling attention to it so that the political processes may act (this is clearly what has been happening in the environmental field). In general, law is dynamic and adjusts to the dominant social pressures and powers, although there is often a lag time. One of the chief attributes of the court system is that its decisions are accorded general respect, authority, and legitimacy. The loser accepts the judgment, knowing that he has had "his day in court," and any person—no matter how unusual his position—can usually receive a hearing.

Partisans in more and more areas are turning to the courts as a means of gaining policy goals—whether it be for welfare reform, abortion liberalization, or environmental protection— in spite of the institutional disadvantages. The irony is that the judicial process is predicated upon a spirit of moderation in society. In theory, it should perform in the interstices of legislative and other governmental actions since, despite the drama of the adversary setting, it is not suitable for the decision of far-reaching social and political questions. The reason for this paradox is that the professed political branches of government have neglected certain social issues because they were either too hot to handle (*e.g.*, segregation, apportionment, contraception) or had too little pressure behind them to be noticed (*e.g.*, legal counsel for the indigent). The result is that the courts have been prime movers in contemporary social issues.[1]

. . . There is a deep tradition in this country that the courts exist to redress imbalances that may remain after the political branches of the govern-

---

* Mailing address: Department of Environmental Engineering, Cornell University, Ithaca, New York 14850.

ment have had their say and played their part. . . . The courts are a penulti-mate resort; after that only demonstrations and riots can possibly work.[2]

"Technology assessment" means different things to different people. I would emphasize its policy aspects and define it as ascertaining the trend of technological change and the resulting implications for all sectors of society, systematically evaluating the consequences (direct and indirect) of such developments, attempting to forecast the possible future trends and consequences, and making social decisions to choose the alternative for the future which would maximize desired benefits and minimize negative effects according to the normative policies one wishes to effec-tuate.

Virtually none of the writers on decision theory include the judi-ciary in their conceptions. They deal with political and administrative decision making; yet, judicial decisions often have political dimensions and lead to rules which govern our conduct. But most commentators on technology assessment minimize discussion of the judiciary as model or mechanism. Most recognize that court actions are assessments (in the broad sense), but the possibilities of the converse have not been met with favor. The standard view is that private litigation simply cannot be relied upon to protect the public interest in this era of technological affluence and rapid social change. Primarily motivated by a knowledge of the procedural and practical difficulties of suits on these issues, such persons see the legislature and administrative agencies shouldering more of the task and formulating standards for protection of the public at large. Only a few writers have seen the use of lawsuits as technology assessment devices, especially in regard to environmental areas.[3]

Courts and Technical Matters

How does the legal system handle new technologies and their asso-ciated social problems?

. . . The first phase of societal response to such social problems has usually been the extension and application of old legal principles to the new prob-lems. Our judicial system has worked out on a step-by-step, trial and error basis new rules of law to mesh new technologies into the fabric of our overall societal structure. When these rules of law have seemed to our legislative bodies to be inadequate, or to be developing too slowly for protection of society, our legislative bodies have superimposed statutory law over the judge-made law by establishing statutory standards of conduct and liability or providing for outright government regulation.[4]

The legal community has not devoted much direct attention to the ramifications of technology as a systematic area of interest, although the New York Bar Association set up a committee on this subject a few years ago. As a result the law has responded to technical change rather than explicitly controlling it. An interesting example is that in 1825 the Supreme Court held that the admiralty jurisdiction of the United States was limited to tidal waters, but this view was overruled in 1851 and the jurisdiction extended to all waters which were navigable because, in part, the intervening invention of the steamboat and its application to commerce had greatly increased the reach of shipping activities.[5]

A panel of the National Academy of Sciences has presented nine guidelines for assessment institutions: develop cautiously; continue evaluations in areas where federal programs play a role; supplement, not supersede, existing mechanisms; stimulate awareness and competence regarding technology assessment in other institutions; be able to elicit cooperation of the corporate and professional communities; be neutral, neither promoting nor regulating technology; operate at a strategic level politically; be open to widest range of interest groups; and be itself able to establish priorities among assessment issues.[6] The courts measure up to these well, except for the last item and perhaps the second. The panel also listed eight specific functions an assessment institution should be able to perform.[7] But the courts can do only one well—reviewing the determinations of other agencies—and cannot do some at all (such as sponsor research or make recommendations), although the adversarial parties to a lawsuit could undertake many of these as part of their dispute. The conclusion might be that court litigation is a suitable mode of performing some aspects of technology assessment even if it is not the answer to all of our needs.

Courts are essentially conservative institutions, and it is not their nature or function to promote change. In fact, their structure also makes promoting causes difficult since they have "neither purse nor sword." Therefore, they are not likely to be sympathetic to technical developments which seriously disturb the status quo or are incipient; for the same reason, they may be more disposed to tolerate already ongoing detrimental effects (like pollution) from a technology which has established itself. Plaintiffs and their attorneys, and to a lesser extent the other side, ought to perform a technology assessment of their own to come up with feasible options that a court can choose since the lawsuit is otherwise apt to be an all-or-nothing situation and a judge may feel that it is irresponsible to chose nothing.[8] In addition courts are poorly equipped to perform early warning functions since there are no motivated parties to clearly present the issues. However, their skill is that of making choices upon evidence which has been presented; this is an expertise which assessors should possess, but the question is whether the courts can transfer it from their accustomed fields to technological ones.

In contrast to the judicial bipolar model, regulatory agencies are tripartite: the agency staff, the public, and the regulated entities. Although the staff is supposed to promote the public's interest, the history of most agencies shows that they tend instead to accommodate themselves to the parties being regulated.

The contemporary literature on the failings of the administrative process—both in theory and in practice—is extensive. It includes work by Ralph Nader, Charles Reich (Yale), Marver Bernstein (Princeton and Brandeis), Matthew Holden (Michigan), and Joseph Sax (Michigan), and others, not to mention popular articles in magazines and newspapers.

Some points made by the critics are: Planning by a regulatory agency is difficult, if not impossible;[9] agencies may hamper private initiative and responsibility; roughly speaking, agencies usually do not attract personnel of as high a quality as the bench; the administrators try to remain unobtrusive and shy away from controversy (most citizen lawsuits of the type we are discussing are against government agencies); agency expertise and flexibility are often touted but sometimes overrated, and their positions may become frozen around interests which arise.

One response has been to try to create better agencies. A newer trend is a return to private vindication in the courts. Here the decision makers are generalists not related to vested interests or constituency pressures. Since the issues involved are not solely technological but involve policy questions, sensitivity in judgment and wisdom are more important than expertise. (In litigation, judges are not asked to make technical judgments, but to rule on evidence and applicable legal doctrines.) Litigation revolves around concrete issues and is one of the few decision mechanisms which can be triggered by an individual citizen or small group.

The Judicial Process

How courts decide cases will not be extensively covered here; a general feeling for the judicial process rather than the complexities of jurisprudential theory will be assumed, based on other presentations. The process of judge-made law, or the "common law," is evolutionary until "we discover that the contour of the landscape has been changed, that the old maps must be cast aside, and the ground charted anew," *i.e.*, that a fundamental decision is required.[10] Experience, not only empiricism but ethical and nonrational motivations as well, has had much influence on the law.

> . . . The life of the law has not been logic; it has been experience. The felt necessities of the time, the prevalent moral and political theories, intuitions of public policy, avowed or unconscious, have had a good deal more to do than the syllogism in determining the rules by which men should be governed.[11]

The law thus grows into new areas. Where it has not yet formulated rules for such an area of social change, the conflict engendered by the change is apt to lead to litigation and the opportunity for law to be made. The order in which cases arise is important because there may be existing doctrinal bridges to build upon or doctrinal gaps which seem to a judge to be too large to leap.

In the courts, as elsewhere, means and ends exist along a continuum. Since the final ends of the law (such as "due process" or justice) are vague, not unlike the "public interest," the means for achieving them are the usual focus of judicial decisions.[12] Although some decisions are obviously concerned with ends (such as whether malapportionment of a legislature is unconstitutional), these ends are not apt to be too far toward the extreme of the continuum. More frequently judicial actions deal with means (as one man/one vote, gerrymandering, whether school boards are to be considered legislative bodies for this purpose, and so on). The judicial process thus has a strong problem-solving aspect as well as the decision-making one for conflict resolution. Since judicial opinions will serve to guide future conduct, the judiciary must be concerned with a great number of questions of implementation and adjustment, although its structure is not well suited for these tasks.

Yet in both of these types of decisions the courts have, in fact, been dealing with value questions for several hundred years; every judgment has an ethical dimension and ethical references.

Usually a court action is not well designed for the exposition of new values; it works best in the context of value consensus, handling disputes which arise within accepted norms. This corresponds to a basic conservatism inherent in the judicial institution and the traditional posture of judicial self-restraint, which tend to reinforce the status quo. In addition, courts rely on numerous procedural devices to keep decisions as specific as possible and avoid broad general rulings. The result is a powerful influence upon the assessment capabilities of the judiciary. In spite of this influence, however, one can readily think of judicial opinions which rest on basic value issues—*e.g.*, individualism versus majority pressures (the school prayer decisions), pluralism and the relationships between various ethnic groups (the segregation cases), and irrelevance of economic criteria to legal equality (the provision of counsel for indigent criminal defendants). It is noteworthy and to the credit of the judiciary that in most of these instances the courts dealt with such value conflicts when other institutions largely ignored them.

Judicial Involvement in Assessment: Standing

Since they exist to settle rather than stimulate litigation, courts do not make their services available to any individual or institution who, for reason or caprice, decides to initiate a lawsuit. A would-be plaintiff must possess the requisite "standing" in order to sue. That is, he must have some sufficient "interest" which he alleges has been invaded or is about to be invaded by the defendant. These principles apply to all cases, not just to those involving technology assessment. Aspects of standing and their relation to technical controversies include:

1. The situation when one or a limited number of individuals suffer the adverse consequences of a technology to a special or greater degree than the community as a whole. For example, people who contract hepatitis as a result of a blood transfusion, have their property values diminished because neighbors pollute a stream they share, or are injured by a defectively designed power tool or automobile, turn to the courts regularly for relief or compensation. Their special damage provides the requisite standing.

    It is probably impossible to find a common law theory of tort liability (*e.g.*, negligence, absolute liability) that has not been successfully levied on some form of technology by an injured individual. In addition, contract actions for breach of warranty, property actions for nuisance and trespass, refusal to submit to eminent domain takings, and even challenges to statutory authority on constitutional grounds have been employed by specially damaged individuals and have resulted in forcing courts to perform technology assessments.

2. Unlike individuals, government instrumentalities have standing to complain about general injury to the community they represent, and actions brought by them constitute a second mode. In the en-

forcement of some criminal laws, such as those relating to the emission of excess automotive exhausts, the courts are used merely to administer the policy embodied in an assessment made elsewhere (*e.g.*, the legislature). Sometimes the government calls upon the court itself to make a technical assessment as part of the enforcement procedure. Courts may also get into such issues when called upon to arbitrate policy conflicts between different governmental layers in our federal system, the status of federally reserved rights to control navigable streams, or the question of whether a municipality may dedicate parts of the public domain to private use without state approval.

A governmental unit can also bring a question of technology assessment before the courts in an action to abate a public nuisance or in other circumstances where an individual cannot show the requisite special damage but the government organ can claim to represent the public generally. Public nuisance has not been used extensively for assessments, perhaps because the government often has the alternative of a criminal prosecution or regulatory process available; in addition, the doctrine of public nuisance has an historical association with the abatement of brothels, gambling dens, etc., and so the case law is not readily transferable to technological problems.

3. Taxpayer action; stockholder's derivative suit; class action.

4. Originally the law recognized three basic protected interests which would support a plaintiff's standing: his person (including mental anguish and privacy), property (especially land), and contract. Recent cases are establishing nonpecuniary interests concerning "the quality of life" as a sufficient ground in certain instances. This may be a reflection of the broad historical movement (assuming that the values of personality have had fairly continuous validity in Anglo-American jurisprudence) from feudal and agrarian societies where land is the basic commodity, to industrial society characterized by the flow of money and contractual transactions, into a post-industrial era concerned with qualitative values.

Modes of Judicial Assessment

There are, in general, four approaches courts take in performing technical assessments.

ONE

The legal system, statutory and common law, infuses all assessments, public and private. It determines the incidence of costs, defining some as internal and others as external, thus underlying every cost/benefit analysis. It defines the probability of responsibility for certain consequences, thus deterring harmful activities or spurring the development of new alternatives.[13] By modifying these definitions, a court performs one aspect of technology assessment, *internalization*.[14] Legal restraints or incentives may be viewed as internalizing mechanisms.[15]

Two legal fields, torts and nuisance, offer examples of this process (although they can also be handled as more complete assessments—see below). A tort is a private or noncriminal wrong or injury, independent of contract, stemming from a violation of some duty owed. The definition of the duty is the key. During the period of industrialization, the courts' reluctance to define it so as to make manufacturers responsible for certain activities related to their operations fostered the growth of manufacturing. For example, negligence predicated on fault became the general standard of care owed, rather than absolute liability; employee injuries on the job were often excused if a "fellow servant" was in any way involved. In more recent times social welfare considerations have been introduced, shifting the analysis from "fault" to "compensation," *i.e.*, asking, in a sense of fairness, who is best able to bear the risk or prevent it in the first place. Thus, in the field of product liability manufacturers have been held liable for more remote injuries because of their ability to absorb such outlays spread over all their products. This internalization, it is hoped, will spur new technologies to increase product safety and so on.[16]

A nuisance is the wrongful interference with another's enjoyment of his interest in land. It has long been employed to internalize external costs.[17] An injunction rather than a damage award would be a more effective stimulus to technological innovation because the defendant would not be able to operate at all unless he could abate the nuisance.

TWO

The second judicial response is to force other agencies to make the assessment. This may be viewed in *procedural* or *substantive* terms, the first concerning which agency should undertake the general task and the second relating to the imposition of guidelines for such a task, although these are not rigid compartments. This second mode reflects a concern by judges that other agencies may not be weighing the full consequences of their actions.

The *procedural* aspects of this power to make others assess is best demonstrated by the judicially developed "public trust" doctrine currently being utilized in some instances for protection of the physical environment, especially insofar as it is publicly owned.[18] Especially in Massachusetts courts have been requiring that there be plain and explicit authority from the legislature to divert public lands (such as parks and marshes) to new and inconsistent public uses (as for highways), that the parcel of land not only be specifically identified but that the legislation indicate an appreciation of the existing use to be foregone as well as the public interest in the new use which is contemplated.

Another procedural aspect of the relationship between the courts and agencies which are performing technical assessments is the pressure exerted by the former in favor of democratization of the assessment process. There are many cases dealing with statutory or constitutional requirements to conduct public hearings, afford the public adequate notice of agency action, and the like. Although a large proportion of such cases have nothing to do with technology, the rules they annunciate would apply to all similar situations irrespective of subject matter.[19]

A final procedural group of cases concerns attempts to expand an agency's subject matter jurisdiction so that it can be forced to consider consequences occurring beyond its accustomed sphere. In *New Hampshire v. Atomic Energy Commission*[20] the agency was held not required to take thermal pollution into account in a proceeding to license a nuclear power plant. However, in *Zabel v. Tabb*[21] the refusal of the Army Corps of Engineers to issue a dredging permit was upheld over objections that it lacked statutory power to consider ecological factors. The cases could be harmonized by saying that courts will accede to the agency's definition of the scope of its concerns, but more cases will have to be decided before a pattern is clear.

A *substantive* consideration also exists in regard to the courts' power to make other institutions undertake technology assessment. The technique used is statutory interpretation, and there is a fair range of judicial discretion possible. In *Udall v. Federal Power Commission*[22] the Secretary of the Interior sought to reopen an FPC licensing proceeding in order to argue that the government, rather than private interests, ought to be permitted to build a proposed power dam at High Mountain Sheep. The opinion was authorized by Justice Douglas, a noted conservationist, and began with a quote from Holmes that "a river is more than an amenity, it is a treasure." Douglas went on to raise the question of whether the dam should be built at all. First he analyzed the possible effects of the dam on anadromous fish, even to the point of making distinctions between salmon and steelhead. He discussed the consequences of a reservoir on other wildlife in the area, and he reviewed various technical forecasts on the needs for future electrical power and its likely sources. Concluding that all of these factors "were largely untouched by the Commission" (*i.e.*, the Court itself was raising the issues), the Court determined that the statute governing the FPC required that the licensing procedure be reopened to consider them as well as the question of who should construct the dam if it were decided that one should be erected.

In the first *Scenic Hudson* case[23] the court sent the matter back to the FPC for reconsideration because the Commission had only looked at engineering and economic factors, ignoring scenic, historic, and aesthetic aspects of the site and its environs.

THREE

The third response courts may give to questions of technology assessment is to perform the assessment themselves. The evolution of certain substantive legal doctrines, as in tort and nuisance, illustrate this mode.

In the development of tort liability for injuries caused by defendants' products, the courts have created a category of dangerous substances or activities which should require a higher standard of care than merely the absence of negligence. This series of cases, long used in law schools to illustrate the growth of the common law by classifying new fact situations in the light of previous cases, represents a separate technology assessment at each step.[24] What risks should have been foreseen? Should the manufacturer bear them because of his superior control over the instrumentality, as through its design, for example? What is a defect? Who should the manufacturer have expected would use the product and in what fashion? This goes beyond cost internalization.

In the evolution of tort liability, the plaintiffs often experienced the wrong in terms of a sudden dramatic situation (an accident, an explosion, etc.). Today, health is also impaired by long-term, low-level exposures to dangerous conditions. How will the courts handle these assessments? Cause-and-effect relationships are often more tenuous, and it is hard to distinguish causative factors from the merely aggravative. The sensitivity of persons differs with respect to given conditions—should the courts protect the weakest sectors of the population (the aged, infirm, infants) or set standards according to the tolerance of the most robust?

For more than two centuries, nuisance was the only common law means for redressing environmental pollution. In handling these cases, the courts made numerous classifications, distinguishing between private nuisance and public (only governmental officials could sue the latter, which were defined as affecting the whole community); looking to see who occupied his property first in time; and tending to excuse "beneficial" offenders in a bias in favor of industrialization. Most interesting, however, was the judicially evolved factor of investigating the current state of technology in order to see if the defendant was doing all he could to minimize the harmful effects the plaintiff was experiencing.

In *Anderson v. American Smelting and Refining Co.*,[25] a group of farmers sought to enjoin the operation of two nearby lead and copper smelting plants because the sulphurous gases they emitted damaged pastures and vegetable gardens. The court carefully reviewed the scientific evidence and concluded by requiring the companies to devise a means of eliminating the nuisance or go out of business:

> . . . I do not believe the limit of improvement has been reached, or that it is impossible for the smelting and farming interests to exist in the same neighborhood to the advantage of both and without discomfort or injury to the farming community. On the other hand, in this period of the world, when the right of every human being to live in comfort has become a universally accepted principle in American life, I am loathe to believe that the law, or the courts in applying it, will condemn any community of citizens to suffer perpetual discomfort or injury resulting from an unavoidable industrial nuisance.
>
> My conclusion is that if the defendants will suggest a method of operation that will overcome the conditions complained of in this case and eliminate cause of further complaint, a decree will be entered accordingly, or if they will suggest a method of operation, or further improvement that gives fair promise of accomplishing the desired result. . . . Failing in either of the alternatives above suggested, a decree will be entered in accordance with the prayer of the plaintiffs' complaint.[26]

This process is not unusual in nuisance actions,[27] although usually the plant is found up to par.

In the recent case of *Boomer v. Atlantic Cement Co.*,[28] the technology investigated was not the technology of cement making as much as that of pollution control. In addition, the case is noteworthy because it not only measured the defendant's operations by the current state of the art, but also attempted to assess his ability to develop new technical innovations within the subsequent eighteen months.

The enforcement provisions of certain criminal and regulatory statutes also require the court to make a technical assessment. For example, enforcing abatement orders under the Air Quality Act of 1967[29] involves a *de novo* determination by the court of the issues.

FOUR

Courts also review assessments made elsewhere by legislatures, administrative agencies, and quasi-public entities.

In *Miller v. Schoene*,[30] the U.S. Supreme Court was confronted with a Virginia statute (*i.e.*, an assessment by the state legislature) authorizing the government entomologist to order certain privately owned cedar trees destroyed to prevent the communication of the plant disease cedar rust to neighboring apple orchards. The judges, mindful of the impressive contribution of apple trees to the state's economy in comparison to that of cedars, reviewed the status of available technology in the field of plant diseases and concluded that the statute was a constitutional exercise of the government's police power. "The only practicable method of controlling the disease and protecting the apple trees from its ravages is the destruction of all red cedar trees, subject to infection, located within two miles of apple orchards." Although fungicide developments have subsequently rendered cedar destruction unnecessary for modern control, the state retains the statute on its books in case resistant strains should arise.

The review of agency determinations is by far the most common type of assessment in this mode.[31] The basic rule of such judicial review is that if there is any rational basis for the administrative decision, it will be upheld; nonetheless, lawsuits have successfully challenged many bureaucratic actions, and the possibility of a legal action may serve to keep administrators responsive to otherwise ignored interests.

Although the courts will usually cast the decision solely in terms of legal issues, there is Supreme Court precedent for addressing questions of technological forecasting, impacts, etc. See, for example, *Radio Corp. of America v. U.S.*, 341 U.S. 412 (1951), especially the separate opinion of Justice Frankfurter at 421.

In the case of *Abbott Laboratories v. Gardner*,[32] the Court created a presumption that Congress intended all administrative decisions to be open to court review where it did not specifically say otherwise. When the rationale of this case is coupled with the expanded notions of standing discussed previously, it is obvious that the courts are going to be asked to make many technology assessments in the future at the request of disaffected groups.

Texas Eastern Transmission Corp. v. Wildlife Preserves, Inc.,[33] illustrates the last subcategory. It was an action of eminent domain by a federally authorized pipeline company against a private nonprofit corporation maintaining, in New Jersey, "the finest inland, natural fresh water wetland in the entire Northeastern United States." The defendant argued that taking the proposed route would cause extensive ecological damage to vegetation and wildlife, and leave an aesthetic scar on the area. It further claimed that an alternative route with less drastic consequences was available. A unanimous court held that courts would not enforce an eminent domain taking if the route selection were "arbitrary" in light of the potential damage to the environment and the available alternatives. The case was remanded to a lower court to develop facts and determine the arbitrariness of the route; it was finally decided in favor of the pipeline company after careful consideration by the judge of construction technology and ecological impacts.

A significant amount of judicial assessment activity has been occasioned by the National Environmental Policy Act of 1969;[34] because this legislation and its interpretation has received extensive commentary in the literature, it will not be explored here.

*Obstacles and Advantages to Effective Technology
Assessment by Courts*

Courts are passive institutions; they do not initiate actions on their own but must await a decision by a would-be plaintiff to complain. This is a severe drawback to effective use of the judiciary for technology assessment. Assessment is predicated upon rational choice at the earliest possible stage of events, yet individuals and groups may not even be aware of their possible grievance until a much later period. Unless groups of consumers, conservationists and the like continue to be vigilant and militant in bringing court cases, the judiciary will have no chance to attempt to handle these technological problems successfully. Governmental agencies will rarely take technology to court, due to political considerations.

Practical barriers are also pervasive. Aside from having his standing questioned, the plaintiff is moving into an area where substantive law is apt to be nonexistent. He has the burden of proof, yet usually begins with access to far less information than his adversary. The controversy is a public one, the press will be present, and he is emotionally as well as rationally involved.

The contest is substantially unequal. The corporation or government agency has virtually unlimited resources of money and all that money can buy —lawyers, expert witnesses, printing, models, charts and other exhibits, and all of the multitudinous goods and services that go into a major law suit. The conservation group must recruit and organize largely from volunteers. It must appropriate from a deficit budget or conduct house-to-house campaigns to raise small sums from large numbers of people.[35]

However, one prominent figure in public interest litigation against the Atomic Energy Commission, David Comey of Businessmen for the Public Interest (Chicago), has stated that the public groups do have several advantages—in his view, they are smarter than the bureaucrats, more flexible and mobile in their operating possibilities, and "right."[36] Ironically money may be more available to such *ad hoc* groups after a disaster has occurred (as in Santa Barbara) than for a preventive assessment.

Because of the passive stance of the courts and the barriers to entry, most technological assessment questions will not reach the courts until the technology in issue is already in general use or is the object of substantial monetary investment. That is, judicial action is most often *ex post facto* in spite of the possibility of preventive suits (such as for injunctions). Private citizens do not seem to be aware of, or aroused by, the secondary consequences of technology until injury actually takes place or construction actually begins. Sometimes courts dismiss actions because damage is not imminent, thus refusing to hear such issues before the technology is put to use.

Such a doctrine may result in a Scylla/Charybdis situation for the plaintiff, for if he waits until the damage is occurring, the court, if it is balancing his interests against the defendant's, may find that the vast monetary investment in the technology impels a decision to allow the operation to continue. Some cases, of course, hold differently, but there is a danger that the courts will give way before such technological momentum. This basic *post facto* stance is thus inadequate for dealing with technological hazards.

Courts are also extremely limited in the nature of the enforcement mechanisms available to back up their decisions. They can award money damages (the collection of which may take years) or issue injunctions to restrain imprudent conduct, but the "judicial processes are somewhat helpless to induce rationality or even, at technical points, to review it."[37] Injunctions are discretionary, and money damages often cannot restore a ravaged ecosystem. Mandating action is not a common judicial remedy. The "declaratory judgment," an actual controversy over the parties' relations in regard to contemplated future—rather than past—conduct, is a recent device to increase judicial flexibility. Here, however, as with injunctions, the courts find it more difficult to define a protected zone of interests as compared to *post facto* situations where there may be damage to display; the issues of standing and the plea of irreparable injury, necessary to support an injunction, are attempts to overcome such problems.

In addition, a related factor is that a court decision is usually of the "go/no go" type rather than the choice of a point on a continuum of alternative positions. The range of intermediate positions for a judge is usually very limited. Courts also cannot easily become involved in continuing operations such as monitoring, evaluation, and periodic adjusting or fine tuning of the parties' relations. This is obvious in the dilemma faced by courts in "ending" racial segregation in the schools. Yet technology assessment would seem to demand such competence, and it may not be sufficient to rely on the successful party to monitor the results. One of the main arguments in favor of regulatory agencies is their ability to perform such functions.

The judicial method of reasoning seems to have similarly negative implications for the effective use of the courts in technology assessment. Precedent frequently burdens the courts with historical logic which may be irrelevant or even ludicrous when applied to modern technology. Liability rules arise slowly and uncertainly and only after actual harm, yet the potential harms today are too vast to experience before they are dealt with.[38] A modern tort suit is likely to differ from its predecessors in presenting injury arising from cumulative, long-term, low-level exposure rather than a sudden and dramatic impact; injury may be non-specific, from multiple possible causes; even if there is one cause which can be isolated, there may be many sources of that causative agent (as sulfur dioxide in urban air) rather than one; thus, there are numerous, often unknown putative defendants.[39] A nuisance action is similarly burdened by history: it protects only property, not persons; the plaintiff must have a substantial interest in the property; the pollutants have to be traced to a specified defendant; causation must be proved; and how are the damages to be calculated?[40] An injunction may be too drastic a remedy while damages are just a minor annoyance to the defendant; an individual may suffer, although the court may not find it significant or irreparable, or it may not be readily demonstrable; if a nuisance is labeled "public," the plaintiff must show special injury or else hope that the public officials will sue in his stead. The adherence to the notion that trespass is a physical invasion has saved many a polluter who emits noise, odors, or gases, from the social costs of his operations, and has permitted sophisticated electronic equipment to be used to invade peoples' privacy without judicial redress. Perhaps the height of folly was reached in a case which awarded the plaintiff an injunction against cloud seeding above his land (*i.e.*, in his zone of ownership), even though his objection had been to seeding elsewhere which affected the rainfall on his parcel.

The tendency of judicial thinking to focus on the unique circumstances of each case further distorts the results of any technology assessment which might be included in the action. This particularism is associated with the incremental inductive character of the common law system. For example, if a plaintiff exhibits contributory negligence or assumption of the risk, or has "come to a nuisance," it may amount to a perfect defense, without a decision on the merits being reached. The defendant's ability to foresee harm, his posting of a warning, or his general intent may either extricate him or result in his being charged punitive damages. Even the legalistic relationship between the parties (*e.g.*, buyer-seller) may be determinative, because a legal recovery requires the prior existence of an obligation or duty of care on the part of the defendant toward the plaintiff. It should be emphasized that courts are primarily designed to adjust relationships between *parties*; a technology assessment involving diffuse and numerous interests and groups presents the problem of how to take *nonparties* into the decision making. As noted above, if a court focuses on the individual circumstances of the parties, a direct assessment will usually be weighted in favor of the expensive large scale technology and against the damage done an individual or small group of plaintiffs. Some scholars have therefore suggested abandoning the fault system of individual litigation in such situations and substituting insurance, workmen's compensation, or trust fund types of administrative procedures.

As long ago as 1901 Learned Hand discussed the anomaly of asking a lay judge and jury to resolve a dispute between experts on a subject about which they know nothing other than what the experts have told them. In the past courts have occasionally cited their technical incompetence as one reason for avoiding questions which we might characterize as technology assessments. They have always been particularly keen to accept the results of assessments made elsewhere; for example, few courts are willing to question the adequacy of AEC radiation standards. If courts begin to narrow the range of discretion open to industry and administrators, their own technical incompetence will be more apparent and they still might be hesitant to become involved in the direction of technological development. Parties can present expert witnesses to "educate" the court, but this is not always easy for citizen groups to do.[41]

Legal proof relies on definite causation, yet in many assessment situations there are only probabilities or statistical evidence (for example, that cigarette smoking is related to lung cancer). This attitude is associated with the court's being familiar with handling individuals and the rights and responsibilities of unique entities, not cohort groups. As a result, the proof of scientific conclusions in court is unduly cumbersome. For example, the hearsay rule bars as evidence what one scientist (not in court) may have told another (who is), treating it like backyard gossip instead of recognizing that scientific knowledge is the product of cooperative intelligence, team projects, professional literature, conferences, etc.[42] The credibility of legal evidence is based on a witness's credentials and demeanor; the credibility of scientific evidence usually depends on validation through replication and statistical testing (although credentials do receive deference). It is difficult to say whether the courts will adjust their rules to account more readily for phenomena such as synergism, or be willing to accept partial or interim technical findings in the key early stages of technological development.

Technical incompetence without doubt contributes to the heavy burden of proof which is placed on those who attempt to challenge technology in the courts. *Probable* harm is usually ruled out as conjectural; damage must be shown to be impending or to have occurred. The rules of evidence, particularly the hearsay rule, may extend trials and make litigation expenses unbearable. In all such actions the party advocating the technology has the technical competence necessary for its employment and, therefore, for its defense. The challenger, on the other hand, may be an individual without such competence who is merely suffering from the secondary consequences. Be that as it may, the general rule is that the challenger must bear the burden of proof, although there are some signs that a more realistic apportionment may evolve, especially through use of the rules of discovery. Recent statutory developments in Michigan and elsewhere are evidence of a changing situation.

Lastly, one might mention the time factor as a disadvantage. Proceedings in courts and agencies can consume a great deal of time, and this is related to the problem of expense (however, a judge in his discretion can greatly accelerate the process). On the other hand, if those opposing an activity can have it halted until a decision is reached, time can be a factor on their side. Not only does delay generally contribute to disrupting the plans which have been made for the technology, but other technologies develop in the interim, altering the likely assessment at the end of the period from that made originally.

Courts present some advantages as decision-making bodies which remain applicable in technical assessment matters. First, they facilitate participation by affected individuals, groups, or interests in assessment. Participation is a social value in its own right. In addition, the alternative to such involvement seems to be decision making by an elite, paternal at best and manipulative otherwise. Participation need not be direct; it could involve the use of advocates or other surrogate relationships. An adversarial form of decision making is an effective mode of realizing this type of participation and also has the advantage of fostering the consideration of normative issues. Courts are essentially the only recourse which can be immediately effective (except for action of the Executive branch, but it is more time consuming to mount the necessary political pressures to motivate these institutions than to file papers in a court). They are free from pressures and working relationships that administrative agencies have with one side or the other. They are not subject to lobbies; for those with limited time and resources, a suit before a single judge may be more feasible than attempting to compete with organized interests engaged in expensive lobbying before scores of legislators. Narrow political interests are minimized in a judicial forum. Courts can, and do, overrule past decisions, and in this manner are far more receptive to admitting earlier error than many other institutions.

Given the desire to facilitate participation in technology assessment and the suitability of the adversarial context in which to realize this goal, the courts present advantages of diffuseness and decentralization. Corresponding to the complexity of our continental society, the judiciary exists in fifty-two separate but related systems (plus those of the territories), each one multitiered with many specially designed courts. There are cross-linkages between state judicial systems, and between these and that of the federal government. As a result there are many points of entry for the public. Decision making is decentralized because the hierarchy of binding court decisions is limited, and all others exist as material to be used to persuade subsequent courts in their decisions.

Courts can, and do, act at the behest of one person, and can ignore any disparity in the numbers of persons on each side (although this is a factor they usually include in any balancing—see below) if the existence of a right is clear. The Constitution and the legal system are largely premised on the protection of the individual and the regulation of individual conduct, even to the extent of fictionalizing huge corporations as "persons" to fit this outlook. This is an admirable posture as contrasted to administrative agencies which are more inclined to view individuals as troublemakers and may make the courts more sympathetic to the social impacts of technological developments. But because the questions are so complex and the problems apt to concern collective rights and responsibilities, the courts will need to become more flexible. They should be able to mandate agency action more readily, insure access to information, authorize safety criteria and preutilization clearance requiring a proof of nondamage prior to widespread application, etc.[43]

The Balancing Factors

As Cardozo has said, in most situations, "after all, there are few rules; there are chiefly standards and degrees."[44] The judge's problem in a technology assessment case is not unlike that which any assessing institution would have to face after all the procedural and structural differences are washed out:

> . . . He must balance all his ingredients, his philosophy, his logic, his analogies, his history, his customs, his sense of right, and all the rest, and adding a little here and taking out a little there, must determine as wisely as he can, which weight shall top the scales. If this seems a weak and inconclusive summary, I am not sure that the fault is mine. I know he is a wise pharmacist who from a recipe so general can compound a fitting remedy. . . .[45]

The courts, after all, follow the same large goals as planning organizations and technology assessment institutions—fairness, the general welfare, reasonableness, etc.—and the concretizing of these concepts in the light of particular factual situations often requires some sort of balance.[46] Legal rules are means for the realization of some of these values but may have consequences which impair others.[47]

Such balancing must occur in technology assessment irrespective of the institutional setting. There is no static hierarchy of ends; there will likely be multiple values on either side, some modal or intermediate, others more terminal; evaluation consists of lining up the values and attempting to judge how much any or all of the social values on the one side will be enhanced or impaired as against how much on the other side.

. . . But I think it most important to remember whenever a doubtful case arises, with certain analogies on one side and other analogies on the other, that what really is before us is a conflict between two social desires, each of which seeks to extend its dominion over the case, and which cannot both have their way. The social question is which desire is stronger at the point of conflict. The judicial one may be narrower. . . . Where there is doubt the simple tool of logic does not suffice, and even if it is disguised and unconscious, the judges are called on to exercise the sovereign prerogative of choice.[48]

What Holmes is saying is that logic—or rationality—breaks down at a certain point. Here it seems that the personal qualities of the assessor may be key aspects of the decision. And it is arguable that this point exists due to the nature of the decision to be made and consequently cannot be avoided by structural or institutional mechanisms. How is the assessor to know when one interest outweighs another? He must get his knowledge "from experience and study and reflection; in brief, from life itself."[49] Most judges take this to mean that they should apply the standards of utility and morality of the community, but it is not clear how these are to be ascertained.[50] And community values change with time, so they should be attuned to current intellectual trends and social sensitivities, as with new concepts of environmental ethics.

Convincing a court to accept a public-interest lawsuit in the environment area is mostly a matter of strategy and of education. As the public becomes more concerned . . . it will follow that judges, reading the same newspapers and magazines, will also begin to want to do something about the problem. Judicial sympathy will go a long way in the determination of whether "standing" is a barrier to a given lawsuit. Public education, therefore, will have a direct effect upon the law as well as upon the public. . . .[51]

In short, the old saw about "a government of laws and not of men" is not quite accurate; the personal factor exists in decision making.

Conclusion

The capability of the courts, as the prime example of the institutionalization of the adversary system, to handle technological issues appears somewhat mixed. In terms of three criteria—their competence, the acceptability of their product, and the personal qualities of the assessor —it can be said that they function adequately, although in a limited area.

The passive nature of the courts, the barriers to entry, and the practical problems which surround their use make it clear that they cannot serve as society's primary instrument for technology assessment. Direct assessment by the courts may be used to accommodate special problems of local concern, but even then the results seem to depend more on precedent and the individual circumstances of the parties than on a total balance between the societal interests involved without any built-in institutional preferences. If the courts are to perform primary assessments, then complainants must utilize preexisting types of legal actions, although there is hope that these can be expanded. The method of legal liability via lawsuit for internalizing the secondary costs of technology seems at best sufficient only to protect individuals from private damage —not society from catastrophe. Socializing these secondary costs among all the consumers or beneficiaries of the technology, or all of society, is particularly difficult; courts (as well as other institutions) have not even begun to figure out what these amount to, no less who should pay them, to whom they should be paid (*e.g.*, effluent taxes). Indeed, the whole idea of internalizing costs as a goal of technology assessment depends upon a theory of market operations which has been increasingly questioned in recent years. The courts have even greater difficulties with other aspects of technology assessment, such as predicting the likely trends of technological developments, their consequences, and attempting to guide or influence these forces.

When courts act as part of the government administrative structure, on the other hand, they seem to have the ability to influence technology assessment. Admittedly, the courts are still passive in the sense that they cannot act until someone decides to institute litigation, but the recently expanded concept of standing moves toward assuring that most controversial decisions will be capable of challenge. Similarly, the distorting effects of historical precedent and the particular circumstances of the parties are largely irrelevant in such actions or at least less important than in the situation of primary assessment. The technical incompetence of the courts may be a reason for the judicial bias in favor of upholding an assessment once made by an agency, but the power of the courts to determine who should participate and what factors should be weighed in the balance have had salutory effects. The burden of proof is still quite heavy in these actions, but occasionally some of it is shifted to the administrators to show that they have considered all the relevant issues. Greater utilization of the courts in this manner is likely.

The argument of this paper is not that the courts should be less concerned with the unique circumstances of each case before them, should abandon the use of precedent, or should otherwise drastically alter their methods of operation. Indeed, with the growing complexities and impersonality of government and society generally, the fact that courts continue to concern themselves with individuals and their unique circumstances is one of their most important characteristics. Rather, the conclusion reached is that in spite of the fact that courts cannot handle the problems of modern technology by themselves, they can play a role in the interstices of an assessment process conducted by other government organs; moreover, they can perform even more substantially in situations where other entities are not assessing or are assessing poorly. In addition to the task of designing adequate institutions to do technology assessment on a primary basis, it is to be hoped that judicial doctrines and procedures will continue to evolve so that the courts may function effectively as secondary institutions to deal with specific situations of hardship or injustice which appear, notwithstanding the overall planning which will be done for guiding technological change.

REFERENCES

1. Portions of this paper relate to materials that the author helped research and that have been published by B. Portnoy as Note, "The Role of the Courts in Technology Assessment," 55 Cornell Law Review 861 (1970).
2. D'Amato, "Environmental Degradation and Legal Action," 26 Bulletin of the Atomic Scientists 24 (March 1970) [Hereinafter cited as D'Amato].
3. There are not many published articles dealing *directly* with this subject. Harold Green of George Washington University is active in this field. In addition to the Note cited in footnote 1, see Tribe, "Legal Frameworks for the Assessment and Control of Technology," 9 Minerva 243 (1971), and Katz, "The Function of Tort Liability in Technology Assessment," 38 University of Cincinnati Law Review 587 (1969) [Hereinafter cited as Katz]. Charles Maechling, Jr., former Deputy General Counsel of the National Science Foundation, presented a paper published in House Subcommittee on Science, Research, and Development, *Technology Assessment* at 342, 91st Congress, 1st Session (1969) [These hearings are hereinafter cited as 1969 *TA Hearings*].

4. Green, "Technology Assessment and the Law: Introduction and Perspective," 36 George Washington Law Review 1033 (1968).
5. *See* J. Hurst, *The Growth of American Law* 8, 9–11, Little, Brown (1950).
6. Committee on Science and Public Policy, National Academy of Sciences, *Technology: Processes of Assessment and Choice* (Report to the House Committee on Science and Astronautics) 90 (1969) [Hereinafter cited as NAS Report].
7. NAS Report at 90–94.
8. *See* D'Amato at 26.
9. *See* Reich, "Law of the Planned Society," 75 Yale Law Journal 1227 (1966).
10. B. Cardozo, *The Nature of the Judicial Process* 178, Yale University Press (1921) [Hereinafter cited as Cardozo]. Note the similar theory advanced to explain the development of technical knowledge in T. Kuhn, *The Structure of Scientific Revolutions*, University of Chicago Press (1962).
11. O. Holmes, *The Common Law* 1, Little, Brown (1881).
12. *See* E. Patterson, *Law in a Scientific Age* 50–53, Columbia University Press (1963) [Hereinafter cited as Patterson].
13. Insurance is a derived assessment mechanism in which the specific risks and the liabilities therefore are translated into periodic premium payments based on experience.
14. *See* 1969 *TA Hearings* at 175.
15. *See* NAS Report at 54.
16. *See* Katz.
17. *Id.*
18. *See* Sax, "The Public Trust Doctrine in Natural Resource Law: Effective Judicial Intervention," 68 Michigan Law Review 473 (1970), and Berlin, Roisman & Kessler, "Law in Action: The Trust Doctrine," in *Law and the Environment* 166 (M. Baldwin & J. Page eds.), Walker & Co. (1970).
19. The Federal Freedom of Information Act, 5 U.S.C. § 552 (Supp. IV, 1969), is similarly germane.
20. 406 F.2d 170 (1st Cir. 1969).
21. 430 F.2d 199 (5th Cir. 1970), *cert. denied*, 401 U.S. 910 (1971).
22. 387 U.S. 428 (1967).
23. 354 F.2d 608 (2d Cir. 1965), *cert. denied*, 390 U.S. 921 (1967).
24. *See* Katz at 625–661.
25. 265 F. 928 (D. Utah 1919).
26. *Id.* at 943–944.
27. *See, e.g.*, Smith v. Staso Milling Co., 18 F.2d 736 (2d Cir. 1927), and Renken v. Harvey Aluminum, Inc., 296 F. Supp. 164 (D. Ore. 1963).
28. 26 N.Y.2d 219 (1970).
29. 42 U.S.C. §§ 1857 (g)-(h) (Supp. IV, 1969). This procedure has been altered by the 1970 amendment to the statute.

30. 276 U.S. 272 (1928).
31. *See* 1969 *TA Hearings* at 355 for an explanation of how agency operations can be seen as technology assessments.
32. 387 U.S. 136 (1967).
33. 48 N.J. 261 (1966).
34. 42 U.S.C. §§ 4321 *et seq.* (1970).
35. Sive, "The Law and the Land," 2 National Environmental Law Society Newsletter 1 (May 1970).
36. Seminar presentation at Department of Environmental Engineering, Cornell University (Fall 1972).
37. Haar, "The Social Control of Urban Space," in *Cities and Space* 222 (L. Wingo ed.), Johns Hopkins Press (1966).
38. *See* Green, "Technology Assessment and the Law: Introduction and Perspective," 36 George Washington Law Review 1033, 1036 (1968).
39. *See* Rheingold, "Civil Cause of Action for Lung Damage Due to Pollution of Urban Atmosphere," 33 Brooklyn Law Review 17 (1966), and Juergensmeyer, "Control of Air Pollution Through the Assertion of Private Rights," 1967 Duke Law Journal 1126 (1967).
40. *See* Katz at 615–622.
41. Sive, "Securing, Examining, and Cross-Examining Expert Witnesses in Environmental Cases," 68 Michigan Law Review 1175 (1970).
42. *See* Patterson at 17–18.
43. *See* 1969 *TA Hearings* at 272–273.
44. Cardozo at 161.
45. Cardozo at 162.
46. Reich argues that a balance is not a satisfactory basis for planning for the public interest, Reich, "Law of the Planned Society," 75 Yale Law Journal 1227, 1238–1240 (1966).
47. *See* Patterson at 52–53.
48. Holmes, "Law in Science and Science in Law," 12 Harvard Law Review 443 (1899).
49. Cardozo at 113.
50. See the celebrated conflict over the definition of "good moral character," as used in nationalization statutes, in the case of an applicant who had committed euthanasia upon his son who was pathetically handicapped, Repouille v. United States, 165 F.2d 152 (2d Cir. 1947).
51. D'Amato at 25.

Scientists as Suppliers of Facts:
Do Lawyers Listen?

DONALD R. MOORE*
*President, Federal Administrative Law Judges Conference
Washington, D.C.*

TITLES CAN BE INTERESTING, EVEN INTRIGUING—WHETHER WE ARE TALKING about the title of an office held by an individual or the title of a paper. I must say that I found the title of the paper assigned to me to be intriguing when Tom Thomas gave me the word one spring day. Today, however, I am not sure that I love it in December as I did in May.

As I struggled with the subject, I was struck by the disconcerting thought that perhaps I would be writing under false pretenses—that I had been selected to discuss such a subject on the basis of a misapprehension revolving around *my* title. At the time that Tom extended his invitation, I bore the title of "hearing examiner." Perhaps Tom thought that this qualified me to answer the question "Do lawyers listen?" Really there *have* been occasions when people thought we tested auditory perception! Now, although I am doing the same type of work that I was doing as a hearing examiner, I have the more descriptive title of "administrative law judge."

I gather that I am selected for this panel in recognition of the fact that many significant cases dealing with scientific issues are resolved by administrative law judges, so that there should be some reference to the administrative hearing process. There are now more than twenty federal agencies that employ nearly eight hundred administrative law judges, and a goodly number of these do get involved from time to time in the resolution of scientific issues.

At this point I should make the usual disclaimers—I am here in my individual capacity and I do not profess to speak either for the Federal

* Current address: Administrative Law Judge, Federal Trade Commission, Washington, D.C. 20580.

Trade Commission or for the Federal Administrative Law Judges Conference. Moreover, I do not intend to judge or to appear to judge any matter that is now before me or that may be presented to me for decision.

No useful purpose would be served by describing in detail the procedures used by the administrative agencies. Although there are some differences between our hearings and court trials, I would say in general that the scientific witness can properly consider applicable to administrative hearings the same principles that are involved in court trials, particularly in cases tried by a judge without a jury.

No one needs to be persuaded that scientists are required as suppliers of facts in legal proceedings, including administrative agency hearings. In fact, I would sustain an objection to the question in the main title of this book ("Scientists in the Legal System—Tolerated Meddlers or Essential Contributors?") as a rhetorical question, and a loaded one at that! I won't undertake to call the roll of all the areas of science and technology that may be involved in cases that my colleagues hear. But, by way of example, just in my own agency—the Federal Trade Commission—science is called on to furnish facts about the safety and the efficacy of such products as foods, drugs, therapeutic devices, cosmetics, assorted poisons, household products, and others. Additionally, economic testimony and evidence are vital to the Commission's antitrust cases. And the areas continue to expand; for example, the question of environmental pollution is one that may be involved in all sorts of regulatory agency cases today—not just EPA proceedings. My colleagues in the Department of Health, Education, and Welfare get deeply involved in disability determinations and other medical questions. And then, of course, scientists will be needed in the new Consumer Protection Agency.

With the fact established that the legal system must rely on scientists as suppliers of facts, why should anyone question whether lawyers listen when scientists speak? To interject a light note, we might look to genetics. Like the scientist who crossbred a lion and a parakeet; when asked what the resulting offspring was called, he responded, "We don't know what to call it, but when it speaks, we listen!"

At any rate, I was surprised by the negative results when by discreet inquiries I sought to obtain from some scientists illustrative instances of occasions when lawyers failed to listen. Perhaps I did not ask the right people. (Let me hasten to note that I did not make a scientific survey!) I tried the same question on some lawyers, and you will not be astonished to learn that none of them confessed to not listening. As a matter of fact, some of them, as lawyers are sometimes inclined to do, wanted to rephrase the question to "Do scientists listen?" I suspect that Tom was using a catchy title to point up a problem of long standing— the frequent mutual dissatisfaction of both lawyer and scientist when they meet in a legal proceeding, whether as co-workers on the same side or as adversaries on opposing sides.

That there should exist such a troublesome conflict between two essential professions seems incredible at first blush but there are numerous explanations, and it may be profitable to explore some of them.

Certain dissimilarities between the two disciplines do exist. Many writers have emphasized the contrast between the inductive process utilized by science and the deductive process utilized by law. But this is an oversimplification; by no means does it explain the conflicts we hear about. In any event, both lawyer and scientist should recognize and respect the differences in the way each approaches and thinks about a problem. Each needs to learn more of and to understand better the objectives and the techniques of the other. And analysis will demonstrate that there are more important parallels in our objectives and techniques than there are differences.

The dissatisfaction that the scientist feels when he is called upon to participate as a witness in a legal proceeding also stems from another contrast—the contrast between the role that he visualizes for himself and the role that he often actually plays. Too often the expert considers himself as one who gives highly specific answers to highly specific questions. As he visualizes the scene, he makes his appearance in the courtroom surrounded by an aura of science; he states his piece with great authority, then departs. The effect is dramatic and impressive as a difficult controversy is resolved by his testimony.

But often the drama plays out altogether differently. He may blame the lawyer, and the lawyer may blame him.

The scientist considers the lawyer to be an ignoramus as to science and the scientific method. There is more truth in this criticism than we lawyers like to admit. With notable exceptions, lawyers need more education in the field of science. Happily there are signs that this deficiency is being recognized. In time you should find the lawyer better versed in scientific matters.

A major part of the problem is a communications gap, if not a communications barrier. This is partly due to increasing specialization. Each profession has been so compartmentalized that it suffers from a sort of professional myopia.

Let us elaborate just a bit on this major problem of communication between the two disciplines. On the one hand, it is reasonable to ask that the lawyer should attempt to understand the basic language of science, but on the other, it is also reasonable to ask that scientists should do their utmost to express their material in simple terms. The difficulties are about evenly divided. For the scientist must distill his scientific material down to its basic principles, which he, all too readily, takes for granted, while the lawyer must make the intellectual effort to follow the basic arguments before attempting to apply them to practical problems. This gets us back to the need for lawyers to receive more basic scientific training.

The conflict may also arise as a "conflict between amateurs" when the lawyer tries to play scientist or the scientist tries to play lawyer. Again, each should respect the role of the other and should not assume an expertise he does not have.

There can be no question that the attorney is the captain of the case. The ultimate authority and responsibility for success or failure rest with him. However, the good captain makes full use of his lieutenants in the areas of their specialties.

The scientist frequently chafes under the usual requirement that evidence must be given by question and answer. The result thus may depend more on the skill of the questioner than of the witness. The questioner is dominant. The form of his questions conditions the form and often the content of the answers. Unless the questioner really understands the subject matter, he may phrase his questions in ways that restrict the scientific witness or misplace the emphasis. At worst, he may ask questions that are unanswerable because to the witness they have no rational content.

To get an intelligent answer, of course, we have to ask an intelligent question. If the answer is to be highly technical, the question itself must be technical in content and must be clearly phrased to bring out the desired answer. With all due respect to the skill of the lawyer in his own field, he finds it difficult to feel at home with the highly specialized language of another field. It is a most distressing experience for an expert witness to be subjected, from a supposedly friendly attorney, to a barrage of questions that really don't mean what the attorney thinks they mean. In fact, they may be technologically unintelligible, while at the same time sounding like the best of the King's English.

The solution is obvious. Communication!

In any communication between an attorney and an expert—in or out of court—precise language must be employed, or at the very least there must be enough exchange of views so that the language has an agreed meaning. Since the attorney and the expert view the problem from different vantage points, it is quite possible that they will see different objectives. These can be reconciled if recognized in time, but the danger is that each may go his separate way, leaving both unaware that they are working at cross-purposes. To be effective, the precision of the scientist and the legal skill of the attorney should focus on the same target.

Obviously, the lawyer should seek the advice of the expert on the wording of questions beforehand, and he should thoroughly understand and heed this advice. Then both will be on target. Too often, however, time limitations on the part of the lawyer or the scientist or both prevent such careful collaboration. But both should insist on it as far as they can.

In some of our proceedings, the problem has been met by permitting the submission of the direct testimony of an expert in writing, sometimes in question and answer form, sometimes in narrative form. Although this technique has suffered by being inelegantly termed "canned testimony," it can be a useful device.

Now as to cross-examination, there are some grounds for complaint. Questions may contain hidden assumptions and thus yield answers that almost contradict a witness's real meaning unless he is quick enough to detect and expose the assumption. Sometimes, by splitting up the question into fragments and compelling the witness to answer each fragment separately, the cross-examiner may mislead the witness into saying almost the opposite of what he intends. At other times, questions may be so confusingly phrased that the witness must get them elucidated before attempting to answer.

Although the scientist, as the expert witness, must be alert to such pitfalls, he has the right to expect the lawyer who called him, and the judge as well, to prevent improper cross-examination. Nevertheless, he must expect fairly wide latitude to be accorded to the cross-examiner. This is because cross-examination has been found valuable, and occasionally devastating, if the cross-examiner really understands his subject. It may force a witness to re-examine the premises on which his opinions are founded or the technique of his experiment. Sometimes it will challenge the scientist to justify a widely accepted theory that he has adopted—perhaps uncritically—and force him to recognize its weakness.

To ensure that lawyers, judges, and juries listen, I proffer this advice to the scientist–witness:

1. Become accustomed to having legal rules and legal logic applied to scientific facts.
2. Your value will be greatest both as an advisor and as an expert witness if you consider your primary responsibility to state with care what you know, the limits of your knowledge, and the reservations that must be attached to your conclusion.
3. Get acquainted with the attorney. Establish rapport. This is primarily the responsibility of the lawyer, but if he does not take the initiative, you must do so.
4. Make sure you and the lawyer speak the same language. Try to translate scientific language into layman's language.
5. Learn as much as you can about the case and where you fit in.
6. Insist that you be fully briefed by counsel on what to expect from him, from opposing counsel, and from the judge.
7. Listen to each question. Don't rush to answer until you're sure you understand the question. In general, answer only the question posed. Stick to facts within your knowledge. Don't guess. Don't be afraid to say "I don't know" when this is the case.

Others will doubtless give further advice and admonitions. My list does not pretend to be all-inclusive. But properly prepared along these lines, the scientist should be an effective supplier of facts, and he will be listened to.

Scientists in the Courtroom

DAVID SIVE*
Winer, Neuburger & Sive
New York

IN VIEW OF THE SUBJECTS COVERED BY OTHERS IN THIS VOLUME, I WILL TRY to confine my remarks to those pertaining to the true interface between scientists and lawyers in the courtroom itself. By in the courtroom I mean within those narrow confines of the litigation proceedings themselves. Other contributors no doubt will consider some of the broader interactions between scientists and lawyers, including those within the political arena. I shall keep my comments within the specific adversary setting, remembering of course that the interface does occur within the much broader framework of political events.

I have one comment, however, concerning the political interface. I agree wholeheartedly that it is necessary to determine the risks of various alternative courses of action before it is actually necessary to determine whether the particular project should be undertaken. This is accomplished by bringing scientific expertise to bear on the problem as early as possible. In an increasing number of cases, however, that may not be the whole answer to the question at hand. In the case of the supersonic transport, for example, the real issue as I see it—and I do not pretend that all other persons who have examined the question may agree with this analysis—is not solely a question of whether there were specific hazards involved. This question of hazards (particularly atmosphere modification, damage due to supersonic booms, and increased rates of skin cancer) that the scientists were called upon to argue was one aspect of the controversy. It seems to me that the more important issue was whether there were any social benefits whatsoever to support such a large expenditure of funds and energy.

* Mailing address: Winer, Neuburger & Sive, 445 Park Avenue, New York, New York 10022.

It is clear that methods are not available for solving all uncertainties. The problem with uncertainty occurs frequently in many environmental controversies. This argument of uncertainty can be used both against and by environmentalists. Two examples: When one is involved in such litigations as I have been, concerning the advisability of expressways to increase automobile traffic, one is always open to the argument that he is killing children. "Unless this highway is built," it is said, "to replace the old two- or three-lane road, do you realize how many children will be killed and by the very reason you are standing up here in the courtroom?" That of course is a very difficult question to answer. It may well be that there *is* increased safety in a four- or six-lane road, and that fewer persons will be run down than on a narrower road. On the other hand, when arguing the advisability of siting nuclear power plants near metropolitan regions, the environmentalist has the principle of uncertainty on *his* side. He then asks, "How many children do you think you will be killing by placing this nuclear facility so close to large population centers?" I bring these two examples forward only to suggest that while we may all decry uncertainty, it does not always work uniformly to the advantage of any of us.

My subject does indeed involve one way in which environmental controversies are resolved, although many others are by way of the purely political process and still others are resolved solely as issues of public or personal behavior—in which the decision is made outside all governmental systems, judicial or political. Nonetheless the judicial proceeding is a necessary way of solving a large percentage of our environmental cases for the very simple reason that the operative words in many of our environmental laws always shall remain somewhat vague. For example, no one has proposed that we change Section 10a of the Federal Power Act to suggest something better than the term "comprehensive plan for the development of a waterway." Similarly, I don't believe anyone will improve upon, at least for a few years, the key phrase "major federal action significantly affecting the human environment" as used in the National Environmental Policy Act.

As the environmental movement matures, however, much as did the civil rights movement, fewer of the issues will be resolved by strictly doctrinaire principles. The social-values and social-conflicts questions, resulting from the "good guys versus bad guys" issues, will increasingly give way to factual issues in which the scientists' participation becomes more and more important.

Within the litigated proceedings, the scientist is an expert who renders expert testimony, which is limited only by the accepted rules of evidence through which the issues are resolved. The basic point to keep in mind is that all evidence in adversary proceedings is either direct or opinion. For example, as a lay witness I can testify that five years ago a certain traffic light was green. That statement involves no opinion. An expert uses facts proven by others and renders an opinion based upon them. The court takes cognizance of the expertise of the witness and allows his opinion testimony to be admitted. These basic rules of evidence in environmental matters are essentially the same as they are in other proceedings involving experts, such as those involving automobile negligence cases where the plaintiff and the defendant or his insurance company bring forth experts to bolster their respective cases.

I like to emphasize this particular point with one of the stories lawyers like to tell each other about a particular automobile negligence claim. The plaintiff's testimony included comments by a physician who indeed did show that the plaintiff's son's leg had been fractured, as he claimed it was, and that there was temporary disability and a high probability of some lasting disability; whereupon the insurance company's doctor gave his testimony to the effect that indeed the leg had been broken, but that the plaintiff was young and that young bones mend quickly to original strength, and that sometimes, because of a patient's youth, mend to a condition even stronger than they were before. On cross-examination the plaintiff's attorney asked but a single question, "Would you say then, doctor, that you advise all your patients to break their legs?"

Recently, Mr. Justice Douglas of the U.S. Supreme Court must have had this old anecdote in mind when he commented during a case brought by the State of Vermont against an alleged polluter of Lake Champlain. According to the record of the oral argument, the polluting company's attorney was stating a fine case to the effect that the sludge being deposited by his client had no effect at all on the waterway; whereupon Mr. Justice Douglas inquired, "Tell me, sir, would you advise each of the United States to fill all their waterways with that sort of sludge?"

Expert testimony is brought forth according to accepted legal principles and rules, including the right of cross-examination. The expert witness who enters the courtroom must recognize that because of their profession the attorneys almost always have the upper hand. Therefore the scientist who accepts the role as expert witness must be aware of the tactics commonly employed during courtroom litigation by opposing attorneys. The most common of these, of course, is an attempt to demean the witness or to make him look silly by confusing him or by asking him apparently simple questions that he cannot answer. Actually what the opposing attorney does, and this is certainly no trade secret, is to state the factual situation to the expert over and over again but each time picking away at it by slightly changing the circumstances upon which the expert bases his opinion.

Thus, if asked if fact A were taken away or fact B taken away or fact C taken away or fact D added, would his opinion change? Now obviously somewhere along the line his opinion must change, just as it would if he were asked to consider increasing the temperature of ice water degree by degree until he felt it would become warm and then hot. The opposing attorney then leaps in and attempts to dramatize the fact that the expert witness's opinion could be altered by that very small single change in the factual circumstances.

I think all that the expert witness need recognize is that this is all part of the accepted legal procedure of ascertaining facts. Most trial attorneys advise their experts never to fight the questioner, never to try to win a game of wits. And above all, the expert witness should never give what he thinks would be the answer favored by his client. The attorney is, through experience, very adept at getting the answers he wants to particular questions, through the phraseology employed and even the tone of his voice.

The scientist in the courtroom should keep uppermost in his mind the fact that lawyers believe that through open expression and examination of conflicting opinions—the process generally known as advocacy—the parties more efficiently will reach the truth and a just result and that this process is carried out by rules that protect both parties by limiting the scope and type of evidence that is to be admitted.

In this respect the lawyers are really doing what scientists do. They pick out of a mass of controversy certain particular issues that can be narrowed until they are of appropriate dimension for resolution; all information that is irrelevant to these particular questions is then excluded. Thus emotional considerations are not given weight. Lawyers have believed for centuries that the best way to resolve many conflicts is to argue the issues openly but within the prescribed rules in a courtroom. Through this procedure the issues can be resolved better than they can by any other means. It is the overwhelming opinion of lawyers today that the technological issues that the courts will face in the future can also be resolved in this manner.

In the larger political controversies, we must accept the reality that some parties have more power, more money, more public relations, and more information on their side. The same persons will have that same advantage also, to some extent, in the courtroom, but not to the same degree because the issues are relegated to their narrowest possible scope and because the judge and opposing counsel are free to ensure that the game is played within the rules. For the expert's convenience, the factual issues are separated from the legal issues, and the expert limits his comment to his field of expertise.

One way to emphasize this point is to present an example from the Storm King Mountain controversy with which I have been involved. Some of the proponents of the project, involving a pumped storage reservoir atop Storm King Mountain, claimed that the project would enhance the aesthetic characteristics of the area by various cosmetic procedures, thus improving over the pristine nature of the Hudson Valley in that region. During the cross-examination of several of the expert witnesses the question was asked, "Have you in your experience as a landscape architect or land-use planner ever had any experience with any piece of land or any body of water that was so unique that it did not need any improvement by man?" The answer invariably was "No."

By thus securing such impressions from the witnesses concerning the relative merits both of the project and of leaving the mountain alone, the inherent biases of the witnesses were open for inspection by the court. The court then could rule with an awareness of the conflict-of-value question in addition to knowledge of the factual issues presented by the expert witness.

Most scientists should recognize, and many of them will understandably have difficulty doing so, that, wrong or right, the basic theory is that by this testing of witnesses the best result ultimately will flow from the legal proceeding. True, many attorneys may appear to be discourteous or even abusive while doing this, but the better expert witnesses merely consider these instances as characteristic of attorneys' zeal and do not let it interfere with their reasoned answers.

One other point should be kept in mind by all scientists who enter the courtroom. All great trial lawyers, in addition perhaps to having a flair for the dramatic, know the subject matter of their cases very well indeed. Every great trial lawyer knows the subject matter of his cross-examination of an expert as well as or even better than the expert does. This is possible because the cross-examiner knows well in advance which specific question he is going to dwell on, within the broad expertise or knowledge of the expert. Thus, he is able to prepare himself extremely well. The cross-examiner makes no pretense that he comes close to matching the expert's overall knowledge of a particular subject, but he does make every effort to know more than the expert about the particular testimony that is central to his case.

He does this by concentrating his total energies on that subject for considerable periods of time—by extensive study and discussions with his own expert witnesses and other scientists. It is said that good trial lawyers never ask a question unless they know what the answer must be. There may appear to be some generalized probing of the expert's opinions at the commencement of cross-examination, but when the attorney focuses his attention on specific points the scientist should never attempt to bluff nor should he ever be afraid to say honestly, "I don't know." Of course, the attorney has no intention of ever mastering the entire subject, and he is virtually certain to forget immediately after the case much of that which he did know. Nonetheless, when he is asking the expert questions, he generally knows as much or more than the scientific expert about the particular subjects of his questioning.

In conclusion, I want to emphasize that scientists should not think that some lawyers' behavior intimates that they do not believe that scientists' opinions are needed in the courtroom. To the contrary, all lawyers experienced in this area realize that the scientific experts' opinions are absolutely essential. So the answer to the question posed by this book is a resounding "Yes—contributions by scientists are indispensable to the resolution of courtroom litigation."

Any scientist who is qualified to act as an expert can further the judicial proceedings by merely paying attention to the rules of procedure while he is testifying. As the scientist gains experience in the courtroom and appreciation for the methods by which the proceedings are handled, he will contribute even more to the process and enjoy being a part of the proceedings rather than on the sidelines. Above all, scientists should never refuse to participate and should not look upon these proceedings as being a lesser form of their professional obligation.

The Time Lag Between Medicine and Law

Edwin J. Holman*
Office of General Counsel
American Medical Association
Chicago, Illinois

Is it true that there is a time lag between advances in law and in medicine? Of course it is. Is this time lag harmful? Can it, should it, be reduced or eliminated?

No two disciplines proceed at the same pace. The history of civilization is a history of the dominance of one art or one science at a given time. Law has stood front stage, center, on many occasions in the past. Music and literature have characterized historical eras. Perhaps some disciplines may have been conspicuous because they were slow in achieving dominance.

Science, less than four hundred years ago, found the Copernican theory without believers. Optical combinations had not yet been discovered. The circulation of blood, the conduction of heat, the laws of motion, and the weight of air were unknown. Society had no clocks and no thermometers. What advances have occurred in the field of science since the 16th century! What advances have occurred in medicine and medical technology in our own century—or in this half of the 20th century!

The discovery and development of antibiotics and broad spectrum drugs and the new vaccines, the improvement of surgical techniques, and, of course, organ transplantation have overshadowed routine, to-be-expected advances. Some of these advances have been accepted within the realm of the law without question or problem. Some have been accepted by the law only after investigation because the law was dubious about them.

---

* Mailing address: American Medical Association, 525 N. Dearborn Street, Chicago, Illinois 60610.

The recent visit of Charlie Chaplin to the United States brings to mind an experience he had shortly before his self-imposed exile. Despite the exclusionary results of scientific tests to exclude paternity, a court permitted a jury to disregard scientific findings and accept the testimony of the mother of a child who, the mother claimed, was Mr. Chaplin's daughter.[1]

For centuries bastardy cases were impossible to defend from the practical point of view. Then medical science demonstrated that blood tests could in some instances definitely establish nonpaternity. Science could serve justice. But courts were slow in accepting the tests. They were slow in permitting the tests to be accepted as conclusive. In more than one instance, the results of the tests which established nonpaternity were introduced into evidence and the mother then was permitted to testify to access and to say the accused was the father of her child. Juries were permitted to choose between the mother's testimony and the results of scientific tests.

About the same time that blood tests for exclusion of paternity became available, chemical tests for intoxication made the scene. Perhaps we have less tolerance for the drunken driver and more sympathy for the unwed mother. In any event, despite repeated and vigorous attacks by defense attorneys, chemical tests for intoxication were quickly and widely accepted.

Strangely enough, in the last quarter century not only have chemical tests for intoxication been accepted, they have twice been strengthened. As originally adopted, a blood alcohol level of 0.15% was the standard to establish that one was under the influence of alcohol. Throughout the years this figure has been reduced to 0.10% or even 0.08%.[2] In addition, all states save one or two have enacted implied consent laws. Statutes provide that those who operate motor cars on the highways are deemed to have consented to the taking of chemical tests if arrested for offenses arising out of an act alleged to have been committed while operating a vehicle under the influence of alcohol.

These are two small examples of what has happened in the immediate past. Law rather rapidly accommodated technological development and any time lag was minimal.

Today there are several other areas where the two disciplines of law and medicine move at different paces. Medicine has gotten well into the area of transplants and the law has not seriously impeded, if it has impeded at all. When Christiaan Barnard performed his first heart transplant, do you think he consulted his lawyer to ascertain whether the proposal was lawful? I have been unable to determine that he did. He was, of course, concerned with the basic ethical propriety of what he intended to do.

In our own country, where perhaps physicians are more conscious of the legal implications (or possible legal implications) of their medical acts than they are in other countries, transplant surgeons have gone into court on several occasions to have a particular transplantation authorized in advance. In these instances kidney transplants were involved and the donors were minors.[3]

In no case was the court critical of the proposed surgery. In all cases authorization was granted. In Michigan a statute was enacted to permit kidney donations by minors with probate court approval. (Incidentally, the first successful kidney transplant occurred in 1954, the first successful liver transplant in 1960, and the first heart transplant in 1967.)

In July 1968 the National Conference on Commissioners on Uniform State Laws approved the Uniform Anatomical Gift Act (UAGA). In the short period of time since then, almost every state has enacted this proposal into law. When the legislatures of fifty states (and Congress acting for the District of Columbia) take action as quickly as this, we can scarcely complain about time lags.

This is especially interesting because heart transplants, which undoubtedly provided popular impetus necessary for rapid enactment of the UAGA, are not being performed to any significant extent today. Kidney transplants and corneal transplants continue to be performed without notoriety.

Heart transplants have also contributed to the beginning stages of law development by accelerating consideration of the definition of death. Medical scholars have suggested refinements to reflect the time of death accurately. For centuries law *and* society have held death to be the cessation of respiration and circulation.

In 1968 the *Journal of the American Medical Association* carried a communication, "A Definition of Irreversible Coma: Report of the Ad Hoc Committee of the Harvard Medical School to Examine the Definition of Death"[4] which pointed out that, from ancient times down to the recent past, it was clear that when the respiration and heart stopped the brain would die in a few minutes, so the obvious criterion of no heartbeat as synonymous with death was sufficiently accurate. In those earlier times the heart was considered to be the central organ of the body, and it is not surprising that its failure marked the onset of death.

This is no longer valid when modern resuscitative and supportive measures are used. These improved activities can now restore "life" as judged by the ancient standards of persistent respiration and continuing heartbeat. This can be the case even when there is not the remote possibility of an individual's recovering consciousness following massive brain damage.

The characteristics of death in the Harvard Report are (1) unreceptivity and unresponsitivity, (2) no movement or breathing, (3) no reflexes, and (4) flat electroencephalogram.

Even these excellent criteria are not completely satisfactory, according to a report of a Task Force of the Institute of Society, Ethics and the Life Sciences which appeared in the July 3, 1972, issue of the *Journal of the American Medical Association*. The essence of that report is that it is still to be hoped that criteria can be developed which will be acceptable to persons holding various concepts of death. The Institute's report cautions against determining death simply because of an isoelectric EEG, especially if it is concluded that "in the absence of a functioning neocortex, as determined by an isoelectric EEG, human life has ceased."[5]

There are many reasons why time of death is important. And because we don't have uniformity among law, medicine, and society on the definition of death, we sometimes have problems—serious problems. Two of these problems are current and are being discussed. (1) When is a person dead for the purpose of removing his heart or liver for transplantation to another? (2) When is a person who is under life-supportive therapy dead so the machines can be turned off?

Medicine has considered these questions. Law has considered them. Neither has reached definitive and mutually acceptable answers. Kansas and Maryland have enacted statutes defining death. There is certainly no indication, no evidence, that other states will rush to enact their own or identical definitions of death.

A trial court in Richmond, Virginia, instructed a jury that death is a cessation of life; that under the law, death is not a continuing process but occurs at a precise time.[6] The judge listed these criteria: total lack of circulation; cessation of other vital functions such as respiration and pulse; complete, irreversible loss of brain function; and whether any of these functions were spontaneous or were maintained artificially. The jury, in this litigation for damages for having taken a body organ for transplantation without consent of the surviving relative, decided against the plaintiff. The case did not define "death." Nonetheless, the absence of a uniform and accepted definition of death, the presentation

of medical expert testimony to give definitions of death, and the submission of this testimony to a jury provoked early reaction, including
an excellent piece by Veatch,[7] who discusses the confusion between
medical and social responsibility.

Besides the questions of transplantation and "pulling the plug," an
acceptable definition of death is going to become increasingly important
in connection with legacies and taxes and with determination and accrual
of possible life insurance benefits.

Indirectly, the definition of death will help establish an acceptable
definition of life so we can determine when life begins. The courts are
in as much confusion as society in general in regard to the right to damages for negligent injury of fetuses. What confusion will be created by
science's tampering with fetuses? What consternation would be caused
if an in vitro sperm-ovum fertilization developed into a six- or twelve-
week "embryo"?

Artificial insemination as a medical procedure posed no major problem to the law although twenty years ago, when the public was first
made aware of the procedure, the suggestions were made that pooled
semen be used to conceal the identity of the biologic father and that the
resulting child be adopted to preclude legal problems. There have been
only two state statutes (in Oklahoma and Georgia) on the broad issues
of artificial insemination and only a few court cases[8] in which artificial
insemination was raised as an issue. What was thought to be a medicolegal problem two or three decades ago did not develop into one.

The press and our professional journals suggest areas of concern for
tomorrow by telling us what is on the drawing board or under development today. Amniocentesis is a developing procedure to determine information about a fetus. It will afford reliable information concerning
the presence of genetic disability in the fetus. Genetic disability, or inheritance of genetic disease or disability, is a rapidly growing field of
science in itself. What problems can reasonably be anticipated in this
emerging subscience?

Not too many years ago a reliable test for determining PKU (phe-
netketonuria, a congenital faulty metabolism, often associated with
mental defects) was devised. The sensational, popular press "emotional-
ized" over the lack of legal requirements for using the test. The widespread enactment of mandatory PKU testing laws resulted. One state
legislature held hearings on a PKU bill and invited representatives of the
medical profession to testify. When a physician said the medical profession did not believe a mandatory testing law was scientifically sound

or would be productive he was booed, literally, by the young matrons who attended the hearing. A legislator-committee member later asked how he or his fellow legislators could possibly vote against the bill. So far as I am able to ascertain, this particular legislation was unnecessary and unproductive. The most that can be said for it is that it caused no harm.

Is it possible that emotionalism will prevail as a result of new information or knowledge about genetics and the transmission of genetic defects? Will premarital-test statutes be amended to include tests to provide genetic data about those who seek license to marry? If such amendments do occur, as I think they will, what will they provide?

Almost an aside, but emphasizing the ability of the law to develop apace with community morals, is the trend that seems to be developing in oral contraceptive litigation. The normal, applicable rule of law is that when defendant's tortious conduct caused harm to plaintiff and in so doing conferred a benefit, the value of the benefit conferred is considered in mitigation of damages. In cases of unsuccessful sterilization procedures resulting in pregnancies and deliveries of healthy children, the courts have applied this rule.[9]

A 1971 decision of the Michigan Court of Appeals, in an action for damages for the birth of a healthy child, takes a different view.[10] (In this case a pharmacist filled a prescription for birth control pills with tranquilizers.) The court's opinion included this comment:

To say that for reasons of public policy contraceptive failure can result in no damage as a matter of law ignores the fact that tens of millions of persons use contraceptives daily to avoid the very result which the defendant would have us say is always a benefit, never a detriment. *Those tens of millions of persons, by their conduct, express the sense of the community.* [Emphasis added.]

A California appellate court said damages was not compensation for an unwanted child but "to replenish the family exchequer so that the new arrival will not deprive other members of the family of what was planned as their just share of the family income."[11]

In the 1970s we are experiencing two problems: drug addiction and the epidemic of venereal disease. Because young people—minors according to law and traditionally unable to consent to treatment for themselves—are conspicuous among the addicted and the afflicted, the medical profession wants to encourage them to seek treatment. The old laws requiring parental consent (or authorization) for medical treatment of minors are an admitted impediment to the seeking of care by minors. Legislatures have been responsive to this need and have revised statutes to permit young people to seek medical care especially for these conditions without first providing parental consent.

Somewhere I've read that there are more than "two million laws" in the United States. I'm convinced there are a lot. There are many instances when medicine seeks special protection or special benefit from law. There are special medical situations which require special laws to resolve the situation. Laws should not be proliferated to accommodate these situations unnecessarily.

There are few developments of medical science which can be foreseen with such clarity that law can be enacted in advance to cover the effects and side effects of those developments. In addition, the United States is a common law country. Our culture demands flexibility even at the expense of delays or some associated inconvenience.

Bad results, according to scientific criteria, are associated with the law's dilatory acceptance of blood tests to determine nonpaternity. (This could be explained as society's reluctance to cast off its chivalrous tradition of accepting the mother's word as gospel in bastardy cases!) Unnecessary legislation because of emotionalism is exemplified by the PKU mandatory test laws. Good results are seen in legislation authorizing medical treatment of minors for certain social problems without specific parental consent.

The recognition of lack of real necessity for legislation is reflected in the lack of legislative activity in the field of artificial insemination. The adoption of the Uniform Anatomical Gift Act is a graphic demonstration of the fact that in certain areas the law with its present flexibility can be rapidly extended to cover brand-new contingencies. Actually the Commissioners of the National Conference were working on drafts of this Uniform Act before the first heart transplant. The finished version of the Uniform Act was approved and available for discussion, consideration, and possible enactment within eight months after the first heart transplant.

The current lack of activity in legal legislative circles concerning a definition of death may well reflect the wishes of society to play a waiting game. It may be that society does not want a rigid statutory definition of death. Fifteen years from now there may be as little judicial or legislative activity here as there has been in the past about artificial insemination.

To debate whether there is a time lag between the advances of law and medicine is a luxury we might dispense with in the light of the history of development of our law. The more practical and the most necessary item on man's medicolegal agenda is to discuss the advances and possible effects of the growth of medical science, widely and deeply, in the literature and forums of both law and medicine.

When trips to the moon have become so routine they rate minimal television attention, when laser has become a working tool of many disciplines of science, when medical advance enters new fields almost daily,[12] the time to cooperate with each other has come.

Yes, there have been time lags between the advances in law and medicine. But these time lags result from our cultural patterns and will continue. We value voluntarism and flexibility. Our system provides these.

By intercommunication among disciplines, by the exchange of knowledge among these several groups, the literature will develop; guidelines can be drafted where desirable and helpful; and laws based on reasoned decision can be proposed, debated, and enacted when essential. Advantage can be taken of time lags, when they occur, to draft good and workable laws when the occasion arises.

REFERENCES

1. Berry v. Chaplin, 169 P.2d 442 (Cal. 1946). *See also* Jordan v. Davis, 57 A.2d 208 (Me. 1948), and Jordan v. Mace, 69 A.2d 670 (Me. 1949).
2. The percentage by weight of alcohol in the blood, expressed as grams of alcohol per 100 cc of blood (% w/v).
3. Masden v. Harrison, No. 68651 (Mass. Supreme Judicial Court, June 12, 1957).
4. "A Definition of Irreversible Coma: Report of the Ad Hoc Committee of the Harvard Medical School to Examine the Definition of Death," 205 Journal of the American Medical Association 337 (1968).
5. "Refinements in Criteria for the Determination of Death: An Appraisal. Report by the Task Force on Death and Dying of the Institute of Society, Ethics and the Life Sciences," 221 Journal of the American Medical Association 48 (1972).
6. The National Observer, June 3, 1972.
7. Veatch, "Brain Death: Welcome Definition or Dangerous Judgment?," 2 Hastings Center Report, No. 5 (Nov. 1972).

8. Anon. v. Anon., 246 N.Y.S.2d 835 (1964), and People v. Sorensen, 66 Cal. Rptr. 7 (1967).

9. Christensen v. Thornby, 255 S.W. 620 (Me. 1934); Ball v. Mudge, 391 P.2d 201 (Wash. 1964); and Shaheen v. Knight, 11 Pa.D&C 41 (1957).

10. Troppi v. Scarf, 187 N.W.2d 511 (Mich. 1971).

11. Custodio v. Bauer, 59 Cal. Rptr. 463 (1967). *See also* Doerr v. Villate, 220 N.E.2d 767 (Ill. 1966), and Coleman v. Garrison, 281 A.2d 616 (Del. 1971).

12. Shelley, "Hippocrates—1984," 58 Bulletin of the Federation of State Medical Boards, No. 9 (Sept. 1971).

The Scientists' Role in Citizen Environmental Advocacy

JOHN S. WINDER, JR.*
Executive Director
Metropolitan Washington Coalition for Clean Air, Inc.
Washington, D.C.

THE CLOSING CIRCLE, AS ARTICULATED BY BARRY COMMONER, DESCRIBES and defines not only the circle of life but also the circle of the living—the roles of all the players. The legal system, I suggest, has been growing to respond to the new, complex environmental issues. As a corollary, it is clear that scientists have been to some extent, and most emphatically must increasingly become, essential contributors to the making of good environmental law. As Commoner states,

In the woods around Walden Pond or on the reaches of the Mississippi, most of the information needed to understand the natural world can be gained by personal experience. In the world of nuclear bombs, smog, and foul water, environmental understanding needs help from the scientist.[1]

This same world needs help from Ralph Nader and is receiving it. Courtrooms, administrative tribunals, and public hearings are now listening to the informed and concerned voices of Nader's Raiders. But where are the disciples of Barry Commoner and René Dubos?

The Center for Science in the Public Interest is a small group of scientists in the nation's capital deeply committed to the infusion of science into environmental and other public interest issues. They operate on an annual budget of approximately $50,000, and the highest paid staff member receives about $4,000 per year. Some three blocks away are located the offices of the American Association for the Advancement of Science (AAAS), operating on an annual budget of $6 million. How is science advancing? Or how do scientists move themselves and science

* Mailing address: Metropolitan Washington Coalition for Clean Air, Inc., 1714 Massachusetts Avenue NW, Washington, D.C. 20036.

into the arena of the public interest, even into the forum of environmental advocacy?

One gap in scientific participation has been identified by Alvin M. Weinberg, Director of Oak Ridge National Laboratory: the "transscientific" area issues "that lie at the interface between science and politics involve questions that can be stated in scientific terms but that are in principle beyond the proficiency of science to answer." Weinberg admits,

We scientists value our republic of science with its rigorous peer group review. The uninformed public is excluded from participation in the affairs of the republic of science rather as a matter of course. . . . But when what we do transcends science and impinges on the public, we have no choice but to welcome public participation. Such participation by the uninitiated in matters that have both scientific and trans-scientific elements may pose some threat to the integrity of the republic of science. To my mind, however, this is a lesser threat than is the threat to our democratic processes that would be posed by excluding the public from participation in trans-scientific debate.[2]

Such a "sunshine" or open door policy can only be healthy in terms of increasing citizen information and participation. However, lest the republic of science be too smug about allowing this increased citizen participation, it should be remembered that for some environmental issues, citizen-lay-public participation has in fact far exceeded scientific participation. Examine your own house and ask how science was "advanced" by participation or lack thereof in the "trans-scientific" issues of the SST or the Alaskan pipeline.

But perhaps beyond the newly freed scientist, what is the new mandate for science itself? What is the old mandate of the AAAS? The sad state of the art of "technology assessment" is itself, no doubt, a mirror of the order, or lack thereof, in the house of science. In *Future Shock*, Alvin Toffler has written that

. . . a set of "positive technological goals" . . . if comprehensive and well worked out, could bring order to a field now in total shambles. By 1980, according to Aurelio Peccei, the Italian economist and industrialist, combined research and development expenditures in the United States and Europe will run to $73 billion per year. This level of expense adds up to three-quarters of a trillion dollars per decade. With such large sums at stake, one would think that governments would plan their technological development carefully, relating it to broad social goals, and insisting on strict accountability. Nothing could be more mistaken.

"No one—not even the most brilliant scientist alive today—really knows where science is taking us," says Ralph Lapp, himself a scientist-turned-writer.[3]

This world of isolationist science was cogently described by William Bevan, publisher of *Science* and executive officer of the AAAS, when he said,

. . . the scientific community had built a closed world of grants and contracts, publications, professional meetings, and committee business that inevitably excluded such matters as public concern and welfare. Thus, when their hand was called on specific national problems—curing cancer, curbing the physical deterioration of the environment, reducing crime rates—they were caught by surprise.[4]

Ask now how scientists, science, or even the AAAS will be changed by this, the 139th meeting of the AAAS.

Bevan further points the finger at the gap between massive public funds for science and the public interest of advancing science. He said:

Scientists had based their justification for the large-scale support of science by public resources on the criterion of utility, but had failed to take into account the principle of public accountability and thus had failed to reconcile the traditional laissez-faire philosophy of research with a need for strategies that relate basic studies to socially useful outcomes.[5]

The message is, therefore, at least from the standpoint of citizen environmental advocacy as observed by Edward E. David,

. . . society is no longer content to allow scientists simply to do what they will, or even to pick and choose their projects from a long list of societal needs. Rather, it will increasingly insist that scientists do what society as a whole demands.[6]

The scientist, not unlike the lawyer, may at times hide behind the shortcomings of the state of the art. For example, the lawyer who loses in the courtroom may blame his loss on bad law, while at the same time the successful litigant will praise the brilliant attorney. Analogously, the scientist whose laboratory experiment is not successful may point to the lack of development of scientific information in this area, while the successful experiment may be due to the clever scientist.

However, as guidelines such as the state of the art of technology assessment become more refined and as the general direction of scientific advancement becomes more orderly, the scientist as an individual citizen can and must make science, as judges make law.

The question becomes, as asked by Frank von Hippel and Joel

Primack in an article entitled "Public Interest Science," "whether individual scientists can contribute significantly to a restoration of a balance of power between the public, Congress, and the executive branch of the government."[7] Surely scientists must contribute on the side of the public, on behalf of the citizen, to seek to infuse public interest science into the military-industrial complex.

Particularly in the area of environmental quality issues, public interest advocates have frequently been either excluded or chastised for alleged lack of fact, data, and/or scientific information. And while environmental issues can and must be decided before every thread of evidence is in, the scientist may still contribute significantly to buttressing the public interest presentations. Alvin Toffler again accurately pleads in *Future Shock*:

The inability to speak with decision and certainty about the future, however, is no excuse for silence. Where "hard data" are available, of course, they ought to be taken into account. But where they are lacking, the responsible writer—even the scientist—has both a right and an obligation to rely on other kinds of evidence, including impressionistic or anecdotal data and the opinions of well-informed people.[8]

The President of the United States recently stated, "The building of a better environment will require in the long term a citizenry that is both deeply concerned and fully informed."[9] The scientific community has, most often justifiably, prided itself on being fully informed. Perhaps, then, what is needed is a scientific community that is concerned—concerned about the public interest, concerned about the environment, concerned not only about permitting public participation in scientific deliberations but also about scientific participation in public deliberations, concerned enough to participate as advocates in the trans-scientific issues of today.

REFERENCES

1. B. Commoner, *The Closing Circle* 48, Alfred Knopf (1972).
2. Weinberg, "Science and Trans-Science" (Editorial), 177 Science 211 (1972).
3. A. Toffler, *Future Shock* 431, Bantam Books (1971).

4. Bevan, "The Welfare of Science in an Era of Change," 176 Science 990 (1972).

5. *Id.*

6. *Id.* at 991.

7. von Hipple & Primack, "Public Interest Science," 177 Science 1166 (1972).

8. A. Toffler, *Future Shock 5*, Bantam Books (1971).

9. Citizens' Advisory Committee on Environmental Quality, *Report to the President and to the Council on Environmental Quality 5* (April 1971).

Who Stole Scientism from Science and Law?

GEORGE S. ROBINSON*
Assistant General Counsel
Smithsonian Institution
Washington, D.C.

AT THE OUTSET, THE ABRASIVE ASPECTS OF PROFESSIONALLY COVETOUS AND parochial views may be vitiated by making the assumption that all scientists and lawyers are well-motivated, hard-working slobs—the former seeking "truth," the latter diligently reinterpreting it. It is important that the highly polished brass of "professionalism" is pushed aside in this assumption. The important point is that the scientist and lawyer—separated, isolated, and defined by their respective professional trade organizations—are well motivated and hard working.

Now that the historical animosities between lawyers and scientists have been brushed aside as irrelevant, it appears that the rather unsubtle, subliminal, cognative dissonance implied in the question, "Scientists in the legal system: tolerated meddlers or essential contributors?" was formulated by a student of "the Law"—for most certainly a man of the laboratory would have phrased the query in a manner such as "Shysters and the use of science and technology: inexcusable bunglers or necessary evils?"

No, it appears that historical asperities characterizing the relationships of natural discipline scientists and lawyers are implicit in this particular topic; for that matter, the topic is inexcusably provocative and certainly not shaped within the ingratiating constraints of Victorian amenities. So, perhaps it is better to brush aside the topical question as well, and rephrase the issue more in the manner of a simple riddle; *e.g.*, "What is the principal objective toward which strivings of scientists and jurists are shared alike?"

Essential to the riddle is use of the word *jurist*, as opposed to *lawyer*. It is one thing to be a mechanic or tailor dealing with a given body of

* Mailing address: Smithsonian Institution, Washington, D.C. 20560.

law; it is quite another to be creator and designer. The first is a lawyer, the second a jurist. The disparity between a jurist, or jurisprudent, and a lawyer is more striking than the differences between the business transactions of a solicitor and those of a barrister. The *lawyer* may use the scientist as an expert witness or as a source of information to substantiate his views and the interests of his client, and even to serve as the foundations of legislation he may be drafting or regulations he is promulgating. Put in another fashion, the scientist is used by the lawyer as an integral component of the adversary mode.

A *jurisprudent*, on the other hand, uses the data and findings derived from scientific methodology to understand the causes for behavior of societal groups and individuals—behavior precipitating the need for responsive legal principles or even entire juridical regimes. The understanding is not based on a need to justify some synthetic preconception of morality and ethic; rather, it is to help recognize and intellectually articulate the reasonably predictable and natural responses of a society to its ecological dictates. Concisely, in the first instance a lawyer's methodology is proselytizing regarding the right-wrong issue—the seemingly immortal question of whose concepts of morality, ethic, and equity are most likely to prevail. In the second instance, the methodology of a jurisprudent is "controlled objectivity"—very close to the methodology of the natural discipline scientists. For that matter law, itself, may rightfully be considered an exacting natural science.

Now that it has been established that the discussion will deal with jurisprudence and not simply the parochial, amorphous, practical constituent thereof known as "the law," it may be simpler and more productive at this point to state a conclusion and then work back to the assumption; *i.e.*, jurisprudence is the synthesis of all natural science disciplines—politics, or the art of compromise, interprets the contemporary value of the underlying data and applies to the jurisprudential synthesis. Query: Why has "the law," or even jurisprudence, not been considered a natural discipline? My answer to the query is, at worst, blasphemous to my academic colleagues; at best, it is a confirmation of the approach some younger members of law faculties and student bodies are tentatively probing to determine the responsive efficacy of their profession.

William James once observed, "We have to live today by what truth we can get today and be ready tomorrow to call it falsehood." It seems this has been the guiding principle upon which much of legal education has been premised in the Western Hemisphere for the past several centuries. Of course, there have been sporadic forays from emphasis on legal positivisms into the arena of various natural law theories, particularly during intervals of international political quietude. These are the moments of relative calm when jurisprudents and "political scientists" are sufficiently secure to play with ideas encompassing the ultimacy of man's interplay with "nature" (*i.e.*, Natural Law) as the basis of all juridical regimes. When bio-ecological dictates catch up with temporary respites from genetically coded inter- or intra-societal antagonisms, jurists immediately resort to the sanctuary of synthetic legal positivisms both to implement and justify the type of societal ordering necessary to meet and control the newly repeated bio-ecological dictates (*e.g.*, cyclical warfare, various assortments of religious and political crusades, etc.).

Even when indulging the multitude of Natural Law theories, jurists always seem to avoid discussion of presently quantifiable aspects of genetic-coding/environmental interplay as being disgustingly Skinnerian or Shockleyian in nature. "Neo-Fascist" seems to be the applicable contemporary vituperation. Many even conclude their learned dissertations on Natural Law with resort to God, Buddha, divine ethic and morality, etc., as consummate law. That is fine for pipe-sucking musing before a drawing room fire on long winter nights, but it does nothing to lead the way to an understanding of why the great civilizations have hastened the otherwise natural causes of violent and unnecessarily wasteful conflict through effective application of their respective legal systems. And those who resort to legal positivisms to explain the origin of, and need for, order do not understand the need to *quantify* the bases of their laws, their intellectually articulated responses to biological dictates. In pursuing the nobility of "the law," jurists and academicians (and more particularly practicing lawyers) have blinded mankind with mysticism to the point that man has become the forgotten animal. As Dr. William Shockley was recently quoted, "The United States is suffering from 'humanism' gone berserk. . . . A central symptom is anti-intellectualism— a concomitant of disrespect for truth. . . ."

Very few law schools in the United States have more than a nominal requirement or elective for a one-semester, two-hour course in what is characterized with the cloak of divine mysticism as "legal philosophy" or, in a more appropriate, latinized form, "jurisprudence." By the time a hapless law student struggles through the new vocabulary in the introduction to Roscoe Pound's works, the course is over and test results pivot on the ability to parrot, rather than understand, the views of the "classic" giants—Kant, Holmes, Brandeis, Frankfurter, Hughes, *et al.* The frustrating and tragic facet of this dilemma is that Roscoe Pound was first and foremost a student and teacher of biology (specifically, botany) who almost fortuitously pursued a career in jurisprudence at a later date. In a great many respects, he was a latter-day Jeremy Bentham, with much to offer in the way of properly directing a new methodology for teaching law.

Almost across the board, legal education has not been responsive to the tools and methodologies that basic sciences and technology, in the form of applied sciences, have provided to measure the origin of juridical regimes and their components. Occasional courses are taught which emphasize the role of science and technology within the overriding framework of "the law," but never where "the law" fits within the philosophical constraints of scientific methodology.

Purveyors of legal fantasies are not totally to blame, however. Scientists, as a rule, are so fearful of their professional reputations that unless every statement and observation is empirically irrefutable, they will not publish reasonable speculation in such a manner that policy administrators, interpreters, and other students of the legal profession can make appropriate extrapolations from laboratory data to the behavior of man. For that matter, the vast majority of behavioral scientists refuse to support any extrapolation and applications to human behavior of empirical data arising from the so-called subhuman species. Apparently, the fear of neo-Darwinism in the form of violent racial disparagements and confrontations is a legacy sufficiently foreboding to send scientists scurrying back to the refuge of their laboratories, leaving the tasks of molding societal stability to the gropings of law makers. This gives to the process an image of a Keystone Kops skit or a Faulknerian fantasy.

If scientists will not help the jurist extrapolate from laboratory data to keep the framework of social order viable, organic, and nonstatic, then the jurist must be prepared to do his own interpreting so that he has something continuously growing in responsiveness to human environmental changes and fluctuations. This must be passed along to the practicing lawyer, who, in turn, must peddle his trade for an understandably corrupting profit. In fact, it means the jurist must be his own scientist; and with the multitude of natural disciplines and subdisciplines held out as contemporary "professions," the jurist must be a veritable product of the Renaissance.

It is not sufficient solely to be a scholar in the application of law to consumer problems, environmental issues, health care programs, and so on. The jurist, alone and collectively with his colleagues through contemporary systems analysis, must understand the chemistry, physics, economics, and societal behavior patterns influencing the shape of such problems, issues, and programs. Throughout recorded history, the non-scientific methodology followed for articulating societal organization and directions has resulted in a mosaic of irregularly juxtaposed abstractions reflecting an inexorable edging toward the extinction of man through self-destruction. Scientists have provided the tools for engineering a synthetic, but acceptable and extremely viable, evolution of man. Why is it not being done?

The first part of the answer, of course, lies in the fact that lawyers, as opposed to jurists, are not interested in the future of the imperial animal—man. Their only interest is perpetuation of the methodology in which they have been trained since long before law was first considered not merely a profession but a reprehensibly crooked one at that. This particular methodology is the "adversary mode."

The practicing lawyer has been forced into the role of representing the parochial interests of his client which are in conflict with the alleged rights and interests of an adversary. Assuming adequate legal representation of all parties with an interest in a given matter, it is presumed (relative talents of counsel in advocacy and proselytizing proceedings notwithstanding) that a hearing before and decision by a peer group will provide a balanced system of justice and equity when viewed as a whole. However, intrasociety, intersociety, international, and inter-regional commercial transactions and cultural dependencies and relationships have become so extensive and sophisticated that the adversary method of decision making is no longer responsive. In fact, it often is sufficiently provocative to precipitate violent confrontations in situations where reasons for such confrontations simply do not exist.

Often in following through the adversary mode of representation, the most expendable facet is scientific data and functional extrapolations thereof. And yet, these data and extrapolations constitute the foundations upon which effectively responsive legal principles rest. The distinction should be emphasized, however, between such bio-ecological foundations of juridical regimes and scientific expertise purchased for advocacy testimony in litigation.

If not the lawyer or the jurist, then to whom can society turn for a correct comprehension and application of "the law"? Is it the scientist? It is worth taking time to justify rejection of this source out of hand.

I have found in the vast majority of my own experiences that the first to cast aside even a pretense of a scientific methodology in the area of political problem solving is the basic research scientist—when he leaves his laboratory. Let it be assumed for the moment that all lawyers/jurists and scientists/technologists are sufficiently cosmopolitan to recognize a basic fact of human behavioral patterns, *i.e.*, man is not totally autonomous—the so-called master of his fate. However, to the extent he *is* autonomous, his basic, genetically coded behavior patterns are unchangeable. Too, we are learning to change and control our environment through basic research data and its application in the form of technology. Such data and technology are applied to the environment in specific ways to affect human individual and societal behavior. This is powerful science and technology. It can fabricate vast numbers of technological mutants presently confused with *Homo sapiens*.

But as B. F. Skinner asked in *Beyond Freedom and Dignity*, "For whom is a powerful technology of behavior to be used? Who is to use it? and to what end? We have been implying that the effects of one practice are better than those of another, but on what grounds? What is the good against which something else is called better?" These are questions not about scientific data, but about how men interpret or value those data. Concisely, the data are pushed into the realm of is-ought consideration. This generally has been considered the realm of the jurist to the exclusion of the scientist—a self-imposed exclusion.

It has taken centuries for the legislator-politicist to evolve his profession to the point of being able to recognize and balance to a minimum acceptable degree the multitude of societal interests and pressures. Suddenly, when science and technology have been supported by enlightened administrative policies to the point where the legislator-politicist is almost incapable of handling the sheer quantity and implications of applied technology, the scientists burst on the scene, demanding center stage for resolution of problems, the parameters of which they cannot even recognize or speculate. And they wonder why their expertise in atom-splitting or in the fanny-side of an echinoderm is not immediately accepted as a conclusive and impeccable credential for sophisticated and extensive decision-making programs.

Many scientists, based upon unrelated frustrations, condemn nonscientists in particular for letting their manifestations of universal and cosmopolitan wisdom drift off as unrecognized cries in the wilderness. They condemn being relegated to a common sharing of wisdom with the community audience in general regarding decision making as to the use to which their scientific endeavors are put. To them, it is inconceivable that any nonscientist would have greater insight and wisdom in such decision making than the scientists and engineers who have provided the data and instruments which are the subjects of such decisions. The unfortunate fact is that most scientists not only have been too long in their laboratories to know the world around them but they also are often so specialized in their subdisciplines of endeavor that they do not know what colleagues in related areas of research are doing, let alone understand—and be creative in response to—the shifting, intricate, and subtle vagaries of value-forming processes that lead to the confusion and failures of national and international politics as we presently experience them.

If one accepts the foregoing general characterizations of technologist/scientist and lawyer/jurist, it can be observed that they are moving apart relentlessly in the arena of public and social administration. They are polarizing in their respective roles. The overwhelming communication of data essential to refined and responsive decision making is driving them apart almost to a positive/negative relationship. Advanced technology, the one tool that can bring scientists and lawyers together in a productive, symbiotic relationship for more realistic development and application of law, is precipitating, instead, aggressive disputation, fruitless polemic exercises, and reliance upon amorphous, shifting concepts of morality and ethic to substantiate judgments in public legislation, interpretation, and administration.

The *answer* to the dilemma? Since law is an exacting science, scientists must teach the law, and in so doing teach themselves. Perhaps, also, in addition to introducing scientism to the law, scientism will be restored to science. *Scientism*, "the methods or doctrines characteristic of scientists; the proposition that the methods of the natural sciences should be used in all areas of investigation." The *dilemma*, itself? Who stole scientism from science and the law?

Science and Society in the Environment Age*

MAURICE F. STRONG†
Executive Director, United Nations Environment Programme
Nairobi, Kenya

SCIENCE IS THE KEY TO BOTH THE UNPARALLELED PROMISE AND PERIL WHICH today confronts mankind. It is entirely true, of course, that science and scientists can no more be blamed for the problems and the threats that have accompanied the creation of what is, in effect, the world's first technological civilization than they can be given full credit for the manifest benefits it has produced. But neither can they validly claim the political innocence they sometimes profess.

To a much greater extent than they like to admit, scientists have always been dependent upon patronage for the pursuit of their professional activities. And equally to a greater extent than they would like to admit, the direction and nature of their work have been influenced by the interests and requirements of the patrons who have provided the resources for it.

Today, the great patrons of science are the state and business and industry, particularly the giant corporations. Thus, it should not be surprising that the principal emphasis of science—the areas receiving the greatest attention and attracting the largest number of scientists—are those which serve the interests of these powerful patrons. Not at all surprising, too, is the concentration of scientific effort on the development of sophisticated weaponry and defense systems, space and areas related to the development and exploitation of resources, and the production and distribution of consumer products.

One result is that the specialized and often narrow objectives of the patrons in their uses of science and the increasing degree of professional

---

* Excerpts from an address to the International Geological Congress, August 21, 1972, in Montreal, Canada.

† Mailing address: United Nations Environment Programme, Uchumi Building, Nairobi, Kenya.

specialization within the scientific community itself have together contributed to a narrowing of the concerns and the perspectives of scientists. This is reflected in the compartmentalization within universities and research institutions and the often poor communication amongst scientists of different disciplines.

This fragmentation and inadequate communication within the scientific community contributes greatly to its difficulties in its relationships with the rest of society. Science too often appears to speak with too many voices, and the name of science is all too often invoked in support of many dubious policies and projects simply because a few articulate individuals have been prepared to speak up when the more authoritative voices of the scientific community chose to remain silent.

Science, too, has its charlatans, publicizers—and even its politicians —and these have a far greater influence on public opinion and public policy than they should. They fill a vacuum left by the failure of the scientific community to give the public and policy makers the benefit of the best guidance and viewpoints available based on the most authoritative range of scientific knowledge and opinion.

I know I tread on sacred ground when I suggest that scientists profess lofty as well as pragmatic motives for this solemn and dignified detachment from the concerns of the public and politicians. This is justified, they say, for the purpose of maintaining the integrity of science; they cannot be involved in controversial public issues and often cannot offer an opinion because not all the necessary research has been completed or because there is no unanimity within the scientific community itself—although I believe that, just as often, there is a problem in the way the scientific community itself is organized to enable it to provide such authoritative assessments.

Can one blame the public for associating scientists with some of the evils that science has helped produce—nuclear weapons, napalm, and environmental degradation—if scientists themselves maintain this aloof detachment from the very issues and concerns which their own efforts are demonstrably producing? Despite the high degree of professional integrity and objectivity that are the hallmark of the scientist, are scientists fully immune from the charge that science is for hire? Can scientists really escape a sense of responsibility for the uses to which their work and the power it creates are directed? In an era in which our whole future depends on the uses for which our scientific and technological power is put—I think not!

I believe that much of our present dilemma derives from the inadequacies—some of which I have referred to—in the relationships between science and society, particularly as they affect the processes by which societies make their choices and determine their priorities. Although scientists as individuals can do much to influence the purposes and objectives of the organizations in which they work, they cannot—as a rule—be expected to speak out against the immediate interests of the organization which employs them. But through their own professional associations they have the opportunity of making their views known on significant issues which bear on their own professional fields.

In my opinion, this calls for a great strengthening of scientific and professional organizations and the much more active participation in them by individual scientists. At the same time, scientists should organize themselves so as to encourage and facilitate much closer communication amongst the various disciplines and in particular between the physical and life scientists and the social scientists. They should strengthen their own capacity to undertake multidisciplinary assessments of significant issues, particularly those as to which society is being called upon to make important choices. The mounting of multidisciplinary teams should not remain the virtual monopoly of the patrons and users of science.

Scientists must also have a better understanding of the political process through which society makes its decisions and take a much greater interest in these processes. I believe it is fully as important for the scientist to understand the political context in which he is firstly supported and secondly used by society, as it is for politicians and for the public to understand the scientific basis for the important political and social choices they are making. This means, too, that even as society and its leaders respect the integrity of science and the professional objectivity which is the basis for scientific enquiry, scientists must have a respect for the validity of the political process and the primacy of the social goals of society.

I have often been disturbed to hear disparaging comments by scientists concerning politics and politicians, revealing, in many instances, that they have not applied the same kind of objective analysis to their attempt to understand the political and social world as they do to their own field of science.

If the present environmental crisis results—as I believe it does—from gross inadequacies in the processes by which society makes major decisions which, in turn, influence its own future, then I believe this is due in large part to the inadequacies to which I have referred in the interface between science and the decision-making processes of society. I do not think it conceivable that we can achieve the physical, economic, and social balances on which the continued health of our society must be based without radical improvements in the way in which the relationships operate at this interface.

Index

A

Abbott Laboratories v. Gardner, 84
Administrative hearings, 97–102
Administrative law judges, 97
Air Quality Act of 1967, 84
Alaska pipeline, 119
Alcohol, blood tests for, 110
American Association for the Advancement of Science, *v*, 20, 44, 50, 118, 119, 120
American Bar Association, 24n. 32, 36, 38, 40, 42, 44, 63
American Medical Association, 111, 112
American Smelting and Refining Co., Anderson v., 83
Amniocentesis, 113
Anderson v. American Smelting and Refining Co., 83
Anon. v. Anon., 113n. 8
Artificial insemination, 17, 113
Association of American Law Schools, 44
Atlantic Cement Co., Boomer v., 83
Atomic Energy Commission, *see* United States Government
Atomic Energy Commission, New Hampshire v., 81
Audley, Jee v., 26n. 1
Automobile safety, 32, 33, 47, 68, 110

B

Bacon, Francis, 9
Ball v. Mudge, 114n. 9
Barnard, Christiaan, 110

Barzun, Jacques, 18
Bauer, Custodio v., 114n. 11
Benefit/cost analysis, 59, 67, 80; *see also* Economic analysis
Bentham, Jeremy, 126
Berry v. Chaplin, 110n. 1
Bill of Rights, 53; *see also* Civil rights
Birth control, *see* Contraception
Blood tests, 110
Board of Education, Brown v., 18n. 38
Boomer v. Atlantic Cement Co., 83
Boston University, 44
Brahe, Tycho, 9
Brandeis, Louis, 125
Brown v. Board of Education, 18n. 38
Burden of proof, 86, 89, 93; *see also* Evidence
Bushell's Case, 8
Businessmen for the Public Interest, 86

C

Cardozo, Benjamin, 1, 13, 91
Center for Science in the Public Interest, 118
Chaplin, Berry v., 110n. 1
Chaplin, Charlie, 110
Chemicals, and health, 46, 50–51, 68, 71, 83, 98, 109
Christensen v. Thornby, 114n. 9
Cigarettes, 33, 89
Civil rights, 17, 26, 27–28, 32, 33, 53–54, 73, 78, 104, 128

Coleman v. Garrison, 114n. 11

Common law, 76–77, 82, 83, 88, 115

Communication, between scientists and lawyers, 35–45, 51, 57, 99–100, 116, 129, 131; *see also* Education

Computers, 13, 15, 17, 56, 60–65

Congress, *see* United States Government

Constitution, United States, 53, 91

Consumer products and protection, 32, 35, 47, 48, 68, 70, 73, 98, 126

Contraception, 17, 114

Cooperation, between scientists and lawyers, *v–vi*, 2, 21–22, 33–34, 67–72, 99–102, 105–108, 116, 119, 124, 126, 129; *see also* Evidence

Copernicus, 9, 109

Cornell University, 44

Corporate/industrial interests, 48, 50, 53, 64, 71, 121, 130

Corps of Engineers, *see* United States Government

Cost/benefit analysis, *see* Benefit/cost analysis

Courts, nature and operation, 26–27, 61–63, 73–93, 104–108

relation to agencies, 69–70, 76, 80–85

standing, 70, 78–79

see also Evidence *and* Judicial process

Custodio v. Bauer, 114n. 11

D

Dams, 81, 107

Darwin, Charles, 9

Darwinism, 126

Davis, Jordan v., 110n. 1

Death, definition of, 111–113, 115

Declaratory judgment, 87

Defoliation, 50–51

Department of Health, Education, and Welfare, *see* United States Government

Department of the Interior, *see* United States Government

Department of Justice, *see* United States Government

Doerr v. Villate, 114n. 11

Douglas, William, 81–82, 105

Drug addiction, 114

E

Economic analysis, 72, 80, 93, 119; *see also* Benefit/cost analysis

Education, of scientists and lawyers, 5n. 9, 15, 42, 44, 52, 57, 125–126

Electronic surveillance, 17, 26, 27–28, 53; *see also* Civil rights

Employees Mutual Liability Insurance Co., Parker v., 30n. 11

Energy, supply and demand, 15, 17, 32–33, 48, 52, 68, 104, 107

Environment, *see* Environmental quality

Environmental Defense Fund, 67, 69, 70, 72

Environmental Protection Agency, *see* United States Government

Environmental quality, 17, 32, 35, 41, 46, 48, 50, 51, 68, 70, 73, 74, 81–85, 92, 98, 104, 118, 121, 126, 131, 132

Evidence, expert testimony, 30, 36, 70, 86, 88–89, 98–102, 103–108, 124, 127

expert versus opinion testimony, 29–31, 105, 110, 115, 121

scientific, 1, 8, 13–15, 17, 21, 26–27, 89

Executive Branch, *see* United States Government

Expert testimony, *see* Evidence

F

Federal Administrative Law Judges Conference, 98
Federal Aviation Administration, *see* United States Government
Federal government, *see* United States Government
Federal Power Act, 104
Federal Power Commission, *see* United States Government
Federal Power Commission, Scenic Hudson Preservation Conference v., 82
Federal Power Commission, Udall v., 81
Federal Reports Act, 49
Federal Trade Commission, *see* United States Government
Fluoridation, 21
Food and Drug Administration, *see* United States Government
Frank, Jerome, 64
Frankfurter, Felix, 84, 125
Freedom of Information Act, 49, 50, 81n. 19

G

Galilei, Galileo, 9
Gardner, Abbott Laboratories v., 84
Garrison, Coleman v., 114n. 11
Genetics, 17, 113–114
George Washington University, 44
Gilbert, William, 9
Government, *see* State government *and* United States Government
Government secrecy, 49–50

H

Hamilton's Principle, 58
Hand, Learned, 88
Harrison, Masden v., 111n. 3

Harvard University, 4n. 5, 111
Harvey Aluminum, Inc., Renken v., 83n. 27
Harvey, William, 9
Health, Education, and Welfare, Department of, *see* United States Government
Hearing examiners, 97
Heisenberg's Uncertainty Principle, 58
Herbicide Assessment Committee, 51
Herbicides, 50–51
Hertz, Heinrich, 10
High Mountain Sheep Dam, 81
Highways, 59, 104
Hiroshima, 46
History, of law and science, 7–22, 26–27, 57, 109
Holmes, Oliver Wendell, 1, 12, 81, 92, 125
Homo sapiens, 128
Hudson Valley, 107
Hughes, Charles, 125
Huygens, Christian, 9

I

Industrial/corporate interests, *see* Corporate/industrial interests
Industrial Revolution, 2
Industrial State, 2
Injunction, 80, 87
Institute of Society, Ethics and the Life Sciences, 112
Interior, Department of, *see* United States Government
Internal Revenue Service, *see* United States Government
International Harvester Co. v. Ruckelshaus, 3n. 13
Intoxication, blood tests for, 110

J

James, William, 124

Jee v. Audley, 26 n. 1
Jordan v. Davis, 110 n. 1
Jordan v. Mace, 110 n. 1
Judicial process, 10, 55, 58–59, 72, 73–93, 127; *see also* Courts, Evidence, *and* Jurisprudence
Jurimetrics, 22, 24 n. 32, 55, 62
Jurisprudence, 55, 60, 123–129; *see also* Judicial process
Justice, Department of, *see* United States Government

K

Kant, Immanuel, 125
Kepler, Johannes, 9
Knight, Shaheen v., 114 n. 9

L

Land use, 48, 68, 107
Lavoisier, Antoine, 9
Law, historical development, *see* History; *see also* Judicial process *and specific laws*
Lawyers, communication with scientists, *see* Communication
compared with scientists, 2–3, 10–14, 20, 35, 41–43, 56–57, 68, 70, 99, 120, 123
cooperation with scientists, *see* Cooperation
Legal system, *see* Judicial process
Linnaeus, Carl, 9
Lundberg, George, 16

M

Mace, Jordan v., 110 n. 1
Macrolaw, 14–15
Maine, Henry, 7
Mandamus, 87
Marshall, John, 63
Masden v. Harrison, 111 n. 3
Massachusetts Institute of Technology, 48

Maxwell, James, 10
Maxwell's Equations, 58
Medical issues, 17, 109–116
Microlaw, 14–15
Miller v. Schoene, 84
Miracles, 27; *see also* Supernatural events
Models, mathematical, 55–65; *see also* Systems analysis
Mudge, Ball v., 114 n. 9

N

National Academy of Engineering, 49, 68
National Academy of Sciences, 19, 49, 75
National Conference on Commissioners of Uniform State Laws, 111, 115
National Environmental Policy Act of 1969, 3, 44, 85, 104
National Science Foundation, v, 36, 44, 68, 94 n. 3
Natural law, 125
New Hampshire v. Atomic Energy Commission, 81
New York Bar Association, 75
Newton, Isaac, 9
Novum Organum, 9
Nuclear energy, 104; *see also* Energy *and* Radiation
Nuisance law, 79–80, 82–83, 87, 88

O

Oak Ridge National Laboratory, v, 36, 43, 119
Occupational Safety and Health Act of 1970, 3
Office of Management and Budget, *see* United States Government
Office of Science and Technology, *see* United States Government

Office of Technology Assessment, *see* United States Government
Operations research, 56, 62; *see also* Computers, Models, *and* Systems analysis
Organ transplants, 109–113; *see also* Medical issues
Orwell, George, 63

P

Parker v. Employees Mutual Liability Insurance Co., 30 n. 11
Paternity suits, 110, 115
Pearson, Karl, 11
People v. Sorensen, 113 n. 8
Pipelines, 85, 119
Pollution, *see* Environmental quality
Polygraph, 14, 28–29
Pound, Roscoe, 125–126
Priestley, Joseph, 9
Privacy, 17, 26, 27–28, 32–33, 53–54; *see also* Civil rights *and* Electronic surveillance
Professional societies, role of, 40, 44, 50, 54, 118–120, 132
Public interest, 5 n. 7, 46–54, 67–72, 118–121; *see also* Cooperation *and* Scientists, as citizens
Public Interest Economics Center, 72
Public interest research groups, 52–53
Public trust doctrine, 81

R

Radiation, ionizing, 15, 17, 29, 31, 46, 51, 52, 89, 104
Radio Corp. of America v. United States, 84
Renaissance, 126
Renken v. Harvey Aluminum, Inc., 83 n. 27
Repouille v. United States, 92 n. 50
Religion, 8, 27, 125

Royal Society, 9
Ruckelshaus, International Harvester Co. v., 3 n. 13
Rule Against Perpetuities, 26–27

S

Scarf, Troppi v., 114 n. 10
Scenic Hudson Preservation Conference v. Federal Power Commission, 82
Schoene, Miller v., 84
Schroedinger Equation, 58
Science, historical development, *see* History
  patrons of, 130
  utilization in the legal system, evidence, *see* Evidence
    expert testimony, *see* Evidence
    general considerations, 1–4, 13–15
    policy making, 2, 16, 20–21, 33, 50, 54, 69, 73, 132
  see also Scientific method *and* Scientists
Science advisers, 17, 47–49
Scientific evidence, *see* Evidence
Scientific method, 1, 10–11, 16, 35, 56–57, 99, 126
Scientific organizations, role of, *see* Professional societies
Scientism, 123–129
Scientists, as citizens, 4, 5 n. 7, 46–54, 68, 108, 118, 120, 121, 130–133
  communication with lawyers, *see* Communication
  compared with lawyers, 2–3, 10–14, 20, 35, 41–43, 56–57, 68, 70, 99, 120, 123, 129, 130–133
  cooperation with lawyers, *see* Cooperation *and* Evidence
  social scientists, 3, 15, 16, 18, 57, 126
Secrecy, governmental, 49–50
Shaheen v. Knight, 114 n. 9

Smith v. Staso Milling Co., 83 n. 27
Snow, C. P., 17, 18
Sorcery, 8; *see also* Supernatural
    events
Sorensen, People v., 113 n. 8
SST, *see* Supersonic transport plane
Standing, 70, 78–79
Staso Milling Co., Smith v., 83 n. 27
State government, 69, 90, 111, 112–
    114
Storm King Mountain, 107
Supernatural events, 4 n. 5, 7–8, 27
Supersonic transport plane, 49, 103,
    119
Supreme Court, *see* United States
    Government
Systems analysis, 56, 58–61, 127

T

Tabb, Zabel v., 81
Technology assessment, 48, 73–93,
    119–120, 132
Technology Assessment, Office of,
    see United States Government
Technology Assessment Act of 1972,
    5 n. 7
*Texas Eastern Transmission Corp. v.
    Wildlife Preserves, Inc.*, 85
Think tank, 49
Thornby, Christensen v., 114 n. 9
Thurber, James, 63
Tort law, 29, 30, 47, 78, 80, 82, 87–
    88, 113
Trans-scientific issues, 5 n. 8, 119, 121
Troppi v. Scarf, 114 n. 10
Trial by ordeal, 8
Trials, courtroom, *see* Courts, Evi-
    dence, *and* Judicial process

U

Udall v. Federal Power Commission,
    81

Uniform Anatomical Gift Act, 111,
    115
United Nations, 3, 5 n. 7
United States v. White, 28 n. 4
*United States, Radio Corp. of
    America v.*, 84
United States, Repouille v., 92 n. 50
United States Government,
  Executive Branch,
    Executive Office of the Presi-
      dent,
      generally, 17, 48–49, 50, 69, 90,
        121
      Office of Management and
        Budget, 49, 50
      Office of Science and Technol-
        ogy, 17
    Executive Departments,
      Department of Defense,
        Corps of Engineers, 67, 80
      Department of Health, Edu-
        cation, and Welfare, 98
        Food and Drug Administra-
          tion, 72
      Department of the Interior, 81
      Department of Justice, 49
      Department of Transporta-
        tion,
        Federal Aviation Adminis-
          tration, 72
      Department of the Treasury,
        Internal Revenue Service,
          6 n. 12
    Independent agencies,
      Atomic Energy Commission,
        29, 52, 80, 86, 89
      Environmental Protection
        Agency, 51, 72, 98
      Federal Power Commission,
        81, 82
      Federal Trade Commission, 98
  Judicial Branch,
    Supreme Court of the United

United States Government–*Cont.*
  Judicial Branch–*Cont.*
    States, 17, 75, 82, 84, 105
  Legislative Branch,
    Congress of the United States,
      5 n. 7, 48–49, 50, 69, 84, 111,
      121
    Office of Technology Assess-
      ment, 5 n. 7
University of California, 56

V

Venereal disease, 114
Vesalius, Andreas, 9
Vietnam, 50–51
Villate, Doerr v., 114 n. 11
Voiceprints, 14

W

Walden Pond, 118
Warren, Earl, 4 n. 5
Watergate affair, 27; *see also* Elec-
  tronic surveillance
Weather modification, 17
White, United States v., 28 n. 4
Whitehead, Alfred, 47
*Wildlife Preserves, Inc., Texas
  Eastern Transmission Corp. v.*,
  85
Witchcraft, 4 n. 5, 8; *see also* Super-
  natural events
Workmen's compensation, 29, 30

Z

Zabel v. Tabb, 81